Driftless Reflection

SUE BERG

Little Creek Press
5341 Sunny Ridge Road
Mineral Point, Wisconsin 53565

Book Design and Project Coordination:
Little Creek Press

May 2026

Follow Sue on Facebook @ Sue Berg/author
To contact author: bergsue@hotmail.com
To order books: www.littlecreekpress.com

ISBN-13: 978-1-969183-08-9

This book is dedicated to my brother Rick; you are gone too soon. We miss your ribald humor, your incredible engineering talent, and your warm presence. Rest in peace.

ACKNOWLEDGMENTS

Thanks to Little Creek Press whose values are so consistent with the Midwest ethos. Kristin Mitchell and her staff consistently produce books that reflect integrity and excellence. Thank you for your attention to detail and your appreciation of the storyteller in all of us.

Thanks to my family and friends for patience and understanding when I don't answer the phone or am late in returning their calls because I am deep into writing. I am grateful to so many readers who have reached out and encouraged me with your timely, supportive comments on Facebook and email. Because of your enthusiasm, people are still discovering the Driftless Mystery Series. Thanks to those readers who have posted reviews online which helps build my readership. As always with every book, I thank my husband, Alan, and my extended family for their support and enthusiasm for my work. Enjoy!

Praise for the Jim Higgins Driftless Mystery Series:

DRIFTLESS GOLD

"… an irresistible tale of lost treasure and the scoundrels who will do anything to get their hand on it."

~Jeff Nania, author of the Northern Lake Mystery Series

DRIFTLESS TREASURE

2021 Finalist Award in The Independent Author Network

"… Descriptive scenes and well-drawn characters in a story of crimes with international implications."

~Greg Peck, author of *Death Beyond the Willows*

DRIFTLESS DECEIT

"… Berg creates a smorgasbord of subplots with characters confounded by real-life issues from family loyalty and faith to forgiveness and love, both lost and found."

~Patricia Skalka, author of the Door County Mystery Series

DRIFTLESS DESPERATION

"An honest portrayal of the crime and rural poverty that exists beneath the bucolic veneer of this unique landscape."

~John Armbruster, author of *Tailspin*

DRIFTLESS INSURRECTION

"... a solid cast of multi-dimensional characters in a plot that kept me guessing. The novel's storyline and characters are as good as anything on the mystery/suspense bestseller list today. Give this author a chance."

~Christine DeSmet, author of The Fudge Shop Mystery Series

DRIFTLESS IDENTITY

"...in this sixth installment of the Jim Higgins Driftless Mystery Series, Jim relies on his team, family, friends, and faith to guide him to find the real killer's identity. Amidst the confusion of the case, he must ensure his family's safety when they survive a dangerous event. Author Sue Berg leads the reader through the investigation while celebrating the beauty of the late summer season along the Mississippi River in the driftless area of Western Wisconsin."

~Susan Apps Bodilly, author, educator, speaker

OTHER BOOKS BY SUE BERG

Solid Roots and Strong Wings—A Family Memoir

The Driftless Mystery Series:

Driftless Gold

Driftless Treasure

Driftless Deceit

Driftless Desperation

Driftless Insurrection

Driftless Identity

The Dirty Business Mystery Series:

Death at the Dentist

Death at the University

FOREWORD
THE DRIFTLESS REGION

The name *Driftless* appears in all of the titles of my books because this region of the American Midwest where my novels take place is a unique geographical region, though relatively unknown. The Driftless Region—which escaped glacial activity during the last ice age—includes southeastern Minnesota, southwestern Wisconsin, northeastern Iowa, and the extreme northwestern corner of Illinois. The stories I write take place in and around La Crosse, Wisconsin, which is in the heart of this distinct geographical region.

The Driftless Region is characterized by steep forested ridges, deeply carved river valleys, and karst geology, resulting in spring-fed waterfalls and cold-water trout streams. The rugged terrain is due primarily to the lack of glacial deposits called drift. The absence of the flattening glacial effect of drifts resulted in land that has remained hilly and rugged—hence the term *driftless*. In addition, the Mississippi River and its many tributaries have carved rock outcroppings and towering bluffs from the area's bedrock. These rock formations along the Mississippi River climb to almost six hundred feet in some places. Grandad Bluff in La Crosse is one of these famous bluffs.

In particular, the Driftless portion of southwestern Wisconsin contains many distinct features: isolated hills, coulees, bluffs, mesas, buttes, goat prairies, and pinnacles formed from eroded Cambrian bedrock remnants of the plateau to the southwest. In addition, karst topography is found throughout the Driftless area. This landscape was created when water dissolved the dolomite and limestone rock resulting in features like caves and cave systems, hidden underground streams, blind valleys and sinkholes, and springs and cold streams.

About eighty-five percent of the Driftless Region lies within southwestern Wisconsin. The rugged terrain comprising this area is known locally as the Coulee Region. Steep ridges, numerous rock outcroppings like the Three Chimneys northwest of Viroqua, the classic rock formations of Wisconsin Dells, and deep narrow valleys contrast with the rest of the state, where glaciers have modified and leveled the land.

The area is prone to flooding, runoff, and erosion. Because of the steep river valleys, many small towns in the Driftless Region have major flooding problems every fifty to one hundred years. Farmers in the region practice contour plowing and strip farming to reduce soil erosion on the hilly terrain.

Superb cold-water streams have made the Driftless Region a premier trout fishing destination in the country. A variety of fish, including brook and rainbow trout, thrive in the tributaries of the Mississippi River system. The crystalline streams are protected by Trout Unlimited, an organization that works with area landowners to maintain and restore trout habitat. In addition, abundant wildlife such as deer and turkeys provide excellent hunting for the avid sportsman.

La Crosse is the principal urban center that is entirely in the Wisconsin Driftless Region, along with small cities, towns, and numerous Amish settlements. Cranberries are grown and harvested in bogs left over from Glacial Lake Wisconsin. At one time, cigar tobacco was grown and harvested throughout the Coulee Region, but foreign markets decreased the demand for Wisconsin-grown tobacco. However, tobacco barns or sheds are still found throughout the landscape and are an iconic symbol of a once-thriving industry. The region is also home to Organic Valley, the nation's largest organic producer of dairy products, organic vegetables, and fruits, particularly apples. Winemaking and vineyards have popped up in recent years, and apple production continues to be a staple in the Driftless economy.

After describing the area's geographical features, you can see why Wisconsin is the perfect setting for a mystery series! It's a wonderland of unparalleled geographical beauty, impressive wildlife, and friendly, memorable people. Enjoy!

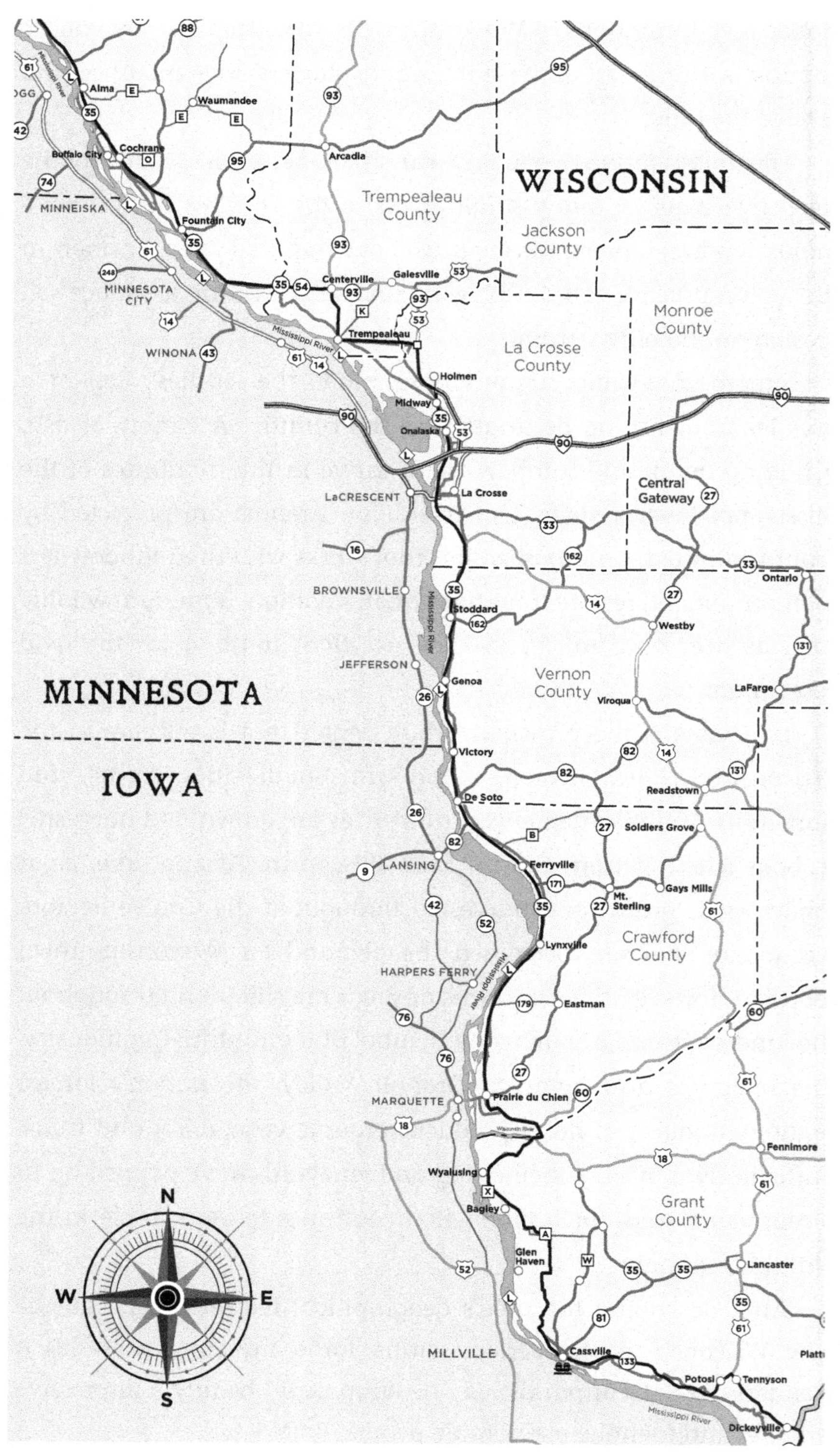
WISCONSIN
MINNESOTA
IOWA
Trempealeau County
Jackson County
Monroe County
La Crosse County
Vernon County
Crawford County
Grant County
Central Gateway
Alma
Waumandee
Cochrane
Buffalo City
Arcadia
MINNEISKA
Fountain City
MINNESOTA CITY
WINONA
Centerville
Galesville
Trempealeau
Holmen
Midway
Onalaska
LaCRESCENT
La Crosse
BROWNSVILLE
Stoddard
JEFFERSON
Genoa
Westby
Ontario
Viroqua
LaFarge
Victory
De Soto
Readstown
Soldiers Grove
LANSING
Ferryville
Mt. Sterling
Gays Mills
Lynxville
HARPERS FERRY
Eastman
MARQUETTE
Prairie du Chien
Fennimore
Wyalusing
Bagley
Glen Haven
Lancaster
MILLVILLE
Cassville
Potosi
Tennyson
Dickeyville
Mississippi River
Wisconsin River
N
S
E
W

"EVIL IS UNSPECTACULAR AND
ALWAYS HUMAN, AND SHARES OUR BED
AND EATS AT OUR OWN TABLE."

W. H. AUDEN

TUESDAY, MAY 15

1

The setting sun dipped toward the western horizon, painting the pink sky with gold and fuchsia swirls. Delta flight 57 banked over the river to prepare for landing at the municipal airport at the wide end of French Island, which sits in the middle of the river southeast of Lake Onalaska. La Crosse, Wisconsin, a small college town nestled along the Mississippi River, is long and skinny, squeezed between the river on the west and the sandstone bluffs on the east.

Geoff LaSarde inhaled deeply and leaned toward the tiny window to catch a glimpse of the wide, winding waterway that snaked its way through the steep forested bluffs on either side. In the distance, the sandstone landmark of the majestic limestone promontory called Grandad Bluff reflected the golden rays of the setting sun.

Geoff was a professional art critic with an intense interest in history, specifically the history of architectural and decorative arts in the United States. His field of expertise was the art and craft of Louis Comfort Tiffany, which included jewelry, decorative items for the home, including stained-glass lamps, glassware, and church windows, an area of mastery of which most Tiffany aficionados were woefully ignorant. Geoff was the exception.

In his master's thesis, LaSarde chose Tiffany stained-glass windows as an area of particular emphasis. Investing several years of study, he'd finally earned a degree in History of Decorative Arts from the University of Chicago, high honors no less. Since then, LaSarde had published several articles about Tiffany windows in *Architectural Digest, Luxe: Interiors and Design*, and *Metropolis*. In Wisconsin, he'd traveled to The Mabel Tainter Memorial Theater in Menomonie, Wisconsin, to study the Tiffany stained-glass windows there, and a few months ago, he'd made a trip to St. Paul's Episcopal Church in Milwaukee, where he stood transfixed by the glorious radiance of eleven of the rarest and most valuable Tiffany church windows in the country. In addition, he'd made several trips to Chicago, where Tiffany church windows were being rediscovered and restored to their former glory.

Regrettably, La Crosse could not boast about any Tiffany church windows within its city limits. However, with the construction of a new art gallery, Feast for the Eyes on the south side of the city in the old Fleischstad meat facility, Geoff hoped to change all that. He was involved in the planning of the gallery, where he served on the board of directors, and had suggested the addition of a modest Tiffany stained-glass window to grace the entry of the gallery. The committee had wholeheartedly approved. However, he had yet to locate and acquire a window for inclusion in the gallery's design scheme.

Currently, he was unemployed, but a generous inheritance from his wealthy parents made worries about a job pointless. Tall and lanky, the thirty-something wasn't exactly handsome, but his narrow face held a pair of inquisitive green eyes, and behind them burned an innate curiosity and a sharp intelligence that drove him in his quest for all things Tiffany. His brown, wavy hair was cut in a classic mullet, but it was rather attractive on him and frequently earned him a second glance from females he met on his architectural expeditions. He dressed modestly in muted colors except for a red T-shirt he'd bought at a convention of interior designers, which flaunted the saying, "It's a Tiffany Thing You Wouldn't Understand."

Three rows behind Geoff on the Delta flight, a distinguished-looking gentleman flipped through a magazine with an air of detached indifference. Lewis Borden uncrossed his legs and waited patiently as the flight attendant walked down the aisle preparing the passengers for deplaning. The man's dark gray business suit was finely tailored, his fingernails were clean and clipped, and his mustache and beard expertly trimmed, but his cold, gray eyes lacked any warmth that would attract anyone to him. He remained aloof and unapproachable, unfazed by the chatter of the friendly flight attendants.

As the plane descended for landing, trays were snapped into place, and people began gathering up their books and magazines, tablets and phones, and placing them in their briefcases and bags. The older man had been keeping an eye on Geoff LaSarde since the luggage auction at the O'Hare International Airport in Chicago late yesterday afternoon. From everything Borden could deduce, LaSarde had no idea he was being followed, nor was he aware of the important information he carried in the luggage he'd purchased at the auction.

The luggage was part of the estate of Howard Ellison, a lumber baron from Oshkosh, Wisconsin, who had built a lavish Victorian home in the city from the profits he'd made at several sawmills in and around Oshkosh. The suitcase, a vintage calfskin throwback, had disappeared and recently come to light when the historical society in Oshkosh discovered it at an auction. They purchased it and then sent it by plane to a museum curator in Chicago who was preparing a display about the historical significance of the lumber industry in Wisconsin at the turn of the century. Unfortunately, the luggage had been taken off the plane, and when the curator had failed to pick it up, it was added to the rest of the unclaimed luggage and eventually sent to a large room on the lower level of the airport where luggage auctions were held every couple of months.

Locating the luggage had been a challenge for Lewis Borden, but last week, using bribery and threats, his contacts found the elusive baggage with the valuable information at the airport's huge unclaimed baggage area. Learning that the luggage would be sold at the auction, Borden had been dispatched to the airport by his boss but had gotten stranded in Chicago traffic and arrived late. He missed the bidding on the suitcase. The realization that he'd failed in his mission left him with a dull ache in his stomach, but he was determined to redeem himself. He'd followed Geoff LaSarde to the boarding area and listened to a conversation he was having with another young thirty-something. When Geoff mentioned La Crosse, Wisconsin, as his destination, Lewis Borden quickly went to the ticket counter and bought a standby ticket.

Waiting to board the airplane, he called his boss and explained his dilemma. The contents of the suitcase held a special interest for his boss, and Borden's orders from his employer when he'd admitted his screwup were to "keep that young kid from doing something stupid with the suitcase he bought. We need what's in it, and I'll not take failure as an option. That's why I'm sending you. Don't disappoint me again."

Lewis Borden smiled to himself. *I am an efficient taskmaster capable of convincing anyone to do anything—with the right amount of deadly force.* Geoff LaSarde was about to find out just how convincing Lewis Borden could be.

Half an hour later, Geoff deplaned, grabbed his piece of luggage and backpack from the overhead rack, and walked to his 2019 Subaru in the airport parking lot. The air smelled of river water and spawning fish, freshly mowed grass, and the sweet, intoxicating scent of lilacs. May was a glorious time of year in Wisconsin, and this spring had delivered a streak of fabulous mild weather, gentle rainfalls, and burgeoning, vibrant greenery among the coulees and bluffs of the Driftless Area. Geoff unlocked his car, opened the back hatch, and placed his backpack and the old suitcase he'd purchased at the luggage auction in the vehicle. He crammed his lean frame in the front seat and drove to his home on the north side of La Crosse near Red Cloud Park.

As an only child of doting parents who were now deceased, he'd inherited a small fortune from patents on his father's medical inventions. He lived comfortably, yet modestly, in his parents' home on a tree-lined boulevard in one of La Crosse's north-side neighborhoods. The house on St. Cloud Street was a low, cozy gray bungalow with a small greenhouse attached to the back of the home. Perennial flower gardens surrounded the small residence and added to its charm. Geoff parked his Subaru in the garage, walked through the breezeway connected to the house, and unlocked the kitchen door.

His cat, Sir Lancelot, a huge tabby male, greeted him with cold, yellow eyes and a husky meow.

Despite the cat's aloof nature, Geoff had a deep affection for the ornery feline. The young man leaned down and affectionately fluffed the cat's ears and stroked his smooth coat, then refilled his bowls with fresh food and water. He walked through the small kitchen and dining room to the living room, turned the thermostat up to sixty-five degrees, and heard the furnace kick in.

Dusk had fallen. Geoff switched on the Tiffany lamp next to the leather couch. The dragonfly pattern glowed as light passed through the intricate pieces of glass causing the colorful insects to glow with an other-worldly luminescence. He walked down the hall to his bedroom, unpacked his clothes, threw his underwear, shirts, and socks in the laundry basket, set his Dopp kit on the bed, and placed the backpack on a hook behind the door.

He always traveled light when he went to luggage auctions. You never knew what the luggage might include inside, and since you were not allowed to open the bags before bidding, what you actually purchased could be surprising, but that was part of the fun of the hobby.

Sometimes he bought more than one piece. Recently, in February, he'd traveled to Cincinnati and bought two huge Samsonite suitcases. One of them had been loaded with expensive, tropical clothing—Tommy Bahama and Vineyard Vines watercolor shirts, Tiboyz Hawaiian shorts, and Driftwood cargo shorts—all with the tags still on them. Unfortunately, Geoff wasn't in the market for a tropical wardrobe in February, when it was still in the lower thirties at night in Wisconsin. Still, he was able to take the upscale clothing to one of the many secondhand resale shops in Rochester, Minnesota, where he sold the merchandise and made a quick thousand-dollar return on his purchase. Not bad for having paid only twenty dollars for the suitcase. The other piece of luggage yielded a collection of cameras and recording equipment, which Geoff stashed on a shelf in the spare bedroom. One of these days, he'd examine them and determine their value.

He strolled back to the kitchen and picked up the vintage suitcase from the O'Hare auction. Something about the luggage appealed to his sense of style—a throwback to a simpler time. It was made of tanned calfskin and was accentuated with brown trim around the edges and corners, and it had a fancy brass key lock beneath the leather handle. Geoff leaned down and read the label affixed near the lock, Anthi Leoni, an old, well-known Italian name in quality leather luggage. The clerk at the auction had to drum up interest in the old suitcase, and after a short, intense exchange with another bidder, Geoff had won the luggage for one hundred dollars. He chuckled to himself. The luggage alone might be worth that in a store that specializes in vintage items.

Geoff carried the suitcase to his bedroom and plopped it on the bed. He carefully opened the luggage, his hands shaking in anticipation. Unfolding the suitcase, he peered at the contents inside.

At first, he was disappointed. There was nothing but some musty, yellowing papers. But then, as he sifted through the paperwork inside the case, his disappointment turned to amazement. A newspaper article caught his attention. He stood stock still for several minutes reading the article about a horrendous fire at an Oshkosh, Wisconsin, lumber baron's mansion in 1904, which resulted in some Tiffany windows disappearing. One of the windows depicted a Knights Templar figure in full armor, and the other windows featured various Templar iconography. A search for the windows after the fire by the Oshkosh police had come up empty. Now, over one hundred years later, despite intense interest by other Tiffany experts and amateur sleuths, the windows were still missing.

Geoff gazed across the room, thinking about the information. He'd read about these windows during his research for his graduate thesis. The Ellison windows had been missing for a long time, and their whereabouts were a continuing mystery in the world of Tiffany. He could never have known the suitcase contained such intriguing information. It was almost as if a stranger had reached over and tapped him on the shoulder, saying, "Look at this. It's right up your alley. Missing Tiffany windows." What were the odds? *About a million to one,* he thought. Geoff grabbed the top papers along with the newspaper article and quickly walked into his study, opened his roll-top desk, and deposited them inside.

Just then his landline rang. He was tempted to let it go to the answering machine so he could get something to eat out of the refrigerator, but he was sure there were several messages to answer already, so he quickly walked back into the kitchen and picked up the phone.

"Hello. This is Geoff."

"Hey, buddy. Where've you been? I've been trying to get a hold of you for two days."

"I could ask you the same thing, Jamie. But to answer your question, I went to an airport luggage auction in Chicago, and I just got back," Geoff replied. Jamie Alberg was an archaeologist friend. The two young men had been on numerous digs together throughout the Tri-State region.

"You know we discovered another vein of buried pottery at Fish Farm Mounds down near Lansing. The items we're finding are pretty significant—some more Oneota pots, pipestone tablets, bone awls, and some turtle shell rattles. Cool stuff. I'm getting a crew together.

Can you help us excavate for a few days?" Jamie asked.

Geoff could imagine the excitement in Jamie's eyes, and he heard the quiver of anticipation in his friend's voice when he spoke about the new discoveries buried in the river silt.

"Well, I guess I could help for a few days," Geoff replied with reluctance, "but I've got a couple of pressing projects that I need to finish in the next few weeks for the new art gallery. I can help until Friday, but then I have other priorities."

"Great! I'll call you tomorrow and explain how to get to the site. See ya," Jamie finished, and the line went dead.

Geoff hung up and stood by the phone thinking about his friend. Brilliant and determined to make a name for himself as a famous archaeologist and treasure hunter, Jamie Alberg was demanding and obstinate. He'd also been involved in a number of cases at the La Crosse Sheriff's Department as a consultant in a couple of mysterious predicaments involving gold coins and ancient Native American ball clubs, things he believed required his expert opinion, even though the police hadn't solicited him. Jamie had audaciously inserted himself into the investigations and had come close to being killed both times. His social awkwardness and bravado notwithstanding, Geoff had formed an authentic friendship with Jamie, and he looked forward to seeing him again.

At that very moment, Sir Lancelot let out a loud mewl, and his hair puffed out and stood on end. Simultaneously, Geoff heard a rustling noise behind him. A strong arm grabbed him around the neck in a choke hold. Despite his resistance, within seconds Geoff slumped into unconsciousness, and the perpetrator lowered him roughly to the floor.

The darkly attired man walked rapidly through the small house, searching for the vintage luggage. Finding the case opened on the bed, he shoved the loose papers that were lying next to it inside, clicked the lock, and walked back to the kitchen. Looking down at the young man who lay crumpled on the floor, he was momentarily tempted to send him into oblivion. Instead, he reached into his pocket, retrieved a syringe of potent benzodiazepine, which he promptly injected into Geoff's rear end. The young man groaned, then fell silent.

However, Sir Lancelot, the cat, had other ideas. The feline suddenly gripped the intruder's leg hard with his front claws and sank his sharp teeth into the man's calf. The perpetrator stifled a scream and kicked at the cat, who scampered away unscathed. Lewis Borden turned hurriedly toward the door and silently slipped into the dark night.

WEDNESDAY, MAY 16

2

On Wednesday morning, Jamie Alberg stood in his garage on Madison Street in La Crosse, carefully selecting the tools he needed for the archaeological dig at Fish Farm Mounds near Lansing, Iowa. His canvas bag lay open on the workbench, and he muttered to himself as he loaded the equipment into the bag. Selecting paintbrushes of various sizes, plastic spoons, string, stakes, a collection of toothbrushes, dental picks, and trowels from his bench, he carefully arranged them in the pockets of the cloth canvas bag his mother had made for him. After he loaded his tools in the car, he went back into the office of his small ranch-style home and gathered up a collection of notebooks and maps of the Fish Farm Mounds excavation site and stuffed them in a backpack along with a couple of digital cameras, blank notebooks, and fine-tipped Sharpie pens.

Jamie zipped up the bag, then suddenly remembered he was supposed to call Geoff LaSarde to give him directions to the excavation site. Instead of a phone call, he decided to drive over to Geoff's house on St. Cloud Street and pick him up. It was only a few blocks away. With the rising price of gas, it made sense to ride share anyway.

Jamie loaded his knapsack and tools into his Volkswagen Golf and drove to Geoff's house. The misting rain that had begun to fall earlier in the morning had turned into a steady, hammering shower. Sitting in his VW Golf next to the curb, Jamie thought about his friend's interest in Louis Comfort Tiffany. No matter what topic they discussed, Geoff would inevitably steer the conversation to his favorite subject. Jamie chuckled to himself. It was a familiar ploy. *I guess we aren't that different. Every conversation I get into with somebody eventually leads to archaeology or hidden treasure,* he thought.

Jamie reached up and pulled the hood of his windbreaker over his head. Opening the car door, he stepped out and walked to the house. He knocked lightly on the front door. Getting no response, he walked around the side of the house to the garage, letting himself in through the side door. He strolled through a glass breezeway and stepped into the kitchen.

Geoff lay unconscious on the floor, his long arms splayed over his head. Sir Lancelot, the cat, appeared and meowed loudly, walking back and forth near Geoff in obvious distress.

Jamie sucked in his breath. "Geoff! Geoff!" he yelled as he knelt down next to him. He gently shook his friend, who groaned and rolled over. "Hey, what happened?" Jamie asked. "Did you get drunk? Did you pass out?"

"What are you doing here?" Geoff muttered, his eyes at half-mast. "Why am I on the kitchen floor?"

"I don't know. I just came over to give you a ride to Lansing," Jamie told him.

"Lansing? What're you doing in Lansing?"

"Don't you remember? You were going to help me at the Fish Farm site today. We were going to do some excavating."

"We were?" Geoff said, totally confused. His eyes were dull, and he was very pale.

"Yeah. We talked about it last night, but obviously you don't remember that conversation," Jamie reminded him as he knelt beside his friend.

"No, I don't remember that," Geoff said. He groaned ominously. "I think I'm gonna puke." Geoff sat up and proceeded to vomit between his legs. The stench made Jamie gag.

"Hey, let's get you up into a chair," Jamie said after a few minutes. "Then we'll get you cleaned up, and I'll take you to the ER to have you checked out."

He got behind Geoff, gripped him under the arms, and helped him to his feet. Geoff wobbled precariously as Jamie grabbed him around the waist and led his friend to a kitchen chair. He had turned another shade of white, and the front of his shirt and jeans was splattered with vomit.

"I feel like I've been hit by a Mack truck," he whispered.

"Just sit there. I'll get you some water," Jamie said. He stepped over the puddle of vomit, found a glass in the cupboard, and returned with water. He handed the glass to Geoff, who sipped it timidly.

After a few moments, Geoff seemed to regain his equilibrium. He stood up, blinked several times, and took a few wobbly steps.

"Need help?" Jamie asked.

"No, I think I can make it," Geoff replied, walking slowly toward the bedroom.

Ten minutes later, Geoff came into the kitchen in a fresh shirt and jeans. Feeling nauseated again, he sat down at the kitchen table and cradled his head in his hands. Finally, he looked up and held Jamie's concerned stare.

"I've been robbed," he said simply. His expression was flat, but his green eyes burned with anger.

"Robbed? Whaddya mean? What was taken?" Jamie asked, alarmed.

"It's a long story, but the short of it is the luggage I bought yesterday at the O'Hare airport is gone," he said.

"Was it valuable?" Jamie asked, scrunching up his face in confusion.

"It must have been to somebody. Otherwise, they wouldn't have knocked me out and risked being caught red-handed in my house." Some color had returned to Geoff's cheeks, and he was beginning to feel the outrage that comes from being attacked and burglarized.

"Holy moly," Jamie whispered under his breath. He considered the seriousness of the situation: His friend had been attacked and robbed. It was obvious even to Jamie, who sometimes struggled to interpret situations accurately, that someone had to take charge. The young archaeologist straightened his shoulders. "Listen, we need a plan," he said. "I'll take you to the emergency room, and then I'll call my friend Lt. Higgins at the sheriff's department. He'll know what to do," he said with authority in his voice.

"But I don't know who did this!" Geoff hissed. "I won't be much help. I can't even give a description of the intruder. He hit me from behind and knocked me out cold."

Jamie waved his hands in front of him. "That doesn't matter. Lt. Higgins is an expert. He's solved some pretty baffling crimes," Jamie explained. *Of course, he had a little help from me,* he thought, smiling to himself. Then he thought a little more and remembered the times Lt. Higgins had rescued him from certain death. *Better not get too cocky, Alberg.* He could almost see Lt. Higgins' blue eyes blazing with fury and hear his voice bouncing off the walls in his office as he dressed him down for some investigative faux pas. Jamie squeezed his eyes shut when the memory of those confrontations flooded into his brain.

"Come on, buddy. We need to get you to the ER so you can see a medical professional," he said to Geoff, who stood up and wobbled unsteadily. Jamie escorted his friend to his VW Golf in front of the house and drove across town to the Mayo ER.

Jamie slouched in a chair in the hallway of the Mayo Clinic waiting for the diagnosis of his friend to be completed. While he waited, he dialed the La Crosse Sheriff's Department on Vine Street. After several transfers, he was finally connected to Emily Warehauser, secretary to the investigative team on the third floor.

"Jamie! What have you been up to? Are you in town again?" Emily asked, rolling her eyes toward the ceiling.

"I am. I've been back for about a month. I got called to an excavation site near Lansing. I'm heading up a dig there, so I'll be in town for a while. I'm living in my house on Madison Street," he said proudly.

"A house? You bought a house?"

"Well . . . my mom floated me a loan . . . sort of," Jamie explained sheepishly. "It's really more of a dumping ground for all my tools, notebooks, and collections of pottery and Native American artifacts. To be honest, I'm not there very much."

"Wow! That's exciting!" Emily said.

"Well, I can't really blame my mom. She was sick of storing all my archaeological stuff at her place, so we found a little ranch house and bought it. Nothing fancy." There was a brief pause, then Jamie asked, "Is Lt. Higgins around there today?"

"He is. I'll connect you. Hold on," Emily said briskly. Putting Jamie on hold, she got up quickly from her desk and trotted down the hall to Jim Higgins' office. Jim was sitting at his desk giving his full attention to some kind of report.

"Lt. Higgins?"

Jim looked up, his reading glasses perched on his nose. "Yes, Emily. You need something?"

"Not really. But Jamie Alberg is on the line, and I wanted to give you a heads up, sir."

Jim cocked his head, made a wry face, then met Emily's stare. "I'll take his call, Emily," he said, taking off his reading glasses. "He's probably on some wild goose chase that he wants to tell me about. Don't worry. I can handle it, but thanks for the warning," Jim said, picking up his landline.

Lt. Jim Higgins, senior investigator for the La Crosse Sheriff's Department, was familiar with Jamie and his eccentric quirks. The mildly autistic archaeologist had become embroiled in a couple of investigations in the department over the last few years. Although the kid's knowledge and expertise had come in handy in both investigations, Jamie's talent for getting himself into tight quarters with criminals had almost gotten him killed twice.

Emily backed out of the office, wondering about Higgins' new and improved attitude toward the young archaeological savant. She knew Jamie had caused the lieutenant considerable anxiety in the past, so she was surprised by his friendly attitude toward the little braggart. *There's only one Jamie Alberg,* she thought as she returned to her desk. *Thank God for that.*

"So, Jamie, what have you been up to?" Jim asked casually. He leaned away from the paperwork on his desk and swiveled the desk chair toward the narrow window that overlooked Vine Street.

"I was hired by MVAC to head up a dig at Fish Farm Mounds down near Lansing," Jamie explained. "We found another vein of pottery that needs to be uncovered, but that's not why I'm calling."

"Okay. So why are you calling?" Jim asked. He propped his feet on the low window ledge as he prepared to listen to Jamie's account. *Here we go again,* he thought. *Another big mystery that needs solving. A bunch of bragging and supposed intrigue.*

"My friend, Geoff LaSarde, was attacked in his home last night on the north side and had an item stolen from his house."

Jim sat up abruptly and put his feet on the floor. "Did he call the city police?"

"No."

"Why not?"

"When I got to his house this morning, I found him unconscious on his kitchen floor. He was out cold. We were planning to go to Lansing today to work at the dig, but when I walked into his kitchen at about nine o'clock this morning, there he was sprawled out like a dead duck. So, I woke him up, and after he puked all over himself, I brought him to the Mayo ER to get checked out. That's where I am now."

Despite Jim's outward calm, he felt a prickle of goosebumps along his arms—an omen of some enigmatic conundrum in which Jamie would try to insert himself, all with possible catastrophic results. Higgins was experienced in dealing with this kid. After all, they had a storied history centered around the resolution of criminal activities that had thrust them into the national spotlight. Dealing with Jamie was never simple. He attracted perpetrators like a lightning rod attracts lightning.

"What was stolen?" Higgins asked in a calm voice despite the growing dread that felt like a tight knot in his chest.

"I don't really understand it all, but apparently a suitcase that Geoff purchased at a luggage auction at Chicago's O'Hare Airport is missing. There must have been something in the suitcase that someone wanted, and whoever it was, he was willing to break into the house, steal the suitcase, and knock Geoff unconscious. Kinda crazy, huh?"

Jim could almost imagine Jamie's expression at that moment—a subtle grin, his eyes wide with wonder. *How come he's never been killed?* Jim wondered.

"Well, that does sound a little unusual," Jim said, although he hesitated to offer his services. He'd already overstepped the boundaries between city police and the sheriff's department on another previous case that resulted in a letter of reprimand in his file. He didn't want another one.

"I need your help, Lt. Higgins," Jamie said, coming to the point. "Geoff can't remember anything. The only thing he remembers is coming home from the airport, unpacking his stuff, and after talking to me on the phone, the next thing he knew he was waking up on his kitchen floor this morning," Jamie explained.

"What was in the suitcase that was so important?" Jim asked.

"I have no idea, and I don't think Geoff really knows either. But if you could come and talk to him, I'm sure he could tell you about it, and you could get to the bottom of this."

"Hmm . . . I'm kinda busy this morning," Jim said, his voice dry and detached, trying to distance himself from the whole affair. "But I can send a city police officer over later when Geoff gets home."

"I was hoping you could talk to him personally, sir," Jamie said insistently.

Jim hesitated, then said, "Call me back when he's done in the emergency room. Maybe I can break free this afternoon and drive over and talk to him," Jim suggested. "What's his address?"

Jamie gave him the address, thanked him profusely, and hung up.

Jim sat at his desk thinking for a moment about the conversation with Jamie. *So much for not getting sucked into another hullabaloo with this kid.* But in all fairness, Jamie's friend was attacked and robbed, and since he reported it, the incident was official police business now.

Jim picked up his cell and dialed Tanya Pedretti, chief of police for the city of La Crosse.

"Chief Pedretti," a pleasant female voice said.

"Tanya. Jim Higgins here."

"Yeah, Jim. What's up?"

"Just a heads up. I got a call from a friend of mine about someone on the north side who was attacked in his home last night. This source of mine discovered him unconscious on his kitchen floor this morning and took him to the emergency room. The situation sounds kind of sketchy. He asked me to talk to the guy. I tried to bow out, but—"

"Jamie Alberg, right?" Tanya said brusquely.

"Yeah, unfortunately, he asked me to check into the situation. You okay with that?" Jim asked.

"As long as you keep me informed. We're stretched to the max right now with drug busts, traffic stops, and domestic calls. I'm short two officers, plus I've got some bank clerk who was brought in this morning on suspicion of embezzlement at one of the credit unions here in town. So, between you and me and the fence post, it's a don't ask, don't tell situation. Can you live with that?"

"Yep. Thanks, Tanya." Jim had no sooner hung up than his cell buzzed.

"Hi, honey," Carol said sweetly.

"Oh, hi," Jim said distractedly. "What's up?"

"I just wanted to let you know Gladys fell at home. She called me after she got up off the floor, and I took her to the emergency room.

She's got a nasty contusion on the back of her head, but you know Gladys. She just brushed it off. I think they'll release her in a few minutes, and then I'll take her home."

Gladys Hanson was a dear friend of the Higgins' family. She had counseled Jim during difficult cases, and he was sure she had offered up many prayers on his behalf over the years. After the death of his first wife, Margie, to breast cancer, Gladys had resolutely stood by his side, allowing him to grieve and vent in the privacy of her farm home on County K. Jim valued her as a friend and confidante. In addition, she had become Lillie and Henri's proxy grandma since Jim's and Carol's parents were deceased.

"You think she'll be all right?" Jim asked.

"Probably, although brain bleeds are very common in the elderly, especially after a head injury. We'll have to wait and see."

"Why is she so darned stubborn?" Jim spat angrily. "You know, I've been after her to sell the farm and move into an apartment."

Beneath the brusque question, Carol could hear the layers of concern Jim had for his old friend.

"Well, honey, the old saying applies: You can lead a horse to water, but you can't make him drink," Carol said. Silence ensued.

Jim sighed loudly, his disquiet about Gladys' situation apparent. "She's been such a good friend," he said wistfully, "I just wish she'd let us help her."

"It's a process, Jim. She's been independent for so long, it's hard for her to accept help, but maybe over time, she'll come around," Carol said. She paused. "Would you stop and check on her on your way home tonight?"

"Yeah, I can do that."

"Okay, the doctor just walked in. I'll call you later. Gotta go," Carol said, and she hung up.

Jim laid his cell down, stood up, and walked to the long, narrow window of his third-story office. The bluffs in the distance reflected the morning sunlight, and several eagles hovered overhead, the warm updrafts lifting them high above the rugged landscape as they searched for prey in the brambles. The distant wail of an ambulance whined on the street close by, and Jim looked down at the traffic on Vine Street below, where a biker was riding dangerously close to traffic, seemingly oblivious to potential hazards. Jim shook his head, thinking about Sam Birkstein's passion for the sport of biking. *That'd be the last thing I'd do with my spare time,* he thought sourly. *Riding a bike next to traffic.*

He considered the circumstances of Jamie Alberg's friend on the north side again and wondered what kind of situation might develop. A home invasion, an assault, and a missing suitcase? It all sounded like a made-for-TV movie script. Jim shook his head in frustration. How did this stuff always land in his lap? He didn't know, but one thing he did know from past experience: When Jamie got involved in police business, the result was usually anything but ordinary. In fact, the result was usually a disaster in the making.

Jim scowled, then turned, walked back to his desk, and continued the paper shuffle. *Everything will reveal itself as events unfold,* he thought. *You can't hurry the resolution of a crime.*

3

After returning to their home on Chipmunk Coulee Road following the visit to the ER with Gladys, Carol wrangled their golden retriever puppy, Latte, into the back hallway. Despite her frustration with the family's new pet, she took a few moments to cuddle the squirming ball of fluff before she put him in his kennel. She thought back to the day early in April when Jim appeared in the dining room with the whimpering puppy under his arm.

Jim hadn't consulted her about getting a puppy, which was unusual, but how he could think that a dog was a good idea at this stage in their lives was beyond her. Their house had just undergone a major renovation after a horrible house fire started by the villainous Devon Williams. While their home had been in shambles for months, they'd stayed with their dear family friend, Gladys Hanson, on her small farm on County K until the renovations and updates could be finished. The new carpet, drapes, and furniture were all fair game to the gnawing, chewing, defecating tendencies of a juvenile dog. Carol could just imagine the damage that might ensue. She'd have to be extra vigilant until the little imp was trained.

When Jim presented the puppy to Lillie and Henri, he was rewarded with squeals of joy. Carol smiled recalling Lillie's reaction.

"Daddy, this is just about the best thing you've ever done," Lillie bubbled enthusiastically, her blue eyes glowing with excitement. Henri looked up at Jim with uninhibited joy on his little face and added, "No, Daddy, this *is* the best thing you've ever done."

Jim shrugged his shoulders, grinned widely, and gazed at Carol. The pandemonium the puppy was causing with the kids around his feet and his wife's scrutinizing gaze made him wonder if he might have overstepped his boundaries.

"They needed something to help them put the fire in the past," he said over the ruckus, "something to help them build new happy memories. Just think of it as emotional support."

Carol considered Jim's reasoning and decided she couldn't argue with him. Their two young children, nine-year-old Lillie and five-year-old Henri, were still struggling to forget the horrible night they'd escaped from their burning house by the skin of their teeth. Lillie and Henri were plagued with frequent nightmares and insecurity from the terrifying incident. Now, eight months later, the house had been rebuilt and redecorated. The living room had been bumped out to accommodate a new baby grand piano for Lillie, and special features like the skylight in the dining room had once again made the Higgins' home an oasis of comfort, light, and love—a place to escape from the pressures of Jim's job and a haven where they could nurture and raise their children, make good memories, and leave their troubles behind.

Carol placed Latte in the kennel and returned to the kitchen. Today was her day off from her work as office manager at the La Crosse County Coroner and Medical Examiner's office. After getting Gladys comfortably settled back at the farmhouse after the ER visit, she stirred up a batch of chocolate chip cookies for the kids to enjoy when they returned home in the afternoon from St. Ignatius Catholic School in Genoa. Humming under her breath, she plopped the cookies on a baking sheet and thought back to the recent family trip they'd taken to Paris last October.

The fall weather and infrequent tourists made the autumn

trip delightful. They walked and biked all over the great city. The children oohed and aahed as they stretched their necks upward to the pinnacle of the Eiffel Tower. Riding up on the lifts, the children enjoyed a 360-degree view of the marvelous city while Jim and Carol sipped on champagne from the bar. Later, Jim and Carol soaked up the magic of the city on a romantic boat trip down the Seine at night holding hands and stealing kisses while visions of iconic Paris landmarks and scenes drifted by: the Eiffel Tower, the Louvre, the Musée d'Orsay, and the Notre Dame Cathedral under reconstruction after the devastating fire on April 15, 2019, that destroyed the iconic landmark.

A trip to a small bed and breakfast on the outskirts of Paris later in the week provided the children with ample opportunities to run and play with chickens and goats while Jim and Carol luxuriated in late morning lattes accompanied by crisp French pastries and evenings of delectable wine, creamy goat cheeses, and fabulous French cuisine. They came home thoroughly refreshed and relaxed. Since then, Jim's infrequent depression had been pushed into the shadows. That, in itself, was worth every dime they'd spent on the trip.

Carol took a pan of cookies out of the oven and poured herself a cup of coffee. She thought about her previous sedate life as a forty-year-old divorcée in a comfortable, predictable job to Luke Evers, the La Crosse County coroner. When Jim entered her life six years ago, her predictable lifestyle took a dramatic turn and revved into high gear.

The daily grind of the Higgins' household was busy and strenuous. Jim's job exposed him to danger and threats, which sometimes spilled over into their family life. Hunting down perpetrators often left him physically exhausted, and the stress from all-night stakeouts and the looming danger of injury and gunshot wounds frequently depleted his energy. Most of the time her husband was easy to love, but recently, the pressures of his job had crept into his mental real estate, and at times, the stress rearranged his temperament and disposition. He was less patient with the ups and downs of life, and having young children later in life often left him irritable. Carol sighed. Lately, it seemed she was always trying to put out fires. The children's schedules, interests, and schoolwork, Jim's demanding work hours, and of course, the unpredictable nature of police investigations sometimes strained their relationship. Carol knew that trying to figure out why people do the things they do could wear on anyone's equilibrium. But she also knew Jim's deeply held moral code and the tenets that guided his work as a police officer did not give him many options. Anyone who had an ounce of moral fiber could understand that.

In addition, maintaining their beautiful home at times left her exhausted and physically used up like an old shoe. But when she compared her life now with her life before Jim arrived on the scene, she knew she wouldn't trade places with anyone. She thought of the old saying her sister Vivian liked to use when counseling her patients: The grass is always greener on the other side of the fence because it's fertilized with bullshit. This truth Carol knew all too well; life was difficult for everyone at times, and anyone who said differently hadn't experienced all that life could throw at you, or they were full of bullshit. Take your pick.

Her cell buzzed on the counter.

"Higgins' residence. Carol speaking."

"Hey, baby. How're you doin'?" Jim asked softly.

"Just baking some cookies for the kids," Carol said, enjoying the sound of Jim's warm, deep voice.

"The Paris effect is still going strong, sweetheart." Jim said softly, "I'm thinking about that night when we got back to the hotel after the boat ride down the Seine."

Carol grinned. "Hey, I was just thinking about our trip, too. That was pretty great, wasn't it? But what about last night?"

"Oh yeah, that was good, too," Jim chuckled, "but you know, Paris gives off a certain . . ."

"Magical mystique?" Carol asked. "Will it solve my puppy problem?"

"Definitely not," Jim chuckled. "So, did you get Gladys back home?"

"Oh yeah. She was more embarrassed than hurt. You know how proud she is."

"Yep. I know all about that. What did the doctor say?"

"Just that she may have a headache today, and then she'll probably turn many shades of purple, green, and yellow in the next week as the blood is reabsorbed into her system. She was feisty and scooted me out the door when I offered to stay a while. You know—that typical Norwegian grit," Carol said. "What have you been up to?"

"Well, guess what? I just got off the phone with none other than Jamie Alberg, child wonder, archaeologist in search of the next great discovery, treasure hunter extraordinaire."

"Oh, boy," Carol said. "That kid keeps showing up like a lost penny, doesn't he?" she said. "What's he up to now?"

"Oh, he's got a minor problem. A friend of his was burglarized last night over on the north side. Sounds pretty straightforward. I'll look into it this afternoon," Jim explained, but a shiver ran up his arms as he thought about the missing suitcase. *What was in that luggage that was so important?*

"Okay. Will you be home by six?" she asked.

"Should be. See you then. Love you," Jim said.

"Love you, too." Carol disconnected and laid her phone on the counter, feeling a wave of concern. When Jamie Alberg inserted himself into Jim's detective work, it was usually a portent of unpleasant events that were about to unfold. Standing in her kitchen, Carol envisioned a flashing amber light blinking a warning: Caution! Danger ahead! *Where Jamie was concerned, nothing was ever simple,* she thought.

4

On Wednesday afternoon, Jim pushed the pile of documents he'd worked on earlier to the side of his desk, grabbed his suit jacket, and headed to the parking lot of the law enforcement center. As he pulled out of his parking stall, Detective DeDe Deverioux arrived in her car and pulled up next to him. She rolled down the window, leaned over, and greeted Jim.

"Did you check in with Williams' attorney?" Jim asked.

"Yep. He says the trial is on the court calendar for late August, so we've still got a little time to get our ducks in a row," DeDe informed him.

"You might want to check in with Sam and Paul. They've been trying to track down some homeless guy over at Hoska Park who appears to be a full-fledged drug dealer," Jim said as he shrugged nonchalantly. "Seems he's operating out of a tent, tantalizing the homeless population with meth and cocaine, all in an attempt to alleviate the fact that homelessness sucks." Jim waved his hand in front of his face in frustration. "I don't know. It all sounds like business as usual."

"Will do, Chief. I'll talk to them." She smiled.

"I'm heading over to the north side to check on a burglary incident that happened last night. See you later," Jim said as he began driving out of the lot.

After the morning rain, the sky had lightened a bit, but a persistent mist continued to fall. Jim reached over and flipped on his wipers while he studied the clouds. Bits of blue were peeking through the gray cover like a bashful child hiding behind their mother's skirt. He thought about the burglary that involved a suitcase. *Doesn't seem credible,* he thought. *But it's been reported, so I guess we'd better check it out.*

Jim turned on West Avenue, the highway that spanned Myrick Marsh, which contained floodwater from the La Crosse River each spring. The marsh had been the fodder of many city council debates. Developers thought the area had potential for untapped commercial ventures, while scientists and naturalists put up a good fight to protect the marsh since it acted like a geographical sponge, soaking up floodwaters, and providing habitat for a number of native plants, migratory birds, and other animals. Bordering the wetland a half mile away, Jim enjoyed the familiar view of the sandstone bluffs that hemmed in the long, narrow city of La Crosse and rose majestically into view. The change in scenery could make a person forget you were only five minutes from downtown La Crosse.

He passed over the causeway near Menard's, and when he spotted a green-backed heron posing motionless on a dead tree limb near the road, he pulled over for a few moments and watched the chunky bird raise its crest and flick its tail. His thoughts turned dark. He recalled a day from the past when a victim had been discovered shot in the head on the state bike trail adjacent to the marsh. *Another time, another crime,* he thought philosophically.

Jim pulled out into traffic again and drove through the north side of La Crosse until he rolled up to a small bungalow on St. Cloud Street where Geoff LaSarde lived. He'd called LaSarde earlier, and as Jim walked up to the home on the shady, quiet boulevard, a tall, young man opened the front door, then waved him inside.

Jim entered the home and picked up the slight scent of vomit in the air. The two men shook hands, and Geoff invited Jim into a small, comfortable living room. Bookshelves flanked a red brick fireplace. The two men settled into gray swivel upholstered chairs that faced each other. A low coffee table between them was stacked with several large art books about Louis Comfort Tiffany. Geoff kicked his ankle up on his knee and leaned back in the chair, studying the senior detective.

Higgins was middle-aged, over six feet tall, and fit, and had a strange mix of gray-blond hair that was styled in a short, funky way. He wore expensive navy wool slacks, a subtle gray and blue plaid wool jacket, and underneath the jacket a pale blue pin-striped shirt which was open at the neck. The detective's perceptive eyes drifted around the room taking in the atmosphere of the home. He had an easy self-confidence about him, but Geoff guessed he could be tough when circumstances required it. You didn't become a senior detective in charge of the investigative department by being a slouch. Higgins' gaze finally settled on the young man, and Geoff squirmed uncomfortably as the detective studied him.

"Thank you for coming, Lt. Higgins," Geoff began hesitantly, breaking the ice. "I understand Jamie contacted you this morning while I was getting checked out in the ER. He told me you've got quite a reputation for solving the unsolvable." The young man studied Jim's face wondering what his reaction would be to Jamie's unapologetic hype.

"Jamie has a knack for overstating the obvious," Jim chuckled, although he could feel the irritation resonate in his chest like a slight electric shock. *Jamie was already at it—embellishing the mundane.* He felt his neck redden with embarrassment at the thought of Jamie's description of him. *What has he been saying about me now?* he thought. *Whatever it is, it's overkill.* He shrugged his shoulders and mentally shook off his misgivings, took a deep breath, and said, "I don't know exactly what Jamie has told you about me, but I am a detective, so tracking down leads and witnesses and hunting for suspects who may have committed a crime is part of what I do. People like to think we get lucky when our team solves a crime. Sometimes we do get lucky, but there is skill involved. To be truthful, luck and skill usually happen in the cases we solve. Some luck, a lot of common sense, considerable skill. But just remember, whatever Jamie says about my abilities is probably mostly fantasy and a lot of claptrap."

"I've known him for quite a while," Geoff said, smiling.

Jim casually crossed his legs and said, "It all boils down to how much of Jamie's balderdash you choose to believe."

"He can lay it out there sometimes," Geoff casually commented.

Jim nodded. "So let's hear your story. Just tell me what happened last night."

Geoff proceeded to give his account of the previous night's events. He explained his interest in airport luggage auctions and the suitcase he'd bought at the O'Hare airport auction on Tuesday. The young man described his return flight to La Crosse and his uneventful drive home. Jim listened carefully. He didn't know anything about luggage auctions, but found the idea interesting. Geoff explained that auctions happened at regular intervals at major airports across the country, though few people knew about them. As Geoff talked, a picture popped into Jim's mind—piles of luggage spewing out the doors of the airport, creating mountains of Samsonite in the streets. He supposed the auctions made sense and eliminated the need to store unclaimed baggage that was left by travelers.

"It must be interesting to find out what's inside the suitcases," Jim commented when Geoff had finished his account.

The young man nodded his head vigorously. "Yeah, it's pretty exciting. Sometimes it's a total wash, but I always enjoy that aspect of the hobby. Not knowing what's inside is a mystery in and of itself."

"So tell me, what *was* inside the suitcase you purchased a few days ago?" Jim asked, his pen poised above the small memo pad he used to take notes. "The suitcase was taken during the burglary, right? Or was some other valuable thing taken from your home, like jewelry or money?"

Geoff leaned forward and rested his elbows on his knees. "I do have other valuables in my home like this Tiffany lamp, but apparently, it was the suitcase the guy was after, and it was taken from the bedroom down the hall."

"Anything else missing?" Jim asked.

"Not that I know of," Geoff answered.

"What was in the suitcase that was so important?"

"Just a bunch of old papers," the young expert explained. "When I first looked in it, I was pretty disappointed, but then I read the newspaper articles inside, and I have to say, the content was pretty fascinating."

"Fascinating in what way?" Jim asked, cocking his head at an angle.

Geoff stood suddenly and headed toward a short hallway that led to the bedrooms. "Wait a minute, and I'll show you." A few minutes later he returned to the living room carrying a small stack of yellowing papers. He plopped into the chair and laid the articles on the coffee table in front of Jim.

"I found these in the suitcase and skimmed them briefly. After I read them, I put them in my desk. I was going to study them later. When the intruder took the suitcase, he probably thought he got everything, but he didn't. I still had this stuff," Geoff waved his hand over the papers, "but I haven't really had a chance to study it. Like I said, at first glance, it looked pretty dull, but when you start reading it, well . . . it gets interesting."

"So these were the papers that got removed from the suitcase before it was stolen, right?" Jim asked. Geoff nodded. Jim spread the papers on the low coffee table in front of the chairs and scanned them quickly. A newspaper article from the *Oshkosh Gazette* dated 1904 caught his attention. He picked it up and began to read:

"Oshkosh Lumber Baron's Mansion Destroyed in Fire"

Late Sunday evening on December 18th, a fire broke out at the Howard Ellison mansion on Winnebago Street in Oshkosh. The blaze destroyed a substantial part of the interior of the lumber baron's Victorian mansion built in 1883. The home was well known for its Queen Anne architecture, elegant furnishings, and modern amenities, including hot and cold water and gas light fixtures. Several valuable Tiffany stained-glass windows lined the library of the home. They also sustained heavy smoke damage in the fire. At the time of the blaze, the family was visiting relatives in Madison. No one was injured during the fire.

The damage is estimated at $18,000. It is not known at this time if Ellison will rebuild. He was not available for comment.

Jim looked up from the paper with a quizzical look. "What's so interesting to you about this article?" he asked.

"Well, I'm something of an expert on Tiffany windows, and the article mentions several unusual stained-glass windows from the Ellison house," Geoff said.

Jim tipped his head to one side, the confusion still there. "Okay, so how does that tie in with the burglary?"

"I've been studying stained-glass windows for about ten years now, Lieutenant. I did my graduate dissertation at the University of Chicago on Tiffany stained-glass lamps and windows. I'd heard about the windows from this home while I was doing my graduate research. The Ellison windows disappeared after the fire, and no one has ever found them. I think I could safely say that I know the location of every Tiffany window that exists in the Midwest, but these windows disappeared into thin air and have never been found."

"How do you know that?" Jim asked. "What proof do you have?"

Geoff rifled through the newspaper articles, picked one out, and handed it to Jim. "Here's an article from the *St. Paul Pioneer Press* written after the fire that talks about the disappearance of the windows from the burn site. Apparently, they were loaded on a wagon and were supposed to be delivered by train to a glass restoration company in Winona for cleaning, but they never arrived. And I know of numerous other scholarly papers that discuss the missing windows."

"Are you saying there's a connection between the stolen luggage and the missing windows?" Jim asked as he briefly perused the article.

"Possibly. I think someone is determined to find out where they are. They either want to find them and put them on the market, or they want them for their own personal collection. Someone must have known the suitcase held important information about the windows' whereabouts, and they followed me from the auction, broke into my home, and took the suitcase to determine the location of the windows." Geoff shrugged his shoulders, but he stared intently at Jim. "Right now, that's the only possibility that makes any sense to me."

"How did you find out about this luggage?" Jim asked.

"I bought the suitcase because I liked the looks of it—you know, it was stylish, aged, and well- made. I was going to resell it at a vintage store. I had no idea what was in it, but I think someone else did and followed me to La Crosse. They broke into my house and walked off with it," Geoff finished. He looked at the floor, dejected and discouraged.

Jim sat quietly for a few minutes absorbing everything Geoff had told him. "Do you have any enemies?" he asked. His blue eyes seemed especially focused on the Tiffany expert.

A shadow passed across the young man's face. His crestfallen expression told Jim he couldn't imagine anyone who disliked him enough to try to kill him. "I can't think of anyone who would want to harm me. I'm not very threatening. I just know a lot about Tiffany stuff," he said, meeting Jim's gaze.

"The problem is someone did try to harm you. Luckily, you escaped relatively unscathed," Jim said seriously. Higgins had moments in his job when his ignorance showed, but if he was going to get to the bottom of the burglary and assault, then his lack of knowledge about Tiffany stained-glass windows was going to be on full display. *So be it,* he thought. *Nobody knows everything about everything.*

"Are these windows valuable?" Jim asked. Geoff's mouth fell open in astonishment, and by the look on his face, it was obvious Jim's ignorance about Tiffany windows shocked the young expert.

Geoff rubbed his hand across the stubble on his chin, and he met Jim's gaze with the confidence that comes from being an expert in the field. "Well, yes, they're extremely valuable, but as with anything old, that depends on their size and, more importantly, on their condition, and I suppose, their disappearance adds to their value. The windows from the Ellison home were very fine renditions of Tiffany's work, despite the damage they may have sustained in the fire. In addition, the subject matter of the windows centered around Knights Templar iconography—rare images, beautifully crafted by none other than Louis Comfort Tiffany, large in size. They contained the finest glass available at the time, using the latest techniques in stained-glass construction and design. To put it bluntly, they'd make any collector of stained glass drool with desire."

"Wait. Did you say Knights Templar? You mean King Arthur and the Round Table?" Jim asked. "That kind of stuff?" He was beginning to wonder where this investigation was going.

Geoff shook his head, and suddenly Jim was somewhat embarrassed by his ignorance about the subject. "The link between King Arthur and the Knights Templar is debatable and is still argued about to this day," Geoff said. "But, to your point, many believe the Templar saga and the Knights of the Round Table were linked during the Crusades of the Middle Ages."

"So would someone want the windows because of the images portrayed on them?" Jim asked, recovering from his embarrassment.

"I suppose that might be one motivation for wanting them," Geoff answered.

"What else?" Jim probed.

Geoff leaned back in his chair, relishing the questions. "Louis

Comfort Tiffany revolutionized the craft of stained glass by perfecting techniques in America previously seen only in the Middle Ages in Europe—windows like the ones in the Notre Dame Cathedral in Paris."

"I've been there and seen them. Those rose windows are unbelievable," Jim said, nodding.

"Tiffany was not afraid to go outside the box, and he experimented with the way sheets of glass were shaded and blended, which made his figures almost three-dimensional. Realistic, yet spiritual. The colors are very vivid. Many of the figures on his windows are life-size, and the light reflecting through them can be almost surreal, like the figures are actually standing before you." As Geoff talked, he got a faraway look in his eyes. "They're incredibly beautiful and very valuable in today's antique market," he finished.

Jim watched the art expert for a few moments, noticing the wistful quality in his voice and his dreamy expression.

Geoff focused his attention on Lt. Higgins.

"So, back to my original question. Can you give me a dollar figure on the value of these windows?" Jim asked, making notations in his small notebook.

"Supposedly there were five windows that went missing. Each window today could range in price from $100,000 to $500,000, depending on condition. If the five windows were to come up for auction today and be in relatively good shape, they might be worth several million dollars. But the subject of these windows is unusual, so that may bump up the price substantially, and they were rather large in size—about six feet high. They could make anywhere from five to ten million, depending on the parties involved and how badly they want them."

Jim whistled softly under his breath. "Well now, *that* is interesting."

"What are you going to do about all this, Lt. Higgins?"

"To start with, I need copies of all this information. My team will start digging into it. But there's one more thing I'm concerned about," Jim said solemnly.

"Oh, yeah? What's that?"

"Whoever broke into your house didn't get everything they wanted," Jim explained. "They may be back when they realize something's missing, so make sure someone checks on you every day, be aware of your surroundings, and take precautions to keep yourself safe."

Geoff seemed to shrink a little into the chair, and his eyes widened as Jim finished his warning.

"I can do that, I guess," he said. He scratched his neck and flicked his hair back.

"Show me where the attack took place," Jim said, suddenly standing up. Then he held up his hand. "Wait. I forgot to ask. How did the intruder disable you?"

"He put me in a choke hold 'til I passed out, and then he must have given me a shot of some kind. The tests at the hospital showed a substance in my blood called benzo . . . something." He waved as if he were shooing away a pesky fly.

"Benzodiazepine," Jim interrupted, "more commonly known as Xanax or Ativan. It's a class of drugs used for managing anxiety and panic attacks, among other uses. So, the intruder was a man?"

Geoff nodded. "I guess so. Must have been. He was pretty strong."

"If he gave you a shot of benzos, you were probably as limp as a rag doll."

"Well, he must have given me a big dose 'cause I was out all night. I never knew what hit me."

Geoff led Jim to the kitchen and stopped by the phone attached to the wall. Jim looked around, examining the walls and floor. The smell of vomit lingered in the air. Something on the wall caught his attention, and he got down on his hands and knees and stared at a small red spot near the floor baseboard.

"Was this spot here before the attack?" Jim asked, his nose about two inches from the wall.

Geoff leaned over Higgins' shoulder and looked at the spot. "I dunno," he said, wondering about Higgins' investigative methods.

"My house is fairly clean, but I'm not that fussy. That spot could've been there for a long time."

Jim whipped out his cell phone and aimed his flashlight at the questionable stain as he examined it. Then he clicked a photo of the spot.

"Did you hurt yourself recently?" Jim asked, straightening up, resting on his knees. Geoff stared at Higgins. "You know, did you cut yourself with a knife or something, enough that you would have bled so some of it might have dripped on the floor or wall?"

"No, not that I remember."

"Do you have any pets?" Jim asked, getting up from the floor.

"Yeah, my cat, Sir Lancelot."

"Bring him in here," Jim said.

"Why?"

"Just do it," Jim ordered curtly. Geoff briefly disappeared and returned to the kitchen carrying a huge, neutered cat.

"Whoa! That's a big cat," Jim said softly. Sir Lancelot watched Jim with wide yellow eyes.

"He's quite a specimen, isn't he?" Geoff said as he smiled proudly, stroking the cat's fur.

"Is he friendly?" Jim asked, leaning away a little.

"No, not usually. He's quite territorial, in fact. Generally, he doesn't take well to strangers."

"Can we look at his claws for a minute?" Jim asked.

"His claws? Why?" Jim frowned at Geoff until the young man held up his hand. Then he said, "I know. Just do it, right?"

"That's right," Jim said brusquely.

Geoff carefully inspected the cat's claws. Jim noticed there seemed to be some darker material under one of the claws on the cat's right paw.

"I know this is an unusual request," Jim said, "but I want you to bring your cat down to the lab at the sheriff's department on Vine Street this afternoon. Go to the second floor and ask for Carl Ettinger." Jim wrote his name on his memo pad and tore out the paper, handing it to Geoff. "I'll tell him you're coming in with your cat."

Geoff shrugged his shoulders. "And I'm doing this because . . .?"

"It's just a hunch at this point, but I think that spot might be blood. I want Carl to get a swab of whatever is under his claw at the lab. I'm also going to have the crime scene people come over and go through your house."

"Okay. You're searching for DNA samples, right?"

Jim pointed his finger at Geoff. "You got it. We might get lucky and find the perpetrator in one of the online databases. If not, at least we'll have the DNA on file."

"Thanks, Lieutenant. I appreciate this," Geoff said sincerely.

"No problem. Remember, take care of yourself, and bring the cat to the lab ASAP."

5

After DeDe Deverioux finished her conversation with Higgins in the parking lot on Wednesday afternoon, she rode the elevator to the third floor of the law enforcement building on Vine Street. When she stepped off the elevator, Emily Warehauser was standing near a group of secretaries shaking her head in disapproval as she listened to the group's gossip. DeDe waved casually and walked down the hall, peeking into Leslie Birkstein's office. She sighed, thinking of her partner who was still out on maternity leave, and her shoulders hunched in despondency at the thought of her absent friend. She missed her, but she understood Leslie's deep desire to be home with their new little daughter, Karina.

The last time DeDe visited with Leslie at her home on the bluff overlooking the Mississippi River a few weeks ago, she'd warmed up to the thought of a child of her own. JuJu, her chef husband, desperately wanted a family, but as DeDe watched Leslie in action, she realized parenting was a full-time job, and right now she had a full-time job as a detective at the La Crosse County Sheriff's Department. Besides, she rationalized, JuJu was so busy with his restaurant, *Si Bon,* on the south side of La Crosse, he barely had time for her, let alone a child. She concluded that a family would have to wait.

She traipsed down the hall to Sam Birkstein's office. He sat with his feet propped on the metal wastebasket near his desk, scrolling on his phone. He looked out the window as the misting rain continued unabated, with occasional gusts of wind slapping against the window.

"Hey, what's up with the drug dealer at Hoska Park?" DeDe asked. "Higgins told me a little bit about it. What's going on?"

Sam laid his phone on the desk. "We don't know if the guy's actually dealing drugs or not. We may have to do some more surveillance, but we've had complaints about him from some of the homeless population."

"It sounds weird," DeDe commented. "Is it going to develop into something?"

Sam hunched his shoulders and began to explain. "Hard to tell. This guy has been living at Hoska for a while. Paul and I learned about him in late April. The rumor from some of the other park residents is that he deals drugs and has women who visit his tent late at night. However, we haven't really staked him out in the evening yet. We're going to try and find him so we can talk to him, but he'll deny all of it."

"Sounds familiar. When are you doing this stakeout?" DeDe asked.

Sam shrugged nonchalantly. "Maybe this week. We'll see."

She paused, afraid to ask what was really on her mind. Since Sam's lightning injury last August, he was reticent to share personal details about his life. His previously open, friendly demeanor had been replaced with something more antagonistic and distrustful. During her heart-to-heart talks with DeDe, Leslie had revealed some rough spots in their relationship, and DeDe wondered how Sam was handling the everyday stress of being a father and a husband. As she formulated a question in her mind, she felt as if she were about to lift the cover off a hive of angry bees. Exposing Sam's vulnerabilities seemed risky and might not be met with a friendly response. She reconsidered, but when she noticed Sam's silent appraisal of her, she asked anyway. "So . . . how's the parenting going?"

"Good," Sam said. His features softened when he thought about his baby daughter. He looked out the window at the misting rain coming down. "Karina is getting so cute. She's starting to coo, trying to talk, smiling a lot. I can't believe she's already seven months old." His eyes drifted back to DeDe. "You know, even though Karina was unexpected, she's been good for me and Lez. We feel very blessed."

DeDe nodded. "You seem totally enthralled with her," she said, noticing the photo of the smiling baby on Sam's desk. "Has she wrapped you around her little finger yet?"

"Totally and completely." Sam grinned.

"And Leslie seems to be adjusting well?"

"Yeah. She loves being home with Paco and Karina. I thought she'd miss her cop work more than she does—the intensity, the chase, the challenge of an intriguing case, putting all the pieces together—but she's gotten a couple of high-powered clients who have commissioned her to do some paintings. And frankly, I think once her art career takes off, she'll make as much, if not more money, doing that. And her chances of getting shot or injured will be almost nil. People generally don't shoot someone if they're disappointed in a piece of artwork, do they?"

"I haven't heard about any murdered artists lately," DeDe said with a chuckle.

"And she can work from home," Sam concluded.

Leslie had discovered her talent for painting when her therapist had suggested a hobby to take her mind off the abuse she suffered from her former boyfriend and her PTSD from her service in the Gulf War. So far, she took to painting like a duck to water, and the hobby helped level out her anxiety. After several lessons with an art professor at the university and hours of dedicated practice, she began selling her work privately, and now her paintings were commanding some very impressive prices.

DeDe's heart sank in her chest. "Well, to be honest, I don't want to lose the only female partner I have. I'll really miss her if she quits." She noticed the concern in Sam's hazel eyes. She leaned forward as she tried to put a positive spin on the conversation. "Maybe she could work in a consultant capacity for the department. You know, when we need research done or military expertise, she could work from home and plug into our investigations. Seems like lots of people are working from home since the pandemic." She tilted her head at Sam, wanting him to approve her plan.

Sam shrugged and lowered his feet to the floor. "That's a nice thought, but the budget would never allow it. But you can go see Lez anytime you want, DeDe. You're always welcome at our house. Besides, she loves your company. Baby talk and dog barks only go so far." Sam smiled widely.

"And how are you feeling these days?" DeDe asked. A shadow passed over Sam's face, erasing his friendly smile. "Just asking as a friend," she added softly.

Sam's face froze into an imposing mask. He stayed silent so long that DeDe thought he was purposely ignoring her question. He chewed on his lower lip, deep in thought. Finally, he spoke.

"I have my struggles. My short-term memory is basically fried, and my temper sometimes gets the best of me. Migraines are still a problem, although they're fewer and farther between. To put it bluntly, my recovery is far from over, but I think this might be the new normal."

Sam's cell buzzed. He listened and then said, "He's probably harmless." More listening. "I'll deal with it when I get home tonight." He hung up.

"Everything okay?" DeDe asked.

"Lez said there's some itinerant gypsy-type guy who's decided to camp at the bottom of our driveway. I guess the homeless are not confined to our city parks. I've heard about this guy—he's been traveling through the area. I think he's harmless. If not, Paco will take care of him until I get home," Sam explained. "That dog could guard Fort Knox by himself."

DeDe chuckled. "Yeah, he probably could." Paco was Leslie's intrepid black lab who had gained quite a reputation throughout the city for his takedowns of perps.

There was a light tapping on the door of Sam's office. Jim peeked around the frame. "Come to my office for a minute. We've got a developing situation I want you to be aware of." Sam wondered if this dilemma involved Jamie Alberg. DeDe followed Sam down the hallway to Higgins' office.

Sitting down in his office chair behind his desk, Jim dug out his memo pad from his suit jacket. "I interviewed a guy named Geoff LaSarde over on St. Cloud Street on the north side who was burglarized last night and had a piece of luggage stolen," Jim began.

Sam's eyebrows creased into a frown. "Since when do we investigate stolen luggage, Chief? Isn't that city's job?"

Jim held up his hand and scowled at Sam. "It is, but I talked to Chief Pedretti about it."

"What'd she say?" Sam said impatiently.

"Just let me finish, okay? This guy, Geoff LaSarde, is some kind of expert on Tiffany antiques: lamps, glassware, and stained-glass windows. Stuff like that. I just finished talking to him, and the circumstances are strange."

"In what way?" asked DeDe.

"He was in his kitchen last night when someone came up behind him, put a choke hold on him, and then gave him a shot of benzos. When he woke up on his kitchen floor this morning, an old piece of luggage was missing. There was information inside the luggage about some very valuable Tiffany windows that have never been found," Jim explained. He continued to roll out the story and his suspicions that Geoff's big cat might have nailed the intruder with its claws or teeth. "That cat is not friendly as cats go, and he's huge. I found what might be blood on the kitchen wall. I'm thinking the cat might have taken a chunk out of the intruder. They're going to run DNA on the blood down in the lab."

"So why are we involved in a case of missing windows? That sounds kinda lame even for us," Sam commented. "I mean, a house break-in. Seriously? An old piece of luggage is missing? We've got bigger fish to fry, Chief. La Crosse County is flooded with drugs and domestic abuse, and we're chasing some unknown perp who's looking for stolen windows?" Sam sat hunched lazily in the chair and gave Higgins a belligerent stare. "Seems pretty lame to me."

Jim leaned forward and rested his elbows on his desk, making a mental note of Sam's demeanor, wondering how his recovery was going. *If his attitude is any indication,* he thought, *the recovery isn't over. There's still room for improvement.*

"Well, I'm not sure what direction this whole thing is going to take yet," Jim began explaining, "and it might not develop into anything at all. It's too early to tell, but I told Tanya I'd keep her informed. She's okay with that. Those windows are worth millions according to LaSarde, and if the wrong person starts rattling cages to locate them, things could heat up."

"So right now, it's on the back burner?" DeDe asked with a puzzled look on her face.

"Yeah, I guess you could say that," Jim sighed. "But keep it on your radar. Keep your ears to the ground."

"Is Jamie Alberg involved in this?" Sam asked.

Jim's head snapped up, and he looked at Sam with an intense stare. "What makes you think that?" he asked gruffly.

"I talked to him over on campus one day last week. He hasn't changed too much," Sam commented. "Always looking for a way to get attention. Did he call you about this?"

Jim cleared his throat noisily. "Unfortunately, he did. That kid . . ."

"Yeah, I hear you," Sam mumbled. "I think we're about to get sucked down another black hole."

6

At five o'clock Wednesday afternoon, Sam Birkstein shuffled to the elevator, glad to be heading home. He felt old, washed-up in an odd sort of way, even though his day of investigating had been relatively uneventful. When he thought about it some more, he decided the day had been strange, with two situations that could develop further and might need more investigation. Higgins seemed worried about the burglary on the north side, but would it really develop into anything substantial? He doubted it.

Sam recalled the facts Higgins had shared about the burglary and the lost Tiffany windows. Despite the fact that the iconic windows had been missing for a hundred years, Sam knew better than to rule out a wild goose chase to locate them. After all, Higgins' team had been embroiled in similar brouhahas before. Two previous cases immediately came to mind: lost gold coins hidden in the bluffs above the Mississippi River and stolen treasures from Iraq's National Museum in Baghdad that had been transported by boat to Galena, Illinois, and siphoned into La Crosse via truck.

Sam shook his head when he thought about tracing the location of the windows. He could imagine road trips around the state and surrounding areas trying to find the famous Tiffany creations. But, if he was honest with himself, he had to admit these kinds of cases were what kept his blood pumping and his mind engaged, and he desperately needed some kind of activity in which he could use the little gray cells. Since the lightning strike, his mental acuity needed additional stimulation, and a puzzling case could provide abundant motivation. There was nothing like a convoluted case to get his brain cells firing on all cylinders.

The wooded bluffs along the river were draped in a curtain of gray fog, and a steady, cold drizzle made the evening particularly miserable. The drive to his home that overlooked the Mississippi River near Genoa each evening along the Great River Road was usually the highlight of Sam's day. He was looking forward to a quiet evening cuddling his little daughter. The windshield of the Jeep kept steaming up, making visibility difficult. Sam flicked the windshield wipers on and cranked up the defroster. This afternoon he'd called *Si Bon,* the restaurant owned by Jude Delaney, DeDe Deverioux's five-star chef husband. He'd ordered takeout: pan-fried shrimp, grilled romaine salad, a side order of creamed sweet corn, and couscous primavera. Expensive but so worth it. Then he remembered the quirky man at the bottom of their driveway who had set up camp, and his attitude took a hit.

All Sam knew about the guy camped at the bottom of the driveway was what Leslie had told him on the phone. His wife made snap judgments all the time in her police work, and usually her insights were uncannily accurate. The guy probably was homeless since he was riding a bike and pulling a shopping cart loaded with junk, and he sounded like a nuisance. According to Leslie, he had erected a shelter using some kind of blue plastic tarp, and the stuff he carried with him was scattered under and around the tarp within a fifteen-foot radius. In his mind, Sam could picture the whole scene, complete with various forms of insect life that were probably hatching out of the detritus this very minute—fleas, maggots, whatever. He shivered, disgusted at the thought. Why did these problems always come at the end of the day when his patience had worn thin? Sam rubbed his neck, hoping the persistent migraines he frequently experienced would stay away.

From several city police officers, Sam had become familiar with the plight of the homeless in the city of La Crosse. Recently, they had invaded Hoska Park near the brewery and had carved out their share of press coverage in the *La Crosse Sentinel* and on the local television stations. The newly elected mayor seemed focused on their plight and was attentive to the various factions in the city who had proposed solutions.

The challenges that plagued the homeless population were substantial—inadequate housing, quarrels that erupted into violent physical altercations, drug and alcohol abuse, shoplifting at local stores in the vicinity of the park, joblessness, and littering. Hoska Park, a once beautiful natural respite for city dwellers, had become a terrible eyesore. The police were frequently called there to check on residents who had been using drugs or selling drugs to others living there. Sam shook his head in frustration. He'd been involved in a number of problems around the city involving the homeless. It seemed almost impossible to stay ahead of the insidious expansion of drug abuse at all levels of society, from teens to the homeless to middle-class kids to hardcore punks and criminals.

Sam wheeled into the parking lot of *Si Bon*, which sat on a small rise overlooking the Mississippi River. Despite the misty rain that still fell softly across the landscape, the beauty of the blue bluffs stacked along the shore of the great river lifted Sam's spirits. He hopped out of the Jeep and walked across the parking lot to the front entrance of the restaurant. The air was saturated with the smell of fried food, and the intoxicating scent of purple lilac hung in the air.

Si Bon was a refurbished, old timber frame barn that Jude Delaney had bought and renovated into a first-class eating establishment when he'd followed his wife, detective DeDe Deverioux, to Wisconsin from Louisiana three years ago. After selling his famous restaurant in New Orleans, he redesigned the old, weathered barn using a variety of recycled materials, adding his own unique flair to the decor inside.

His creative ingenuity in preparing locally grown meats, fish, and vegetables into mouth-watering entrees had resulted in *Si Bon* soaring to the top of the La Crosse culinary scene. People for a hundred miles around enjoyed Jude's tasty cuisine.

Inside the restaurant, people were taking seats at round tables covered with white tablecloths accentuated by bouquets of fresh spring flowers. A huge limestone fireplace on one wall soared upward to the roof of the barn. Old timbers in the ceiling of the structure glowed with an aged patina and added a nostalgic atmosphere to the laid-back vibe of the place. Customers were studying the menu, ordering drinks, and carrying on lively conversations. Laughter rippled through the atmosphere, and it should have been appealing to someone as outgoing and friendly as Sam. Instead, it all seemed overwhelming, like an overloaded circuit sparking and shorting out his senses—another fallout effect from his lightning injury last fall. The noisy cameraderie of the crowd made him nervous and restless.

Sam waited in line for fifteen minutes, then approached the hostess and asked for his takeout order. She was a lovely gal, accommodating and polite. She checked her list, and a slight frown appeared on her forehead.

"Sam Birkstein? I don't seem to have an order for you, sir. When did you call?"

Sam grabbed the book, flipping it in his direction. The girl jerked away. Her shoulders stiffened, her brown eyes widened. She was clearly shocked by his aggressive behavior.

"It's right here," Sam said impatiently. He pointed to a line farther down the page, his finger tracing the outline of his name. "Sam Birkstein," he said loudly. "It's right there. I called at four o'clock." He jabbed his name in the notebook with his finger again, his impatience on full display.

The hostess, whose name was Luann, reached over and retrieved the book. "I apologize. I didn't see it there. We've been pretty busy tonight. I'll check and see if your order is ready, sir." Sam glared at her. "If you could just wait over by the bench, then I can keep checking people in who have reservations." Her brown eyes were wide with embarrassment, her cheeks flushed pink.

Sam shuffled his feet and mumbled a clumsy apology. *Get a grip*, he thought to himself as he raked his fingers through his curly brown hair. He turned, and the customers waiting in line stared at him, parting like the Red Sea so he could pass through the crowd on his way to the bench. He plopped down, sullen and embarrassed by the scene he'd created.

As soon as Sam paid and got his order, he tucked the bag under his arm and walked quickly to the Jeep. On the drive home, he berated himself for his bad behavior. Lez would have been appalled if she'd witnessed that outburst. Somehow, he needed to get a handle on his impatient, angry outbursts.

When Sam approached his driveway, the vagrant who'd traveled by bike with a shopping cart hooked on behind had taken up residence in the ditch next to Sam's driveway, his garbage scattered around him in casual nonchalance. Sam gaped. Piles of clothing, a dented, rusting Weber grill, a mound of plastic takeout containers, a couple pairs of rubber boots, and other random items lay strewn in a wide circle under a blue plastic tarp that was held up with a couple of aluminum ski poles. *How does he get all that in his cart?* Sam wondered. *Why the hell does he need a grill?*

Rolling to a stop at the bottom of his steep driveway, Sam stepped out of his Jeep and walked cautiously toward the chaotic encampment. He stopped in his tracks when the homeless man swooped out of the tent waving his arms wildly, hissing like a mad goose.

"This is private property!" the man shouted, spittle flying. "The homeless are being marginalized. They are victims of a society rampant with greed and evil." As he spoke, his arms punctuated the air in wild gesticulations.

Sam held up his hands. "Easy there, buddy," he said calmly, his hazel eyes cautious. "Your notion that this is private property is a little off base. This," Sam pointed at the ground, "is highway right-of-way. The driveway is mine. I live at the top of that hill," he finished, pointing up the steep incline that ended at his comfortable cottage.

The belligerent vagrant held Sam's stare with unsettling resolve. His brown eyes flashed with conviction and righteous anger. Matted, greasy dreadlocks hung loosely around his handsome face, one that reminded Sam of a Roman aristocrat, similar to an image he'd seen on some old coins in Leslie's collection. His clothes were tattered and predictably filthy. He was barefoot. An unpleasant odor of sweat, grime, and sour food drifted toward Sam and made his stomach turn over.

"I have every right to occupy this ground," the man snarled. "I spend the time I have left on this earth defending the poor. I bring awareness to their plight because the privileged and rich hold the keys of power and subjugation over those less fortunate than themselves."

Sam nodded, casually agreeing. "What's your name, buddy?" he asked calmly.

"I am Wanderer," the man stated, standing at attention like a soldier taking orders.

"Okay, fair enough. Listen, Wanderer, I don't have a beef with you, but my wife was a little alarmed at your presence at the end of our driveway this morning," Sam explained. "How long do you intend to camp out here?"

Wanderer thought for a moment. "As long as it takes for people to acknowledge the poor and needy among us. That is the mission I have been given by God." Wanderer plunked his hands on his hips and met Sam's gaze with eerie calm. *He looks like a Roman soldier,* Sam thought. *A soldier on a mission.* Fragments of the hymn "Onward Christian Soldiers" drifted into Sam's memory, and he began to hum the tune softly. The vagrant tilted his head in confusion as he listened to the tune. Sam quit humming. *Pick your battles,* he thought. *I've hit a new low arguing with a vagrant living in a road ditch.*

"Alright. I've got bigger fish to fry. I can live with that," Sam said. "I hope your message gets across. Good luck." He scanned the disastrous scene once again, then turned and climbed back into his Jeep. When he reached the top of the hill, Paco, their black lab, bounded toward the truck, barking with joy at Sam's return home.

"I'm in here, Sam," Leslie yelled when he walked through the side door of the house from the detached garage. Sam hung his rain jacket on a hook in the hallway, set the bags of food on the counter, then strolled through the kitchen and living room and walked into the art studio on the northwest side of the house. The bank of windows that faced the river was streaked with misty rain, the scenery to the west smudged into a muted wash of green and blue. Leslie was sitting at her easel, dabbing mauve and purple highlights on a stunning river scene. Baby Karina lay on a folded comforter on the floor, kicking and cooing, her little legs churning with energy.

Sam bent over and picked up the baby girl, taking in her sweet, milky smell. He kissed Leslie and plopped into a recliner near the window. Late afternoon light fell on one of Leslie's paintings—a gorgeous river scene—that hung on the wall opposite the bank of windows facing west. Suddenly Karina grabbed a fistful of Sam's hair and tugged with surprising strength.

"How's the happy wanderer at the bottom of the driveway?" Leslie asked, continuing to dab paint on the canvas.

"Funny you should call him that," Sam said, making a disgusted face. "That's what he calls himself—Wanderer."

"Really? You talked to him?"

"Yep. He's on a mission of some kind. He yammered about saving the homeless from the decadent, upper ruling class, or some socialist crap like that. He seems harmless, but I hope he's gone in the morning."

"Don't count on it. I saw Mrs. Beiderfeld at the grocery store in Stoddard, and she said the guy camped up by Viroqua on Highway 14 for almost a week before he moved on." Leslie continued to paint while she talked, switching to a fan brush as she added details to some bulrushes in the foreground of the painting.

Karina grabbed Sam's lower lip and tugged. "Ouch! You little twerp!" Sam said, loosening Karina's fingers from his face. He lifted her high in the air and listened to her giggle. Drool streamed from her mouth and landed on Sam's shirt collar.

"Look out below! Boy, you're a messy little thing," he said to no one in particular.

Leslie stopped painting, her brush poised in midair as she watched Sam and Karina interact. The birth of their daughter in mid-November had been such an unexpected blessing, and Sam's moods, although rocky at times, had leveled out largely due to the baby. She watched him tenderly wipe the drool from Karina's chin with a Kleenex and cuddle her close to his chest. Their eyes met, and Leslie realized once again how fortunate she was to have a man like Sam in her life. Her turbulent past receded a bit when she thought of the challenges Sam had faced last year. Now she wasn't the only one who was damaged by life's circumstances.

"You been painting all day?" Sam asked. Karina giggled with infectious baby innocence when Sam tickled her tummy.

"No," she chuckled. "I did some laundry this morning and other stuff, and then I painted this afternoon until you walked in the door."

"Dinner's on the counter. My treat from *Si Bon*. We'll just have to nuke it a little in the microwave."

"How nice. Let's eat," Leslie said, standing and taking Karina.

Over dinner, Sam and Leslie discussed the new case that was confronting Higgins and the team.

"This window thing could turn into something," Leslie said. "I'll call Higgins tomorrow and see if I can do some research from home."

"That reminds me. When are you coming back to work? You've been on leave for almost seven months, honey," Sam commented, chewing a mouthful of grilled lettuce.

Leslie looked over at Karina jumping enthusiastically in her bouncy seat near the table and groaned. "I don't know, Sam. I'm so torn. Leaving Karina in the care of someone else just goes against every motherly bone in my body. Is that weird?" She stared out of the kitchen window, a forlorn expression on her beautiful face, her blue eyes sad. Sam noticed and stopped chewing. He reached across the table and tenderly took her hand in his.

"No, it's not weird. In fact, I'd say it's totally normal."

"Are you okay with me quitting my job at the sheriff's department?" Leslie asked.

"It's up to you, sweetheart, but I'll support you in whatever decision you make. You know that."

"Some help you are," she grumped, stuffing another shrimp into her mouth.

"Always glad to be of service."

THURSDAY, MAY 17

7

Lewis Borden slumped in the plastic chair at the Thorsen Memorial ER clinic on West Irving Street near the Alta Vista Terrace neighborhood in Chicago on Thursday morning. His leg was on fire, infected from the cat bite he'd received when he bushwhacked Geoff LaSarde at his home in La Crosse. *Just my luck,* he thought bitterly. Ever since the mission to retrieve the luggage from the O'Hare airport, his good luck seemed to have evaporated into thin air. He remembered the words of his commanding officer during his stint in the U.S. Army: "Luck is not an option that will serve you well. Preparation and planning are the keys to a successful outcome." *Yeah, right,* Lewis thought. *If that's the case, then I've failed miserably on this mission.*

The clinic was crowded with patients of various ages with a variety of ailments—kids with runny noses and coughs, a little old lady whose hands were crumpled with arthritis, another middle-aged man who had a huge bandage on his forearm, and Lewis with an infected cat bite, of all things.

"Lewis?" a nurse called over the murmur of fussing babies and muted conversations. Lewis rose from his chair and painfully hobbled after the nurse down a short hallway to an exam room.

After recording his vitals, the nurse said, "The doctor will be with you shortly." Lewis smiled blankly, a gesture lacking any warmth. The door clicked shut. As he waited to be examined, he rolled up the leg of his jeans. The wound was ringed with red, angry splotches, and yellow pus oozed from the bite marks. The area was swollen and hot to the touch. *That damn cat,* he thought. *I should've gotten rid of him when I had the chance.*

Within a few minutes, a physician entered the room, his manner brusque and harried. He had jet black hair, dark brown eyes, cappuccino-colored skin, and thin pink lips, which left Lewis to conclude his ethnicity was probably Middle Eastern. The doctor looked at the wound on Lewis' leg. "What bit you?" he asked abruptly.

"A cat."

The doctor stared at Lewis. "Really? I've never heard of a cat biting anyone."

"Well, now you have," Lewis said with a coldness in his voice.

"Are the cat's shots up-to-date?"

Lewis shrugged. "No idea."

"It wasn't your cat?" the doctor asked. Lewis shook his head. "Well, let's hope it didn't have distemper. Your leg is obviously infected." The doctor poked the wound, pressing around the site of the punctures. Lewis grimaced and squeezed his eyes shut. "I'll prescribe an antibiotic and give you some antibacterial cream for the wound. Keep it clean and change the dressing every day. Take Tylenol for pain. The wound might continue oozing some pus, but once the antibiotic takes hold, the drainage should disappear. If things don't improve within the next few days, come back."

He sat at the small wall desk, scribbled furiously on a prescription pad, ripped a page from the pad, and handed it to Lewis. The doctor glanced at him and said, "Avoid cats. There's something about you they don't like." He gave Lewis a sardonic grin, stood up, and bustled from the room.

"Smart ass," Lewis whispered through clenched teeth. His shoulders slumped at the thought of the choices ahead of him. His boss, Charles R. Tewalt Jr., was the CEO of Tewalt Technologies, a small but highly profitable Chicago company that manufactured computer chips for a variety of technological gadgets. Lewis had a shadowy, but lucrative, position as Tewalt's personal assistant. His role included fixing problems that usually involved random illicit affairs by his boss, paying off gambling debts Charlie had racked up at the dog races and other sporting events, and many other diversions that Lewis was sure neither the board members of the company nor Tewalt's wife knew anything about. Nothing had changed over the years—Charlie always wanted what he couldn't or shouldn't have.

Tewalt's latest craze was the construction of his lavish mansion in a new development about twelve miles north of Lakeview in the Chicago suburb of Winnetka. The building had consumed his out-of-office interests for over two years. The mansion, which Lewis had only seen from the curb, was a fifteen-thousand-square-foot Georgian monstrosity. It was a showplace with precise architectural details and an overblown presence in a neighborhood that screamed privilege. The sprawling home was situated on a twenty-five-acre rise in the landscape and offered a distant view of Lake Michigan. Rumor had it that the home contained a huge gourmet kitchen, loft apartment, sunroom, theater, wine cellar, and personal gym, besides the normal amenities, which included multiple bedrooms and bathrooms. The crowning glory of the home was a library, which was to be completed with five authentic Tiffany windows and a collection of reading material that would be the envy of any Ivy League university. Lewis was sure the mansion would have a price tag of well over fifteen million dollars.

After his appointment with the doctor, Lewis walked gingerly to his Lexus RX 3501 parked in the lot at the clinic. The bright orange sports car caught the attention of almost everyone who saw it, garnering oohs and ahhs from kids and jealous glances from men who could only dream of owning such a vehicle. Lewis was a careful, observant driver and had never gotten a moving violation in all the years he'd lived in the Windy City. But the countryside—now *that* was a different story. Recently on a long stretch of highway southeast of Chicago, just beyond the outskirts of the city, he'd wound out the Lexus' horsepower. The car had guts, cruising easily to 120 miles per hour in just over ten seconds. Risky, but *so* satisfying.

Leaving the clinic, he drove several blocks, parked at a scenic overlook near the lake, and took the antibiotic prescribed by the doctor, washing it down with several gulps of bottled water. Through his windshield, Lake Michigan sparkled in the spring sunshine. Several sailboats were out for an early test run, their colorful sails taut from a stiff wind. White-crested waves rolled toward shore. A couple of joggers dressed in skimpy clothes ran along the sandy beach. His thoughts drifted to the angry exchange with Charlie, his boss, at his Lake View office earlier in the morning.

When Lewis walked into Tewalt's office at eight-thirty, his boss was sitting behind his mahogany desk, his gray suit creased and pressed, his white shirt crisp, his luxurious burgundy silk tie impeccably knotted. He was just beginning to gray at the temples, but he was still a handsome man, virile and fit. Charlie leaned back and seemed relaxed, but Lewis noticed the glint of steel in his icy blue eyes, and he knew immediately Tewalt was furious about something. Tewalt's gaze traveled from the top of Lewis' prematurely silver hair to the bottom of his Nike Air Force 1 running shoes.

"How are you, Lewis? The leg? Is it better?" Charlie asked, his patronizing tone barely concealing his fury. He picked up a pencil and began quietly tapping it on the desktop as if he were trying to release his pent-up frustration and anger.

"Actually, my leg isn't better. It's worse. I'm going to need to get it looked at this morning," Lewis replied, returning his boss' stare.

"Be careful. Don't tell anyone how you got that wound. The police would have a heyday with you if they discovered what you've been doing for me." Charlie put the pencil down, placed his elbows on the desk, then rested his chin on his clasped fists. He continued to stare at Lewis.

“So what am I here for?” Lewis asked. “Did you get the information you needed from the suitcase?”

Several moments passed in complete silence, and despite Lewis’ professional grace under fire, he began to worry. He felt a tremendous urge to shift positions, to stand up or cross his legs, but that would be considered a sign of weakness, and the last thing he wanted was to give his boss the opportunity to hold him over a barrel like a squirming fish. Outwardly, he remained calm and self-assured, but panic was beginning to build in his chest. *Calm down. Stay in control,* he reminded himself.

“The suitcase contained some interesting facts, but it was useless to me. The location of the windows was not revealed in any of the articles or other information, nor was there a contact name where I could get further information.” Charlie lifted his chin, his gaze penetrating Lewis’ tough exterior.

“Not my problem, really,” Lewis responded with disdain. He pulled nervously at his earlobe. “You wanted the suitcase. I got the suitcase. What was in it was of no concern to me. I just did as I was told.”

Charlie leaned forward suddenly, smashing his fist on the desk with a loud bang. His coffee cup jumped, and the liquid sloshed across the polished mahogany desk. “The guy who bought the suitcase must have taken some things out! The location of the windows was not there! I need that! It’s essential for me to finish my house!” he yelled in a fit of juvenile fury. “Those windows were supposed to be the embodiment of my classical Georgian-style home. The photo shoot for *Chicago Magazine* is only two months away. Those windows are crucial to the whole design scheme of my house,” he shouted, his face red with frustration.

Lewis, angered by the accusations, leaned forward. He kept his voice low and slow. “Listen, Charlie. I’m your go-to guy when you get in a jam. How many times have I delivered your sorry butt out of trouble and kept you from being investigated for fraud, bribery, extortion—”

"What's your point?" Charlie snarled, his face scarlet.

"My point is this: I got the suitcase. You never asked me to look at the information contained inside. Someone else obviously failed in that directive, but don't lay that at my doorstep. I. Won't. Own. It." Lewis got up and began limping toward the door.

"You walk out of here now, you're done," Charlie said quietly, delivering an ultimatum.

Lewis paused with his hand on the office doorknob, but only for a moment. He opened the door and walked to the elevator, punching the button to the ground floor.

Now sitting alone in his car, he wondered whether he'd made the right decision. He'd been an invisible employee of Charlie's for over eight years. They'd served together in Iraq early in the '90s when both of them had been involved in clandestine operations for the U.S. Army, extracting information about enemy movements from sympathetic Kurds. Now Lewis felt the ground shift under him as if he were back undercover again. Dangerous but exciting days. Days of exhaustion and exhilaration. Days of camaraderie and esprit de corps. Somehow, his termination from Charlie's employment reminded him of the day they'd parted at Camp Justice in Adhamiyah, Iraq. Lewis thought then, as he did now, that he'd never see Tewalt again.

He considered his options. Obviously, the purse strings had been severed. However, he had plenty of money having lived frugally despite his six-figure salary from Tewalt Technologies. He had a beautiful row house in the Alta Vista Terrace District of the city. He could easily sell it for over $800,000, but he'd miss the house's comfort and charm—the hardwood floors, two fireplaces, the tin ceiling in the kitchen, and all the sundry features of living in a historically distinctive home. The tree-lined streets and the allure of residing in a well-known district, one of Chicago's finest, would be hard to give up. He'd learned early in his career that money could buy all the security, safety, and charm you desired if you were willing to pay the price attached to it.

Lewis watched the white puffy clouds form and re-form in the sky above the lake. He was still considering his options when suddenly a thought wormed its way into his mind and made the image of his comfortable row house fade to a corner of his brain.

What if I find the windows and beat Charlie to the punch? Go rogue? He knew the obsession that gripped Charlie when he set his sights on something he couldn't have. *Hmm, now that's an interesting idea.* After all, he knew where Geoff LaSarde lived, and the guy *was* an expert in all things Tiffany. A cold, cruel smile spread across Lewis' face, and his expression changed from worry to excitement. Perhaps the challenge of a new task was just what the doctor ordered. *That might prove to be a very interesting mission—interesting and lucrative,* he thought, chuckling to himself.

8

"Can't you hold him still?" Carl Ettinger barked. He took a couple of steps backward. Sir Lancelot hissed at him, mewed loudly, and swiped his large paw through the air when the CSI lab technician approached him with a swab. Geoff LaSarde stroked the huge cat, trying to calm the killer instincts of his oversized feline.

"How much does he weigh anyway?" Ettinger asked as he leaned on the counter, a swab dangling from his fingertips mid-air.

"Probably close to twenty-five pounds," Geoff answered.

"What are you feeding him?"

Geoff frowned. "As the saying goes, anything he wants."

"You might want to reconsider that strategy. Sir Lancelot is very overweight," Ettinger said with an air of superiority as he crossed his arms over his chest. "My girlfriend has a cat, and she is extremely careful about its diet. Does he get any exercise?"

Geoff harrumphed and gave Carl a look of growing disgust. "Look, I don't need any advice about pets, and I'm not here to win you over with my huge cat," Geoff said, irritated at the string of suggestions about his cat's health. "You're supposed to be getting a swab of whatever's under his claws."

"Well, I would if he would quit trying to have me for lunch," Ettinger snarled.

"Give me the swabs," Geoff said, holding out his hand. Geoff donned a pair of gloves, and Ettinger dropped several swabs into his upturned palm. Geoff calmly and efficiently swabbed the curled undersides of the claws on the large cat, then dropped them into Ettinger's clear plastic bag.

"Thank you for your cooperation," Carl said with brisk efficiency.

"Not a problem. I hope you can figure out who broke into my house and rendered me unconscious," Geoff said. Then he murmured in the cat's ear, "Come on, Lancelot. Let's blow this place and get a tuna shake."

Ettinger rolled his eyes. "See ya," he grumped, twiddling his fingers. Then, under his breath, he whispered, "Good riddance."

Sheriff Elaine Turnmile hung up after her phone conversation with Police Chief Tanya Pedretti on Thursday morning. She sighed and shook her head when Tanya told her about Higgins' interest in a home break-in within the city. *What part of police jurisdiction does Higgins not understand?* she thought. Tanya was happy to let Jim handle it. Apparently, her plate was full to overflowing, and she appreciated a little give-and-take among law enforcement agencies within the county and city.

Since her tenure as La Crosse County sheriff began over a year ago, Elaine had worked hard to improve her interpersonal communication skills with the public, although the path had not been rosy. She still had bouts of extreme sarcasm and impatience, but she gave credit for her improved reputation within the department to Senior Detective Jim Higgins. His honest suggestions about how she could connect on a deeper level with her officers had been right on target. In the process, she had developed a grudging admiration for the man. Higgins knew how to lead, which was proven by his faithful, loyal team who followed him unfazed through the smoke and fire. Their success in solving some very puzzling crimes was legendary within the ranks of local law enforcement, and Higgins consistently demonstrated his deep understanding of human nature in his policing strategies and his interactions with the public. *Now, if he'd get his act together and quit interfering in city affairs, we'd be making some progress*, Turnmile thought.

Be *honest, Elaine,* she continued thinking to herself. *Without Higgins, you would have been sitting on a curb with your bags packed and a bus ticket in your hand for destinations unknown.* She sighed and leaned back in her chair, studying the ceiling tiles. Yes, she did owe much to the lieutenant. He'd single-handedly rescued her reputation, which had plummeted with each new encounter with the public. She was learning to be more patient and kind—new territory for her. She turned her attention to her phone messages and reviewed the text Higgins had sent her this morning informing her of the full-blown CSI work-up at Geoff LaSarde's home on St. Cloud Street. *That seemed a bit heavy-handed,* she thought. And all of it over a suitcase? What was that all about?

Turnmile twisted a strand of blonde hair that had come loose from her French braid and reached for her phone. *No time like the present to find out what's going on,* she thought. She dialed Higgins' number.

"Jim Higgins," a deep baritone voice said.

"Hey, just wondering about your decision to send the CSI team over to LaSarde's house this morning? Seems a little bit much to me," Turnmile began. Her grating voice caused Jim to grimace. "I'd like to hear your justification for that."

Jim fingered the knot on his tie, grateful he could hide within the confines of his office rather than deal with Turnmile face-to-face. He began to explain. "Well, after the seminar in Milwaukee about using DNA to nail the perpetrators of property crime—specifically house break-ins—I thought there was no time like the present to give it a shot. Carl did a great job with the team, and we got quite a bit of stuff from the house that could come in handy down the road," Jim replied calmly.

"Oh, yeah? Like what?" Turnmile asked rudely.

"We've got blood samples that might lead to the perp. There was—"

"Wait—blood? I didn't think anyone was hurt."

"LaSarde was rendered unconscious with drugs," Jim countered, "but I have a theory about the blood. I think LaSarde's cat may have attacked the intruder. Geoff brought his cat down to the lab this morning, and Ettinger got a sample of some blood that was embedded under his claws," Jim explained.

There was an uncomfortable silence that neither of them attempted to fill.

"So now we're investigating an attack cat?" Turnmile asked with contempt. "Are you serious?"

Why did I bother to explain? Jim thought. He continued, "No, we're not investigating the cat, but LaSarde has a very unfriendly, predator-type cat which may help us identify the perpetrator if the blood from the cat's claw matches the blood I found on the wall near the phone."

"You mean this cat is like a pet lion or something? Are you for real, Higgins? Seriously?" Her disdain for the idea was obvious.

"No, he's not a lion, but he is one huge cat with sinister intentions."

Turnmile chuckled, a rarity Jim had only heard a few times in the last year. Suddenly, Turnmile seemed to capitulate. "Okay, I guess I'll trust you on this one."

"Thank you. I appreciate that," Jim remarked.

"So—the suitcase? What was in it? Diamonds? A stash of cash? Drugs? Porn? What?"

Jim cleared his throat and prayed for patience. "Nothing remotely criminal." He waited for the explosion he was sure would come.

"So why are we paying so much attention to this incident then? Seems like the city guys could have handled this," Turnmile complained. But before Jim could answer, the sheriff continued. "Frankly, Higgins, I don't get it, so I'll return to my original point. It seems like a case of gross overreach to me, to say nothing of the city jurisdiction problem."

"I can understand your thinking, ma'am, but there was information in the suitcase about some missing Tiffany windows that are quite valuable. This LaSarde guy is a Tiffany expert, and knocking him unconscious and stealing the suitcase hints that there might be more trouble brewing at some point . . ." Jim's voice trailed off. He realized his justifications sounded terribly lame. *Here it comes. I'm going to get nailed to the wall,* he thought. Turnmile did not disappoint.

"There might be *hints* of trouble?" the sheriff sneered. "That's not what we're paid to investigate, Higgins. We don't do hints or suggestions or insinuations or innuendos or—"

"Got it, ma'am," Jim said brusquely. He gritted his teeth and rolled his shoulders to alleviate the tension that was building in his chest.

"Keep an eye on it, but let's move on. We can't afford to waste any more resources on something so vague, especially when it's city's problem," Turnmile concluded.

"Understood."

"Good." The phone call ended abruptly when Turnmile slammed down the receiver.

Jim hung up and willed his racing heart to return to its normal cadence. Dealing with Elaine always got his hackles up. Rude, demanding, and caustic were the only ways to describe her, but Jim continued to believe that somewhere under that hard shell was a kind person just waiting to emerge. *Dream on, Higgins,* his inner voice told him. *When it comes to Turnmile, your quixotic dreams of reforming her behavior are just pie in the sky.* Then his thoughts turned to Jamie Alberg. *When are you going to learn? Every time you get embroiled in a situation with that kid, you end up looking like a bumbling twit. One of these days, he's gonna get killed, and then what are you going to do?*

9

Sam squirmed restlessly in the front seat of his Jeep Cherokee on Thursday morning; his hands clutched the steering wheel in frustration. He was parked in front of Paul Saner's small mid-century bungalow on Market Street in La Crosse. The early morning blue skies promised a sunny, bright day, but it did little to alleviate Sam's anxiety. Trying to track down Kevin Chroniger, the drug-selling homeless resident, who was last seen at Hoska Park, would most likely be a crap shoot. He imagined drifting through tent city, talking to the residents, trying to find out information from a population that was reticent in revealing any information about the people who called the park their home.

Relax, he reminded himself. *You're gearing up for another migraine. Take it easy. It'll all work out.* He laid his hands in his lap, leaned back in the seat, and did a series of deep cleansing breaths. Then he twisted his head from side to side, trying to relieve the tension in his tight shoulder muscles. The advice his doctor had given him last week at his three-month checkup was nothing new—avoid stressful situations, practice mindful thinking, advocate for your needs, eat healthy, and exercise.

"Have you considered yoga to relieve some of your anxiety?" Dr. White asked.

Sam glared at him. "Yoga? Really, Doc?" he sputtered. His eyes hardened at the suggestion that a few meditative poses could possibly change his outlook on life.

"Many of my patients have really benefited from it. I wish you'd consider it. I could give you the name of any number of excellent teachers who have studios within the city and offer lessons," Dr. White responded.

"No thanks, Doc. Twisting my body into positions that resemble a snake isn't my idea of relieving tension."

Dr. White gave Sam an empathetic glance. "A big part of recovery from a lightning strike is accepting the ways your body has changed, Sam. Think about the yoga thing. It's better than the alternatives," he said.

"Which are?" Sam rasped.

"Broken relationships, stress, anger, panic attacks, migraines . . ."

"I hear you, Doc," Sam said, sighing softly.

"By the way, how are your relationships these days?" Dr. White asked. His brown eyes seemed to plumb the depths of Sam's personality and feelings.

"My relationships at work are fine, and my wife, Leslie, is very understanding. She's had her own PTSD issues from her military service overseas, so she gets me. And Karina, my little seven-month-old daughter, keeps me on the straight and narrow—and keeps me laughing." Sam smiled for the first time during the conversation. "I'm very thankful for her presence in my life."

"Good. That's encouraging. You need to appreciate your friends and family," Dr. White said as Sam slipped down from the examination table. "Be sure you get out once in a while in a relaxing social setting."

"No need for a lecture, Doc. Without my friends and family, I probably would have given up a long time ago." He thought about his tantrum last night at the *Si Bon* and cringed. *It's a good thing the doc doesn't know about that,* he thought.

Without Leslie's understanding and insight into traumatic injury, he wasn't sure where he'd be. He remembered the arguments they'd had about honesty; Leslie insisted on a frank assessment of the daily stress he experienced so they could come up with some solutions as a couple. And Lt. Higgins relied on his forthrightness about his condition if he wanted to continue in his role as detective at the La Crosse County Sheriff's Department. After all, it was a well-known fact from numerous studies in the field of police performance that the challenges and threats a cop experienced while interacting with the public took a toll on the officer's health and well-being, particularly in the area of cardiac conditioning. Higgins was a bulldog when it came to ongoing police training, especially in the area of stress management and interpersonal relationships. He recalled Higgins' blue-eyed gaze when Sam tried to sidestep the training. "You're not getting out of it, Sam," Higgins lectured, his voice hardening. "We have a responsibility to our families and friends to do all we can to lessen the effects of the threats and stress we face on the job. This training will not only improve your marriage and relationships—it will make you a more empathetic person. Sign at the bottom of the page," he ordered, handing a pen to Sam.

Higgins stared at Sam as he pushed the consent form across the desk for the next training session, noticing the chiseled, painful expression on Sam's handsome features. To think he didn't need the refresher course was, in Higgins' opinion, asking for trouble. Lately the young detective's curt arrogance and aloofness bothered Higgins at a visceral level. If he was this belligerent with his boss, what were his interactions with the public like? Sam, on the other hand, wished he had an explanation for the resentment he felt about the compulsory workshops. He wondered sometimes if he had overstepped his boundaries with Higgins and was on a short list for dismissal or a leave of absence.

Leslie noticed the dark circles under his eyes and his worried countenance this morning. Sam couldn't hide from her love and concern. She knew him too well.

"How are you feeling today, hon?" she asked gently at the breakfast table.

"I'm all right," he commented brusquely. He took a sip of coffee and looked out the living room window at the wide Mississippi flowing south, hoping the peaceful surroundings would calm his troubled soul. Lez raised her eyebrows at his brusque response to her question, but she stayed silent. She stood up and walked to the kitchen sink with her dishes, pausing a moment to gaze at the backyard with its huge pine trees and the craggy sandstone bluff that bordered their property on Warner's Bluff.

Sam came up behind her, set his dishes in the sink, and placed his hands on her shoulders. He turned Leslie toward him. "Please don't worry—"

"Really? Don't worry?" Leslie blurted. "Sam, why wouldn't I worry? You're my husband, remember? What bothers you, bothers me." Her blue eyes flashed with conviction, and tears welled at the corners of her eyes. She reached up and pulled him toward her, placed her hands on his cheeks and gave him a firm kiss. "Are you going to be all right today?"

Sam pulled her close and hugged her long and hard, burying his face in her long, loose blonde hair. "I don't know if I'll be all right," he said into her shoulder as he rubbed her back. "I don't know what I'll come up against today, but I know you're in my corner, so that helps me cope, I guess."

"If you need anything, you call me, okay?" she said softly.

"Got it," he said. "I'll call."

Sam drove to Paul's house to pick him up. He exhaled a quick breath and glanced at himself in the rearview mirror as he waited for Paul to emerge. Sometimes he felt like he really didn't know himself anymore. He heard a screen door slam. Sam jumped, then looked over as Paul Saner jogged quickly down the sidewalk to the Jeep. He opened the door, hopped in, and buckled his seat belt.

"Sorry, Melody had to play me a little tune on the piano before I left," he said.

"Got it. No problem." He hesitated, then took a deep breath and waded in. "Listen, Paul, I need to bounce something off you, if you don't mind."

"Absolutely. Shoot," he said simply. Paul noticed the haggard look of his friend, and his heart went out to him. Despite their frequent disagreements on a number of political and social issues, Sam was his brother in blue. No matter what, he had his back.

"After the ball club murders, do I seem . . . distant? You know, like angry and frustrated?" Sam asked.

Paul nodded his head and pulled his lips downward. "A little more than usual, you mean?"

"Yeah. It's hard for me to evaluate how I'm handling the public and the stress of the job. I think I'm being effective, but I seem to have lost my ability to tell . . ." He let out a short grunt. "I don't know. Maybe I need some time off to get it together. What do you think?" He looked over at Paul.

Paul felt the seriousness of the question. He paused briefly, then asked, "Everything okay at home?"

"Yeah. Truthfully, without Lez, I'd be lost. But, how do you think I'm handling the job?" Sam asked. "You know, from one cop to another?"

"I'd say you're handling things as well as can be expected. Everyone's tolerance for the job changes from day to day. We have family problems, financial problems, and physical ailments that all factor into our stress levels. You've had a lot on your plate, adjusting to your lightning strike and a new baby. I'd say asking for my assessment about your job performance is a healthy sign that you still care, and you want to do a good job."

Sam studied his friend's dark hair and clean-shaven profile. He was a fastidious dresser: crisp shirt and tie, pressed slacks, and polished shoes.

Now Paul turned and locked eyes with Sam.

Sam held up his hand in a high-five pose, and Paul slapped it enthusiastically. "Thanks. I needed that," he said softly. Sam leaned over, started the Jeep, and pulled away from the curb. "Know anything about yoga?" he asked casually.

"Got a cop friend in Kansas City who swears by it," Paul said.

"Really?"

"Really."

Sam drove south on West Avenue to Jackson Street, then wove his way behind a series of industrial complexes to the Hood Street viaduct, which led to Hoska Park located on the north end of Green Island in the Mississippi River. The morning was clear, and cotton-ball clouds skidded across the sky. Ahead, a tall dead oak hung over the water, and a bald eagle sat regally on a gnarled branch watching the surface of the river.

Up ahead along the perimeter of the park, a John Deere skid steer end loader was moving mountains of debris into a huge windrow near the edge of the grass. Sam parked the Jeep, and he and Paul stepped down from the vehicle. They walked toward the operator of the skid steer. When they got his attention, they waved at him. He shut down the engine, crawled out of the machine, and walked over to the two detectives.

"Yeah, you need something?" he asked. The driver of the skid steer was short and stocky. He wore a plaid flannel shirt with a Carhartt vest thrown over the shirt and a pair of jeans. A thatch of thick red hair stuck out from beneath a black stocking hat that was perched on top of his head, and his brown eyes looked curiously at the two men.

Sam waved his hand over the scene of mounded garbage, tents, and refuse, turning up his nose. "Looks like you're cleaning up the place," he commented.

"Yep, the housing authority issued an evacuation order for all the homeless in the park last month. We've been coming and shooing these people out of their shelters a couple of times a week, trying to get them to move on. Finally, today we just started pushing stuff into piles. The La Crosse landfill will come and load it up when we get done."

"So where did the people go who lived here?" Paul asked.

The operator shrugged his shoulders. "Don't know, don't care. My job is to get all this crap moved out of here so it can become a park again. That's all I know. Those are my orders from the powers that be. Who're you guys?" he asked.

Sam and Paul explained their role at the sheriff's department and their concern about finding Kevin Chroniger. "We've had numerous complaints about the guy from some of the people in the neighborhood. Apparently he's been doing some dealing and some possible sex trafficking of minors. We were told he was living here, but . . ." Sam's voice faded as he looked at the mess in front of him.

"Like I said, I don't know any of these people. I'm just here to clean up the mess they left behind," the city worker said.

"Sure, we get that. Thanks for your help," Paul said. The two detectives shuffled back to the Jeep and climbed in. Paul scanned the scene in front of him—a row of portable toilets on the edge of the encampment and mounds of refuse that had been scooped into a long, narrow pile. He thought it was a sorry commentary on the lives of those who had no home. "How do people get to the point of being homeless?" he asked quietly.

"Must be a gradual slide downhill, or a catastrophic event that lands them in the street," Sam commented. "I guess I really don't know."

"Well, there are certainly people who will take advantage of the situation," Paul said. "People like Kevin Chroniger."

"The piranhas are out there, that's for sure. What's our plan now?" Sam asked, leaning over and starting the Jeep.

"Wait a minute. Who's that guy over there?" Paul asked, pointing in the distance.

"Don't know. You wanna talk to him?"

"He might know this Kevin guy, or at least know what he looks like," Paul said.

Sam opened his door and stepped out again. "Let's go," he said.

The two detectives approached a Black man calmly sitting on a torn leather upholstered truck seat quite a distance from the clean-up operation. His dirty dome tent sat opposite him, the flap of the tent blowing in the wind. He was staring aimlessly at the scene before him, drinking a Big Buddy soft drink. His face was pockmarked from a teenage case of acne, and he sucked on the straw of the soft drink while he watched Sam and Paul approach.

"Hi. We're detectives from the sheriff's department," Sam informed him as he flashed his ID. "We're looking for a guy named Kevin Chroniger. Do you know him?"

"Why'd I know somebody like that?" the man asked crossly. His voice was deep and raspy, and his comment was followed by a coughing jag that rumbled through his chest.

"We'd just like to talk with him. We have a few questions for him," Paul said, watching the man closely.

"I ain't seen him since they come and started clearin' us outta here," the man said, pointing at the skid steer, waving his hand over the scene as if he could erase it.

"Could you describe him?" Sam asked.

The Black man looked up at Sam for the first time. "He drives a black van, a Chevy, I think," he said brusquely.

"Year?" Sam asked.

The man shook his head. "Don't know, but he lives in his van and drives around, stopping here and there."

"Does he deal drugs?" Paul asked.

The man shrugged casually. "Maybe."

"You buy from him?" Sam asked.

"Nah. Don't have money for that. I'm lucky if I can buy my cigarettes."

"Know where he is now?" Paul asked.

"He cleared outta here like everybody else. I'm the only one left now."

"Can you describe him?" Sam asked again.

"White dude, tall, medium build, wears those big glasses like a pilot . . ." the man said.

"Aviator glasses?" Paul asked.

"Yeah, I guess so. They're big, that's all I know." The man continued to stare ahead at the refuse piling up along the strip of grass on the edge of the park.

Sam sighed loudly. "Okay, thank you, sir. We appreciate the help."

Sam and Paul turned and walked slowly back to the Jeep. "Kevin seems to be like a ghost—appearing and disappearing at will," Sam commented.

"We'll find him eventually. At least we know what he's driving. We can put out some feelers to city police and see if they spot him," Paul said.

"Yeah, maybe," Sam said.

⊠

Toward noon, Sheriff Elaine Turnmile appeared on the third floor of the law enforcement complex. She rarely visited the upper levels of the law enforcement center, so when she approached the reception desk, Emily cringed, but she rose to the occasion, giving Turnmile a healthy dose of her professionalism.

"How can I help you, Sheriff Turnmile?" Emily asked crisply. "We don't see you up here very often."

"I need to talk to Sam Birkstein. Is he in?" the sheriff asked brusquely.

"Yes, he should be in his office," she pointed down the hall. "The third door on the right, ma'am."

Turnmile pivoted away from Emily and walked briskly down the hall. She stopped at Sam's door. "Birkstein? You got a minute?" Turnmile asked gruffly.

Sam took in her presence and the in-your-face attitude. *Is she ever going to learn how to get along with other people?* he thought sourly.

Most people learn that in kindergarten. He crossed his arms over his chest in a defiant gesture. *Bring it on, lady.*

The sheriff noticed Sam's posture, took offense at his aloof stare, and dove into the conversation. "I was going to bring this topic up earlier, Birkstein, but the opportunity didn't seem to present itself. Anyway, when is your wife going to return to work? Her eight weeks of maternity leave are used up. She's been gone six months. Is she ever going to come back to work?" If not—"

Sam interrupted. "Might I remind you, ma'am, that I also had eight weeks of paternity leave, which I gave to my wife, so she's really only been out of leave for two months," he reminded her as he gritted his teeth.

"Need a decision from her soon—like by the end of this week," Turnmile said in a crisp tone, her hands planted on her wide hips.

Sam's jaw rippled, and his eyes turned cold. "We were just discussing that yesterday, and—"

"And what? Is she comin' back or not?" Sheriff Turnmile barked. "'Cause if she isn't, then somebody else—"

"Elaine! I thought I heard your voice," Jim said, standing behind Turnmile in the hallway. "I think this is a discussion that would be more appropriate in your office, Sheriff, with someone from the personnel committee representing Sam and Leslie's interests." Jim had interrupted when he noticed Sam's rigid posture and red face. "Could you contact Herb down in HR and set something up for later this week?" His eyebrows arched, and he leaned toward her ever so slightly. Turnmile backed up a few steps and nodded silently. Then she spun around, maneuvered around Jim, and headed down the hallway.

"Your suggestions about common courtesy are not having the desired effect, sir," Sam said, watching her blow down the hallway like a cold north wind. "How did she ever get the sheriff's job, anyway?"

"She was elected by the voting public, but that's a discussion for another time," Jim commented. They stood for a few moments thinking thoughts that were better left unsaid.

"So what now, Chief?" Sam asked.

"I'm thinking about a sandwich and a good cup of coffee," Jim said. "Let's head over to the Peddler and get something to eat."

"Sounds good."

They drove to the Peddler restaurant on Mormon Coulee Road, and once they were settled in the dining room of the restaurant and had ordered their food, Jim took his first sip of coffee. It was hot and delicious.

Jim's cell buzzed. He answered and had a brief conversation with Paul, who informed him about their trip to Hoska Park. When Paul hung up, Jim continued his defense of Leslie. "By the way, Turnmile does have a point. We're going to need Leslie's help with this window case if it develops into something. I'm going to approach Turnmile and ask if Leslie can work from home for a while. How's that sound to you?"

"Really? You'd do that for her?" Sam asked, his mouth gaping open.

"Well, sure I'd do that for her. We need her research skills and expertise on every case. And if this Tiffany window thing revs up, we'll need her knowledge about the art world. Anyway, what can Turnmile do but say no?"

"Are you serious? She'll probably have you for lunch—with all the fixings. I can already hear the shouting from here. All I can say is, better you than me."

"No, no, no," Jim began, his finger wagging back and forth like a metronome, "I'm not going to bat for Leslie alone. You're going with me, so don't get on your high horse too quickly."

"Me?" Sam rested his hand on his chest and gave Jim a stare of disbelief. "You want *me* to come along?"

"Well, don't you think you should defend your wife? This proposition needs more than my lousy, inadequate attempts. I need your backing, Sam," Jim explained reasonably, but he shuddered inwardly when he thought about the possible reactions the persnickety sheriff would have to his request. The shouting. The insinuations. The distrust. All of it wore Jim down in a way he couldn't explain.

Sam pushed his sandwich away and slumped in his chair. "I just lost my appetite. Isn't there any other way to accomplish this?"

"Nope. So prepare yourself. This afternoon the hammer comes down. I already contacted Buzz Hanson in HR, and Turnmile agreed to meet this afternoon." Jim grabbed the tab and stood up. "You ready?"

"I guess so," Sam said. He pushed himself away from the table, left a tip, and followed Jim out to the parking lot. On their walk to the car, Jim glanced at Sam and noticed his worried demeanor.

"Come on, Sam. Turnmile is formidable, but she's made some progress. It might not be as bad as you think it's going to be."

"That's like thinking a root canal is going to be a walk in the park. It never is," Sam said. "It's always hell on wheels no matter how much Novocain they give you."

10

Geoff LaSarde plopped wearily on his leather sofa Thursday evening, kicked his feet up on the coffee table, and flicked on the television. He watched a rerun of *MASH*, then decided he had better things to do with his time than stroll down memory lane. Getting up, he went to the kitchen, got a Pepsi out of the refrigerator, and carried it to his home office.

The articles he'd removed from the airport luggage lay untouched on his desk. He sat down and flipped through them. Nothing caught his eye—at least nothing that would help him locate the iconic stained-glass windows. The smell of old newspaper and ink drifted in the air as he sipped on his soft drink. After fifteen minutes, he was beginning to wonder where this whole mess would lead. *Probably nowhere*, he thought. *Everyone's getting wound up about nothing, especially me*. But he couldn't hold back the thoughts he'd had about the possibility of finding the windows. He knew if he found them, his career would take off like an F-35 rocketing into the sky. *My career could rise to meteoric levels of fame, and my status as a Tiffany expert would go through the roof.*

Leaning back in his chair, he stared at the wall. It was all so tempting. But along with the thoughts of fame and his burgeoning career as a Tiffany expert, other thoughts crowded his mind like the warning Lt. Higgins had given him. Make sure somebody checks on you every day, the astute investigator had told him. Watch your back. LaSarde doubted that anyone would want to harm him, but then he recalled the monetary and historical value of the windows. He'd already been harmed once. Would the perpetrator try again? *I suppose it's possible,* he thought. He recalled the conversation he'd had with Jamie Alberg on the way home from the archaeological excavation site at Fish Farm Mounds in Iowa earlier in the evening.

"You mean to tell me you haven't studied the stuff you took out of the suitcase yet?" Jamie asked. The accusation made Geoff bristle with irritation.

"When would I have had time to do that?" he fired back. "Between being knocked out with benzos, visiting the ER, cleaning up my own puke, talking to Lt. Higgins for an hour, and helping you excavate ancient artifacts, there hasn't been any time to even think about it." He stopped his tirade momentarily, then started up again. "Oh, and then there was the hour when I took my cat down to the law enforcement center to that idiot in the CSI lab."

"I could help—" Jamie began.

"No," Geoff barked, making an angry sweeping motion with his hand. "This is not your problem, Jamie. I brought the suitcase home, and now I've got to figure out who wants it and what they want it for. Besides, this involves Tiffany windows, something I don't think you know too much about." Geoff sniffed, his arrogance on full display. He watched the river scenery whiz by the car window as Jamie drove down the Great River Road back to La Crosse. Dusk was descending, and the western horizon was brilliant with pinks and oranges, the burning ball of the setting sun, and the bluffs which cast a striking silhouette against the radiant evening sky. Geoff was hungry and sweaty. He was in no mood for Jamie's uninformed opinions on the subject of Tiffany. After all, *he* was the expert on that topic.

"I'm just concerned that you don't get yourself in a jam you can't get out of," Jamie responded. He looked at his friend and raised his eyebrows. The look suggested he had gained some hard-earned wisdom about risky situations.

"I take it this is the voice of experience speaking," Geoff said, lifting his nose in the air.

"Hell, yeah. I've been in more jams than I can count. Not everybody has a friend like Lt. Higgins who will come charging in and rescue your sorry ass when you've made some stupid mistakes."

"Well, you would know," Geoff said, his sarcasm just below the surface, "the voice of experience."

"Well, I've learned a few things since my last narrow escape."

"Really? You have?" Geoff asked, watching the side of Jamie's face. The young archaeologist looked so innocent—that curly hair, those inquisitive, hazel eyes, that maddening, seemingly innocent persona. Geoff had to admit that it was hard for him to accept Jamie as a colleague on equal footing, a mature, rational adult, even though Jamie was twenty-six years old and extremely smart. LaSarde remembered reading somewhere that men's frontal lobe, the prefrontal cortex to be exact, didn't fully mature until they approached the age of thirty. Rational decisions in the areas of work, relationships, and distinguishing between good and better and best seemed to lag behind female cohorts of the same age. This was especially true when it came to the ability to suppress urges. Maybe that explained the bare-chested, beer-drinking, drunken, obnoxious behavior of some of the young men Geoff had seen last fall at a Packers game in Green Bay. He shivered at the memory of his only sports-related venture—a visit to Lambeau Field during a Packers-Vikings game when temperatures hovered around twenty degrees, and spitting snow made it seem a whole lot colder than November. It was a spectacle he would never forget. *I'll watch it on TV from now on*, he thought with a smile.

"Did you hear what I said?" Jamie asked.

"Yeah, you said you'd learned a few things," Geoff commented. Jamie was silent, perhaps recalling the wisdom he'd acquired. Finally Geoff asked, "Like what? What'd you learn? I'm all ears." Geoff pulled the lever on the side of the seat and reclined a bit farther, folding his hands across his stomach.

"Well, I've learned that the best laid plans can go down the tubes really fast, and you have to be anticipating where things might be going, or you'll end up in a world of hurt." Visions of the wide, cold Mississippi River flashed through Jamie's mind. Suddenly his skin prickled with goose bumps at the memory of his narrow escape from death almost four years ago. He could feel the water weighing him down, the gasping, panicked breaths, the strong, malicious current sucking him under.

"You mean when you got thrown in the river, and everybody thought you'd drowned?"

"Yeah, but it didn't help that I was totally smashed at the time," Jamie said grudgingly.

"No, I'm sure it didn't. And what about that escapade in the cave? That was a classic screwup, too," Geoff reminded him.

Jamie's face flashed with anger. "Hey! As I said, things can go south in a hurry, as you found out the other night when you were rendered unconscious by some dude who broke into your house!" Jamie's voice had risen in volume, and his face turned pink with embarrassment. "I'm just trying to help you!"

Geoff waved Jamie's criticism off with a frustrated gesture. "Listen, let's not do this. Let's not argue. If we're honest, then we have to admit we've both had our share of botched situations. The thing is, Lt. Higgins warned me that the person who disarmed me with the drugs might be back. You know, he might not be done looking for whatever he was after."

"The quicker you figure out what he wants, the better off you'll be. 'To be forewarned is to be forearmed.'"

Geoff stared at Jamie in the glow of the car's dash lights. *Where does he come up with this stuff?*

Jamie glanced at his friend as if he'd read his thoughts. "Abraham Tucker. 1768. A quote from *The Light of Nature Pursued.* I do read, you know. Quite voraciously."

"Whatever," Geoff said, depressed at the thought that someone was out there aiming to get him for something he might have, which was still a total mystery to him.

"I could help you look through the stuff from the suitcase. Maybe something will jump out at me," Jamie suggested.

Geoff silently nodded his head in agreement. "Okay, but not tonight. I'm too tired. Maybe over the weekend. I'll call you."

Now it was late on Thursday evening, and he'd arrived back home from the dig. He was too exhausted by the day's dramatic events to search the material for clues tonight. Instead, he made a to-do list for the following day: Home Depot to get a surveillance camera, call Jamie and arrange a meeting time, get cat food and groceries, and contact the CSI department about the blood sample. He tore the list off the pad and strolled to the kitchen, laying it on the counter.

Sir Lancelot wound himself around Geoff's leg, meowing noisily. Geoff reached down and stroked the feline's glossy fur. "No, you don't get any more treats today," he said. "Apparently some people think you're fat." Sir Lancelot growled and disappeared into the living room. "Besides, you're the least of my worries," Geoff said, snapping off the kitchen light.

11

On Thursday evening, Sam Birkstein stood in the doorway of the bathroom, leaning against the frame, his arms crossed casually over his chest as he watched Leslie corral Karina's wiggling arms and legs into her pajamas.

"You're kidding?" Leslie said as she finished dressing Karina after her bath.

"No, I'm not kidding," Sam said. "I can hardly believe it myself. Turnmile gave her stamp of approval for you to work from home . . . on a limited basis. Her approval is very surprising. Do you think Higgins has some dirt on her, and he used it to leverage this whole deal?"

"Sam, you've been talking to way too many lowlifes lately if that's what you're thinking. Higgins would never do something like that."

Sam thought about Higgins. He'd never run into anyone who had as much integrity as his boss, except his father, but he was a pastor, for Pete's sake. "Hmm, I don't know about that. He's not perfect—none of us are—but when it comes to Turnmile, all bets are off. This whole deal seems a little out of character for Higgins. Negotiating with the enemy is not his style."

“Well, first of all, Turnmile is not the enemy,” Leslie commented calmly. She lifted her eyebrows and tilted her head, waiting for Sam’s response.

Sam’s eyes flashed with anger. “Yeah, right. You weren’t there to see the humiliation. Why do we have to beg for every little concession? Do you know what she said about—”

“Sam, get a grip,” Leslie interrupted. “Nobody’s perfect, and remember, Higgins is short-handed since I had the baby. I’m just glad that I can help and do it from home.” She handed Karina to Sam and began picking up the bath things. “Her bottle’s on the kitchen counter. See if you can get her to sleep, okay?”

Sam cuddled his baby girl to his chest, retrieved the bottle from the kitchen, and walked into the living room, where he sat down in the rocking recliner. He willed his unkind thoughts about the truculent sheriff out of his mind. *Don’t give her any more of your mental real estate*, he thought. The sun was sinking toward the horizon, painting the sky with a blaze of pink and red hues. The dark bluffs cut a sharp profile against the flaming sunset. The lights from a tow glowed in the dusk as the monstrosity pushed its cargo steadily downstream.

Paco, ever watchful, plopped in a heap at Sam’s feet and stretched out on the wooden floor, emitting a long groan. Sam noticed lately that Leslie’s intrepid companion was slowing down. The aging process was at work. The faithful canine tired more easily and had put on a few pounds, but the black lab was still a formidable protector. His loyalty to the members of the Birkstein family remained steadfast and unquestioned.

“Tough day, boy?” Sam asked, as Karina drank her bottle.

Paco lifted his head in acknowledgment, thumped his tail on the floor, and stretched out, closing his eyes in utter relaxation. Sam sat in the chair watching the sun set. Despite his attempts to ban negative thoughts, the conversation with Sheriff Turnmile that had taken place at the end of the workday in her office came roaring back into his brain.

"What's your justification for making this request?" Turnmile had asked with brusque impatience.

"We've got this window deal on our hands, which is bound to get tangled up with road trips and interviews. We need someone to do some background work, and that's Leslie's strength." Jim studied his fingernails, then gave the sheriff a cool stare. Sam sat in the corner thinking murderous thoughts. Jim looked at him expecting a comment of support, but he stayed quiet.

"What is it about your team, Higgins? Somebody isn't pregnant again, are they? Don't you people practice birth control? People are having babies around here every couple of months. DeDe's the only person who hasn't gotten pregnant yet, except for me, of course. Goes without saying." The sheriff smiled weakly.

Neither man responded to the challenge hidden in Turnmile's comments. *Boy, could I have a heyday with that remark,* Sam thought. Instead, both detectives pasted on a blasé expression and waited for her response. In the end, after fifteen minutes of vigorous arguments from both sides, the sheriff conceded, limiting Leslie to thirty hours a week with no benefits. Sam wanted to fight about insurance benefits, but Jim laid a hand on his arm, cutting off his comments before he could hang himself with his words. Jim's perfectly timed gesture hit the mark, and Sam shut up.

Leslie walked into the living room, sat down on the couch, and muted the TV. "So what are the conditions of this part-time gig?" she asked as she leaned over and touched Karina's downy hair with her fingertips.

"Thirty hours a week max, no benefits, seventy bucks an hour," Sam said.

Leslie tipped her head in thought. "I can live with that," she answered. "When do I start?"

"Tomorrow."

"No rest for the wicked, huh?" Leslie quipped.

"You got that right. And just remember, honey, the wicked are going at it as we speak."

FRIDAY, MAY 18

12

Friday morning dawned bright and sunny on Chipmunk Coulee Road. The temperature was warm for May, and the trees along the backyard at the edge of Jim Higgins' property were filled with chirping, chattering flocks of birds busily building nests and incubating their eggs. Jim stood on the backyard limestone patio in his stocking feet, boxers, and T-shirt waiting for Latte to relieve herself along the edge of the woods. There were advantages to living in the country. Like standing on your patio half-naked enjoying the beginning of the day. Or, every once in a while, taking a whiz off the back deck—something Carol knew nothing about. Jim smiled at the peeing conspiracy. He loved Carol with a vengeance, but a man needed some territory that was totally his own without any female interference.

While Jim waited for the puppy to finish her business, he enjoyed the morning light and the burgeoning green of the lawn and trees. A plum tree near the patio was heavily laden with pink blossoms that would burst open any day now. At the base of the tree lay the plaque dedicated to his first wife, Margie. *Would she even believe the life I have now?* he thought. The years had morphed into a blur since he'd married Carol, but every once in a while, his life with Margie materialized in front of him and sent him on a trip down memory lane. He'd never forgotten her, and despite his happiness now, there was always a shadow of sadness when he remembered his first wife and the life they'd shared.

He shook his head, and his thoughts turned to the summer season that was almost upon them. In a few weeks, the kids would be out of school, and they could fire up *The Little Eddy* for a test run out on the Mississippi River.

The boat was a gift from his dad, and Jim treasured the vessel, keeping it clean and in top form, tuning the engine until it purred like a kitten. He remembered the many trips they'd taken as a family along the great waterway—fishing, swimming, camping, exploring random islands, and observing the plant and animal life along the great Mississippi.

Ten minutes later, Latte returned to the patio, interrupting Jim's reverie of past summer adventures. The young retriever bounded up next to Jim and then obediently sat down near his feet when Jim snapped his fingers and gave the "sit" command. Jim smiled. He leaned down and thumped the canine's side. The dog was learning. *Must be those obedience classes Carol invested in,* he thought. *Now if we could get the kids in line, we'd be doing something.*

Jim turned and entered the house through the patio door, followed by the spunky puppy. Walking through the living room, he stepped into the kitchen where he ground coffee beans and began his morning java routine. While the coffee brewed, he strolled through the dining room, walked to the front porch, and picked up the *La Crosse Sentinel,* the city's only daily rag, and the *Wisconsin State Journal.* Back in the dining room, he scanned the *Sentinel* with interest, wondering if there was any mention of the break-in at Geoff LaSarde's home.

Latte began to pull on Jim's sock with canine impatience. She nipped his toe, and he grabbed a stuffed penguin chew toy from a box in the corner and shoved it toward the puppy. Grabbing the toy, the puppy retreated under the table where she gnawed on it with gusto. A moment later, Carol appeared in the dining room.

"Hmm, that coffee smells so good," she said. Giving Jim a quick embrace, she asked how he'd slept. He didn't answer immediately. Instead, he spent a few moments taking in Carol's beauty. Although her dark hair was streaked with the first signs of gray, her luminous skin glowed with a blush of pink, and her brown eyes were bright. When she turned to go to the kitchen, he reached out to her and pulled her close, noticing the faint scent of lavender. He tenderly kissed her.

"So . . . you didn't answer me. How did you sleep, honey?" she asked again.

"After that hot shower and your fabulous back rub, I slept like a rock."

"Good. What's on your schedule today?" she asked, turning toward the kitchen.

"Murder and mayhem as usual," he commented as he sat at the table and turned his attention again to the *Sentinel*, scanning it for any references to the police work that went on in the city.

"Murder? I didn't hear about any murder."

"Well, no murder yet, but plenty of mayhem," Jim responded casually.

"Pancakes, eggs, or oatmeal this morning?" Carol asked while she rummaged around in the cupboards.

"Oatmeal with raisins, please," Jim muttered, still reading.

Lillie appeared in the doorway of the dining room, her hair tangled into a mass of golden curls that cascaded down her back. Her rumpled nightgown hung loosely around her skinny legs, but her wide blue eyes were intently fixed on Jim.

Jim looked up from the newspaper. "Mornin', peanut."

Lillie continued to stare. When she didn't greet him, Jim zeroed in on her expression. He felt his stomach flip over. From a very young age, his precocious adopted daughter had demonstrated an uncanny ability to "see" things that hadn't happened yet. Jim and Carol truly believed Lillie's premonitions were God-given. They had never shared her unique aptitude with anyone, although some of the investigative team had been unknowingly privy to some of her predictions. Still, as parents, Jim and Carol felt it was their duty and responsibility to protect and shield Lillie from any undue attention. Jim shuddered when he thought about the day someone would find out about his daughter's gift and make her the center of a full-blown exposé. He could imagine the headlines already: "Child's Premonition Guides Investigative Team." A chill ran up his back at the thought of his daughter being subjected to the intense scrutiny of a rabid press titillated by anything unusual, to say nothing of the general public's fascination with anything out of the ordinary. Then there was Sheriff Turnmile. He couldn't even imagine the reaction such a revelation would have on his boss. There would be no peace in the Higgins' household if any of this ever got out.

"Lillie? What's the matter? Are you sick?" Jim asked.

Carol heard Jim asking Lillie questions, came into the dining room, and stood in front of her daughter. She felt Lillie's forehead while she balanced her coffee cup in her other hand. "You don't have a fever. Are you okay?"

Lillie shook her head slowly, watching Jim's face very carefully.

"So . . . what's wrong?" Jim asked, lowering the newspaper. His skin prickled at the thought that another cryptic conjecture was about to tumble from his daughter's lips.

"I dreamed something, but I don't know what it means," Lillie said, her eyes filled with confusion.

Jim laid the paper on the table and opened his arms. "Come here, sweetheart," he said, crooking his finger at her. "You know, not everything we dream necessarily has a hidden meaning." Lillie walked over and perched herself on Jim's lap. She leaned against his chest, and Jim gently rubbed her back, noticing her tight muscles.

"I'm here for you. You know you can tell me anything," Jim said softly, his blue eyes deep pools of wisdom. Carol stood by the table waiting for Lillie's explanation as she sipped her coffee.

Lillie looked into Jim's eyes, finding an anchor there.

"You've had those before," Carol said. "Go ahead, Lillie. Tell Daddy. He'll know what to do."

"In my dream, there was this old shack—it was deserted and falling down, and nobody lived there anymore—but there were these beautiful windows in the building. They were all kinds of colors, and the light was shining through them. They were really, really beautiful," Lillie said, ending her description in a whisper. She turned toward Jim. "Why would an old building that's falling down have such beautiful windows?"

Jim looked into Lillie's eyes. "That's a good question, but I don't know the answer to that."

A few moments passed. Finally Carol interrupted the silence. "But Daddy will remember your dream, and who knows? It might come in handy somewhere down the line." Lillie nodded her head and seemed satisfied with that explanation. To Jim, it seemed she had given in way too easily.

"Maybe you'll use it to catch some bad guys?" Lillie suggested, tilting her head.

"You never know," Jim said casually, but the goose bumps on his arms belied his casual attitude.

"Okay, I'm trusting you, Dad. I guess you'll figure it out." Turning to Carol, she said, "What's for breakfast, Mom? I'm starving." She jumped out of Jim's lap and skipped into the kitchen.

Jim breathed a sigh of relief that Lillie had so easily accepted Carol's remark, but he worried about her latest dream. He thought about the lost windows that Geoff LaSarde had described to him. The Tiffany windows presented a quandary to the investigative team. Where were they? How had they disappeared? Were they hidden somewhere in the Oshkosh vicinity? Whoever had attacked Geoff was still roaming the landscape undetected, along with the missing suitcase. Jim could feel the weighty implications of the situation: the mystery of the lost windows, the unsavory characters who were trying to find the valuable antiques, and the danger of conflicting parties with conflicting motives. To Jim, it seemed like the endgame was just as big a mystery as the lost windows.

Jim was thankful as their familiar morning routine got back on track and rolled along. Henri and Lillie verbally sparred about a variety of topics as they ate their bowls of oatmeal. In the kitchen, Carol unloaded the dishwasher, made the children's lunches, and scrambled to get the kids out the door to catch the school bus. Jim retreated to the bedroom and dressed in a lightweight navy linen jacket, a white shirt with a subtle gray stripe, a pair of gray trousers, and his favorite Nordic tie in shades of blue, maroon, and gray. He strolled into the dining room where Carol stood by the window waving to the kids as they climbed on the bus.

"Finally, some peace and quiet," Jim said, coming up behind Carol, watching the bus pull out of the driveway.

"What do you think about Lillie's dream?" she asked, turning to face him.

"You got me, honey. It might have something to do with those missing Tiffany windows, but that's not even an official case yet. Nothing's come of it since the burglary at Geoff LaSarde's place Tuesday night," Jim said. "Besides that, Sheriff Turnmile put the kibosh on any more investigating in that area. I think her exact words were 'We can't afford to waste any more resources on something so vague.' But if Lillie's dream is any indication, the whole thing isn't over yet. It's about as vague as the nose on your face."

Carol stared at Jim. "You seem awfully calm about this, Jim. Usually Lillie's prognostications send you into overdrive," Carol commented, wondering at her husband's placid demeanor.

Jim shrugged and sighed. "Well, I guess I'm learning to pick my battles, especially when it comes to Turnmile—and Lillie. I'm suspending judgment on this whole Tiffany window situation until something else happens that moves it into new territory, or it fades into oblivion, which usually doesn't happen."

Carol was skeptical about Jim's reaction. She listened carefully while Jim continued explaining. "You know that Bible verse about worry: 'Who of you by worrying can add a single hour to his life?' or the other one from Matthew, 'Do not worry about your life, what you will eat or what you will drink or what you will wear.'"

Carol's eyebrows lifted, and she tilted her head. "Is that the one that says if God feeds the sparrows, he'll also take care of you, oh ye of little faith?"

"Yeah," Jim said, grinning. "Jesus' Sermon on the Mount. I'm impressed, honey."

"So that's your new philosophy?" Carol asked. Jim nodded. "Does that apply to your job, too?"

Making a wry face, he said, "Well, it should apply to my job, but I'm starting with my personal life first. One thing at a time, sweetheart."

"Okay," Carol said. "Whatever you say, but that'll be the day when you don't worry about what you're gonna wear."

Jim's temper suddenly flared. "Whaddya mean? I've got to develop some kind of strategy to deal with the crap that gets dished on my plate, especially from Turnmile," Jim said. Carol could hear the frustration beneath the words. "I've been hoping she'd change and come around, but until that happens—"

"This is your new way of coping?" Carol said gently, finishing his sentence.

"Yep, and I'm stickin' to it," Jim finished. He leaned over, kissed her, then kissed her again, lingering a little bit, and headed to the garage. "I'll grill tonight if you take some hamburger out of the freezer," he said over his shoulder. "See you later."

By eight o'clock Friday morning, Jim had arrived at the law enforcement center after a brief stop at Kwik Trip for coffee. He was in his office conversing on his cell with Leslie Birkstein about the Tiffany windows.

"I need you to get some background work done on Louis Comfort

Tiffany. You know, his windows are world famous. There's a glass restoration place in Winona called Gorgeous Glassworks. They do restoration work on church windows and other stained-glass pieces. Give them a call and see what you can glean from them about these specific windows. They might know something about them." He gave Leslie the address and phone number. "We'll talk more when you get some information gathered up."

"Got it, Chief. I'll call when I get something concrete." Leslie hung up.

Jim wondered how working at home would play out for Leslie. He knew an arrangement like that would never work for Carol. His wife was a tiger when it came to keeping work and home life separate, but Jim's profession made it increasingly difficult to achieve.

"Honey, we need to have some boundaries between our public and private life," she'd said recently over their evening cup of tea. Jim had taken a number of calls during the evening, which had interrupted his reading time with Lillie and Henri.

"It's not for lack of trying, Carol, but crime is increasing everywhere, and it's really hard to not let it spill over into our home life. I know these violent situations can do a number on my patience and equilibrium, but that's the fallout you get when you do this kind of work. Remember when I got shot in the quarry?"

"How could I forget that?" Carol said bitterly. Her placid face changed to something harder, more angular.

"Well, I haven't forgotten it either, but these things go with the territory." Jim reiterated again. "I wish it was different, but I'm making a concerted effort not to drag my work stuff home and parade it in front of our kids. They see enough violence on the evening news. Besides, you have to admit that I never discuss my cases in front of them."

Carol's expression softened. "Yes, that's true. You're very careful about that, Jim. Thank you, honey."

"So are we all right for now?" he asked, tired of the verbal sparring.

They'd been over this subject many times. He doubted that Carol would accept his analysis of the whole situation.

"Sure, I can live with that as long as we're both on the same page," she said, looking over the top of her mug.

"I think we are, so let's leave it there." His comment squelched any further conversation on the topic.

While Jim waited for DeDe Deverioux and Sam Birkstein to arrive at the office, he pulled a folder from the stack on his desk and flipped through the information about the missing Tiffany windows. Considering his daughter's dream, he thought it might be a good idea to get as familiar as possible with the facts of the original disappearance of the famous windows from the stately mansion in Oshkosh. He'd barely gotten started when Sam walked through the office door and parked himself in a chair next to Jim's desk. He scrolled through his phone and sipped an energy drink. A moment later DeDe walked in behind him. Paul was already at his desk in his office cubicle, reviewing the facts from their latest case, lining up their evidence for the court proceedings scheduled for August.

"Mornin', Chief," DeDe said. She was dressed in black slacks and a powder blue tunic, which was accentuated with a large, black pendant necklace and black loopy earrings. In contrast, Sam looked thrown together as if he'd dressed in five minutes, which was a distinct possibility. His pale yellow dress shirt was wrinkled, and a bright, gaudy red and blue striped tie hung loosely at the neck. He'd opted for a pair of faded blue jeans, and he was wearing his famous lemon yellow Air Force 1 Nike running shoes with the bright orange shoelaces.

"Been visiting Goodwill again, Sam?" Jim asked, wondering if the question would have any significant effect on his choice of attire.

"Nope. All this stuff just screamed to me this morning from my closet," Sam said innocently, glancing up momentarily from his cell.

"Screamed being the key word," DeDe said, frowning, giving him a sideways glance.

"Well, once in a while, I need to reassert my avant-garde position for worst-dressed detective on staff," Sam said defensively. "Nobody else seems interested in challenging me for the title."

"You got that right," Jim said, staring at the yellow sneakers. "Good thing we're not doing any stakeouts today. They'd see you coming a mile away."

"Hey, I'll have you know my clothes are the perfect undercover getup down at Hoska Park when I socialize with the homeless and take drug dealers off the street. We're looking for Kevin today, so I'll fit right in."

"Now, that I believe," DeDe said with a straight face.

"By the way, you locate this Kevin . . . what's his name again?" Jim asked, squinting his eyes at Sam.

"Kevin Chroniger. We went down there yesterday, but the city moved out the homeless, and the city park and recreation guys were cleaning up the place. We talked to a homeless guy. He gave us a few leads, but we struck out. Couldn't locate him. We'll keep looking," Sam said.

Toward the end of Sam's explanation, Paul walked into the office and leaned against the door frame. "Carl Ettinger from crime scene called this morning while I was organizing my desk and filing some stuff," he said. "The blood you found at Geoff LaSarde's house was not his. Carl plugged the info into the DNA data bank and came up with a hit."

Jim listened carefully. "Wow, that's a surprise," he said, feeling hopeful. "So who's the culprit who broke into his house?"

"I looked up the guy online. The intruder was a guy named Lewis Borden. Army veteran. According to his service record, he did a stint in Iraq as an undercover liaison officer and interpreter between the U.S. Army and the Kurds. Negotiated with them and kept U.S. forces informed about enemy movements and operations. Since coming home from the war, he's worked for Tewalt Technologies, a Chicago-based firm that builds digital components for specialized gadgets.

Borden's role in the company was somewhat vague . . ." Paul's voice tapered off.

"What do you mean?" Jim asked, squinting off in the distance as he listened to Paul.

"Well, Borden was on the payroll until a few days ago. When Leslie tried to get information about his employment at the company, she hit a dead end. She was told he was no longer employed at the company, but no one would tell her what his exact duties were when he was there. She's going to call the company again and have a direct conversation with Tewalt. However, she did learn that Lewis Borden and Charles Tewalt were army buddies—rangers no less."

"So, this Lewis guy is skilled in subversion, hand-to-hand combat, and reconnaissance." Jim took a swig of water and wiped his lips on the back of his hand. He felt a chill run up his back as he recalled another veteran, Wade Bennett, who'd created havoc in Leslie's life and had sent the investigative team on a mission in which Paul was nearly killed in a valley down toward the tiny town of Avalanche.

". . . and highly competent with assault rifles." Paul finished. "Sound like somebody else we know?"

"Unfortunately, yes," Jim said, "but fortunately for the general public, Bennett is sitting in a prison cell in Boscobel. Good work, Paul." He paused for a minute, thinking about the information. "Borden's ranger status explains the ease in putting Geoff out of commission. That's assuming he was the one who stole the suitcase from his house. But why was Lewis Borden retrieving a long-lost piece of old luggage from a guy in La Crosse?" Jim asked. "That sounds crazy, at best."

"Apparently, someone wants those Tiffany windows," Sam commented dryly. True to his nature, Sam began weaving a possible theory. "Borden's on some kind of mission—probably to discover the location of them before anyone else does. Either he wants them for someone he's working for, or he wants them for himself, or he has a buyer who will pay the going rate for Tiffany windows. Take your pick. The last time I checked, according to Jamie Alberg, Geoff

LaSarde was looking for them, too. All of this could mean trouble, Chief. Big trouble."

"Get Leslie—"

"She's already on it," Sam interrupted. "She's researching Charles Tewalt and his business this morning. She should have something concrete later this afternoon."

"Great," Jim said. "Now let's all get familiar with the original crime when these Tiffany windows disappeared into thin air." Jim opened the file of the information he'd received from Geoff LaSarde. At that moment, Emily appeared at the door. She took one look at Sam's getup and shook her head.

"Don't jump out from behind any doors," she said. "Your clothes would be enough to give somebody a heart attack."

Sam returned the criticism with a cool smile. "You know what they say: Life is too short to wear boring clothes."

13

Leslie Birkstein walked into her studio on Tuesday morning after Sam had left for work. Smells of paint thinner floated in the air. Brushes and tubes of oil paint in a variety of colors littered the small table next to the easel. The morning sunlight filled the studio with a warm, yellow glow—the promise of a beautiful spring day. Leslie walked to the large window and balanced her coffee cup in one hand while she watched tows move up and down the great waterway and fishing boats race across the sparkling water. Close to shore, a small dory bobbed lazily in the water, the fishermen patiently casting their lures.

Leslie walked back to the canvas on the easel and studied it with a critical eye. The large river scene she'd been working on for the last few months needed a few more details, although it was nearing completion. She decided the water could use more muted purple shading to reflect the movement of the clouds and the moody sky overhead. While Karina took a morning nap, Leslie spent some time adding details to the painting. After half an hour, she decided she'd better use the quiet time to contact Tewalt Technologies in Chicago. She dialed the number she'd found on her internet search of the company.

A voice reflecting the expected professionalism came over the line. "This is Tewalt Technologies. Sarah Fletcher speaking. How may I help you?"

"Hello. This is Leslie Birkstein calling from La Crosse, Wisconsin. I'm a detective at the sheriff's department here. I need to speak with Charles Tewalt, please."

"May I ask what the nature of your call is?" Sarah asked.

"No, you may not," Leslie said firmly. "The nature of our inquiries is confidential."

In an icy, clipped tone, the secretary said, "One moment, please."

A few moments later, a deep voice came over the line. "This is Charlie Tewalt."

Leslie explained her role at the sheriff's department and began asking questions. "Mr.

Tewalt—"

"Oh, please call me Charlie," he interrupted. "We're not that formal around here."

"Mr. Tewalt," Leslie said firmly, keeping the interview formal, "I have some questions for you about an employee of yours—Lewis Borden. Could you describe your relationship with him?"

"Yes, of course. I *was* his employer, but I don't have a relationship with him as of last week. Lewis and I had a serious disagreement, and he is no longer employed at my company."

"What was the problem that led to his termination?" Leslie asked.

"He didn't seem to be able to follow company policy. I had to fire him for insubordination."

"It's my understanding you were army buddies and friends. Is that correct?" Leslie asked.

"Yes, that's correct. We served together in the military in Iraq and Afghanistan. We were friends for many years."

"What role did he play in your company?" Leslie asked. "What were his duties?"

"Just exactly what are you investigating, ma'am?" Charlie asked, avoiding Leslie's pointed questions. "Are you looking for something specific?"

"Yes, we are. Our department is investigating an attack on a La Crosse resident who was rendered unconscious in his home with drugs. He had an item stolen from his home as well. During our investigation of the break-in and assault, Mr. Borden's DNA showed up at the scene. We need to locate him so we can talk to him."

"About what?"

"About his presence in the home, of course," Leslie explained. "It seems he might have been on a mission to discover the location of some very valuable antiques. An old suitcase full of information went missing. Do you know anything about that, sir?" The line was silent. "Mr. Tewalt, are you there?" Leslie asked.

After a brief pause, Charlie answered. "Why would that concern me?"

"It may, or it may not," Leslie said carefully, noticing his expert maneuvering to avoid giving pertinent information. "We're doing a complete history on Lewis Borden to get a clearer picture of him, and that includes his past employers and his years of military service. We're not sure right now why Mr. Borden was in La Crosse. We're investigating the circumstances that precipitated the robbery and assault . . . and whether you were involved. Have you had any contact with Mr. Borden in the last few days?"

"Not since I fired him."

"Do you know where he is?"

"No, he did not leave a forwarding address, although he has a home in the Alta Vista Terrace neighborhood, I think. Our split was very sudden. Like I said, Lewis and I had a disagreement, and he is no longer employed at my company," Charlie explained, but his voice was gritty with impatience. Clearly, he was done with this line of inquiry.

Leslie continued grilling Charlie Tewalt, trying to find a topic that would give her access to the executive's insulated world, but she could tell from experience he was a master of evasion.

“I have some rather pressing matters I need to attend to, detective. I regret I can’t be more helpful. Lewis always held his cards close to his chest,” Charlie explained after several minutes of sidestepping. “I’m sorry to hear that he might be involved in some kind of criminal activity.”

“Well, we’re not sure of that yet, but we really need to speak with him, so if he contacts you, please get in touch with our office, Mr. Tewalt,” Leslie instructed. She left her contact information with him and hung up in frustration. Completing her notes from the conversation, she logged her minutes, walked to the large canvas waiting on her easel and picked up her brush.

SATURDAY, MAY 19

14

Geoff LaSarde and Jamie Alberg sat at Geoff's kitchen table on Saturday morning snacking on cinnamon rolls from a bakery down the street and drinking freshly brewed coffee. A pile of old, brittle newspaper articles and other paper ephemera that had been removed from the airport suitcase sat between them on the table. While they were doing that, Sir Lancelot, the overgrown cat, meowed persistently at Geoff's feet. Jamie looked over the edge of the table where the cat paced nervously below. Sir Lancelot looked up at Jamie, his yellow eyes bright with perceived neglect. He mewed a pathetic wail.

"What's the matter with your cat?" Jamie asked. "Has he got a gut ache?"

"Of sorts. He's on a diet, and he's not a happy camper."

Jamie eyed the cat, while Sir Lancelot continued his loud screeching complaints.

"Maybe you should feed him," Jamie suggested when the cat refused to stop bellyaching. "It's hard to concentrate on this stuff when he's having a conniption about eating." Geoff leaned down and hoisted the cat onto his lap. Jamie's eyes widened when he realized the size and heftiness of the animal. "Jeez, he's a monster," he said softly. "What *do* you feed him? Steak? Hamburger? Tuna?"

"All of the above."

"Is that diet recommended by your vet?"

"No, but Lancelot just loves to eat, and I hate depriving him and then listening to his howling and bitching. He's perfectly healthy; he just thinks he's being starved," Geoff explained as he kept reading one of the newspaper articles.

"Well, you can't put him on a starvation diet and expect him to like it," Jamie said.

"I thought you said he was a monster. Now you're defending his eating habits?" Geoff raised his eyebrows and continued to stroke the golden fur of Sir Lancelot. "You can't have it both ways, Jamie."

"Put him down and let him go outside. He can go mousing for a change," Jamie suggested.

"Mousing?" Geoff sneered, crinkling his nose at the suggestion. "That's disgusting. That's what alley cats, abandoned cats, and feral cats do."

Jamie scowled. "He's a cat, for Pete's sake. His natural predatory instincts will kick in when his stomach starts growling. He'll eat mice if he gets hungry enough. Every desperate cat does. Some cats even enjoy it." Jamie pulled an article from the pile of papers and began reading again. "Trust me, it's for his own good."

"What would you know about having a pet?" Geoff sneered impatiently.

"Well, my mom has a cat, and I can tell you, it looks nothing like yours. Of course she is a female, so she's smaller by design."

Geoff plopped Sir Lancelot onto the floor, then headed to the back door. The cat followed obediently until he reached the door, where he stopped and looked up at Geoff, who tipped his head and waved his hand toward the open door and the backyard. "Out. Come on. Get your butt out there and hunt," Geoff said.

Jamie smiled as he listened from the kitchen. *People and their stupid pets,* he thought. *A bunch of drama over a dumb cat.*

Geoff walked back into the kitchen. "We'll see what comes of this hunting idea."

Jamie was concentrating on an article from the *Oshkosh Gazette*, which reviewed the details of the Tiffany windows and their disappearance from the Burlington Northern Railroad.

"How could a railroad lose five large windows? Didn't they know the value of Tiffany objects?" Jamie asked. He shook his head. "It still sounds like some kind of inside job to me."

"What does the article say?" Geoff asked.

"Well, it just says the windows were scheduled to be delivered to a stained-glass studio for repair in Winona, but they never got there. It *must* have been an inside job. If they were loaded on the train and didn't arrive at their destination, then somebody must have taken them off the train somewhere along the line," Jamie finished.

"Makes sense," Geoff said. "So where do you think they ended up?"

"Don't know. What we probably should do is study the train route from Oshkosh to Winona and try to figure out a possible place where they could have been removed."

"That sounds extremely difficult and time-consuming unless we can find the name of a person in one of these articles who was responsible for the windows' safe delivery to the stained-glass workshop," Geoff suggested. "You know, like someone on Ellison's staff or a person who worked for the railroad."

"Well, by now, they'd be dead." Jamie sat back and looked thoughtful.

"Yeah, they would be," Geoff said. "But some of their relatives might still be alive. They might know something. That's probably the only way we're going to figure out what happened to them." Geoff sighed despondently when he thought of the magnificent windows lying in some god-forsaken shed somewhere, covered in dust and bird poop. "It feels like looking for a needle in a haystack."

"Yep. I would agree with that," Jamie concluded, bobbing his head up and down. "That's exactly what it's like."

15

Lewis Borden looked in the mirror and nodded his head in approval. His hair, once prematurely white, was now a rich dark brown, along with his eyebrows. He'd shaved off his mustache, ditched his middle-age dress slacks and cashmere sweater in exchange for a Badger sweatshirt, comfortable blue jeans, and athletic shoes, which complemented his trim and fit body. There was nothing about his eyes that he could change, even if he wanted to—one was blue, and one was green, but most people didn't notice since colored contact lenses made them appear gray.

He'd rented a small cabin tucked in a quaint little coulee just southeast of Coon Valley. The cabin was comfortable and had a small kitchenette where he could cook some simple food. A trout stream about a hundred feet from the front door was the perfect guise for a fly fisherman on vacation. He'd made sure he had rods and lures appropriate for trout. The owner of the cabin promised him a session with some pointers for catching trout in the morning, and he'd played along with the idea. After all, he was simply here on a relaxing weeklong break from his stressful job in Chicago—a much- needed getaway from the hassles of big city life.

Tomorrow, Lewis planned on getting a better handle on Geoff LaSarde's comings and goings while keeping a low profile. The next time they met, Lewis would extract the information he needed about the hidden Tiffany windows from LaSarde and begin his own quest to find them. He frowned when he thought about the large, pernicious cat who'd torn up his leg. An evil smile turned up the corners of his thin lips. "Here, kitty, kitty, kitty," he said under his breath. He chuckled wickedly at the thought of the payback he'd planned for the feline. Then he became serious again. *The cat is the least of your worries, you knucklehead. Don't get distracted by something so stupid.* Without a job and with no money coming in, failure was not an option.

A trip into La Crosse tomorrow might yield some important information that would help him locate the troublesome windows, recover them, and move on with his life.

First things first. He walked to the rented car and began unloading his bags and fishing gear. It all appeared perfectly normal. Only he knew the true extent of this cover-up, but that was the way he wanted it. By the time everyone else figured it out, Lewis Borden would be long gone.

Bubba and Kay Starch lived in Cheyenne Valley near Ontario, Wisconsin, which was a stone's throw from Wildcat Mountain State Park located just south of the tiny village. Here, the Wisconsin topography was bisected by the Kickapoo River and displayed a dramatically rugged side of the state characterized by deep gorges, pine forests, and sandstone bluffs topped with limestone. About ten miles farther north, the Elroy-Sparta Bike Trail wandered through the countryside, the first rail-to-trail conversion in the United States, completed in 1967.

Moon Ridge Road was a quiet country highway that meandered up and down and around the rolling hills, limestone outcroppings, and bubbling creeks of the Driftless Area. The landscape here appealed to Bubba, so when he began looking for a place to build a retirement home, the forty-acre parcel he purchased from his father-in-law was the perfect spot—near enough to civilization, but far enough away from large populations of people—to satisfy his preference for quiet woods, slow streams, and abundant wildlife.

Bubba Starch was a Vietnam veteran. As a vet from that era, he had lingering effects of PTSD, but the disease had never debilitated him the same way it had for some of his buddies. He'd been able to stay away from the booze and drugs that plagued many of his army cohorts. His wife, Kay, was a quiet, simple woman who enjoyed the same things he did, except for church. Kay loved church and church activities and was always pestering Bubba about his faith. They'd come to an uneasy truce about that, and discussions about God and Bubba's belief system seemed to have been shelved for the time being, much to his relief.

For the last several months, Bubba had taken on a project to clear an old logging trail near his property, which had fallen into disrepair. It was a great trail through pine forests and rock outcroppings, but over the years it had become choked with brush and downed tree branches from frequent storms. Equipped with his chainsaw and a couple of shovels and axes, Bubba enjoyed the hard physical work of clearing the trail, burning the brush, and removing rocks that had surfaced from repeated frosts and thaws.

On Saturday afternoon, while Bubba was working on the trail and roaming in the area beyond his property on his utility four-wheeler, he came across a small, deserted church just off the trail about fifty yards. The decaying remains of a logging camp to the north probably explained the presence of the building in the vicinity. To the right of the chapel, a low-lying swale was populated with marsh marigolds, arrowhead, maidenhair ferns, and clumps of sedges. In one corner of the marshy area, a group of cattails swayed gracefully in the wind. The church sat on a small hillock above the marsh and was surrounded by several large white pines, which towered over the simple edifice. Farther down the trail, a limestone outcropping was topped by a pine tree that leaned precariously over the trail.

Bubba found the discovery of the church to be rather odd. When he'd purchased the land a couple of years ago, his father-in-law, Willie Bradford, had never mentioned the building. Surely, he must have known about the chapel—he'd lived in the Kickapoo River Valley most of his life. Bubba found it unusual that Willie hadn't told him about it.

He shut off his UTV, dismounted, and approached the building slowly and deliberately, expecting the place to be occupied by some kind of wild animals. Underneath his feet, the pine needles from the huge evergreens felt like a soft carpet, and the air was perfumed by the sharp scent from the towering pines nearby. The sturdy limestone foundation of the chapel was in good shape, but the cedar clapboard siding had faded, its paint peeled away, leaving the boards weathered and gray. The roof had rotted away in some places, so parts of the interior had been exposed to wind and rain. Simple four-pane windows along the sides of the church let in some light. The frame around the bleached door had deteriorated, and the door hung crookedly on its hinges. Despite its poor condition, the tiny chapel radiated an air of permanence, stability, and peace. *The presence of the Lord*, Bubba thought, though he wondered if such a thing really existed. He supposed someone who was religious, like Kay, would find this place comforting.

The wooden steps leading into the tiny church were dry-rotted and rickety; he didn't trust them to hold his weight, so he stood on the ground and pushed the door open with his hand. A squirrel skittered along the wall inside the church and disappeared through a hole toward the back of the building. Bubba grabbed the rotted steps, which disintegrated in his hand. He threw the boards aside and hoisted himself up onto the door frame. He stood there for a moment, silently taking in the interior. It was very quiet except for a blue jay who cawed at him loudly from a nearby tree, interrupting the peaceful, reverent feeling of the place.

Once inside the chapel, he walked around, carefully avoiding spongy areas of the floor. The place was small and mostly empty except for animal droppings, dust, and a few wobbly chairs. As Bubba turned to leave, his eye caught a large canvas draped over something that was leaning against one of the walls of the chapel. He walked that way, grabbed the corner of the canvas, and carefully folded it back.

At first, what he saw didn't make any sense. Several large windows were leaning against the wall. Bubba pulled the canvas back some more until he could see the glass within the frames. He squinted, then reached for the small Maglite tucked in his tool belt. He rubbed the grit and grime from the glass with his hand, then drew in a sharp breath when he scanned the glass with the flashlight.

Bubba was no art connoisseur, but it didn't take a rocket scientist to see that the windows in front of him were special—very special. He rubbed a larger area free from dirt. The stained glass that was exposed was beautifully rendered into an exquisite scene of a knight in full medieval armor. As the sunlight shone through part of the rotted roof and fell on the glass, the window shimmered with a dazzling presence, almost as if the knight were alive. Bubba realized he was holding his breath, and the hair on the back of his neck was standing up.

At that moment, his cell phone vibrated in his pocket, and he jumped, startled by the sensation. Irritated by the sudden racing of his heart, he saw it was Kay calling. He relaxed and let out a long sigh.

"Yeah, what's up?"

"Where are you, Bubba?" she asked breathlessly.

"What's wrong? You sound out of breath."

"Dad had a heart attack at home and died sometime this morning. The neighbor found him on the kitchen floor. Can you come home?" she asked. Bubba sensed she was crying, and his heart went out to her.

"I'm on my way. I should be there in half an hour."

Bubba tucked his cell phone into his shirt pocket, replaced the canvas over the windows leaning against the wall, jumped down from the building, and walked to his UTV. Before he started for home, he looked back at the unassuming, decrepit building. A treasure trove of masterpieces lay inside, and he was probably the only one who knew about it. He shook his head in disbelief and drove down the logging trail back to his home on Moon Ridge Road.

SUNDAY, MAY 20

16

Sunday morning dawned cloudy and cool. It was early when Leslie walked into the living room of their home on Warner's Bluff in Genoa. She stood by the window that overlooked the Mississippi River. Pulling her robe around her against the early morning chill, she noticed several eagles soaring on updrafts above the river searching for movement in the water below. After his romp in the backyard, Paco lay in utter relaxation outstretched on the living room rug. When Leslie turned from the living room window, her trusty companion lifted his massive head slowly and emitted a low groan. He padded across the rug to the window, and Leslie reached down, thumped his side, and scratched behind his ears.

Paco had been Leslie's canine companion for several years during her stint in the U.S. Army overseas in Iraq during the Gulf conflict. She couldn't imagine her life without him. Yet she was realistic—her dog was beginning to show his age, and his wounds from his service in the military often caused him pain. Sometimes he walked with a limp, the result of shrapnel he took during a fierce battle in Fallujah, and his muzzle showed signs of gray. But he was infinitely patient with Karina, who pulled his ears and fur with gusto, squealing with delight. Sooner or later, Leslie knew they would have to deal with his worn-out body and wartime wounds. The action he'd seen as a working police dog since his retirement from the army had made Paco a rock star when it came to apprehending perps. His capacity at the La Crosse Sheriff's Department was unofficial, but he often accompanied Sam and Leslie during their investigative duties. As a result, he'd been in more skirmishes with criminals than Leslie cared to remember. But his contributions fighting crime and holding criminals captive until help arrived were well known throughout the law enforcement community.

"What's up, boy?" Leslie whispered softly, bending down to talk to him. "You feelin' old?" The dog stretched his neck up and gave her a wet kiss. There was a rustle at the bottom of the stairway that led to their bedroom. Leslie looked up and watched Sam walk into the living room in his boxers and T-shirt.

"You're up early. You could have slept in," Sam said. "I would have handled Karina." He came over to Leslie and kissed her tenderly, thumping Paco on his side.

"I know," Leslie said, looking in his hazel eyes. "I could have sacked out another hour, but I was slept out. You know me—I can't just lie in bed and relax. I had to get up and make coffee—and let Paco out for his morning whiz." She heard the gurgle of the pot and pointed to the kitchen. "It should be just about done brewing."

"That was a good thing you did. I need some of that," Sam said, turning toward the kitchen. "I'll bring you a cup."

The coffee pot hissed and sputtered noisily on the counter as it reached the end of its cycle. Paco padded along behind Sam and headed for his dog dish in the corner, where he crunched on his kibble. Sam poured two mugs of coffee and took a cup to Leslie, who made herself comfortable in the recliner.

"I forgot to ask you about your doctor appointment last week," Leslie said. She knew Sam would make an effort to protect her from any distressing news concerning his recovery, but she asked anyway. *Lightning bolts tend to mess with the hard wire of your nervous system*, she thought. She waited for his response, which didn't come immediately. Instead, Sam flopped on the couch, silently staring out the window at the broad, dark river winding south.

Throughout the last year, as Sam grappled with the hard realities of his physical and psychological injuries, Leslie had been a rock of comfort and reassurance in a sea of unknowns. More than once, Sam had found himself floundering in hopelessness and despair, especially when his physical recovery lagged behind his high expectations. The migraines, muscle weakness, and unpredictable mood swings had required a truckload of patience and gritty determination on the part of his wife, but she'd delivered big time. Sam just hoped he had expressed his thanks and love adequately for all she'd done to keep him on an even keel.

Now, when the silence persisted, Leslie felt a stab of panic. *Uh-oh,* she thought. *Must not be good news.* Sipping her coffee, she refused to fill the silence that had descended with mindless chitchat. Sam's reluctance to share information about his health issues made her hackles rise, but she tamped down the urge to wheedle a response out of him and instead waited patiently for her husband to respond. Leslie had learned not to hassle him or rush him. *Intimacy takes time . . . and patience . . . and trust,* she thought.

Leslie's azure eyes softened when she looked at Sam. He was so handsome. His curly brown hair and deep hazel eyes, his ready smile, and his indomitable positive spirit were all things she loved about her husband, but since his accident, he'd changed. His confidence had dwindled into an uneasy suspicion, and she found it tough dealing with his reticence. They'd always been able to communicate through the awkward moments, but since his lightning strike, it had become increasingly difficult to navigate his mood swings—his stubborn, tight-lipped grit and caustic impatience. However, she was determined to listen without judging. After all, he'd been down the same road with her, and he'd stuck with her through the thick and thin of her PTSD issues and her beating and near-death experience by a former boyfriend.

When Sam realized the silence did not perturb her and would wait him out, he began his explanation. "Dr. White said my vitals were good, and because of my cycling and running regimen, my muscle memory allowed me to experience a quicker-than-usual recovery in the areas of coordination and strength."

"Well, that's great," Leslie said, giving Sam a wide smile. She sipped her coffee. After a long moment when no other information seemed forthcoming, her smile faded. "What else did he say?"

Sam groaned and rolled his eyes. *Wasn't that enough?* he thought sourly. He took a sip of coffee and looked over his cup at her. His wife had the patience of Job, and he knew better than to try to dodge her questions and concerns. He sighed, struggling with the stilted atmosphere between them. "He asked me about my relationships."

Leslie's eyebrows lifted. "And you said?"

"I praised my wonderful wife who understands what it's like to . . ." Sam hesitated, searching for the right words.

". . . experience anxiety and over-the-top reactions to situations that otherwise would not—" Leslie prompted.

"Bother you," Sam said, finishing her sentence, huffing with irritation. He thought about his reaction to the homeless vagabond at the bottom of his driveway and his impatience and rudeness with the hostess at *Si Bon*. If Leslie knew about that, she might question the progress she assumed he'd made.

"Did he make any recommendations about how to deal with those situations?" Leslie asked.

When is she going to stop grilling me? he thought, gritting his teeth. But instead of giving a curt response, he said, "His suggestion was that I take a yoga class." He held up his hand in a stop motion when he saw Leslie's surprised expression. "And before you say anything, I had a conversation with Paul, who has a cop friend who swears by it. He gave me his number, and I might call him later today."

"Wow, that's great, honey. You could stream a yoga class on our TV, record it, and do the exercises whenever you wanted."

"Yeah, I could, but there are other forms of therapy that work just as well."

Sam smiled at his wife and then crooked his finger at her. He was suddenly feeling guilty about his less-than-gracious attitude toward Leslie's genuine concern. "Come here for a minute," he suggested, patting the couch cushion next to him. Leslie watched his face and read the message written there.

"I know that look, Sam," she said, getting out of the recliner. "I can read your thoughts, you know." She walked over to the couch, opened her robe, and lowered herself to Sam, who gave her a fervent kiss, his hands tenderly caressing her back and rump. He fumbled awkwardly as he tried to undo the hooks on her bra.

"Mmm, that was a nice kiss. Is this the kind of therapy you're talkin' about?" she asked, giving him another long kiss.

"Yeah, for the next half hour you're going to give me the best therapy I could ever want."

MONDAY, MAY 21

17

Sam woke early on Monday morning as was his habit, rolled over in bed, and cuddled up next to Leslie. Her golden hair cascaded onto the pillow, her placid face free of worry and concern. In the early morning light he whispered a prayer of thanks and gently kissed her shoulder. *There's nobody better than Lez, Lord. Thank you for her presence in my life.*

Sam smiled when he heard Karina cooing in her crib in the nearby nursery. Their little daughter buoyed their hopes when the mundane, tedious tasks of fighting crime got them down. The baby girl confirmed the belief that their lives could be filled with goodness, kindness, and joy. They had been blessed beyond anything they deserved, and their daughter's bright, drooling smile and innocent antics were just the right medicine to heal what ailed Sam. Fortunately for them, she was a happy baby, well-contented and healthy.

Sam pulled the covers back and quietly got out of bed. He leaned toward Leslie and placed a tender kiss on her forehead, then walked to the nursery and picked up his daughter from her crib. She greeted him with coos and smiles and a tug of his brown, curly hair.

Sam descended the stairs to the kitchen with Karina in his arms and started the coffee maker, then let Paco out for his morning constitutional. He was in the middle of changing the baby's diaper when his phone vibrated on the kitchen counter. He finished the diaper change, picked up Karina, and walked rapidly to the phone and dialed Paul.

"Saner. You call?"

"Yeah, I thought I might still catch you at home. Heard anything new about the break-in on the north side?" Paul asked.

"Nope, nothing earth-shattering yet. It hasn't developed into anything substantial at this point. When you comin' in?"

"Probably get there when you do. We should take another trip through town and see if we can spot Chroniger. I only say that out of a sense of duty. "

"Yeah, I know chasing dealers around town is not your favorite aspect of being a cop. Actually, in all truthfulness, it's a good way to get shot. But I suppose you're right; it is our duty, but right now it seems like a dead end. Drugs are being sold every day in our fair city, but we should talk to this Kevin guy, if we can find him."

"Yeah, that'll be the challenge—finding him," Paul said, chuckling.

They talked another ten minutes about kids and family and wives and the upcoming season of the La Crosse Loggers semi-pro baseball team until Sam felt the minutes ticking by. Hanging up with Paul, he continued his morning routine.

Late yesterday afternoon, he'd called Tom Lawry, the cop from Kansas City who swore by the benefits of yoga to deal with the on-the-job stress of being a cop. During the conversation, Tom made a valiant effort to convince Sam to give yoga a try. Sam remained skeptical, despite the glowing testimonial from Tom. He hung up, still unconvinced that yoga was the be-all and end-all to his problems. He had a hard time believing that doing a downward dog pose would help alleviate his anxiety.

On Sunday evening, Leslie decided to take a trip to Oshkosh on Monday morning in an effort to dig up any information she could about the Tiffany windows that had gone missing from the Ellison mansion after the 1904 fire that had gutted the historic home. She lined up a babysitter for Karina and decided to start her investigation at the historic Sawyer Home in Oshkosh. The landmark home was a fixture in the community—an English Tudor Revival mansion—which had been donated to the city as a museum by the Sawyer family in 1924. The interior of the mansion had been designed by Tiffany Studios of New York and included a collection of stained-glass windows, in addition to wall treatments, carvings, bronze grilles, and light fixtures. Perhaps someone at the museum could add information about the Ellison mansion and the Tiffany windows that had disappeared after the 1904 fire.

By seven-thirty, Sam descended his steep driveway and turned north on U.S. Highway 35. The morning breeze coming off the Mississippi River was brisk and cool. Wanderer, the itinerant vagabond, waved nonchalantly from the base of the driveway, his blue plastic tarp rattling in the wind. Sam hoped within the next week the vagabond would move on, although he was sure some of his garbage would remain scattered in the ditch next to his driveway after the man's departure. Although his junk irritated Sam, what was important in the general scheme of things fought its way to the top of his agenda.

It was a beautiful spring day. Sam cracked his window open and breathed in the moist river air. A flock of red-winged blackbirds noisily squawked their *konk-la-reee* song from a patch of cattails in a marshy area along the highway that was edged by low-lying banks. The birds' musical ditty came in the partially opened window and filled Sam with a burst of happy enthusiasm. Farther down the road, a red fox darted across two lanes of traffic. Sam braked, secretly rejoicing that the vixen had dodged a bloody demise from the busy traffic that roared along the highway. When Sam reached the Gas & Go near Stoddard, his mind wandered back to the night almost nine months ago when a billion volts of electricity entered his body and permanently altered his constitution. The ordeal was surprisingly fresh in his mind, and it didn't take much to jolt his senses back to that moment in time. He sniffed loudly and gritted his teeth. "I'm still here, so bring it on," he muttered softly to himself.

On his way into the Vine Street building, Sam thought about what Leslie had uncovered on Friday about Lewis Borden, the former army ranger. The details about Borden weren't earth- shattering, but they triggered concern and gave the team something to work with on the missing suitcase dilemma.

On the third floor of the law enforcement center, Jim and DeDe were setting up the classroom where Sam had arranged the facts and photos on the whiteboard Saturday morning pertaining to the break-in on the north side. All of it seemed unpromising at this point, especially since Sheriff Turnmile had squelched the investigation. Despite the sheriff's truculent warning to steer clear of the affair, Jim continued to subversively collect as much information as he could from his own sources. At this point, however, unless something else developed, the flimsy information on the board seemed destined for the scrap heap. Something more serious would have to happen before their efforts at unraveling a possible motive for the break-in would become clear.

When Sam walked into the room, Jim was pleased to see him looking refreshed and energized. All too soon the task of gathering evidence would dull their senses, and their enthusiasm would probably fizzle. Catching perpetrators of wrongdoing was usually an exercise in futility and frustration, with glimpses of hope, mountains of boredom sifting through seemingly prosaic items, and moments of sharp revelation thrown together in a stew of uncertainty.

"Mornin'," Sam said, addressing Jim. "As soon as Paul gets here, we're headin' out for a drive around town to look for Chroniger."

"Who?" Jim asked, his eyebrows gathering in a frown.

"That guy who's been selling to the homeless people down at Hoska." Sam shifted on his feet, giving Jim an uneasy glance. "Of course by now, the homeless have been chased outta there by the city parks crew, so who knows where Chroniger is. He could be anywhere."

"Oh yeah. I remember now. You told me about that," Jim said. "Sounds like an exercise in futility. By now he could be five counties away from here. When you get back, we'll talk through what we know so far about this home invasion. Any chance Leslie could do a conference call this afternoon?"

"She decided to head to Oshkosh this morning to learn more about those windows and how they went missing. Don't know when she'll be back," Sam said.

"Oh . . . all right. Later then." Jim turned his attention back to the information gleaned from Geoff LaSarde. DeDe helped Jim organize the information into categories—suspects, motives, evidence like DNA and lab documents—although at the moment it seemed pointless.

About nine o'clock, after avoiding the paperwork on his desk for an hour, Sam shuffled down the hallway to Paul's small cubicle. He walked in, sat down in one of the ragged club chairs next to Paul's desk. "You ready to take a drive around town and try to find Kevin Chroniger?"

Paul looked up from his computer screen. "And what do we hope to accomplish with this little jaunt around town?" Paul tugged at his tie and gave Sam an intense stare.

"Locate another drug pusher and get him off the streets," Sam said grumpily, shrugging his shoulders. "Make the world safer for your kids and mine. That's our job, isn't it?" he asked, giving Paul a sour stare.

"I'll give you two hours of my time, but then I have to get back to this paper chase. Gettin' our stuff put together for the trial on the ball club murders, although from the looks of it, Little Hawk has lined up his lawyer, and he's pleading self-defense. So who knows where all this will go," Paul said, finishing with a defeated tone in his voice. "Why do I always feel like my efforts are pointless? Are we really making any headway in the fight on crime?" When Sam declined to challenge in his questions, Paul stood up, closed the cover on his laptop, and grabbed his suit jacket off the back of his chair. "All right, I'm ready. Let's hit it, buddy."

Although the weather on Sunday had been cool and cloudy, the sky this morning was a deep blue with cotton-ball clouds and warmer temperatures. Sam breathed the spring air deeply into his lungs as they walked across the Vine Street parking lot. Climbing into his Jeep Patriot, he rolled out onto the street, drove over to McDonald's on Losey Boulevard for coffee and apple pies, and then began the tedious job of canvassing the area. From Sam's contacts in the city police department, he'd learned that some of the homeless were congregating downtown in the stairways of parking ramps and at the abandoned City Lodge motel over on Rose Street. As Sam and Paul drove north through the city, they kept their eyes peeled for any sign of Chroniger and his black Chevy van.

After an hour of cruising on the north side and spotting nothing, they drove through the downtown district again, stopping briefly at the Third Street parking ramp, where they talked to a number of homeless individuals. Learning nothing there, they headed south on Mormon Coulee Road until they came to the Oak Leaf Motel, another abandoned accommodation where a few homeless had recently decided to squat. Driving into the parking lot, Sam found a spot to park and shut off the engine. The motel was sagging with neglect, the roof shingles peeling and curling. The blacktop parking lot had faded to gray, and tufts of quackgrass poked up through the cracks in the pavement. Near the dumpster in the corner of the lot, a rusty, abandoned patio set had been thrown in a heap, and when Sam pulled in, a squirrel ran out from under it and climbed a tree nearby, chirring his irritation at the Jeep.

After a few minutes, a short, stout man dressed in gray sweats and Tingley rubbers came out of one of the motel rooms. Sam opened the door of the Jeep and stepped out. Paul followed. They walked toward the man who was heading to the river along the railroad tracks behind the motel.

"Excuse me, sir. Could we talk to you for a minute?" Sam yelled in his direction.

The man turned and stopped, eyeing the two men with suspicion.

"Do you know a guy named Kevin Chroniger?" Paul asked, walking up to the man.

"Who wants to know?" the man spat, his eyes hard with frustration.

Sam dug his ID out of his jacket pocket and held it up to the man. "We're trying to find him. We understand he's been selling drugs over in Hoska Park, but since everyone's moved out of there, we've lost track of him," Sam explained. "Know where he might be?"

"Do I look like a user?" the man asked belligerently, laying his hand across his chest. "I mean, come on. I might be down on my luck, but I'm not a drug user."

There was a pause in the conversation. Paul looked the man over, and finally said, "In my experience, looks don't usually come into the drug-user equation too often unless you're on meth. Then it becomes pretty apparent. So, have you seen Kevin lately?"

"No, but I hear he hangs out at Goose Island sometimes. Drive through there—maybe you'll spot him. He drives a black Chevy van," the man said, turning back toward the railroad.

"Thanks for the tip," Sam said, glad another person had confirmed the drug dealer's mode of transportation.

Sam and Paul climbed back into the Jeep and headed to Goose Island Park and Campground three miles south of the city along Highway 35. As Sam negotiated traffic along the Mississippi River, the conversation turned to yoga.

"Did you call that guy in Kansas City I told you about?" Paul asked. "The yoga guy?"

"Actually, I did," Sam commented.

"And . . ."

"I'm thinkin' about it. Lez thought it was a great idea, and I guess it's worth a try, although I seem to be handling things pretty well right now."

"Keep it in mind," Paul said as Sam turned into the Goose Island County Campground.

Goose Island was part of the backwater system of the Mississippi River. This section of the Mississippi formed an ever-changing labyrinth of intersecting sloughs and backwaters. The morning sun glinted off the marshland and channels as Sam drove to the entrance of the park. Above the hills to the east, the Guadalupe shrine reflected the morning rays of sun against the backdrop of the lush, green trees. A couple of fishermen angled their poles toward the water on one of the bridges, casting and reeling with an efficiency and seriousness Sam found fascinating. Someone was jogging along the blacktopped road into the campground entry, and in the opposite direction, a couple of bikers were intensely pedaling out of the park toward U.S. Highway 35.

The road to the park sliced the area in two from north to south. The north part of the park, along Wigwam Slough, included four picnic shelters, two playgrounds, multiple campsites, and the park's registration and concessions buildings. South along Hunter's Point Slough, the campsites continued, and included several bathhouses, a beach, and more playgrounds.

"Let's start at the registration building and talk to the manager. Maybe he's seen Chroniger's vehicle in the park," Paul suggested.

Sam drove up to a T in the road and parked the Jeep. Both men got out of the truck and walked across a small paved parking lot to a log structure that served as the registration station for the campground. As soon as they entered the office, things got interesting. A middle-aged woman stood at the service counter crying while she talked to a young man who apparently was in charge of the place. Sam and Paul hung back, listening carefully as the woman told her story.

"Just take your time and tell me what happened," the young kid said calmly, pulling a yellow notepad across the counter toward him. He picked up a pen and asked, "Where did this happen in the park?"

The woman pointed to the south as she talked. "It happened at the bathhouse across from the playground on Hunter's Point Slough." The young manager listened carefully, jotting details on his notepad. He nodded, encouraging the woman to continue. "I was just going to take a quick shower before breakfast," the woman continued. "When I went into the women's side of the bathhouse, I noticed a pair of very large loafers next to one of the shower stalls. At the time I didn't think too much about it—I just thought, *Wow! That's a big lady who has very big feet.*" The woman stopped briefly and wiped her eyes with a Kleenex, then took a big, calming breath. The young man swiped his hand across his forehead and pushed his hair away from his forehead.

"Keep goin'," he said. "I'm listening."

The woman started again. "I went into a shower stall and undressed and started to shower, but I dropped my bar of soap, and it slid across the floor into the next stall. That's when I realized the other shower was not running, although I knew someone was in there because I leaned over and saw two very big feet." She paused again as the manager listened carefully to her story. He nodded, encouraging the woman to continue.

"I started getting this really icky feeling about the whole situation," the woman said. "Whoever it was next door kicked my soap back to me under the shower stall. I finished cleaning up and got dressed. When I opened the shower stall door and stepped out, I was confronted by a tall, blond man who had a towel wrapped around his waist. He stood in front of me and just stared at me. I shouted, "What are you doing in here? This is the women's side." He whirled around, grabbed his clothes, and left. But I'm telling you—for a minute there—I didn't know if he was going to attack me or expose himself, or what."

The manager looked shocked. "I'm so sorry. We've never had anything like this happen before. I'm just glad you weren't hurt."

Sam cleared his throat, and the woman camper and manager turned to look at him.

Sam said, "Sorry to interrupt, but I couldn't help overhearing your story. We're detectives from the La Crosse Sheriff's Department." He pointed at Paul and held up his ID. "We're looking for someone who's been selling drugs to the homeless communities in La Crosse. We were told he might be camping here at Goose Island." Sam looked at the distraught woman again. "Could you describe this individual who was in the bathhouse?"

"Oh . . . I don't know . . . I was so upset, I barely noticed," she began. "I just felt . . . very unsafe."

"That's understandable," Paul said gently, noticing the woman's wide eyes and pale complexion.

"Well, like I said, the guy was over six feet tall. Slim build, and he was wearing a towel." She stopped abruptly, then let out a rush of air. "I'm sorry. I really don't remember anything else. I was so startled and scared, I guess I forgot the important details."

"Did the man say anything to you?" Sam asked.

"No. When I yelled at him, he just grabbed his stuff and took off." The woman scowled. "Good riddance, the damn pervert."

Paul nodded. He wasn't surprised that the woman couldn't recall specific details of the encounter. Witnesses frequently could not recall basic details immediately following a stressful encounter in which they felt threatened. Sometimes, later on, they could remember more, so Paul handed his card to the woman camper. "Here's my card if you remember something later."

She tentatively reached out and took the card, thanked the manager, and left the building in a hurry.

"Man, this is terrible," the manager said. "We've never had anything like this happen before. We get people who get drunk and rowdy and crank their music. But we've never had a man hiding out in the women's part of the bathhouse." He gave the two detectives a harried look as he ran his hand through his hair. Sam noticed his name tag on his shirt.

"Cory, we're looking for a man named Kevin Chroniger. Drives a black Chevy van. Have you seen a van like that anywhere within the vicinity of the park?" Sam asked.

"Well, I don't really get out in the park very much," Cory said. "I'm on the administrative side of things, and I'm usually here behind the counter taking registrations, collecting fees, helping out in the little convenience store next door. You know, stuff like that. But I'll tell the personnel who work outside about the guy in the bathhouse and this other guy you're looking for."

"Sounds good. We're going to take a drive through the park. We'll let you know if we find anything," Paul said.

"Okay. That's fine," Cory said.

Sam walked away, but suddenly he turned around and faced Cory. "I'd suggest you make a formal complaint with the La Crosse Sheriff's Department and inform other campgrounds in the area about the incident with the man in the women's bathhouse," Sam told the manager. "The guy might try that stunt again somewhere else. You never know."

"Yes, I'll do that," Cory said. He took his cell phone from his pocket. "I'll do it right now."

Sam and Paul walked to the Jeep and drove slowly through the park, observing the campers scattered at various sites. They slowly drove south along Hunter's Point Slough to the boat landing. A black Chevy van sat a short distance from the fishing dock under the branches of a large, sprawling white pine. Paul pointed and lightly touched Sam's arm.

"Looks like the van," Paul whispered. "We got lucky." It was silent for a few moments. No one else was around, although a fisherman in a small boat was floating about a hundred feet out in the slough. The gravel crunched beneath the tires, and Sam felt his anxiety spike. He eased the Jeep to a standstill and parked next to a split rail fence about fifty feet from the van.

"That looks like the van that guy at the Oak Grove motel told us about," he said softly. "So what do you think we should do? You have a plan?"

"Let's just sit here a minute and see what happens," Paul suggested.

After five minutes of complete silence, Sam interrupted. "Enough waiting. I'm gonna check it out. You comin'?" Sam opened the driver's door and hopped out, looking across the seat at Paul.

"Do I have a choice?" he asked, grouchy about a confrontation that would probably go nowhere.

"No, you don't have a choice. You're a cop, and there's probably a drug dealer in that vehicle, which could be stolen. The guy's sitting in a public place waiting to be arrested. Do you see anyone else who's going to apprehend him, or did you want to call in reinforcements?" Sam asked sarcastically, his nostrils flaring with irritation.

Paul pushed the door open, then slammed it with a bang.

Sam grimaced. "So much for a quiet, stealthy approach," he snarled.

"Just giving him fair warning," Paul hissed. He walked around the front of the Jeep. "You armed?"

Sam pulled his jacket open. His department-issued Glock pistol was tucked snugly under his arm in a holster. "Anything else you wanna know before we swarm the suspect?" he snapped.

"Look, I'm just following recommended protocol. Getting shot isn't high on my list of priorities," Paul said quietly. "Been there and done that, and I don't care to repeat it."

"Got it. I'll lead. You get on the other side of the vehicle while I approach the driver's side. Ready?" Sam asked.

"Ready," Paul said curtly. As they walked toward the vehicle, Paul tried to remain calm, but his heart began to thump in his chest at an alarming rate, and a light sweat broke out on his forehead. *Easy,* he thought. *Just take it easy.* He felt a chill run up his back. *Damn, I hate these wild goose chases.*

Sam crept along the driver's side of the van and approached the window, but there was no one in the front seat. He shrugged his shoulders and carefully opened the door, then noticed a funky odor—the smell of something sweet and subtle, but beneath the sweetness was a noxious undercurrent of vinegar and window cleaner. Paul picked up on the smell, too, when he opened the passenger door. He crinkled his nose in disgust.

"Let's look in the back," Sam said quietly, pointing his thumb over his shoulder.

Paul opened the back door of the vehicle and groaned. Sam looked over his shoulder and saw Kevin Chroniger prostrate on the floor of the van. His eyes were half-mast, lifeless in their sockets, his mottled skin had turned blue, and his limbs were askew like a rag doll who'd been tossed in a corner. Paul jumped up into the vehicle and crouched next to Chroniger, feeling for a pulse in his neck. Nothing. Looking at Sam, he shook his head.

"He's dead," Paul said. "Probably at least eight hours, maybe more. Looks like an overdose to me, but Luke will have to determine the cause of death. I don't see any visible signs of a struggle. I'll call Luke. You call the chief and tell him where we are. This might take awhile. We're gonna tear this van apart and see what we can find."

"Sounds like a plan," Sam commented, averting his eyes from the dead man.

18

"You're where?" Higgins asked, squinting in the bright sunshine that was streaming through his office window. "Goose Island? How'd you get stuck down there?" He turned away from the window and sat down at his desk. As he listened to Sam's explanation, he picked up a pencil and began drumming an irregular rhythm on the surface of his worn, scratched desk. He glanced briefly at the walls of his office. Pictures of family, city officials, and several casual poses with former Sheriff Davy Jones occupied one wall. His collection of Native American arrowheads, axes, and spearheads was displayed in an attractive arrangement on an adjacent wall. He tuned back into the conversation with Sam.

"We went looking for Chroniger's van, and while we were driving through the park—boom—there it was parked near the dock on Hunter's Point Slough. We found Kevin in the van. He's dead. Looks like a possible overdose, but Luke is on his way. He'll determine the cause and time of death. We might be stuck here awhile," Sam explained. "We're going to go through the van and see what we can find."

"Right. You need anything from me?" Jim asked.

"Nope. We'll wrap this up and try to get back to the office as soon as we can," Sam said.

Jim hung up the landline, then started reading the articles about the Tiffany windows he'd gotten from Geoff. Five minutes later, his phone rang again.

"Higgins."

"Chief, it's Leslie. I just arrived at the Oshkosh Museum. I'm going to visit the Sawyer Home, which is on the museum grounds. From the outside, it's pretty impressive, sir," she said as she gazed out her windshield at the English Tudor Revival. Red brick sidewalks and carefully groomed shrubbery led to the home's massive oak door. Leslie wondered what she would find inside.

"I'm sure it's impressive," Jim commented. "It was probably built at the height of the lumber era back at the turn of the century. That's when most of those monstrosities were constructed."

"Well, I have an appointment with the curator who's going to show me the Tiffany windows in the home and fill me in on the history," Leslie said. "Whether she'll be able to tell me about the lost windows Geoff LaSarde told you about from the Ellison mansion is questionable at this point, but it's worth a try. There might even be something about their disappearance in the city's historical records. I'll see what I can dig up."

"You do that," Jim said. "I'll expect a full report when you get back."

"Right, Chief. Talk to you later," Leslie said, and she hung up.

Jim leaned back in his chair and studied the sky outside his narrow office window. In the distance, vivid green trees and undergrowth were bursting with new leaves and stood out in stark contrast against the chalky limestone bluffs in the distance. Grandad Bluff rose majestically above the river city, the American flag at its summit whipping in the wind. Back on the ground, the traffic on Vine Street was zipping by the law enforcement center in a constant clamor of rumbling traffic. Jim heard the beeping backup warning device on a piece of construction equipment a block away.

His thoughts turned to the burglary on the north side—an interesting conundrum. Would it develop into something more? Would murder, extortion, kidnapping, or some other criminal outrage be the result? Who knew. How far were people willing to go to locate the windows? Jim knew once someone found them, the trouble would begin in earnest. According to LaSarde, they were worth millions. Still, it all seemed rather improbable, but Jim wasn't completely ignorant. From his years on the job, he was convinced that people did a lot of stupid things in the name of money and greed. He didn't think the whole affair was dead in the water. Of course, someone had to find them first, and after more than one hundred years in the shadows, he seriously doubted the windows would be found, especially in the Driftless Area. What were the chances? But then he remembered other fantastic events during his years as an investigator that had propelled his team into state and national recognition—a missing gold shipment and pilfered Iraqi treasures for starters, and those turned out to be true, as improbable as they seemed to be at the time.

More often than not, situations like this reached a tipping point when curiosity morphed into deeper, more sinister motives. That's when people went missing, got hurt, or killed. He sighed deeply with weary resignation. To him, it seemed that Sheriff Turnmile, his cantankerous boss, had shoved a sign in the sand—No Digging Here!—when she'd called Jim and his team off the investigation, and he had no intention of fighting her for the right to do so. For the time being, he was flying under the radar, letting the sheriff enjoy her tentative grasp on power for a little while longer. He was sure it would change—either the mystery of the stolen Tiffany windows would blow away in the wind like a crumpled leaf, or the situation would intensify into a real case. *Que sera, sera,* Jim thought. *I've got plenty on my plate. Whatever will be, will be.*

Leslie sat in her car in the parking lot of the Oshkosh Museum and texted her babysitter, Mrs. Benson. She was nervous about leaving Karina in the care of anyone but herself or Sam for a whole day, although they had hired Mrs. Benson before, and she seemed entirely competent and caring.

"Just checking in. How r things going?" She waited a few minutes and heard her phone chime.

"All's well. K is a good baby. Don't worry. Mrs. B"

"Easier said than done," Leslie mumbled under her breath. She stuffed her phone in her pocket, grabbed her bag, and stepped out of the car. She walked quickly to the front entrance of the museum and went in. Following the signs on the wall, she found her way through a back hallway to the office of Victoria Krumholz, the museum's curator. The office door was open, and inside, a petite woman dressed in a maroon shirt, blue jean jacket, and khaki trousers was talking on the phone. When Leslie walked through the door, she held up her index finger and continued talking. When she hung up, she stood, walked around the desk, and held out her hand.

"Detective Birkstein, I presume?" she asked, smiling brightly.

"Yes, that's me," Leslie said, shaking her hand. "Thanks for taking time to squeeze me into your schedule on such short notice, but as I said in my email, we're puzzled about a crime in La Crosse that involves Tiffany windows. I was hoping you could share your knowledge about Tiffany, and possibly give us some information that might be useful in the case."

"A crime that involves Tiffany windows?" Victoria asked, leaning forward with interest. "Wow! That has to be quite unusual, isn't it?"

"Well . . . not for our team, but we're not sure how everything ties together yet. That's where you and the archives here at the museum come in. Any information you can share would be helpful," Leslie explained.

"I got your email, and I've studied it," Victoria said. "I called on some of our volunteers, and they've been poring through our paper ephemera in the basement looking for connections to the Ellison mansion. We'll talk to them in a little bit, but just to reassure you, I'll do all I can to share what we know about the windows here in Oshkosh," Victoria said.

She pointed to a comfortable upholstered chair. Leslie sat down while Victoria settled herself behind a large ornate desk. She looked at Leslie with anticipation and asked, "So, what is it you'd like to know specifically about Tiffany?" She clasped her hands together and rested her elbows on the desk. She was a picture of calm and self-assurance. Leslie could see by Victoria's unruffled presence that she was more than capable of leading a team of community historians and archivists intent on preserving their heritage and history.

As Leslie listened to Victoria, she was reminded of her mentor, Dr. Rochelle Drummond, U.S. Army antiquities recovery expert. Drummond had taught Leslie a considerable amount about the value of rescuing and preserving historical artifacts when she worked with the archaeologist in Iraq during the Gulf War. During those years, Dr. Drummond had unknowingly fostered Leslie's love of art. *She'll probably never know how much she influenced me*, Leslie thought. *Now I'm painting up a storm and selling my work for big bucks.* Suddenly she realized Victoria was waiting for a response. Leslie blushed with embarrassment and blinked rapidly.

"Oh, I'm sorry. My thoughts went down a rabbit hole, I guess," Leslie stammered. "You remind me of someone from my past—I apologize. I took a trip down memory lane."

"Not a problem," Victoria said. Something like curiosity passed over her features. "So where do you suggest we start? After all, I'm sure you have a goal in mind for this visit, right?"

"Absolutely." Leslie suggested a strategy. "Maybe we could start with a tour of the Sawyer Home, where the Tiffany windows are, and you can fill me in about Tiffany stained glass as we go through the place?" Leslie asked.

"Kill two birds with one stone?" Victoria countered.

"Exactly," Leslie said smiling.

"Let's go." Victoria stood and walked into the hallway, then led

Leslie out of the building. It was a short walk to the historic home, which was situated near the museum itself. While they walked down the red brick pathway, Victoria shared some of her expert knowledge.

"The Sawyer Home was designed by William Waters, and Tiffany Studios of New York was hired to furnish the interiors, which included several stained-glass windows," Victoria began. "Actually, the landscape window located near the staircase of the home was designed by a woman, Agnes Northrup, one of the Tiffany designers at the time. She also designed the Wisteria Window, which we'll see as we enter the home. This stained-glass piece is unique because it's an archway that frames double doors to the conservatory. It's quite spectacular. I never get tired of seeing it."

In a few minutes, the two women reached the entrance of the home. Victoria led the way inside the mansion. Leslie was not prepared for the beauty of the interior of the home. Every surface gleamed—the polished wooden floors, the exquisite furnishings, lamps, wall treatments, and draperies, and the iconic stained-glass windows. All of it drew attention to the creative, enigmatic style of Louis Comfort Tiffany. Leslie slowly turned in a circle, her mouth gaping in awe, as she took in the luxurious grace and elegance of the home.

Victoria smiled, enjoying Leslie's reaction to the majestic mansion. Several times every day in her capacity as museum director, she was privy to similar reactions from visitors at the museum and the historic residence.

"Wow! This is really something," Leslie whispered in hushed admiration.

"Yes, it does take your breath away, doesn't it?"

Leslie now understood why someone might want to steal Tiffany windows and squirrel them away somewhere.

"I know a little about Tiffany, but tell me more about his style," Leslie said, turning to Victoria. "He was certainly a master of the stained-glass genre. That arch is spectacular." She pointed to the curvature of glass with its wisteria blossoms and intertwined vines gracefully arching over the double doors that led into the conservatory.

Victoria nodded in agreement. "When you consider that his New York studio only operated from 1893 to 1928, the amount and quality of his work is astounding," Victoria explained. "He was a visionary in every sense of the word. I think today we might say that his philosophy embodied the 'more is more' concept. His techniques revolutionized the stained-glass industry."

"They did?" Leslie asked. "So what did he do that was so different from everyone else?"

Victoria looked beyond Leslie to the beautiful glass glowing in the morning sunshine. The reflections from the purple flowers and twisted vines of the arched window glowed on the walls and polished wooden floor. As Victoria began her explanation, her expression reminded Leslie of Dr. Drummond when she talked about the ancient artifacts they'd recovered—a dreamy, contemplative look.

"Up until Tiffany arrived on the scene," Victoria said, "stained glass was made by painting glass with enamels and then firing it to set the color. Tiffany introduced opalescent glass to the market. Some at the time called it American glass. This style of glass varied in color and texture, and Tiffany chose specific glass to represent foliage, fabric, water, or the setting of the sun over the horizon," Victoria explained. "Sometimes he would double, triple, or even quadruple layers of glass to get the effect he wanted. For instance, in windows with figures of people, the fabric of their clothing with its folds and textures seems almost real enough to touch." She stopped briefly, and Leslie nodded. "Instead of painting *on* glass, he painted *with* glass. His techniques revolutionized the stained-glass window industry."

Leslie walked farther into the room and gazed at the arch again. Standing in front of it, she said, "I know this sounds crazy, but when the sunlight hits the glass in the window, the whole thing seems to come alive. It's as if I could reach out and touch the flowers and vines."

Victoria nodded her head in enthusiastic agreement. "Yes, that's exactly what it's like," she said. "You've hit the nail on the head."

"I must admit, it's very impressive, but . . ." Leslie said glancing nervously at the time on her phone, "I still have to meet with your volunteers in the basement of the museum and see if they found anything useful."

"Right. Let's head back there and see what they've found," Victoria suggested.

They returned to the museum, took an elevator to the bottom floor, and stepped into a large room. Along the edges of the room, built-in shelves were stacked at eye level and were filled with files of letters and journals and drawers of old newspapers and other historical city records. In the middle of the room were two long worktables pushed together to form a large area where newspaper articles, letters, and other paper ephemera could be laid out and studied. A small team of three people looked up expectantly when Leslie and Victoria walked in.

"Hey, everyone! This is Detective Leslie Birkstein from the La Crosse Sheriff's Department," Victoria said. A few waved a greeting, and there was a nod of heads. "She's on a tight schedule. We're wondering if you found anything of interest about the Ellison mansion."

A short man with a trimmed goatee and a head of silver hair spoke up. "We located the 1904 newspaper article describing the fire at the mansion." He pushed the article toward Leslie, who leaned over and quickly scanned the account.

"Yes, we have this article in our file of information," Leslie said. She stood up again and began explaining their predicament. "Let me fill you in on what's happened so far." She told the small group about the burglary at Geoff LaSarde's north-side home in La Crosse and the missing suitcase filled with tantalizing bits about the Ellison Tiffany windows.

"The windows mentioned in the article have been missing since 1904 and have never been found?" a big-boned, rotund lady asked. "That seems quite fantastic to me . . . pretty hard to believe." Her skepticism was apparent in her tone of voice and her dubious facial expression.

"Yes, that's what we thought, too," Leslie responded. "But we've had other cases that pushed the envelope, so I guess we're learning to take it in stride."

Another woman spoke up. She had a tiny birdlike appearance with small, alert eyes, a petite, pointed nose, and a ruffle of thinning white hair that stuck out from her head like a cloud. "I did my own research about you guys," she said, crossing her arms over her tiny chest. "Your detective team is pretty well known for solving some weird cases. Some of them were thought to be unsolvable . . . like that lost gold shipment."

"Well, yes. That's true. But that's not why I'm here." Leslie stammered, trying to get the conversation back on track. She was surprised that anyone from Oshkosh would know about Higgins' investigative team in La Crosse. "Is there anything else you discovered in your research about the Ellison windows that you think might help us?"

"You mean like how the windows disappeared in the first place?" the silver-haired man asked.

"Right. Anything about that in all this stuff?" Leslie asked, sweeping her hand over the information displayed on the large table.

"Well, the windows were put on a train—the Burlington Northern—bound for Winona, Minnesota, and then they disappeared along the way," the large woman responded. "Says so right here." She slid another article toward Leslie. "Makes for fascinating reading and a lot of speculation, but that probably won't get you very far."

"Yeah, that's what we've learned, too," Leslie said, scanning the article. Her disappointment must have shown in her dropped shoulders and deep frown, because the petite lady suddenly spoke up.

"What about the servants employed by Ellison?" she asked. "Seems to me that if the windows disappeared from the train, somebody must have put them on the train and somebody took them off somewhere along the way. Maybe a staff member planned the heist—and got away with it."

Leslie got a faraway look in her eyes, then gave the petite lady a perceptive look. "*That* is a very good thought, which gives us a whole new direction. So, what about the servants? Find out anything about them?"

"There was a staff of nine people who carried out the household duties. The head manager of the staff was a man named Bradford, but we couldn't find anything about him once the news of the fire died down," said the large woman. "We assumed they retained their jobs when the house was being rebuilt and repaired, although there is nothing about that in any of the articles we found."

"I looked in the city census records for 1900, and a William Bradford was listed, along with his wife and son. But by the next census for the city of Oshkosh in 1910, the Bradfords weren't listed anymore," the petite woman piped up. "That leads me to believe that after the fire, they may have moved on and settled elsewhere."

"What about the glass company in Winona? Has anybody talked to them yet?" the man with the goatee asked.

"That's my next inquiry," Leslie said. "Gorgeous Glassworks has a sterling reputation, so I have serious doubts about their involvement in a major heist of something as important as Tiffany windows, but we'll check into it." A moment of silence fell across the room as everyone thought about the predicament facing the detective team. "So . . . I guess we're back to square one," Leslie said dejectedly, cutting through the quiet.

Victoria entered the conversation for the first time. "We'll keep looking. I have your contact information, and I'll call you if anything develops on our end. I'm sorry the visit didn't generate any new information."

Leslie smiled. "Not a problem. We'll keep in touch. You never know what might turn up. Keep us informed if you find anything new." She turned to the volunteers. "Thank you so much for all your help."

"Hey, all we have to offer is our time, and we have plenty of it," the petite woman said with a grin.

Victoria and Leslie returned to the ground floor of the museum. As Leslie prepared to leave, Victoria laid her hand on her arm. "Please keep us informed. We have many Tiffany admirers here in Oshkosh. They'll be fascinated with anything you find out," she said, "especially if you actually find the windows. That might create a situation you're not prepared to handle."

"Will do, and thanks again," Leslie said. She turned and walked out into the warm sunshine. The things she'd discovered on her trip to Oshkosh didn't seem to be significant at all, but as she considered the beauty of the windows and their ability to mesmerize the beholder, she reconsidered her premise. *There's a quality about those windows that draws you in,* she thought. *Considering their value in today's market, it's not surprising someone out there is trying to find them. It's the kind of thing someone might even kill for.* For a brief moment, she thought of Jamie Alberg—the archaeologist's brash confidence in solving the seemingly unsolvable. She wondered what he'd think of this latest quandary they'd found themselves in. *Higgins will have a fit if Jamie gets wind of this,* she thought.

A shiver ran down Leslie's arms as she buckled her seat belt. She started her vehicle and headed back to La Crosse. *Were those iconic windows hidden somewhere in Wisconsin, maybe even in the Driftless Area?* she thought. That hardly seemed possible, but she'd been an eyewitness to situations that went from probable to possible to reality in the blink of an eye, and often the consequences were dangerous and life-threatening. Maybe all of the hullabaloo over the Tiffany windows would just die down and fade away, and they could go back to more predictable things like drug dealers, embezzlers, drunk drivers, and domestic abuse. *Fat chance,* she thought. *Since when has my job ever been predictable?*

19

On Monday afternoon, Geoff LaSarde pushed the vacuum cleaner over the imported Italian rug and around the leather furniture in his cozy living room on St. Cloud Street in La Crosse. When he finished there, he moved to the bedroom. As he stooped to plug in the vacuum cleaner, he noticed a piece of paper lying just beneath the edge of the bed. He picked it up, opened it, and read the name on the yellow scrap: William Bradford.

He stood still for a moment and wondered about this discovery. Did this paper inadvertently fall out of the airport suitcase and get shoved under the bed unnoticed? If so, this might be a clue that could unravel the location of the missing Tiffany windows or, at the very least, give him a direction in his search for the lost windows. Geoff felt his heart trip in his chest as he considered his options.

Several questions came to mind. What were the implications of finding the windows? Was he prepared for the repercussions that such a discovery would make in the art world? He was sure the windows had appreciated considerably over the years, and their reputation as original, early Tiffany productions had probably pushed their value to dizzying heights. The last time he'd checked the market, windows of the same size and quality as the missing ones were well over a quarter of a million dollars each. That would make the entire set of missing windows valued at close to two million dollars. But Geoff had been to Tiffany auctions, and many times the values soared much higher if two determined bidders were in the room.

His thoughts turned dark, and he tamped down his optimism. What about the guy who tracked him down and attacked him in his own home? Would the stalker come back and make another attempt on his life? Was he adequately prepared for the possible physical threats that might come his way because of his decision to pursue the hunt for the windows? These questions raced through his mind in a blip of time. The slip of paper with the name on it seemed to burn his fingers. Suddenly he felt like he was standing on a railroad track about to be run over by a charging locomotive hurtling toward him at top speed.

He thought about his friend, Jamie. He'd share this information with Jamie later, but not now. Not until he could do his own research first. Geoff left the vacuum cleaner standing in the middle of the bedroom, rushed into his study, and opened his laptop. For an hour, he used a variety of search engines trying to identify the name on the brittle piece of paper. From the look and feel of the paper, it was old—perhaps turn of the century. That fit into the timeline of the 1904 fire at the Ellison mansion in Oshkosh and the disappearance of the priceless windows. He read and reread the names and personal histories produced by the search. Finally, after a few hours of sifting through several references, William Bradford I from Oshkosh, Wisconsin, turned up on the Oshkosh Historical Association website.

Geoff opened a document from the website, which described life in the early 1900s in Oshkosh. The information there led him in another direction, a specific diary outlining the duties of domestics in the many huge mansions being built in the city early in the twentieth century. Then, according to another newspaper article about the Ellison mansion, Geoff found in the *Oshkosh Gazette* in 1902, William Bradford was listed as the head of the domestic staff at the estate. The staff consisted of nine people in various positions:

three maids who cleaned and took care of the laundry, a cook and her assistant, two gardeners, one bookkeeper and secretary, and William Bradford, the general manager of the household.

At the time of the fire in December 1904, the staff of nine were all employed full-time. Bradford not only was in charge of the day-to-day operations of the large mansion and grounds, but according to the newspaper article, he frequently advised Mr. Ellison about the acquisition of fine art for the home—paintings, sculpture, light fixtures, rugs, furniture, and of course, the Tiffany windows, which were the crowning glory of the ornate mansion.

Geoff was encouraged that the name might lead him closer to the discovery of the windows. Obviously, Mr. Bradford was dead, but some of his family might still be alive. If so, they might know some of the shadowy details about the mysterious disappearance of the windows. Geoff leaned back in the swivel chair and stared out the small window of his home office.

The weather outside was bright and sunny, but Geoff felt like he was wandering in a fog of shifting information. He noticed a bed of bright, yellow tulips lining the driveway next door. Then his thoughts turned a corner, and he remembered the morning Jamie had discovered him sprawled on his kitchen floor, unconscious. A shiver of dread raced up his arms. He realized he was at a crossroads: He could take action on the information he'd found or leave the mystery to someone else—someone like Jamie who had the grit and brazen determination to carry out a plan of attack.

As he contemplated the choices before him, his eyes wandered to a book on his shelf: *Awaken the Giant Within* by Tony Robbins. *Yeah, right,* Geoff thought. *Easy for you to say, Tony.* He remembered reading the book while working on his doctorate. He reached over to the bookshelf and took it down. Randomly flipping through the pages, he stopped and read a quote Tony had written at the beginning of a chapter: "It is in your moments of decision that your destiny is shaped."

Geoff leaned back, shut his eyes, and thought deeply for several moments about the choices confronting him. Finally, a sense of peace came over him. He opened his eyes and smiled to himself. The decision he'd so dreaded had been easier to make than he'd thought. *Destiny, here I come.*

20

Leslie arrived at home from her road trip to Oshkosh later in the afternoon. Mrs. Benson gave her a report about her day with Karina and left. Leslie spent half an hour cuddling her daughter until she fell asleep, and then she laid the baby girl in her crib and walked to her studio. Picking up the phone, she dialed Jim Higgins at the law enforcement center.

"Higgins."

"Chief, I'm back from Oshkosh. You wanted a report," Leslie said.

"Yeah. What did you find out?" Jim asked. As he listened, he straightened his desk into piles of the file folders and loose papers that were scattered across the top.

"Well, truthfully I didn't find out anything earth-shattering," Leslie said. "What I found out we already know. The Tiffany windows disappeared after the 1904 fire at the Ellison mansion. They were loaded on a train bound for Winona, where they were going to be repaired, and they disappeared and have never been found."

"Yeah, that's a repeat of what we've got here," Jim said wearily. "So basically you got nothing?"

"Well, I wouldn't say that. There is one thing," Leslie said, reviewing her notes from the meeting with the volunteers.

"What is that?" Jim asked.

"One of the volunteers mentioned the staff at the Ellison home, in particular, a Mr. William Bradford. Apparently, he was the head of the household servants and directed the daily activities of the mansion. It's possible he could have been involved. By 1910, according to the census, Bradford had moved away from Oshkosh. Maybe he moved because he lifted the windows and wanted to get out of town before someone figured it out?"

Jim could hear the skepticism in Leslie's answer. "It's a big leap from Bradford moving elsewhere to suspecting he left the area because of some kind of criminal activity. People move all the time for various reasons, most of them generic. We'd have to find documentation from family records or newspapers or other public records about the reason for the move, but it's possible, I suppose. Although, it will take a lot of time and effort to verify, which I'm not sure we can afford or that Sheriff Turnmile will tolerate. Take your pick. But I'll admit it's an interesting sidebar, anyway. I'll ask Geoff if he knows something about this Bradford guy," Jim said. "Anything else?"

"Not really, but there is one thing I couldn't help thinking about—the drawing power of those windows. If the missing windows are anything like the Tiffany windows I saw at the Sawyer Home today, then I'd say a person could be swayed to do things he normally wouldn't do. Like—" Leslie said.

"Stealing them and hiding them in an obscure place?" Jim suggested.

"Yeah. I think that's a real possibility. I'm tellin' you, Chief, those windows draw you in and mesmerize you," Leslie started to explain, and her voice became dreamy with the memory of the images. "When the sun shines on them, the images seem to come alive. It's not surprising to me that a person could become totally obsessed with them."

Jim turned his office chair toward the long, narrow window that overlooked Vine Street and put his feet on the sill. He thought about the enthusiasm of Geoff for anything Tiffany. The guy wasn't a nut as nuts go, but he was a connoisseur of fine craftsmanship, and he seemed committed to locating the treasures.

"You know, I remember the first time I saw the Rose Windows in the Notre Dame

Cathedral," Jim said. "Carol and I were on our honeymoon, and I agree with you. There's something about the colors and the sunlight streaming through them that can have a powerful effect, even on someone like me who's basically ignorant about art."

"Well, I wouldn't say you're ignorant, Chief. You know what you like," Leslie said. "You have opinions, and that's a good thing."

"Yeah, and I love the oil painting you did for us of the old rowboat in the cattails along the river," Jim said. "It's my absolute favorite. I love it, and I admire it every day."

"See? People can get hooked on this stuff. But to get back to it, sir, I really believe the whole motivation behind this heist is the beauty of the windows themselves."

"That, and the value of them. They've skyrocketed in price since they disappeared," Jim reminded her. "Apparently, the windows have sparked somebody's interest, and they've already taken some considerable risks to figure out where they might be."

"I agree, but I think initially someone somewhere became fixated on the *beauty* of the windows, and their compulsion led to stealing and then hiding them away in some obscure place," Leslie said.

"That seems kind of hard to believe, but I suppose that's one explanation for their disappearance," Jim commented as he thought about Leslie's theory of a possible motive.

Leslie continued. "Before today, I'd never seen anything Tiffany, but I have to say those windows I saw today at the mansion were the most beautiful objects I've ever seen, and I've seen a lot of art in my day, Chief."

"That's true, you have," Jim said, remembering Leslie's work in the U.S. Army locating and rescuing stolen art objects. "Just think about World War II. Plundering and stealing art is nothing new in the human catalog of crime, so why should we be surprised that someone would want these windows for themselves?"

"Agreed," Leslie answered. "I guess my trip to Oshkosh wasn't a success in terms of new information, but in terms of motivation, I think we're on to something."

"Yeah, I think we are," Jim said thoughtfully. "So what about that stained-glass restoration place in Winona? Do you think that's worth visiting?"

"Yep. I think so. There might be someone there who would remember the Ellison event and be able to point us in a new direction," Leslie said.

"Good. You do that then. Take a trip over there in the next few days," Jim ordered.

"Will do. I'll talk to you later." Leslie hung up and stood up, stretched her arms over her head, trying to get the kinks out of her back and neck from the drive home. Walking to the large living room window, she watched the river traffic moving slowly. A large tow chugged its way north, pushing several barges riding low in the water. Leslie noticed a deer browsing along the hillside below their home and, farther down the driveway, Wanderer had disappeared inside his makeshift tent. She wondered when he would pull up stakes and leave. She heard scratching and whining at the back door, so she walked through the kitchen and let Paco inside. He slathered her hand with kisses, and then promptly puked on the kitchen floor.

Leslie leaned over and inspected the vomit. Wet clumps of paper and aluminum foil lay in the sticky mess, a brown oozing substance creating a puddle on the tile. After she'd cleaned up the mess, Leslie walked down the driveway with a garbage bag in her hand to Wanderer's encampment. She stopped on the driveway next to his tent and shouted, "Excuse me. Anybody home?"

While she waited for Wanderer to appear, she scanned the disaster surrounding the blue tarp—an old grill with a dented top, a pile of mismatched boots and shoes, Cool Whip containers and other plastic detritus, an empty box of Wheaties—all scattered haphazardly next to their driveway. A sudden gust of wind rattled the tarp and sent the Wheaties box into the dense ground cover next to the driveway, where it got wedged in a clump of tall June grass.

"Anybody home?" Leslie repeated loudly. *Home?* she thought. *That doesn't apply to a place like this, does it?*

Suddenly from beneath the tarp, Wanderer swooped into view. His tangled hair and dirty, ragged clothing made Leslie back up a few steps and reconsider this confrontation. The vagrant's eyes glowed with irritation at the disruption, although Leslie couldn't imagine what he did under his shelter all day long. *It's not like he's doing anything important under there,* she thought disgustedly. Suddenly, she felt a red-hot anger. She brushed her flushed cheeks, swallowed hard, and reined in her frustration, remembering her de-escalation training.

"I'm home. Whaddya want?" Wanderer snarled rudely.

"What I want is for you to clean up the chunks of paper and garbage around your tent. I think my dog ate something of yours, and he was just sick and puked on my kitchen floor," she said calmly from the driveway, her blue eyes challenging the belligerent attitude of the drifter.

"I doubt it," the man sneered. "Why don't you keep your mutt tied up? Then he won't be sniffing around my property where he don't belong. He's been shittin' on my stuff."

"My dog has been trained to stay on our property. If he's been down here, it's because *you* are camped on *our* property, and I'm sure your stuff is a temptation for him to snoop and investigate," Leslie said, keeping her voice evenly modulated, although her eyebrows arched above her blue eyes at the high-handed opinion of this bum. "He is a dog after all, and Paco takes his duties seriously."

The man leaned over and spat a stream of black, tarry tobacco juice in the high grass near Leslie's feet. She thought of her police training again—always try to defuse a tense situation. De-escalation is the key to a better ending. She realized the man was baiting her, trying to start an argument that could explode into violence.

"When are you going to move on, sir?" she asked, gritting her teeth at his uppity attitude.

"I haven't decided yet," he said, glaring at her. He sniffed arrogantly as if he were in the presence of a nuisance.

"Well, here's a little hint—a garbage bag," Leslie said. "Please use it to clean up around your tent." Wanderer suddenly seemed to shrink back, intimidated by Leslie's commanding voice. He gingerly took the bag when Leslie handed it to him.

"Thank you for your cooperation," Leslie said politely through gritted teeth. She turned and trudged back up the steep hill to the house, all the while fuming at the man's attitude of entitlement. *Where does he get off,* she thought angrily, *camping on our property, spreading his crap everywhere, and then acting as if that's his right?* By the time she reached the house, her temper was boiling over. She walked into the house and heard Karina crying in her crib. Her cell phone rang in her pocket, and she answered it as she walked into the bedroom.

"Birksteins," she barked.

"Lez, honey—" Sam started to say, but Leslie interrupted him. She picked up the crying baby as she stuck the phone between her ear and her shoulder.

"When is that guy gonna move outta here?" Leslie asked loudly, trying to shush Karina as she talked. Her words tumbled out in a torrent. "I've had about all I can take of Wanderer. Do you know he actually thinks he has a right to camp on our property, Sam? Do you believe that? I am so done with him!"

"Whoa! What's going on? What happened that got you so fired up?" Sam asked, hearing the anger and disgust in his wife's voice.

"Paco got sick this afternoon on something he snacked on down there, I'm sure of it. What are you going to do about this, Sam?" she rasped. "This situation is getting intolerable."

"Whoa, honey. I wasn't there, or I would have handled it. So Paco got sick?"

"Yeah, he puked all over the kitchen floor. That's not like him, Sam. I can count on one hand the times he's ever vomited in the house," Leslie reminded him. "When is this guy gonna leave?" she shouted into the phone.

"I don't know, but I'll call Officer DeFlorian down at the Genoa police station and have him make a visit," Sam said. "I agree. The guy is pushing his luck. Maybe the appearance of a squad car and another cop will get his attention. How does that sound?"

"Well, it can't come soon enough. I've had about all the backtalk I'm going to take from that guy," Leslie said brusquely. "When are you going to be home?"

"I'm leaving in about fifteen minutes. Need anything from town?"

"If pancakes and bacon are all right for supper, then I don't need a thing," Leslie told him. "Except you."

"Sounds good. See you in an hour." And Sam clicked off.

21

St. Cloud Street on the north side of La Crosse was quiet on Monday evening. The warm weather hinted at the promise of summer, which was just around the corner. Dusk was settling over the busy neighborhood, and most of its inhabitants had retreated inside their homes and apartments. The streetlights hummed and sparked on, the orange glow creating bright ovals on the pavement below. Lewis Borden sat in the dark between the streetlights in a plain brown Chevelle. He was hoping his car was boring enough to blend in with the dark surroundings in case someone should happen to remember seeing it later. He'd rented the nondescript vehicle from Enterprise, telling the agent he wanted something low-key and cheap. They'd delivered.

Lewis had been sitting too long. His butt was numb, and his legs felt like pieces of wood. He opened the driver's door, stepped out, and began walking down the sidewalk toward Geoff LaSarde's home. He studied the environment around the small bungalow, hoping to see the big yellow cat lurking in the bushes somewhere, but he didn't see the nasty feline who'd ripped a hole in his leg and caused the painful infection. *Too bad. I'd like to wring its everlovin' neck,* he thought bitterly. His leg had improved somewhat, but it was still tender.

He met a young couple who were holding hands, talking quietly, laughing occasionally. Lewis nodded to them but kept his head down, his baseball cap shadowing his features. He was still mulling over his strategy. He'd considered breaking into LaSarde's home again, but by now the Tiffany expert had probably invested in some sophisticated surveillance equipment, and getting caught on camera was not something Borden was willing to risk.

He'd learned from his search online that LaSarde served on the La Crosse Area Arts Council board of directors and was involved in the renovation of the defunct Fleischstad's meat plant facility located on the south side of town on Mormon Coulee Road near Gundersen Lutheran Hospital. The red brick structure was being transformed into a first-class art gallery. He'd driven past the building today. He had plans to visit the place tomorrow and ask a few questions.

Lewis took a deep breath of the fresh night air. The smells and sounds were subtle but distinct: the cooing of doves in a nearby tree, the crack of a bat and the cheers from a crowd at a local ballpark nearby, the smell of popcorn, the sweet fragrance of blooming lilacs. *Peaceful,* Lewis thought, *just like my neighborhood in Alta Vista.* When he'd walked six blocks, he turned around and doubled back on the opposite side of the street, wondering what LaSarde had discovered about the location of the windows. He had no doubt that the Tiffany expert was fully engaged in the search, investing his time, energy, and money. Lewis had done his research on the man; he was educated, knowledgeable, passionate, and articulate. A difficult task like this would not deter someone as enamored with Tiffany as LaSarde. Lewis sensed the expert was on the hunt, and he intended to capitalize on his efforts.

Lewis arrived back at his car and got in behind the steering wheel. Moments later, a Volkswagen Golf rolled to a stop in front of Geoff's house, and an energetic young man hopped out of the car and jogged to the side entrance of the garage. Lewis watched closely as the man walked through the breezeway and into the kitchen. Obviously, this was someone who was very familiar with the layout of the home. A good friend? A confidante? A co-conspirator in the window search?

Lewis lightly pounded the steering wheel with his fist in frustration. This was getting complicated. Why couldn't anything ever be easy?

While he waited, he took down the license number of the Golf. He debated his next move, then boldly got out of the car and walked across the street. The car was unlocked. He opened the passenger door on the Golf and rifled through the glove box. Inside lay the title. Lewis noticed the name—Jamie Alberg. *Hmm? Who's this guy?* Another fly in the ointment.

Lewis stuffed the title back in the glove box, quietly closed the car door, and walked back to the rental car. He wrote a few comments in a small notebook and sat for another hour watching the home. By ten o'clock, he was beginning to tire, and he decided to head back to his cabin near Coon Valley. He'd do some research on Jamie Alberg later, although he was beginning to realize his approach to the problem would have to be reconsidered. He'd have to break it down again and rethink his strategy—come up with new alternatives. For some odd reason, he realized this problem and its challenges were tailored to his strength—thinking on his feet, going with the flow, letting possibilities reveal themselves in their own good time. He smiled to himself in the darkness.

Complications and problems were the lifeblood that flowed through his veins. It was what had made him so effective as Charlie Tewalt's personal assistant and as a covert operator in the military. Whoever this kid was, he was no match for a former army ranger and troubleshooter. *Let the games begin,* Lewis thought darkly. *Good luck, sucker.*

22

"Where'd you find it?" Jamie asked Geoff as he sat across from him in his living room late Monday evening holding the scrap of old paper in the palm of his hand. Jamie had stopped over to Geoff's house after he'd told him about the discovery of the name written on a piece of old paper. Now Jamie studied the name of William Bradford scrawled in dark ink across the scrap of yellowed, fragile paper.

"I told you. It was under my bed. I was about to vacuum the carpet this afternoon when I noticed it lying under there."

"Maybe it's something from one of your other boxes of stuff you had out when you were doing your research for your doctorate," Jamie suggested.

"No, it's not. I would've remembered something like that. And besides, when I vacuum, I go way under the bed, so this is something that's only been there a few days. It was right along the edge of the mattress. The only logical explanation is that it fell out when I opened the old suitcase and looked through the papers inside after I got home from Chicago."

"Well, you know what this means, don't you?" Jamie asked, his blue eyes widening with a challenge.

Geoff sighed. This was exactly what he thought would happen. Involving his friend in his search for the missing Tiffany windows was a disaster in the making. Geoff should have known better. Jamie was about to go off the deep end. After all, the kid had been in more serious life-threatening escapades than Geoff could count on one hand. *Why did I call him and tell him about this?* He berated himself, inhaled deeply, and met his friend's intense stare. Leaning forward, resting his elbows on his knees, Geoff began to explain.

"It means that we don't really know anything yet," Geoff said patiently as if he were addressing a child. "I've done a little preliminary checking, and I think I might have found out who this guy actually is, but it's not a sure thing at this point. Right now it's just a—"

"Guess? A theory?" Jamie finished his sentence. "Well, you can't solve this problem without some kind of hypothesis. So listen to this—this is what I think." Jamie sat forward and mimicked Geoff's position, elbows on his knees. The two men stared at each other.

Geoff noticed Jamie's excited demeanor—the excitement in his eyes, the flushed cheeks. The young archaeologist was flush with the possibilities that lay before them.

"Jamie—" Geoff interrupted before he could get started, but his friend continued on, unfazed.

"Here's what I found out this afternoon," Jamie began. "William Bradford worked in the Ellison household. He was a valued member of the staff and had the confidence and trust of his employer."

Geoff's anger steamed as his friend rambled on with his theory. His impassioned, ardent speech and piercing hazel eyes unhinged Geoff in a way that was hard to explain. How many times had this kid inserted himself in other people's affairs, plunging headlong into situations that had very nearly gotten him killed? Now he was at it again.

"Who better to plan a heist of the windows after the fire than Bradford?" Jamie asked. "I think Bradford used his position to steal the windows and—"

Geoff shook his head and waved his hands in front of him, interrupting his monologue. "Jamie, you're getting carried away before you really know any of the facts."

"But I *do* know some of the facts," Jamie retorted impatiently, pointing his index finger at Geoff's chest. "After you told me about the name this afternoon, I did my own research—"

Geoff rudely interrupted again. "Jamie, this is not your problem to solve. I'm conducting my own research into the name. When I get more information, I'll let you know." The room suddenly became very quiet.

After a few moments, Jamie stood abruptly. "You don't want my help? Fine then," he said curtly, his words sharp with disdain. "But I have the name, and I know some of the history, and you can't stop me from looking into it myself."

Geoff stood and noticed the spark of anger reflected in Jamie's eyes, his clenched fists, and his belligerent stance. "Look, I appreciate your interest," Geoff said more gently, "but like I told you before, this is my battle to fight, not yours."

"Well, good luck with that," Jamie said sharply. "When I find out more—and I will—I'll let you know." He turned and stomped out of the house. The door slammed loudly after him.

Geoff stood in the living room and swore to himself. He looked at the ceiling, his hands on his hips. "Yeah, I'm sure you'll find out more, buddy. Just don't get yourself killed in the process," he whispered as he plopped back on the couch.

The same night in the countryside of Ontario, Bubba Starch sat in his darkened office staring at his computer screen. A desk lamp illuminated the work surface of his sturdy, antique desk. Other than that, the rest of the house was dark and quiet. He'd snuck out of bed about midnight without disturbing his wife, Kay, and quietly walked to his office and shut the door silently until the latch clicked. Now, at two o'clock in the morning, he continued scrolling through several websites, trying to discover any information about the stained-glass windows he'd uncovered in the old lumber camp chapel.

He stopped infrequently and read some tidbits of information about missing or lost Tiffany windows from several websites he'd discovered during his online search. There wasn't much information, and he wondered how much of it was actually reliable. Not only were the windows probably hidden in an obscure location, but the information about them seemed hazy and vague, too. *This is about as clear as mud,* thought Bubba. He made a *tsking* sound with his tongue, stretched back in his chair, and pushed his arms to the ceiling, loosening the tight muscles in his back. *What am I going to do?*

He sat up straight again and made one last attempt to find out more about the perplexing, infamous windows. After clicking on several websites, he noticed a want ad for stained-glass windows. Clicking on it, he read the ad, trying to tamp down the spark of hope in his chest. A Presbyterian church in Milwaukee, Wisconsin, was searching for windows to enhance their new parish hall—preferably stained glass, historical, and artistically significant. *Bingo. That's it,* thought Bubba. *That's the solution to my problem.* The contact name and number were given at the end of the ad.

Bubba leaned back and studied the ceiling for several minutes. Then he opened a new document, composed his thoughts, and began to write:

Dear Mr. Hanakee,

I found your ad on the internet and decided to contact you. I think I have some windows you would be interested in for your church building project.

TUESDAY, MAY 22

23

The remodeling job at the old brick Fleischstad's meat plant on the south side of La Crosse was bustling with carpenters, plumbers, sheet-rockers, and electricians on Tuesday morning. In the midst of a group of workers, Trisha Fanella leaned over a long table and pointed to blueprints and issued orders, her fingers flashing with diamond and gold rings, her nails painted a deep maroon. She was a petite size two redhead dressed in a form-fitting teal suit, her tiny feet encased in two-inch alligator heels. Her hair gleamed with highlights and was cut in the latest style. She made eye contact with each worker as she issued orders. Her frank, commanding stance went unchallenged by the men.

Despite the signs that said "Authorized Personnel Only," Lewis Borden let himself into the building and stood to one side, leaning against the wall, watching the tiny redhead spew orders. He had chosen his wardrobe carefully today, determined to make the right impression on whoever was in charge of this project. He wore a pair of casual black dress pants and a Tommy Bahama luminescent silk shirt in a gray and black leaf pattern. He didn't glow in the dark, but he did stand out among all the working-class guys dressed in Walmart T-shirts, Carhartt jeans, and Red Wing work boots. Observing Ms.

Fanella, Lewis concluded she was the one who might know about Geoff LaSarde's involvement in the construction of the art gallery.

Lewis strolled casually around the perimeter of the gallery, keeping an eye on the drama between Fanella and the construction crew. Her expertise didn't seem to impress too many of the blue-collar workers. Some of the guys rolled their eyes in frustration, some dipped their heads and stared at the floor silently as if questioning her judgment, while others were taken in by her authoritative presence and simmering sexuality. *Crawling in bed with her,* thought Lewis, *would probably be like crawling in bed with a poisonous snake. No thanks.*

When the crew had gone back to their designated areas after the construction powwow, Lewis approached the petite authority figure. He held out his hand, but she declined the gesture, giving him a steely stare instead.

"Hello. I was watching you with the guys," he began, dropping his hand back to his side, "and I think you're the one I need to talk to."

Trisha looked at him coldly. Her dark brown eyes held no warmth, and her petite mouth was tight-lipped with intensity. "This area is restricted to the public. You really shouldn't be in here. Didn't you see the sign?" she asked, pointing to the entrance. "What do you want to talk about?" she said brusquely.

Lewis kept his voice low-key, but his temper was bubbling beneath the surface at her cold rebuff. "I represent a client from the Chicago area who is searching for some genuine Tiffany windows. Any size will do. They're actually for his library. I heard through the grapevine you have a Tiffany expert on the local arts board, and I wondered if you would mind sharing some information about him. Perhaps he would be willing to assist me in my search," Lewis explained with a tentative smile. He stood in front of Trisha waiting for the blast of rejection he was sure would come. Instead, he was pleasantly surprised at the sudden warmth in her voice and the sparkle in her eyes.

"Oh, you must be referring to Geoff LaSarde," she said pleasantly, the name rolling off her tongue with exuberant familiarity. She suddenly moved closer to Lewis, a hint of friendliness in her voice. "I'm Trisha Fanella, the director of design here at the museum. Geoff is extremely knowledgeable about anything Tiffany. We're so lucky to have him on our board. What kind of information were you looking for exactly?" she asked, tipping her head to one side.

Despite Lewis' attempt at remaining aloof and professional, her brown-eyed gaze flustered him. *Don't waffle now*, he reminded himself silently. "Well, as I said, I need his expertise in locating a Tiffany window. My client prefers something large, dating from Tiffany's earlier period of design— anything that was produced at the founding of his stained-glass window studio—something from the late nineteenth or early twentieth century."

"Geoff is very enthusiastic about anything Tiffany, especially windows. He'll talk your ear off if you give him a chance. I'm sure he could help you locate something or at least point you in the right direction. Let me give him a call," Trisha suggested warmly.

Wow! She really is a lovely person when she smiles, Lewis thought. "That would be great. I really appreciate this," Lewis said, returning her smile. "Maybe I'll just look around a little, if that's all right." He raised his eyebrows and gestured toward the gallery.

Trisha swept her arm in front of her. "Of course, take a look at what we're doing." She held her cell phone to her ear and turned toward the large windows facing the street. After an extended conversation in which her head bobbed up and down along with a few furtive glances at her visitor, she approached Lewis, her heels clicking rhythmically on the cement floor.

"I talked to Geoff, but unfortunately, he's out of town at the moment. I told him about your interest, and as soon as he returns from his trip, he'll give you a call," Trisha said.

Lewis reached into his shirt pocket and gave Trisha a business card. "I really appreciate your help. My client will be excited about this," he said graciously.

Trisha took his card, thanked him, and turned when one of the construction crew called her name. "Sorry, I've got to run," she said, pivoting on her heel. "Nice to meet you."

Lewis watched her sashay toward a guy holding a junction box in his hand. *She just warned off LaSarde,* he thought. He gritted his teeth and swallowed hard. The thoughts roaming through his head at the moment were nothing he'd want anyone to know about, least of all Trisha, but he was beginning to realize the players in this whole affair were smarter than he'd anticipated.

Jamie Alberg rummaged through his tools in his garage on the north side of La Crosse, Tuesday morning, looking for a particular dental pick that he needed for the dig in Iowa, one that wouldn't damage the delicate pottery they'd found buried beneath layers of river silt. His enthusiasm about heading up the dig at the archaeological site had dampened substantially since the argument he'd had last night with his friend, Geoff. *Sometimes he can be so cocky. He might be a Tiffany expert,* Jamie thought scowling, *but he ought to listen to me once in a while. I wasn't born under a rock.*

Jamie didn't have many friends, so the ones he did have were important to him. He worried that the friendship he enjoyed with Geoff might have been damaged by his eagerness to assist him in his research into the Bradford family. Still, he didn't view his involvement in the search for the windows as adversarial. Rather, he was pursuing the identity of William Bradford as a favor to Geoff so he could reach his final goal—the location of the valuable windows.

Jamie understood what unexpected discoveries could do for your reputation and career. After all, his assistance in locating a cache of 1868 gold coins hidden in the bluffs overlooking the Mississippi River had launched him from obscurity into the limelight. His reputation in the field of archaeology and treasure hunting soared to new heights. It opened doors he'd never imagined—interviews on national television shows, a fellowship in archaeological studies at the University of Cairo in Egypt, and the opportunity to write several articles in national archaeology and treasure-hunting magazines featuring his discoveries of the lost gold coin cache. People in his field knew his name, and they trusted him and were impressed by his achievements and credentials. He had taken risks in his career, but it had paid off in unique opportunities, prestige in his field, and recognition on the national stage.

Jamie picked up the corner of a tarp that was lying on his workbench. Underneath it he found the pick he was looking for. He walked back into the house and put the tool in his small duffel bag, then decided he'd better take a lunch. He quickly made a peanut butter sandwich and threw a banana in the bag. Zipping it up, he headed for his VW Golf parked in the garage.

As the garage door slowly opened and Jamie backed out onto the street, he looked in his rearview mirror and noticed a brown Chevelle sitting near the curb about fifty feet down the opposite side of the street. For some unknown reason, Jamie thought he'd seen the car before. He ignored the little bell dinging in his brain and continued to drive south through La Crosse, eventually hooking up with Highway 35, which followed the flow of the Mississippi River south.

As he drove toward the dig site in Lansing, Iowa, Jamie thought about the discoveries he'd uncovered late last night during his computer search for William Bradford. Based on his research, he was confident that William Bradford was the man who'd orchestrated the heist of the Tiffany windows from the Burlington Northern Railroad train, which had been on its way to Winona. His conclusion was based on the fact that William Bradford was a reliable employee of Howard Ellison, and he not only had the trust of his employer but also the seniority needed within the household staff to plan and execute the robbery.

In Jamie's genealogical search online and his subsequent construction of the Bradford family tree, he'd uncovered a grandson, William III, currently living in Ontario, Wisconsin, about thirty miles west of La Crosse. Jamie smiled. The search had been relatively easy, but then an unsettling thought robbed the joy of his discovery. Geoff didn't seem to put much weight in the discovery of the Bradford name he'd found on the scrap of paper under his bed, let alone the likelihood that Bradford was involved in the missing window mystery. Jamie sighed and softly pounded the steering wheel, frustrated with his friend's refusal of his generous offer to help. *People can be so pigheaded.*

To Jamie, the argument he'd had with his friend last night temporarily cut off any opportunities he might have had to share his findings with Geoff. Would he listen to reason? Would Geoff accept the research he'd done to try to solve the Tiffany conundrum?

Jamie sighed and impatiently ran his hand through his curly hair. He knew his assumptions were presumptuous, but in past cases involving lost treasures, his hunches and theories had always proven insightful. He had no reason now to disbelieve his own hypothesis. No other name had risen to the surface during past attempts at solving the window mystery, despite the fact that many Tiffany experts had investigated the famous missing windows and come up short with anything persuasive.

He turned right on Highway 82 toward the city of Lansing, driving through the Winneshiek Bottoms that made up the long approach to the Black Hawk Bridge, which arched across the great waterway. The morning sun sparkled on the sloughs, ponds, and backwaters of the Mississippi River. Sections of cattails, brown sedge, and wool grass swayed in the early morning breeze, and a couple of eagles soared high above the bluffs in the brilliant, cloudless sky. Even at this early hour, fishermen had positioned their boats along the shore, casting and reeling for walleye and pan fish. The rumble of the morning traffic over the sixty-eight-foot-high bridge left Jamie feeling uneasy about his hypothesis. Was he correct? Could Bradford be the one who had duped everyone? Were the windows so well hidden that no one had ever discovered them?

Jamie's thoughts returned to his friend. What would it take to convince Geoff that William Bradford I was the culprit who'd stolen the Tiffany windows? Jamie groaned in frustration. His friend seemed comfortable in his foregone conclusions, and he could do little to change it. *I guess the only way he'll change his mind is if I find the grandson and locate the windows.* But somehow, despite the dazzling morning sunshine, that course of action seemed fraught with danger. A shadow of uncertainty made Jamie pause. He recalled the words of caution he'd spouted to Geoff earlier about assessing the risks and being aware of danger. *To be forewarned is to be forearmed. Yeah, right,* he thought skeptically. *You'd better take your own advice, buddy.* When all was said and done, tracking down the grandson, William Bradford III of Ontario, was the only way to prove his allegiance to his friend and move the case of the infamous windows forward to a conclusion.

Jamie crossed the narrow high bridge over the Mississippi River and turned right toward the Fish Farm Mounds archaeological site. He glanced in his rearview mirror and noticed the brown Chevelle following two cars behind him. The driver was too far away to make out any facial features, but Jamie was certain it was the same car that had been parked across the street from his house this morning. Chills ran up his arms. He wondered where the perp was who had broken into Geoff's house. Was he back in the area searching for the windows? The hairs on the back of Jamie's neck stood up. Maybe the perp who broke into the house and knocked Geoff unconscious was the same guy who was following him in the brown Chevelle. If so, then things were suddenly a whole lot more complicated than he'd bargained for. After he crossed the bridge, he breathed a sigh of relief when the car turned onto a side road and disappeared.

It's just your nerves, he reminded himself. *You're getting all worked up over nothing. Nobody even knows you're looking for the windows. Relax. It'll all work out if you don't lose your focus.*

24

Kay and Bubba Starch stood quietly at the graveside of William Bradford III. The mild spring sunshine shone down on their heads, and Bubba could feel the warmth of the rays on his shoulders through the fabric of his suit jacket. It felt good after the long, cold winter. The trees were bursting with new leaves, a verdant green that appeared on the budding tree branches only in spring. A robin sitting in a flowering crab tree by the entrance of the cemetery tweeted his cheer-up warble. A small crowd had followed the family to the graveside, and now they stood quietly waiting for the pastor to begin the graveside committal. Kay grasped Bubba's hand firmly, her tears a silent tribute to a father she'd dearly loved.

"Please join me in the Lord's Prayer," Pastor Hedlund said. "Our Father who art in heaven, hallowed be thy name . . ." The crowd joined in. Throughout the prayer Bubba mouthed the familiar words, but his mind wandered back to the stark white envelope he'd received in the line at the funeral home from Jared Browning, Willie Bradford's attorney. The lawyer had slipped the envelope into Bubba's hand while he stood next to the casket with Kay greeting the mourners. The lawyer's instructions were simple: "Read it later when you're alone." His serious expression revealed nothing more, but his somber demeanor made Bubba wonder what it contained. He slipped the envelope into the inner pocket of his suit jacket.

Now, as the graveside service ended, Bubba's curiosity about the envelope was almost too much to bear. Like a child anticipating the opening of birthday presents, he wanted to hurry home, be alone in the quietness of his office, and rip open the envelope. But Kay lingered after the final prayers, talking to friends and relatives while picking roses from the flower arrangements that were draped over the coffin.

"They're so beautiful," she said softly to her husband. "It's a shame to let them go to waste."

"Here, let me hold them for you," Bubba said, reaching for the flowers. Kay stood quietly next to the oak coffin, her thoughts jumbled and confused.

"Are you okay, honey?" Bubba asked.

Kay turned and looked at him, her gray eyes sad. "No, I'm not okay, at least not right now, but I'll be all right after a while. It's all just so sudden. I thought I'd have more time with Dad. I guess I wasn't ready to let him go yet." Bubba nodded with sympathy, then waited as she continued to gather the flowers. After fifteen minutes, his hands were full of roses, and he was bursting with impatience.

"Are you ready to go home? I think you should lie down awhile and rest," Bubba said. Kay kissed him tenderly.

"Yes, I think that might be a good idea," she said, turning away from the grave. The cemetery was deserted now except for the men who would lower the casket into the dark hole and fill the grave with dirt. Kay grabbed Bubba's free hand while he clutched the flowers tightly in the other. They walked to the car, then drove five miles out of town until they came to Moon Ridge Road. During the drive, smells of spring drifted into the car window—lilacs, cut grass, and the cool crisp cleanness of the spring air. Bubba parked the car in the garage, and they went inside the house. Kay took the flowers and found a vase which she filled with water. She stood by the counter and carefully arranged the roses one by one.

"Can I make you some coffee?" Bubba asked.

"No, I don't want anything right now. I'm going to take these flowers to the bedroom, and then I'm going to lie down, maybe take a nap." She sighed, turned, and walked down the hall carrying the vase of roses.

Bubba heard the click of the bedroom door as it closed. He fussed around the kitchen for ten minutes until he was sure Kay was resting. Then he walked rapidly to his home office and made himself comfortable at his old oak desk. Loosening his tie, he reached inside his suit jacket, retrieved the envelope, and ripped it open with shaking hands. Bubba took a deep breath and began to read:

Dear Bubba,

By the time you read this, I will have been dead for several days. Please take care of Kay. She has made me very happy over the years, and I hope you love her as much as I do.

What I have to tell you next is not easy, but I trust you will do whatever you think is necessary to safeguard this information.

You didn't know my father, Willie II, very well although you met him a few times at family functions. What you didn't know is that he was the keeper of a terrible legacy—one that may be very hard for you to believe. When you bought land from me and built your dream retirement home, I meant to tell you . . . but I couldn't do it. So I guess my cowardice shows in the writing of this letter.

In 1904, my grandfather, William Bradford I, lived in Oshkosh, Wisconsin, and worked for Howard Ellison, a fantastically wealthy lumber baron. Ellison had a beautiful home in the city, and my grandfather oversaw his estate. He was a very trusted employee who directed the activities of the entire staff.

In December of that year, a terrible fire destroyed much of the luxurious Ellison home. Damaged in the fire were some priceless Tiffany windows. My grandfather took charge of the windows, and under his watchful eye, they were loaded on a train to Winona bound for a stained-glass studio where they were scheduled to be cleaned and repaired. However, they never arrived at the studio.

My grandfather was blamed for the loss and accused of orchestrating the disappearance of the windows. He was fired from his trusted position in disgrace. He returned to Ontario a broken and disheartened man. Whether he was responsible or not, no one is sure, but the windows were never found.

Why am I telling you this? Perhaps you have the grit to dig into this sad family legacy and find out the truth. There have been rumors down through the years that the windows are hidden somewhere in the Ontario countryside, but that is very hard to reconcile with the facts of the case, unless my grandfather was involved. Anyway, good luck to you. Maybe you can clear the Bradford name once and for all and erase the cloud of suspicion that has hung over our family for generations.

Willie

Bubba sat in his chair gripping the letter. The magnitude of the contents left him gasping in shock and surprise, and the challenge his father-in-law had given him was disturbing. What did this mean? How could he already have discovered the missing windows, yet his father-in-law claimed he knew nothing about them? What was he supposed to do with the windows he'd discovered in the decrepit chapel? Hide them? Sell them? Report the discovery to the police? What? All of these thoughts passed through his mind in seconds.

Further complicating his predicament was what to tell his wife, Kay. He was sure she knew nothing about this. In the forty-two years they'd been married, Kay had never revealed any knowledge about their family legacy. Their marriage had always been an open book; they trusted each other implicitly. If he lied about the windows or failed to tell her about them, then the very foundation of their relationship would be jeopardized.

Bubba shook his head in frustration. He suddenly wished he had a faith in God like Kay possessed, because right now he knew any decision he made was bound to be flawed. Without some kind of divine guidance, he felt doomed to fail.

He heard the door of his office open. Kay walked over to him, noticing the letter in his hand.

"Bubba, what are you reading?" she asked.

He looked up at her and saw the trust in her eyes, a trust he could not violate. He gently clasped her hand. She noticed the slight tremor in his touch.

"Bubba, you're shaking. What's wrong?"

"Sit down, honey. I have some things to tell you."

25

Jim was late getting home from work on Tuesday evening. He'd promised Carol he would look in on Gladys Hanson after her fall at home and her subsequent trip to the emergency room yesterday. He drove through the valley on County K south of La Crosse until he came to Gladys' eighty-acre farm. Pulling into the driveway, a flock of chickens of varying colors and breeds scattered, clucking and flapping their wings in excitement. He parked the Suburban under a huge soft maple near the white clapboard house and stepped out of the vehicle.

As Jim approached the steps to the porch, Gladys appeared at the door. Her fly-away hair encircled her head like a wispy halo. Her wide body moved slowly these days—arthritic hips caused her pain and discomfort. She wore a traditional bib apron over a paisley house dress that was probably thirty years old. The apron was older, and Jim was sure the slippers on her feet had traveled with Noah on the ark. She smiled widely as Jim climbed the steps. Gladys was Jim's person—a steady rock in his life who faithfully prayed for him and listened to him when he needed her counsel. In addition, she acted as a grandmother to his two young children.

"Heard you had an up-close-and-personal encounter with the floor yesterday," Jim commented laconically as he glanced at the familiar face he'd grown to love over the years.

"I s'pose Carol told you all about it, huh?" she answered gruffly. Jim nodded silently, "Well, don't just stand there. Come on in."

Jim followed her into the outdated but familiar kitchen and found a chair at her round, oak table. The smell of a freshly baked pie, Gladys' gruff but caring demeanor, and the ticking of the kitchen clock put Jim at ease. He stretched his legs out under the table, leaned back, and folded his hands in his lap.

"Just made a cherry pie. Want a piece?" she asked.

"Is that your way of avoiding the subject of falls?" he asked as she puttered at the kitchen counter dishing up a piece of pie perfection.

"Absolutely. Who wants to talk about being clumsy enough to trip on a rug and land on your backside and then lie there on the floor like a beached whale?" she answered, her eyes sparkling with humor.

Jim smiled. "Well, when you put it like that, I guess no one would want to admit that," he said.

Jim dug into the pie while Gladys poured him a glass of milk. When she was done fussing, she plopped down at the table and watched him eat. Jim looked up at her. "How's the bump on the head?" he asked.

"It's there," Gladys answered tersely.

Jim laid his fork on the plate and lifted his eyebrows as he stared at Gladys.

"What?" she snapped. "Spit it out if you've got something to say."

There was nobody in Jim's life who understood him and the pressures he endured at his job like Gladys. She'd been a social worker in La Crosse County for over thirty years, and in those years she'd seen a lot of dysfunctional families with a variety of problems—alcohol and drug abuse, physical and mental damage inflicted on wives and children from drunken or drug-crazed men, neglect, and abandonment. The problems facing society today weren't anything new to Gladys. She'd seen it all. Now Jim wondered how she would react to what he was about to say, and if she would accept his suggestion. Despite his doubts, he was determined to find out by giving her a dose of her own medicine. Her gruff exterior might scare others off, but the one thing Jim always knew he'd get from Gladys was the frank truth spoken in love.

After several moments in which Gladys held her tongue and Jim munched on his pie and drank his milk, he finally spoke. "Listen, Gladys, we're all concerned about you. You're getting older, and you live here on the farm all alone. Otto's gone, and your nearest neighbor is three miles away. If you're determined to stay here, then I want you to get a Lifeline, so you can call for help when you need it." His suggestion was met with stony silence. Jim continued to sell the idea. "You could fall out in the chicken coop and lie there for days. Or what about the bathroom? What if you fell in the tub?"

"Somebody would get a birds-eye view of my awfully big ass," Gladys retorted. Jim chuckled but stopped when the kitchen suddenly became ominously quiet. Gladys fiddled with the corner of her worn-out apron, her eyes downcast, avoiding Jim's gaze. When she looked up at Jim, tears glistened in her kind eyes. He reached out and enfolded her wrinkled, calloused hand in his large one.

"Tell me what you're thinking so I can help you," Jim said tenderly. The clock ticked quietly on the wall.

Gladys pursed her lips together tightly, keeping her emotions in check. Finally, she spoke with a conviction in her voice that told Jim he'd hit a raw nerve.

"Do you have any idea how hard it's going be for me to give up my stubborn independence—my life here on the farm?" she asked quietly as the tears slipped onto her wrinkled cheeks. "I've lived here successfully without Otto now for almost five years." Her voice wavered with emotion. "I feed my chickens, gather my eggs every morning, and plant and harvest my own garden. I drive myself to town and church. I don't want to lose that."

Jim nodded in agreement. "I can understand that losing those freedoms would be scary."

"And sad," Gladys added. "Not to go all sentimental on you, but a few lines from Dylan Thomas come to mind: 'Do not go gentle into that good night. Old age should burn and rave at the close of the day; Rage, rage against the dying light.'" She smiled sadly. "I have a natural affinity to rage."

"Didn't know you were a lover of poetry," Jim commented. "But that sounds quite apropos to the situation. Still the fact remains that in the end it's not the years in your life that count. It's the life in your years." Jim smiled.

"You got me there," Gladys said softly, smiling back. "Good ol' Abe Lincoln."

"Right. But poetry is not going to solve your problem of living alone out here in the country. You can rage all you want, but in the end, if you fall and get hurt, it could be . . . well, it could be bad. A broken hip or a broken leg or a brain bleed is nothing to sneeze at. So will you think about getting a Lifeline?" Jim asked, skeptical that Gladys would accept his suggestion without a fight, or at least more discussion.

She nodded her head slowly. "I'll give it some consideration."

"Good, that's all I'm asking for. We'll talk again in a couple of weeks." Jim glanced at the wall clock. "I gotta get home. Carol hates it when I'm late for supper." He got up from the table and gave Gladys a hug and a peck on the cheek. "Don't trip over any more rugs," he said gruffly.

Gladys patted his arm thoughtfully. "I'll try not to. Thanks for stopping, Jim."

By the time he'd driven home, it was almost six o'clock, but, to his surprise, he hadn't missed the evening meal. Lillie's piano lesson in La Crosse after school had delayed Carol in town. She was just starting dinner when Jim walked into the house.

"Just go read the paper or something," Carol suggested when Jim explained why he was late. "I'll call you when everything's ready."

Jim settled into the swoopy black chair with the newspaper and a beer while Henri played quietly on the carpet with a tub of Legos. The smell of frying onions and garlic permeated the air, and the sounds of sizzling meat and the clang of kettles made Jim's stomach rumble with hunger. Henri was concentrating on building a pontoon boat when he stopped and gave Jim an intense stare. Jim glanced over at the little tyke and asked, "What are you thinking about, Henri?"

"Lillie got in trouble at school today, and she had to go to the principal's office," he explained.

"Really? What'd she do?" Jim asked. Lillie's behavior and decorum were usually top-notch, so Jim was surprised to hear this tidbit of news. *The teen years are right around the corner,* he thought. *Maybe Lillie's trying out a few strategies.*

At that moment, Lillie walked into the room and stood by Jim's chair. "Henri, I hear Mom calling you to set the table," Jim said.

"I didn't hear anything," Lillie said, frowning.

"Chop, chop, little buddy. Go check with Mom," Jim repeated. After Henri left the room, Jim put the newspaper in his lap. "Tell me about what happened at school today."

"Henri, you little tattletale!" she yelled in the direction of the kitchen.

Jim held up his hand. "Forget Henri for the time being. Just tell me about your trip to the principal's office. No frills. Just the facts."

Lillie recognized the investigative tone in her father's voice. She crossed her arms over her chest and gave Jim a blue-eyed stare. "Is this an interrogation?" she asked, tipping her head at an angle.

Jim fought down a grin. "You might call it that. So come out with it, toots. How'd you get sent to the principal's office?" He could see Lillie churning up a story to explain her behavior.

She took a big breath and began. "During social studies, we were taking turns telling about our parents' jobs, and I told the class that you were a famous detective who solved very hard cases, and that sometimes you had to shoot at people and take them down and handcuff them and put them in jail."

"Okay. That might have been an exaggeration, but go ahead," Jim said patiently. "Tell me the rest."

Lillie looked away for a moment, and Jim could see tears shimmering in her blue eyes. "After social studies at morning recess, Shiloh Gavin came up to me on the playground and told me I was a damned liar, and he smacked me on the arm. I told him he was a shit-faced monkey, and he could go to hell."

Jim took a deep breath, then said calmly, "Well, that was an interesting choice of words, but you know how your mom and I feel about cursing. Is that why you got sent to the office?"

She nodded. "Shiloh ran to the teacher on the playground and lied about what he said," Lillie spouted, her voice getting louder. Jim could clearly see she was outraged by Shiloh's behavior. The pace of her story increased until she was tripping over her words. "He lied about hitting me, and then he told—he told Sister Miriam that I swore at him, but he swore first, and it was totally unfair." Jim suddenly held up his hand for her to stop.

"I got the picture," he said solemnly.

Lillie shrugged her shoulders. "It wasn't that big of a deal, Dad. I just missed afternoon recess." As soon as she said the words, Lillie knew she'd made a grave mistake. She saw the glint of anger in her father's eyes, and suddenly she felt very small.

"Well, it's a big deal to me," Jim said seriously, leaning forward, his blue eyes burning with conviction. "I know you were angry, but telling someone to go to hell is not something I would expect from you, Lillie."

Lillie bit her lower lip, and the frown on her forehead deepened. She finally met Jim's steely-eyed gaze. "Well, I just got so mad when he hit me and then ran off and told a bunch of lies," she said, the tears beginning to spill onto her cheeks as she began crying in earnest.

"I can understand that, but telling someone to go to hell is a very serious statement. And it's certainly not what Jesus wants us to do, is it?" Lillie shook her head slowly. Jim continued. "Jesus wants everyone to understand how serious their sin is and how very terrible hell is. Telling someone to go to hell when we're angry with them doesn't help them understand how much Jesus really loves them, does it?" Jim said.

"No, I know that, Dad. But I was just so mad," Lillie mumbled. "I'm sorry."

"I accept your apology, but after dinner you will spend the rest of the evening in your room. No TV. No piano. No bike riding down the driveway. Understood?"

"Yes, sir," Lillie said, snuffling quietly. "Can I read or draw?"

"Sure," Jim said gently, getting out of his chair. "Come here, baby." Lillie walked over to him, and he put his arms around her and kissed her gently on the top of her head. "I will always love you, peanut."

Lillie sighed loudly, wiping the tears from her cheeks. "I know, Dad, even when I say bad things . . . even though it was the truth."

"Even when you make a bad choice," Jim said gently.

"Can we go and eat now?" Lillie asked.

Later, after the evening meal, as Lillie disappeared down the hallway to her room, Jim's cell rang. He had cocooned himself in his den and was reading more about the missing Tiffany windows.

"Jim Higgins," he said curtly.

"Lt. Higgins. It's Geoff LaSarde. I wanted to bounce something off you."

"Sure, go ahead. What's up?"

"I got a call from Trisha Fanella, the director at the new art museum being constructed at the old Fleischstad meat facility on the south side of Mormon Coulee Road. Are you familiar with it?"

"I'm aware of it," Jim said dryly.

"Well, some guy visited the museum this morning asking about me, but I think it was the guy who attacked me in my home."

A chill ran up Jim's arms. "That's interesting. I wondered if he'd show up again. What are you going to do now?" he asked.

"Wait a minute. You knew about this guy, and you didn't bother to tell me? What kind of police protection is that?" Geoff snapped.

"I just became aware of him a couple of days ago," Jim explained patiently. "The blood spot on the wall in your home belongs to him. His name is Lewis Borden. Apparently, he's the one who disarmed you and took the suitcase. Our lab tech got a hit when he entered Borden's DNA in the national registry. And just so we're clear," Jim continued, his voice tightening with authority, "the sheriff called me off the break-in at your home claiming it comes under city police jurisdiction, and she's right. It really is a city police matter."

"Why didn't you tell me all this?" Geoff's voice had risen in pitch, and he sounded agitated and scared.

Jim could understand the anxiety Geoff was experiencing. He wondered what the Tiffany expert would think if he knew about Lewis Borden's considerable skills as a former army ranger.

"We didn't know the perpetrator's location. We thought he'd left town, but apparently he's back in the area again—or he never left at all. What do you want me to do about it, Geoff?"

"Well . . . well . . . I don't know," Geoff stammered. "But I know some other stuff about the windows that I didn't know before. I wanted to sit down with you and explain it, so we're on the same page."

Jim leaned back and stared at the ceiling. "Like I said, it's really out of my hands. I've been taken off the case, but you might schedule a meeting with Police Chief Tanya Pedretti—maybe tomorrow morning? I'd be glad to sit in. Maybe Sheriff Turnmile would come, too. Call me once you get something set up."

"That's fine, but what do I do in the meantime?" Geoff asked. "Is this Lewis guy dangerous?"

Jim hesitated to tell Geoff what he knew about Lewis Borden, but at the same time he didn't want to be complicit in giving him a false picture of the dangerous man who seemed to be following him. "I'll have a city officer patrol your street tonight. Do you have a surveillance camera outside your home?" Jim asked, avoiding Geoff's pointed question.

"Yes, I installed one next to my front door over the weekend, and there's one mounted on the corner of my garage."

"Good. Take your cell phone to bed with you. If something happens, call 911. But I think you'll be okay. He's probably already checked out your house and noticed the camera. He won't want to get caught on video—"

"Trisha already captured images of him on her cell phone when he visited the museum," Geoff interrupted. "She took a couple of photos of him and sent them to me."

"That's good. Bring those with you tomorrow morning to the meeting. If you really don't feel safe, go and bunk with a friend for the night or go to a hotel. Can you do that?"

"Yeah, I guess I could."

"That might be your best bet. You can make a plan tomorrow with Chief Pedretti," Jim said.

"Okay. Thanks, Lieutenant."

"No problem," Jim finished. He hung up and sighed. Obviously things were heating up in the Tiffany window case, but he didn't know how he could help since Sheriff Turnmile had told him the case was off limits to anyone in the sheriff's department. *Politics,* he thought. *Just a bunch of stupid politics.*

Against his better judgment, he picked up his cell and dialed the city police department, explained the situation to the officer manning the night desk, and asked that a patrol car periodically check LaSarde's residence on St. Cloud Street throughout the night. When he was assured that would happen, he hung up. But the thoughts of Borden slinking around the city left him feeling rattled. They certainly didn't need a murder to add to the investigation, especially one in which the victim had called and asked for police protection.

It was still early in the evening. Jim picked up his cell and dialed Tanya Pedretti's number.

"Jim? What's up?"

"Sorry to bother you at home, Tanya, but the victim of that house break-in on St. Cloud Street last week just called me. We traced a blood sample from his home to a guy named Lewis Borden. He showed up at the new art gallery this morning looking for Geoff LaSarde. Apparently he's back in town and is trying to connect with him."

"Oh boy, that doesn't sound good. So, what are you saying? You're dumping this back in my lap?" she asked, sounding irritated.

"Hey, just so you know, Turnmile pulled my crew off the case, even though you gave me permission to do the initial investigation, so I had no options but to tell Geoff to contact you in the morning to set up a meeting."

Pedretti cursed softly under her breath, then said, "Okay, I guess I can live with that. What other choice do I have? You comin' to this meeting?"

"I can if you want me to," Jim said.

"I want you there. I'm still short a few officers, and I could use your help, but let me talk to Turnmile again and see if we can work out some kind of arrangement. I could really use your help in this case, Jim. Maybe my relationship with Turnmile can actually result in something positive, instead of me just listening to all her problems." She chuckled softly. "Life's just a big bowl of cherries, huh?"

"Yeah, something like that," Jim chuckled. "Listen, I gotta go. My wife's waiting for me in the tub."

"Oh boy! I'd like to hear about that sometime," Tanya said, laughing out loud.

"Don't get your hopes up. My love life is private, but when I see Roy, I'll share my plans for the ultimate romantic bathroom, complete with a soaking tub and skylights."

"Well, I can tell you he'd never spend the money, although if he gave it a try he might like it. Me? I'd love it," Tanya said, laughing.

"He might like it more than you think," Jim said, smiling. "I'll talk to you later."

He got up from his desk, flicked the lights off, then walked down the hall and checked on the kids. The rest of the house was dark, and it was finally quiet after a long day. Jim never tired of the huge tub in the middle of the en suite master bathroom with its generous skylights that delivered a magnificent view of the stars in the inky sky overhead. Carol had dimmed the lights and lit candles. The room smelled divine, like lavender and sandalwood. Her eyes were closed, but she opened them and watched Jim undress.

"What took you so long?" she asked lazily.

Jim slid into the warm, sudsy water. "Just a couple of unexpected phone calls. Nothing that has anything to do with us or this moment." He clasped her hands. He loved the tenderness in her brown eyes and her bare shoulders that were peeking just above the water.

"By the way, why was Lillie in her room all evening?" Carol asked. "Did you send her there?"

"Yeah. She had an incident on the playground at school and got sent to the principal's office for using profanity," Jim explained.

"Really? What did she say?"

Jim repeated the colorful language to Carol, who blanched in shock. "Jim, we're paying good money to send her to a school that builds character, and she comes home swearing like a sailor. How does that work?"

"Don't worry. I made it perfectly clear that what she did was unacceptable," Jim said casually. "That's why she spent the evening in her room."

"Where in the world does she get these ideas?" Carol asked.

"The bus, the playground, other kids, and unfortunately, there are plenty of adults who fling around bad language at the drop of a hat." Carol continued to frown at Jim as if more of an explanation was needed. "Honey, you can send her to the finest religious school in the country," Jim continued, "but there will always be somebody there who's going to test the waters. People are flawed, and their bad behavior is not going to miraculously disappear when somebody waves a crucifix in their face. Lillie's pushing the boundaries as all children do, but as her parents, we just have to reinforce the boundaries when she forgets. Our expectations haven't changed. She found that out tonight. She'll be fine."

They soaked in the warm water for a few minutes, and then Jim grabbed Carol's hand and pulled her toward him. He kissed her on the lips. "Let's talk about something else," he suggested, kissing her again.

"Hmm. You need a little distraction from all your worries?" Carol asked, moving into Jim's arms.

"Distraction? Yeah, that sounds like a great idea," Jim said, kissing her intensely.

"One of the little joys in life," Carol whispered between kisses.

"Little?"

"You know what I mean, big guy."

"Big guy. That's better," Jim whispered.

WEDNESDAY, MAY 23

26

Sheriff Elaine Turnmile sat at her desk on late Wednesday afternoon in her stark, boring office waiting for Higgins to show up after the meeting they'd had with Police Chief Tanya Pedretti and Geoff LaSarde, in which they'd discussed the missing windows and Lewis Borden's recent reappearance in La Crosse. She leaned back in her office chair and fixed her eyes on the yellowing ceiling tiles, then glanced around the room. The threadbare carpet and dull beige paint did nothing to cheer her up. No family pictures graced the walls or credenza, and if she had interests other than law enforcement, it was not evident in the decor. She groaned with pent-up frustration when she thought back to her recent session with her therapist last night after work.

Her session with Dr. Gillespie was the latest in a long series of appointments Elaine had had with Dr. Gillespie at Jensen Family Counseling Services in Holmen. She had slouched in her chair like a surly teenager. The counselor's wide smile seemed inappropriate considering Elaine's tight-lipped reticence about her relationships. Trying to uncover the reasons for her extreme aversion to human intimacy was the fly in the ointment that never seemed to get resolved.

The psychologist tented his fingers and brought them to his lips as he leaned back in his chair. *Maybe there will be a change soon,* Dr. Gillespie thought. *We're on the cusp of a breakthrough.* He sat for several moments studying the woman in front of him. Elaine had been one of the most difficult patients he'd had in several years of practice, but he held out hope that she could gain some insight into her personality and put some of her horrible past behind her.

Dr. Gillespie leaned forward, placed his elbows on the desk, and said, "Elaine, you cannot continue to push people away and expect them to come back for more." Beneath the soft tone of his voice was a thread of irritation. "Sooner or later, others will quit trying to reach out to you. You have to be willing to meet people halfway, so to speak. Without risk and trust, relationships can't exist."

That's easy for you to say, Doc, Elaine thought as the doctor prattled his hackneyed advice. His empty platitudes filled her with a deep resentment. *What do you know about what I face every day?* she thought. *You sit here in your little ivory tower and analyze everybody else's problems. What about your relationships, Doc? How's that going, huh? You got any problems that seem unsolvable?* Instead of responding honestly to the doctor's suggestions, Elaine chewed on her bottom lip and remained silent, stewing in a soup of bitterness and angst. Dr. Gillespie rambled on until Elaine finally tuned in to what he was saying.

"I think we're finally getting somewhere," Dr. Gillespie was saying. "Tonight you expressed some of your frustration about your mother and sister. You're starting to deal with the past, which is a good sign."

Elaine watched the therapist with flat, dull eyes, her facial features reflecting a weary boredom. *I'm doing it again,* she thought. It was exactly what the doctor had warned her about—walling herself off from any real feelings, avoiding intimacy at all costs. She tipped her head to one side and studied Gillespie, who was blabbing up a storm from behind his desk. *We're no further now than we were six months ago,* Elaine thought, *and I've spent almost a thousand dollars listening to this rambling chitchat.*

She was beginning to think no one could help her develop genuine, intimate relationships with other human beings. In retrospect, she realized Higgins had helped her more than all the psychological blather and counseling she'd invested in over the years. What was it about Higgins that put her at ease? For some reason, he seemed to understand her, or at least, he empathized with the difficulties she had in navigating human relationships. When she thought about it, she realized her biggest problem was one of trust. She didn't believe others could actually like her, let alone love her. Once they'd penetrated the attractive facade—her beautiful, smooth skin, her golden hair, and her deep, green eyes—what they found was a deficient, sterile, and cold human being. Although Higgins wasn't what she'd call a friend, at least he seemed to understand how terribly lonely she was. In his own clumsy way, he'd treated her with more respect than any of her family ever had, and somehow, she knew he was sincerely trying to help her.

There was a light rapping on the office door. Elaine twirled around in her office chair. Higgins stood on the threshold waiting for an invitation to enter. Elaine waved him in with one hand. "Come on in, Higgins. I've been waiting for you."

Jim walked in. Elaine noticed his carefully coordinated ensemble: black dress pants, a white shirt with tiny gray stripes in a luxurious fabric that made you want to touch it, a muted gray and maroon checkered silk tie, and a classic wool suit jacket in a lovely gray English tweed with threads of maroon woven through it. *Expensive,* she thought. *How does he afford those high-priced threads on his salary?* She continued to stare at Jim until he squirmed uncomfortably.

"Have a chair, Higgins," Elaine ordered curtly. Jim looked around, found an upholstered armchair next to the wall, and plopped into it. The suggestion from Dr. Gillespie about meeting people halfway floated into Elaine's brain. *Maybe I should give that a try.*

"I understand you talked to Pedretti last night. Is that right?" she asked. Jim nodded, but before he could comment, she hurried on.

"She told me about your fabulous bathtub. You've got some kind of spa in your house? Is that right?"

Jim reddened with embarrassment and cleared his throat. "I remodeled my bathroom for my first wife, Margie, when she was suffering through breast cancer treatments," he answered quietly. "It seemed to help her for a while, but then . . ."

"But then . . . what?" Elaine blurted rudely, leaning forward in her chair, waiting for some delicious tidbit of juicy gossip.

"Well, then she passed away," Jim said softly. A shadow of pain and sadness passed over his handsome features. Elaine noticed the change in his expression—a combination of wistfulness and sorrow, although she had no idea what to say to Higgins in response.

"After she was gone," Jim continued softly, "I thought it was all a pretty stupid waste of money, but then I thought about how much she enjoyed it while she was living, and I decided it was a pretty good investment. You can't put a price on the happiness of a woman, especially when she's your wife. Thinking back, it was worth every dime I spent to give her a few hours of enjoyment."

"You still use it?" Turnmile asked, an odd expression on her face.

"Absolutely. My wife and I use it quite often," Jim commented, wondering where this conversation was going. *Has she ever had an intimate relationship with another person, because I could swear she doesn't have a clue what's involved in a romantic encounter.*

"Together?" Turnmile asked, her green eyes shining with titillating curiosity. Jim squirmed with discomfort at the sexual innuendo.

He frowned. "What do you mean—together?"

"You get in the tub together?"

"Yeah, we do sometimes, although Carol uses it more than I do." Jim cocked his head, trying to understand the purpose of this exchange. *Since when are my private habits the fodder of a conversation with my boss? Was this some clumsy attempt at connecting?* he wondered. If she continued this line of questioning, things could get real personal in a big hurry. Jim felt a spasm of panic, then anger. He attempted to turn the conversation away from the intimate details of his escapades in the tub with Carol, hurrying to fill in the awkward lull in the conversation. "Was there something specific you needed from me this morning, ma'am?"

"Yes, after the meeting in Pedretti's office, I've reconsidered my position on the LaSarde house break-in on the north side," Turnmile said in a more business-like tone.

"You have?" Jim asked, surprised at her concession.

"Mm-hmm. I've decided you can keep tabs on the investigation, but don't go overboard. Just put it on your watch list and keep me informed if things heat up."

"I can live with that," Jim said. He stood up to leave and walked toward the door, but Turnmile had other ideas.

"Wait a minute," the sheriff said suddenly.

Jim grimaced, then pasted a weak smile on his face and turned back to face the petulant sheriff.

"What did you think of that meeting with Chief Pedretti and that Tiffany art guy this morning?" Turnmile asked. The question seemed like a fishing expedition to Jim since she'd been a participant at the meeting. He wondered why she needed his opinion about something that was so straightforward.

"I can understand LaSarde's concern," Jim began. "Like I said this morning, he was attacked in his own home, which can be upsetting. And it appears that Lewis Borden is back in town again looking for a way to connect with him. Frankly, I'd be nervous about meeting that guy, too."

"Have you been trying to find this Borden guy?" Turnmile asked, twirling her reading glasses in one hand.

"We thought he left town, so we wrote the whole thing off. The guy is slippery, and he has skills that the average citizen is not prepared to deal with. He's careful and connected, but until he contacts Geoff directly, there's not much we can do," Jim explained, although his statement sounded like an excuse.

"Do you really think these missing windows are hidden somewhere around here? That seems like a fantastic stretch of the imagination," Turnmile said, plopping her glasses back on her face. She pushed a strand of hair away from her face as she stared at Jim. Her icy green eyes bothered Jim at a visceral level. *I should be used to those stares by now*, he thought.

"According to everything we've examined—newspaper articles and other historical documents from Oshkosh—the windows have never been recovered," Jim said. "Where they are is anyone's guess, but as you heard this morning, Geoff has uncovered a name—some William Bradford from Ontario—and he's investigating the man's connection to the window scheme, so maybe he'll come up with something. It's hard to tell at this point. One thing I do know—whether it's jewelry, lamps, vases, or stained-glass windows—anything with the Tiffany name scrawled on it commands huge prices on the antiques market. Just watch *Antiques Roadshow* if you don't believe me. Those windows are worth millions, and as we know, money is usually a motive when it comes to crime."

Turnmile was quiet for a moment, evaluating Jim's comments. She sat back in her chair, which squeaked loudly under her weight, and stared at Jim until he wondered what was passing through his boss' mind. To Jim, it seemed like the sheriff constantly questioned his ability to carry out investigative tasks forthrightly despite the fact that his team had a stellar reputation of dogged determination and effectiveness in unraveling some of the most peculiar crimes in La Crosse history.

"How does all this stuff seem to land on your plate, Higgins?" the sheriff finally asked. She was in some kind of philosophical mood—something Jim rarely saw in her. "People thrown in the river, victims getting whacked with ancient ball clubs, gold coins hidden in the bluffs, a crazy woman who buried a hatchet in Sam's front door, and now, Tiffany windows worth millions tucked away in some obscure hiding place." She leaned forward toward Jim. He backed up a couple of steps. "How does all this weird stuff fall into your lap anyway?"

Jim shrugged. "I don't know why these things keep coming my way, but this window deal seems to be heating up. In my experience, that usually means someone somewhere is going to do something stupid, and we'll have to figure out why, but I'll keep you in the loop as things develop," Jim promised.

"So that's Plan A?" she asked, dipping her chin as she peered at Higgins over her reading glasses.

"Yep, and if plan A doesn't work, the alphabet has twenty-five more letters."

"Well, that's a philosophy of crime I've never heard before," Turnmile commented sarcastically. "Good luck with that, Higgins." She pushed her glasses up on her nose and focused her attention back on the stack of paperwork spread out across the desk. Her parting comment was impersonal and not meant to encourage. Instead, it was the dismissal of someone who'd taken up too much of her precious time. Turnmile rifled through more documents from the stack on her desk. It was evident her conversation with Higgins was clearly over.

How could one person be so good at making someone feel so insignificant? Jim thought. He shuddered, then took the opportunity to escape any more caustic remarks as he marched out of her office. When he arrived back at his office on the third floor, he was surprised to find Carol sitting in a chair waiting for him.

"Hey, what's up?" he asked. Although Jim and Carol worked in the same building, their paths rarely crossed during the workday. The last time his wife had shown up in his office was almost two years ago when his older daughter, Sara, was abducted by a crazed drug dealer. Jim hoped the reason for the visit today was something less alarming.

Carol stood up and quietly closed the door. As she walked toward him, Jim felt a shiver of anxiety. "Emily said you were in Turnmile's office. I figured you probably needed a little shot in the arm after your session with Miss Elaine, since she usually doubts everything you say."

"That's true, she does," Jim said, "and she didn't disappoint today, either." He paused briefly, and Carol noticed his strange expression. "Something weird's going on."

"Whaddya mean?" Carol asked, frowning.

"Well, today Turnmile actually seemed to be trying to make a personal connection with me, which is very strange."

"Oh, yeah? Maybe her sessions at Vivian's clinic are resulting in something positive."

Jim shook his head. "Nah, I don't think so," he said flatly. "Right out of the blue, she asked about our tub. Don't you think that's weird?"

"Our tub? You mean our bathtub? How'd she find out about that?" Carol asked, her nose crinkling in confusion.

"Oh, I mentioned it to Tanya last night when she called, and today Elaine asked me some stuff about it," Jim said.

"Boy, that is weird," Carol said grumpily. Then she did a double-take. "You told Tanya about our tub?"

Jim swiped his hand dismissively through the air. "It was just an offhand comment. Anyway, the conversation with her today was strange. As you well know, I can't seem to convince her that I'm competent at my job and that my experience and record speak for themselves, but she's got the guts to question me about my tub. Go figure."

Carol came around Jim's desk, wrapped her arms around his waist, and gave him a warm kiss.

"You didn't tell her what we do in the tub, did you?" Carol asked, raising her eyebrows slightly.

Jim sighed loudly. "No, for Pete's sake. Why would I share our personal intimacies with someone like Elaine?"

Carol shrugged. "Well, telling her about the tub probably opened another whole can of worms you're not ready to deal with."

"Maybe. But to get back to it. Why are you here?" he asked. Jim wasn't sure what Carol had in mind, but things were going in a good direction, so who was he to question the motives behind her shot-in-the-arm plan? Carol kissed him again. Finally, Jim pulled back from the embrace.

"Seriously, honey, why are you here?" he asked again.

"Your brother, Dave, called about an hour ago. You're supposed to call him when you get a chance. And Lillie said something this morning after you left for work that I thought you should know about."

"Oh yeah? What was that?" he asked.

"She said to tell you that what you're looking for is closer than you think."

Jim focused his gaze on Carol, and his eyes widened slightly. "Excuse me? What's that supposed to mean?"

"Hey, don't shoot the messenger. I thought you'd know what it meant," Carol said, "or at the very least, you'd find it encouraging."

"I have no idea what Lillie is talking about. Sometimes her one-liners are not always clear until later, after everything comes out in the wash," Jim commented. "From my experience, it's not always something you can act on in the present."

"Well, remember that dream about some beautiful windows in an old shed?" Carol asked. "Maybe that's what she's talking about."

"Yeah, I remember when she told us that," Jim said softly. He thought back to the morning Lillie had come into the dining room looking pale and distraught. Frankly, he'd been so busy lately he'd forgotten all about her dream. *Beautiful windows in an old shed?* He was skeptical about the idea. *Nothing is ever that easy.* Besides, hundreds of old tobacco sheds peppered the countryside throughout the Driftless region, reminders of a time when high-volume tobacco production gave farm families some extra income. To think that Lillie's dream could actually lead them to the priceless, lost windows in some out-of-the-way shed out in the countryside was inconceivable at this moment, given the little information they had. Still, it was . . . *something.*

Carol interrupted his thoughts as she untangled herself from the hug. "I need to get back downstairs. Will you be home by six?" she asked.

"Should be, unless something else blows up in the meantime, which is a distinct possibility," Jim commented.

"I hear you," Carol said. "You never know what's going to happen, but try to stay out of Elaine's office." She walked to the door, but not before Jim could thank her.

"Hey, the shot in the arm was just what I needed. Thanks," he said, grinning.

"See you at home," she said, twiddling her fingers over her shoulder.

After Carol left, Jim picked up his landline and dialed Jensen Family Counseling Services in Holmen, which was run by Carol's sister, Vivian Jensen, a certified psychologist specializing in anger management, relationship healing, and marriage counseling.

After explaining his need to talk to Vivian personally, the secretary who answered the phone connected him to Vivian's office. He was still fuming about the conversation he'd had with Sheriff Turnmile about his bathtub activities. In fact, the more he thought about it, the madder he got. He chewed on the inside of his cheek in frustration as he waited on the line.

"Dr. Jensen. May I help you?"

"Hey, Viv. It's Jim."

"Wow! I haven't seen or talked to you in over a month. Where have you been?" Vivian asked.

"I've been doin' what I always do. Tied to my desk with a ball and chain, puttin' one foot in front of the other trying to survive the rat race, which isn't easy when you're chasin' criminals around the city and countryside," Jim said.

"Needing some advice?"

"Well, maybe not so much advice as a shot of reassurance," Jim grumbled.

"Mmm, that's an unusual request coming from someone as competent as you. Let me guess—Turnmile? What'd she do now?"

Suddenly, Jim felt the urge to unload. "What hasn't she done?" he spouted angrily. "What planet did she come from anyway? I've been trying to befriend her for months—I mean, literally months—but this time she's gone too far." He could feel his cheeks redden with anger and embarrassment as Elaine's awkward questions flooded back into his mind.

"Uh-oh," Vivian said. "She's trampled on your sex life, huh? Asking intrusive, personal questions? She didn't come on to you, did she?"

There was a pause that a Mack truck could have driven through. "Well, not exactly, but, honest to God, Viv, that woman has more chutzpah than . . . well, than anybody I've ever met. Either that, or she's incredibly stupid, which I don't think she is, or she's unfulfilled."

"Sexually? Well, I'd say with her personality, such as it is, she's definitely unfulfilled sexually. So, what set you off?"

"She asked about our bathtub, going so far as to ask what we *do* in the bathtub," Jim sputtered. "Can you believe that?"

"Well, if you didn't have such a reputation for being a great big Romeo hunk, you might not get asked questions like that," Vivian responded quietly, smiling to herself.

Jim slammed his fist on his desk. "I hardly think that my sex life, bathtub or not, should be the topic of a conversation in a meeting with the county sheriff," he barked loudly.

"Maybe she's just curious, or she's got a crush on you, but I think she's pullin' your chain, Jim," Vivian said gently. "I'm surprised you didn't figure that out."

"Well, you had to be there. I interpreted her comments and questions differently—it seemed like a clumsy attempt to connect on a deeper level," Jim said with a huff.

"Hmm, could be that, too, although I don't think Elaine has evolved to that level of relational intimacy and sensitivity or deepness yet. Do you? Connecting is not her thing." Vivian chuckled. "Maybe you can change that," she finished.

Despite his anger and frustration, Jim started to laugh. "That'll be the day. Dream on, Viv," Jim said. It felt good to laugh at the whole farce, and as the tension dissipated, Vivian continued.

"Seriously, though, you should be proud of the way you've tried to help her navigate the sheriff's department, Jim," Vivian said. "Working with a bunch of law enforcement personnel takes a strong constitution, and her people skills are seriously lacking. But you've tried. You really have, and I give you all the credit in the world. If I had a ribbon, I'd pin it on your chest."

"Come on, Viv," Jim groaned. "Spare me. I don't take pity well."

"Are you looking for advice, because I'm assuming that's why you called."

"Yeah, I guess so. I just don't know what to do anymore." Jim leaned forward and put his elbows on his desk, then propped his head on his hand, waiting for Vivian's suggestions. "I've tried everything except ripping her up one side and down the other when she makes a dumb remark. I mean, really, I've been gritting my teeth ever since she arrived in the department, and my staff wants nothing to do with her, either. Nothing works. I mean, nothing."

"I can't divulge too much—patient confidentiality—but she's had a horrible set of circumstances to deal with from her past. She's—" Vivian stopped short. "I can't say, sorry."

"It's okay, Viv. I'm just venting, I guess. I've been waiting and hoping she'd start understanding the ins and outs of human relationships and quit giving me fits, that's all. The questions she asked today were really weird, and the way she said it was very strange and clumsy."

"Might be a breakthrough moment, although I'd have to see it to believe it, but you never know."

"I'll take that as an encouragement, I guess." He chuckled again. "Thanks, Viv."

"No problem. Should I bill you for this, or are we off the record?"

"This is definitely off the record," Jim said. "Have a good night, and don't be a stranger. Carol wants to get together soon."

"You got it. I'll call her. Bye-bye."

Jim sat in the office for several minutes reflecting on the conversation with Vivian. He studied the limestone bluffs in the distance and thought about the people he'd dealt with during his career in law enforcement. The criminals who'd been abused and beaten to within an inch of their lives, who had addiction issues, who couldn't control their anger and used their fists—or a weapon—to solve their problems, the ones who got a particular thrill out of lying, cheating, and stealing, the ones who were just plain mean. He expected that kind of behavior from that segment of society. But Turnmile was attractive, relatively intelligent, and actually, pretty good at her job. So, what had happened to her that damaged her so badly? Jim didn't know, but the better angel of his nature pitied her, although he was sure that wasn't what she needed. He wished he knew how to reach her, so she wasn't so lonely and so godawful irritating.

He sighed loudly. Standing up, he grabbed his suit jacket, slung it over his shoulder, and walked through the third-floor lobby to the elevator. Emily had already left for the day, and the office was quiet. Riding down to the first floor, he let himself out the back entrance of the building and walked wearily to his vehicle. *Elaine Turnmile, Sheriff of La Crosse County. Huh. Now there's a woman for someone who's looking for a mission in life, but that wouldn't be me,* he thought.

27

The sun was hot and beat on Jamie Alberg's shoulders as he hunched over the hardened dirt on Wednesday afternoon at the Fish Farm Mounds archaeological dig site in Lansing, Iowa. Sweat trickled under his curly hair and ran down the sides of his face. He wiped his face with his shirt sleeve and continued to carefully pick at the edges of a partially-exposed ancient Oneota pot. The ancient globular vessel was slowly being revealed. Its fire-blackened edge and zig-zag decorations made with a stick were exposed to the air now. Despite his excitement in finding a new vein of lost artifacts buried in the river clay, his mind frequently returned to the quandary of the lost Tiffany windows. A volunteer near him looked over and attempted a stilted conversation, but Jamie was distracted, and the girl finally gave up when he continued giving her one-syllable answers.

After working for a couple of hours in relative silence, Jamie stood up, his back stiffened and sore from his cramped position over the pot. He stretched backward, easing the tightness in his shoulders and glanced at his phone—three o'clock. He addressed the small crowd of college students and volunteers.

"Hey, everyone. I'll be leaving in a few hours, so let's wrap up whatever you're working on. We'll pick it up tomorrow morning at about eight." The volunteers nodded and went back to their excavation tasks.

At five o'clock, Jamie walked across the parking lot of the Fish Farm Mounds excavation site and opened the hatchback of his VW Golf. He loaded his tools, climbed into the car, and drove out of the lot. The sun was still blazing in the late afternoon sky, and puffy clouds passed over the wooded bluffs, creating shifting shadows on the scenery.

The man in the rented Chevelle who'd followed Jamie to Lansing started his vehicle, keeping his eye on the young archaeologist. He'd parked his car in a lane choked with overgrown blackberries next to the parking lot and slept on and off since morning. Now as the car engine roared to life, he carefully followed Jamie, staying back, remaining unobtrusive. While he tailed the archaeologist, he thought about the elusive Tiffany windows, but he hadn't formulated a plan yet to uncover their location. From everything the man had learned online and from articles written about the intrepid archaeologist in trade magazines, Jamie Alberg was an enigma: brilliant, impulsive, daring, and unpredictable. Some of his past escapades defied logic and luck and seemed based on nothing more than a whim, so trying to determine his plan for locating the missing Tiffany windows was like trying to predict a curveball from a competent pitcher.

The tantalizing reward of finding the stolen windows kept the stalker focused on the money that could be his. He'd done his research, and the results he'd discovered about the rare Tiffany windows were beyond anything he'd originally estimated. From his web searches, he'd found out that each window could have a price tag of $500,000. Using that estimate, the entire group of windows would yield almost three million dollars, but the range of prices depended on who was interested and how much they were willing to pay. The risks associated with finding them and reselling them were enormous. Fortunately, with his many underground criminal connections, he would have the means and knowledge to distribute the windows without any incrimination on his part. He smiled. *I am going to find the damn things—with Jamie's help—and then I'm going to sell them and cash in.*

Driving up the Great River Road to La Crosse through the south side, Jamie arrived in the familiar north-side neighborhood near Red Cloud Park, where he lived, oblivious to the car following him. As he approached his small ranch home, Jamie punched the garage door opener. The door went up, Jamie pulled his car in, and the door went down.

The stalker parked the brown Chevelle a few blocks away, then doubled back on foot until he found a bench at a bus stop a block away, which gave him a good view of Alberg's house. He sat casually on the bench, reading the *La Crosse Sentinel*, giving the impression he was waiting for a bus.

Inside the house, Jamie walked to the living room window and carefully parted the curtains a few inches. The man on the bench looked out of place. Was he really waiting for a bus? If so, he couldn't be a local, because everybody who was anybody around here knew that the bus route had changed over two months ago, and it no longer stopped in the Red Cloud neighborhood. Who was this guy? What was he doing here?

Jamie let the drapery fall back in place, grabbed his cell phone out of his pocket, and dialed.

"Jamie, how'd you get my cell number?" Jim Higgins asked.

He sounded irritated, but when Jamie considered the challenges facing the lieutenant, he decided it was perfectly normal for him to be harried and brusque. After all, keeping the residents of La Crosse County safe was a huge undertaking. Who knew what havoc the perps were planning? Higgins had weathered bombings, abductions, clandestine meetings on Granddad Bluff, murderers in quarries, and God knew what else.

"I've had your cell number for a long time. You know that, Lieutenant," Jamie replied coolly. "Besides, I only call you when it's absolutely necessary."

The line stayed quiet for a few moments until Higgins sighed and asked, "Okay. So what's going on? What are you calling about?"

"I've done some research, and I've reconstructed the Bradford family tree tracing a grandson who still lives in Ontario—"

"Whoa, whoa, whoa, Jamie. Time out. Who are the Bradfords?" Jim asked.

"Well, I was about to tell you—" Jamie began, but Jim rudely interrupted again.

"Keep it short and sweet. I'm about to walk outta my office and go home." He didn't really have time for a long-winded explanation about someone's family tree, even though he knew he'd get one, especially from someone as meticulous as Jamie.

Jamie began explaining William Bradford's role in the day-to-day operation of the Ellison household in Oshkosh, the Tiffany windows that went missing after the tragic fire, which Jim already knew about, and the termination of Bradford from Ellison's employment when he was suspected of orchestrating the heist of the precious windows.

"I know most of that already. So what?" Jim said bluntly after he'd heard Jamie's spiel.

"Well, Lt. Higgins, surely you—with your brilliant mind and analytical skills—can understand the implications of the family's appearance in Ontario when William Bradford I was terminated from his job in Oshkosh. If he arranged for the windows to be taken off the train, and he settled in Ontario, then the windows are somewhere in the Ontario area just waiting to be discovered," Jamie said, his voice hoarse with passion and excitement. "The windows are—"

"Missing, Jamie. They're missing," Jim hastily interrupted. "They've been missing for over a hundred years, and the likelihood of them showing up in Ontario is, by my calculation, pretty slim. Nobody's found them yet, so what makes you think you're going to find them now more than a hundred years later?"

Jamie gritted his teeth when he heard the challenge in Lt. Higgins' voice. *Why are people so obstinate in their ignorance? Why won't they listen to a reasonable solution to a difficult problem?*

Higgins rushed on. "Jamie, you are treading on thin ice, buddy. I know you. Right now, you're questioning my thinking and analyzing your chances of convincing me of this wild theory you have that the Tiffany windows are hidden somewhere in Ontario, Wisconsin. Really, Jamie? Come on. I'm telling you that there are other people involved in the search for these windows. Some of them are bad players, like the guy who overpowered Geoff in his home and drugged him. There are others as well, and they're dangerous, Jamie. They have skills you know nothing about." Jim stopped briefly, waiting for an interruption from the young archaeologist, which didn't come, so he continued.

"My advice to you is to continue to do what you do best—digging up ancient artifacts down at Fish Farm Mounds and interpreting them for the public. Stay out of this window affair. It's only going to cause problems for you." Jim's diatribe was met with silence at the other end of the line. "Jamie, are you there?" Jim asked.

"I'm here, sir. I know this all sounds incredible; it even sounds incredible to me. But as you know, incredible discoveries still happen. Your own record speaks volumes to that truth—lost gold, pilfered Iraqi treasures . . ."

"Jamie, if that's meant to be a compliment, then it's misdirected," Jim interrupted again. "I never went in search of the things that were hidden. They were revealed to me in the natural progression of my job—in investigations about criminal activity. Remember, Jamie, slow and steady wins the race. Turtles, not hares."

"Well, here's one for you, Lt. Higgins. Something an old treasure hunter once told me. When nothing is certain, then everything is possible."

Jim heard a click. "Jamie? Jamie? Wait—"

Jim's shoulders dropped as he pocketed his phone. Based on experience, he knew his conversation with Jamie was an exercise in futility. The kid had made up his mind, and there wasn't much Jim could do to stop him. Dealing with Jamie's determination and brazen bravado was familiar territory. *How many times have we been through this?* he thought. Jim stood at his desk wondering what kind of predicament Jamie would get embroiled in now. He rubbed his face with his hand, then grabbed his suit coat and slipped out of his office.

Outside, the brilliant sunshine should have filled Jim with optimism. Spring was here. The earth was being renewed. Hope springs eternal. Blah, blah, blah. But none of it erased the dread that had gripped him. He thought again of Lillie's advice: "What you're looking for is closer than you think."

If there was any truth in Lillie's theory, then maybe Jamie and his daughter were both right. Maybe the windows were hidden in Ontario, but Jim had the distinct feeling it was all leading to something awful that he couldn't prevent. Feeling despondent, he climbed into the Suburban and drove south out of La Crosse toward his home on Chipmunk Coulee Road.

28

As soon as Jamie hung up after his conversation with Lt. Higgins, a strong arm grabbed him around the neck and squeezed with an iron grip. A deep voice in his ear cautioned him, "Don't do anything heroic. It won't go well."

Jamie stood still and considered his options. He could feel his heart racing in his chest. He supposed the man who was restraining him was the same man who had been sitting at the defunct bus stop outside of his house. From the crushing grip around his neck, Jamie knew his chance of escaping was a physical impossibility—the man was as hard as iron. However, Jamie also assumed the information he possessed must be valuable, or this guy wouldn't be threatening him to within an inch of his life.

"Could we discuss this?" Jamie whispered hoarsely, struggling to breathe.

"Discuss it?" The man laughed with brazen arrogance, tightening his arm around Jamie's neck. "No, discussion is not an option," he snapped through gritted teeth. "You're going to give me some information about the Tiffany windows, and then we're going for a little ride."

"Sounds reasonable," Jamie peeped, standing on his tiptoes. "I can live with that."

"That's the only way you *will* live," the stranger snarled.

Gradually, the man relaxed the stranglehold on Jamie's neck, and he was able to breathe a little easier. At the same time, Lt. Higgins' words ran through Jamie's mind—there are some bad players involved in this window deal. Stay out of it. *It's too late now*, Jamie thought.

"All right, here's what we're gonna do," the deep voice instructed. "I'm going to let go of you, but I'm warning you, I have weapons, and I know how to use them—quite proficiently, as a matter of fact—so don't be stupid. Walk over to the couch and sit down," the man said. The authority in his frigid voice sent chills up Jamie's spine.

When the man loosened his grip, Jamie rubbed his neck, walked to the couch, and plopped down. His first glimpse of his captor surprised him.

The man sitting in the worn-out La-Z-Boy opposite Jamie was powerfully built and exuded a threatening, dangerous vibe. He had dark hair streaked with gray, and his blue eyes were like cold, hard steel. He wore black jeans and a black sweatshirt. Despite his casual dress, Jamie sensed this man was used to being in charge. Obviously, he meant business. Whatever he was after, Jamie was sure he was capable of getting it by whatever means necessary.

Jamie swallowed hard, fear clenching his gut. He must be one of the bad players that Lt. Higgins warned him about. Was this the same man who had overpowered and drugged Geoff? He thought about the ramifications of this confrontation. After several uncomfortable moments of silence in which the man studied Jamie as a coyote might study a rabbit, Jamie crossed his arms over his chest, gave the glowering man a cool stare, and spoke.

"What are you going to—"

"Shut up! I'm asking the questions, not you," he instructed loudly. At that moment, Jamie noticed the revolver the man held in his right hand. The little O of the barrel was pointed at Jamie's midsection, and it focused his attention in a way that was hard to explain. Jamie squirmed uncomfortably, squeezed his eyes shut, and clenched his fists into tight balls. *How could you be so stupid?* he chided himself.

"Tell me what you know about the location of the Tiffany windows," the dark-haired man said gruffly, "and don't leave anything out." He leaned forward and stared at Jamie with hard eyes. The man did not lower the pistol; he kept it aimed at Jamie's stomach.

Jamie took a deep breath and began to tell the stranger everything he knew about the Bradfords, emphasizing that his ideas were only theoretical at this point—nothing was hard and fast and sure yet. The man listened and seemed to relax somewhat as Jamie rolled out his hypothesis about the robbery of the iconic windows. Granted, some information was real. The Bradford family did exist, a William Bradford had been employed in a high position within the Ellison household, and his grandson still lived in Ontario, Wisconsin. Old man Bradford was fired from his position based on the suspicion that he'd stolen the windows off the train and hidden them somewhere. Beyond that, everything turned to mush. No one had hard and fast proof that the original Bradford had anything to do with the disappearance of the famous windows. If someone could prove that, then Jamie's theory would become less tentative and enter the world of possibility.

"So you don't know for certain that old man Bradford actually carried out the heist of the windows and then hid them somewhere around here?" the man asked, flashing the gun in an arching movement toward the living room window. "Is that right?"

Jamie grimaced at the wave of the gun and shook his head. "No. I just discovered Bradford's possible connection to the robbery a couple of days ago, and I haven't really had time to investigate it thoroughly. Whoever took the windows is still in the shadows, but I think that Bradford is as good an assumption as any. Of course, it could be someone totally different." Jamie sighed in frustration, and a look of despondency darkened his face. "To be honest, no one knows for sure who took the windows or where they are."

His captor had been listening without interrupting. Now he became animated. Tucking the gun in a holster hidden under his sweatshirt, he leaned forward, placed his elbows on his knees, and clasped his hands together. "We're going over to Ontario, and we're going to find this Willie Bradford," he said.

"There's no guarantee he'll know anything about the windows. You realize that, don't you?" Jamie asked.

The dark-haired stranger nodded. Despite his skepticism about Jamie's theory, he was impressed by the plucky spirit of the young archaeologist. Even in the face of threatening circumstances with a gun pointed at him, Jamie was calm and thoughtful, rational and confident. This impressed the dark-haired man, and he was not the sort who was easily impressed.

The man leaned back in the chair and studied the kid's soft curly hair, his innocent hazel eyes that burned with intelligence, and his confident demeanor. Despite all that, the intruder had found him to be an easy target—gullible, oblivious to his immediate surroundings—an abysmal failure when it came to reconnaissance and self-defense.

"I have one question," Jamie said curtly, interrupting the man's analytic thoughts.

"Yeah? What's that?"

"Who are you?"

The dark-haired man chuckled. "Let's just say I'm a businessman who has an interest in historical artifacts, especially Tiffany windows."

Jamie lifted his chin and looked down his nose at the stranger. "We might get along better if you'd tell me your name. After all, you know mine," Jamie said reasonably. "If we're going to be working together, it'd be nice to be on a first-name basis. That's how I handle all the people who help me in my excavation work and at my dig sites. I develop a working relationship with them. Names help."

The man waited a long moment, and a slight smile creased his face. Then he answered. "Charlie. You can call me Charlie."

THURSDAY, MAY 24

29

Jim sighed as he drove to the law enforcement center along the Great River Road. He was tired this morning, and he yawned widely, his eyes bleary from exhaustion. He'd slept fitfully, awakened in the middle of the night by his concern and worry for Jamie Alberg's safety and his wild, crazy window theory. *How was this all going to end?*

He'd tossed and turned in bed until Carol finally asked him what was wrong.

They'd talked for a while in the dark as Jim laid out his theories, suspicions, and concerns. Eventually the talking relaxed him, and Carol snuggled up to him, throwing her arm casually across his chest. He fell fast asleep only to be awakened by the buzzing of his alarm clock a couple of hours later.

In addition to the rough night, Lillie and Henri came into their bedroom early in the morning arguing about Lillie's visit to the principal's office. Lillie adamantly defended her use of bad language and blamed Henri for getting her in trouble. Irritated by the interruption and the tone in Lillie's voice, Jim had hollered at them unnecessarily, hurting everyone's feelings, making him feel like a genuine heel. He apologized at the breakfast table before he left for work.

"It's okay, Daddy," Lillie answered, her face soft with emotion. "I forgive you. I know you're worried about lots of stuff, and it didn't help when I got in trouble at school." She carefully watched Jim's reaction to her statement.

"We've already discussed that. You know what we expect," Jim said. "No more cursing."

He thought about his daughter's skill set; she'd make a great interrogator someday. Her blue eyes radiated an odd confidence for a nine-year-old. Henri listened to the conversation at the breakfast table, remaining quiet, but his big brown eyes shifted between Jim and Lillie during their conversation.

Carol watched her son and thought, *He's soakin' it all in. That's our little boy. Silent but deep.*

After a few moments, Lillie tilted her head and asked, "Is someone in trouble?"

Goose bumps prickled Jim's arm as he anticipated another one of Lillie's untimely predictions.

"I suppose lots of people are in trouble, but I only know a few of them. Are you thinking of someone in particular?" Jim asked, folding the *Wisconsin State Journal* together and laying it on the table. He focused his attention on his daughter.

Lillie nodded her head slowly. "Mm-hmm. It's someone who has a bunch of tools. Do you know anybody who has a bunch of tools?" Lillie looked across the kitchen table at her father. Jim met her direct gaze with the confidence that comes from dealing with a precocious child.

"Tools? You mean like hammers and stuff?" Jim asked. "Like Doc Wycowski?"

"Yeah, but most of the tools are little," Lillie explained. "Like something a dentist has. Is a dentist in trouble?" She looked off into the distance and squinted her eyes as if she were watching someone.

Jim shifted in his chair and crossed his arms. "Tell me more. Maybe I can help you," he suggested.

"I had a dream about someone who was digging in the dirt with some little tools. He was about to get in a lot of trouble."

Jim stayed outwardly calm, but his mind was racing. *Jamie. She's talking about Jamie Alberg,* he thought. "Well, I'll have to think about that, but thanks for telling me, peanut. You'd better get your things gathered up. The bus will be here soon," he finished in a calm voice. Lillie gave him a frustrated stare. He knew the day would come, maybe sooner than he'd like, when Lillie might start using her incredible gift to her own advantage, but right now, her motives seemed pure and innocent.

"I know when you're giving me the brush-off, Dad," she said sourly.

Jim flicked his hand at her in a hurry-up gesture. "The bus will be here any minute. Better get a move on, toots."

Carol looked at him over her coffee cup and raised her eyebrows after Lillie had gone into the hallway to get her backpack.

"What?" Jim asked.

"I didn't say anything," she said softly.

"You don't have to. I got the message," Jim said, his irritation revving up again.

Her brown eyes softened with sympathy for Jim's plight. When he was in the middle of a demanding case, his patience wore thin, and his normally unflappable demeanor changed to something less gracious. There was a tightness around his mouth, and that familiar squint and frown appeared on his handsome features as he thought about hunting down another criminal.

The bright yellow school bus rolled up to the end of the driveway, its flashers blinking. Lillie and Henri shoved the door open, yelled their goodbyes, and ran down the driveway, stepping onto the bus.

"Do you think there'll be any more cursing today?" Carol asked as she stood by the dining room window watching the bus pull away. She sipped her coffee as the bus disappeared around the first corner.

"Can't guarantee it, but I'm pretty sure Lillie got the message loud and clear last night," Jim responded from behind the newspaper.

"Well, if she's like most kids I know, she'll keep on swearing and just get better at hiding it from us." Carol came back to the table. She sat down and stared at the backside of the newspaper.

"Mm-hmm, you're probably right," Jim said casually, continuing his perusal of the paper, "but she can't hide from the Lord."

"Let's hope she remembers that *before* she starts her lingo," Carol said.

By nine o'clock, Jim, Paul, and Sam were in the office on the third floor of the law enforcement center, where Jim was relaying the information he'd been told by Jamie yesterday about the Bradfords of Ontario.

"William Bradford? From Ontario?" Paul repeated when Jim finished. "Never heard of him."

"Neither have I," Jim said, "but Jamie thinks this guy who lives in Ontario might know something about the windows, which I suppose is possible. After all, he is the great-grandson of William Bradford I."

"Possible, but not probable," Sam finished, looking peeved.

"Exactly." Jim shook his head in frustration. "You know how Jamie can be," he said, rolling his eyes and rubbing the back of his neck. "Always goin' on about some big idea that's mostly bullshit."

"Yeah. He's a royal pain," Sam said, confirming Jim's opinion of the daring archaeologist.

"Not so fast, guys," Paul said, injecting his opinion into the conversation. "Jamie's talent seems to gravitate at times to wild theories based on . . . well . . . based on illogical and inconclusive notions which he calls facts, but you have to admit that a lot of the time, he ends up being right. He follows his hunches."

DeDe walked into Jim's office carrying a cup of coffee. "Who you talkin' about?" she asked, laying some loose papers on Jim's desk.

"Jamie. He *thinks* he's found the man who hid the Tiffany windows," Jim told her.

DeDe shrugged. "His track record speaks for itself, sir," she commented. "You've got to admit that a lot of times he finds out stuff we don't know, which moves our investigations forward."

The men looked at DeDe but stayed silent. "You know I'm right," DeDe said, taking a sip of coffee.

"Maybe," Sam said skeptically.

"Bullshit," DeDe said with a subtle grin. "I could give you lots of examples when Jamie found out things we probably never would have discovered on our own."

"Okay, okay," Jim said impatiently. "Jamie has had his moments in the sun."

"There. Are you happy now?" Sam asked gruffly, giving DeDe a harried look.

"Leave it to a woman to actually come through with an honest appraisal," DeDe continued.

"Enough," Jim interrupted. "Let's move on." Jim gave everyone their assignments for the day, and the team left the office. Half an hour later, Emily Warehauser, Jim's secretary, delivered a pile of documents for the court case in August when his team would be giving their expert testimonies on a previous case. Jim was straightening the stack of papers to the side of his desk when his landline rang.

"This is Lt. Higgins. Can I help you?"

"Jim, it's Doc Wycowski. How are you?" a pleasant voice asked over the line.

Jim smiled widely at the sound of his voice. Doc Wycowski had been a major player in solving some nefarious criminal activities that included murder, arson, and kidnapping along the Mississippi River near the fishing towns of Stoddard and Victory last year. Doc had an interesting life story—one that included a prestigious career as a plastic surgeon and an unsolved case of identity theft. As a result, he'd ended up divorced and penniless, wandering along the Mississippi River until he'd pushed the reset button of his life. Now he made his home in the small river town of Stoddard in a simple cabin along one of the backwater sloughs.

"I'm fine, Doc. How've you been? Doin' any fishing?"

"I don't have as much time to fish as I used to, although I did catch a nice mess of pan fish yesterday morning down where the Bad Axe dumps into the Mississippi. But I've got some other news," Doc said.

"Oh, nothing bad, I hope," Jim answered.

"No, no. It's just . . . well, I decided to buy into the boat works down here in Stoddard. I was calling to see if you need a tune-up on *The Little Eddy,*" Doc said.

"That's great news," Jim said. "Congratulations. You know, I've been meaning to get the boat tuned up myself, but I've got a case I'm working on now that's stealing every spare minute I've got. Would you mind going to the Pettibone Park Marina and giving the *Eddy* a checkup? It's slip #62. The keys are in the little lantern next to the pilot house door."

"Sure, I can do that. How's the family?"

Jim thought briefly about Lillie's streak of bad language. He was sure Doc wouldn't give two hoots about that, so he filled him in on the new puppy, Latte, and the family's trip in October to Paris.

"When can you come over and have a meal with us? I'd love to hear about your new venture into the boat business," Jim said.

"You've got my cell. Just call me after you talk to Carol. I'm free most evenings," Doc said.

"You got it. Gotta go. You know how it is."

"Sure do. I'll tune up *The Little Eddy,*" Doc said, and he promptly hung up.

Jim leaned back in his office chair and thought about Doc Wycowski's life. A brilliant, technically savvy plastic surgeon, the man had survived a triple whammy—a nasty lawsuit by an unappreciative patient, an unsolved case of identity theft in which his financial assets had been wiped out, and a wife who divorced him when his money disappeared. Jim admired him for his grit and determination in rebuilding his life after being homeless for over a year. When he walked into the small river town of Stoddard, he was destitute and penniless. Jim shook his head in amazement. He wondered how he would have handled such a fall from grace.

When he thought about it, he decided he'd had plenty of his own misfortunes over the years. The death of his beautiful wife, Margie, from breast cancer, the alienation from his daughter, Sara, after she'd been abducted by a lunatic, and a brush with death when he was wounded in a gravel quarry in Vernon County. He was still fightin' the good fight, and for this he was thankful. Sometimes when the smoke cleared, he couldn't believe he was still standing. Of course, his faith had sustained him, but he couldn't discount Carol and his children, who were all factors in his continued positive outlook on life. And then there was the team—a bunch of strapping, feisty young cops who refused to quit in the face of insurmountable odds. He shook his head at the sheer wonder of it all. The mercy and grace of God was an awesome thing.

His phone rang. *Nothing like the blip of technology to interrupt a moment of gratitude,* he thought.

"Higgins."

"Dad? It's Sara," a soft voice said on the other end.

"Hey, how are you, sweetheart? I haven't heard from you lately." Jim leaned forward over his desk.

"I was wondering if you'd have time for a sandwich at noon. Rudy's Drive-in? I could meet you there."

"I'd love it. 12:30?"

"I can be there by twelve. I have an American Lit class at 1:10."

"I'll be there, honey."

"See you then," and Sara hung up.

When Sara disconnected, all Jim's angst about his relationship with his older daughter came back to him in full living color—her abduction by a degenerate named Maddog Pierce, her disappearance for almost four days in the rugged bluff country of La Crosse County, her dramatic rescue at a gravel quarry in Vernon County where Jim was injured, and the emotional baggage Sara carried with her that had never really gone away. The more Jim thought about it, the sadder he got.

As a policeman, Jim understood the important role he played in society, the enforcement of the law and the protection of the citizens in his charge. Hunting down criminals was his job, but it was the after effects of criminal activity that haunted him—the murder victim's family who grieved every day for their loved one who would never come home, the loss of innocence and the trampling of trust for those who suffered from the debilitating effects of violent crime, the relentless bleeding of criminal activity into the fabric of society. The wounds of the victims, both seen and unseen, haunted Jim at times, threatened to upend his determination to continue the fight for justice and righteousness. However, he also knew, according to the 2023 FBI statistics, that the murder rate had decreased by 13 percent, and violent crime was steadily trending downward despite the average citizen's perception that crime was running rampant. Part of that belief, Jim believed, was due to the unrestrained blitz of the twenty-four-hour news cycle via television and the internet. Jim chuckled to himself. *News can be hazardous to your health,* he thought, *and it doesn't give the public the best perception of the work police do.*

But on the brighter side, Sara was married now. Jerome Knight, her husband and a former Catholic priest, seemed to be a rock of stability and grace when Sara felt waves of fear and uncertainty toss her around. Jim was thankful for Jerome. After his daughter's abduction, he agonized over whether she would ever be able to lead a normal life. Thankfully, she had moved on and seemed happy in her marriage and teaching position at Logan High School. But with this latest phone call, he wondered if everything was as copacetic as it appeared. Was she really doing well, or was it all just a big front that was meant to alleviate his concern about the aftereffects of violent crime? He'd have to wait and see what his daughter told him at lunch. He'd just begun to get back to the paperwork on his desk when Emily appeared in the doorway. Jim sat up straight, shaking off the momentary daydream he'd indulged in.

"Lt. Higgins? Sorry to interrupt," Emily said.

"Yes, Emily. Did you need something?" he asked, pushing his reading glasses on top of his head.

"No, but Trisha Fanella is on the line."

"Who?"

"The director of that art museum over on the south side—you know, the old Fleischstad meat plant they're converting?"

Jim nodded his head. "Right. Got it." He leaned over and picked up his landline. "Miss Fanella, what can I help you with?"

"Hello, Lt. Higgins. I was waiting to hear from you. How did the meeting go with Geoff and the chief of police?"

"I'm not in the habit of sharing investigation information with just anyone. What did you want to know exactly?" Jim said curtly, wondering why she cared.

"Well, it's just that I'm good friends with Geoff, and I know he's quite worried about this Lewis character running around town looking for him. Have you located him yet?"

"No, we haven't. Do you know where he is?" Jim asked.

"Why would I know where he is?" Trisha stammered.

"I don't know, but I thought maybe you were calling to tell us something we don't know yet."

"You mean like a tip or something?"

"You could put it that way," Jim said. There was a lull in the conversation, and Jim patiently waited it out.

"No, I don't know anything about the whereabouts of this Lewis character. Will Geoff be okay? I mean—this Lewis guy sounds kinda dangerous," Trisha said.

"He seems determined to find the lost Tiffany windows, which could lead to lots of questionable situations," Jim replied. "I'm guessing Geoff's safety wasn't high on his priority list since he knocked him out and left him sprawled out on his kitchen floor."

"How could somebody do something like that?" Trisha sputtered with indignation.

"Believe me, Ms. Fanella, criminals do things that are a lot worse than that. Geoff was fortunate he wasn't seriously hurt." Anxious to wrap up this conversation, Jim asked, "Is there anything else you want to tell me?"

"Not really, but I do remember this Lewis guy explaining that the windows were for his boss. I don't know who that is, but . . ."

"We'll look into that. Thanks for the call. I appreciate your concern for your friend," Jim said. "Take care."

"Yes, I will."

Jim hung up and leaned back in his chair. Was it possible Lewis was acting on his boss' behalf—this Charlie Tewalt character? Jim doubted it, since Lewis had been fired without a satisfactory explanation from Tewalt. Could Mr. Tewalt already be in the area looking for a way to horn in on the iconic treasures? Jim groaned to himself and shook his head. *That's all we need is another bad player,* he thought. He leaned forward, picked up his phone, and dialed Leslie.

"Hello, this is the Birksteins," Leslie answered.

"Leslie, it's Higgins."

"Yes, Chief. What do you need?"

"I just got a call from Trisha Fanella. She mentioned Lewis Borden's boss as another possible interested party in the Tiffany windows. What do you know about that?" Jim asked.

"Well, my conversations with Tewalt were pretty ambiguous. He denied all involvement with Lewis' possible criminal activities, although we both know that's a bald-faced lie," Leslie said with a disgusted tone. "Believe me, he's smooth—and slimy."

"Okay, that was my take on it, too. Anything from Gorgeous Glassworks yet?"

"Yes. In fact, I just got off the phone with Benton. The only thing he's dug up so far was an old railroad schedule. He's studying it to see if he can tie it in with the work order for the Ellison windows," Leslie said.

"Tie it in how?"

"Well, we've been trying to figure out how the windows were taken off the train. If we can find the railroad company in charge of shipping the windows to Winona, we might be able to figure out where they were taken off the train and . . ." Leslie's voice softened.

"And what?" Jim asked brusquely.

"And . . . well, to be honest, I don't know. I haven't gotten any further with that theory, sir."

"Right. Keep at it. Something will break, I hope."

"Will do." Jim heard crying in the background.

"Gotta go," Leslie said. "Karina needs a bottle and a nap."

"Right. Talk to you later," and Jim hung up.

⊠

Jim sat in the parking lot at Rudy's Drive-in on La Crosse Street waiting for his daughter, Sara Knight. Rudy's was an iconic establishment in the city of La Crosse, a classic root beer stand with a dine-in restaurant and an outdoor awning where people pulled up and ordered their food from the convenience of their vehicle. The place was filling up for the noon specials. The wait staff, clad in Rudy's T-shirts and jeans, wore roller blades on their feet, and were zipping here and there among the parked cars taking and delivering orders. Jim found a spot under the awning, and a few minutes later a girl rolled up to Jim's window.

"Can I take your order, sir?" she asked politely.

"Actually, I'm waiting for someone. When she gets here, we'll order," Jim explained.

"No problem. Just push the green button on the post, and someone will come over," she said.

Jim smiled and nodded. After waiting a few moments, he saw Sara approaching. She opened the passenger door of the Suburban and slid onto the seat. Leaning over, she brushed Jim's cheek with a quick kiss.

"Have you ordered? I'm starving," she said.

"Nope. Waitin' for you, honey. The regular?"

"Yep, two hot dogs with onions, mustard, and ketchup, an order of onion rings, and a large root beer."

Jim leaned over and punched the green button on the post. When the waitress came over, he placed their orders, then turned and looked at Sara. She had classic Scandinavian features: long, blonde hair, striking blue eyes, and fair, beautiful skin.

"How's everything?" Jim asked, tentatively.

"Busy. School stuff keeps me up late. Who knew teaching American Lit. would involve so much prep?"

"I can only imagine. But you love to read, so you enjoy it, right?" Jim asked.

"Yeah, I do, and I have to say the kids are growing on me. They can be little shysters sometimes, but that's the way it is with all kids, right?" She looked out the window at the traffic passing on La Crosse Street.

"Everyone has their issues," Jim responded. It grew quiet as they waited for their lunch to arrive. "So, how are Jerome and Bobby?" Jim asked, filling in the uncomfortable silence.

Jerome, Sara's husband, had left the Catholic priesthood to marry her. It had caused quite a stir among the local parish in Genoa. Jim and Carol's initial reaction was one of shock and then delight. Jerome was a principled man who loved Sara and seemed delighted to be her husband. As for Bobby Rude, Jim had befriended him during an investigation in which Bobby had provided crucial eyewitness testimony that helped identify the killer of two people at a funeral home on La Crosse's south side. Bobby had been Sara's student at the time, and after he'd been orphaned by a complicated set of circumstances, Jerome and Sara had taken the teenager into their home, raising him as if he were their own son.

"Bobby is really blossoming, Dad. He's probably going to get on the 'A' honor roll this quarter, and it'll be fun watching him play Legion Ball this summer. You guys need to come to a few games. I'll get you a schedule."

"That'd be great. We'd love to come," Jim said. "And Jerome? How's he doin'?"

The waitress suddenly rolled up to Jim's window with a tray of food and drinks. Jim paid her and passed out the food. They enjoyed a few bites before Sara began to share.

"You know, Dad, marriage is not what I thought it'd be," Sara began.

Jim groaned inwardly, wondering what the devil Sara was going to say next. Whatever it was, it didn't sound promising.

She continued. "When we got married, I expected it to be like you and Mom—you know, supportive, both pulling in the same direction, a little lovey-dovey here and there, a few arguments about the checkbook . . . that kind of stuff."

Jim was shocked at Sara's analysis of his marriage, but then, this was a subject that Jim assumed most parents and children never talked about. It took every fiber of his being not to interrupt and revise the picture Sara had painted of his marriage to Margie. Somehow, she made it sound so *dull.*

"But Jerome is surprisingly strong. He's decisive when he needs to be and incredibly sensitive about things that are hard to talk about. I suppose that's the priestly tendencies in him. We have a lot of fun together—cooking, hiking, even cleaning the house. It's just not the same old same old that I thought was waiting for me at the end of the walk down the aisle."

Jim stayed silent for a few moments, not sure if Sara expected him to respond or not. *Just wait,* he thought. *The same old same old will come your way, too.* Finally, he said, "That's great, honey. Every couple has to find a way to make it work. I read somewhere that you have to raise your kids so they can live successfully with someone else. And I think there's a lot of truth in that." He took another bite of his hot dog and chewed thoughtfully.

"Yeah, that's a nice saying, isn't it, but what about the hard times? That's where the fabric, as a couple, can rip and tear. Right?" Sara chewed thoughtfully on an onion ring, then glanced at Jim. He wasn't sure if she was asking for advice or not, so he dipped his head and thought carefully before he answered.

"Hard times can reveal qualities about your mate that you either didn't realize were there or were there but lying dormant," Jim said. "It can be tough, but if you can get through it, it makes you stronger and closer."

"The voice of experience. Right now, Jerome and I don't see eye to eye on having kids, but maybe down the road . . ." Sara said, her voice drifting off.

Holy cow, that would make me a grandpa. Wait a few years, Jim thought. Instead, he said, "You'll figure it out. If Jerome is as sensitive as you say he is, then you'll be fine."

"Yeah, I s'pose. So how are Carol and the kids?" Sara asked.

"Lillie mentions you a lot. She misses you, and Henri . . . well, Henri is quiet. Doesn't say too much, but when he does, he makes it count."

"Sounds like a chip off the old block," Sara said. She glanced at her phone. "Aw, Jeez, Dad, look at the time. I've got fifteen minutes to get back to school. Gotta go," she said as she opened the passenger door.

Jim grabbed her arm, and she turned to look at him. Those blue eyes always got to him. "I'm fine, Dad. Really. Don't worry about me. Jerome has my back now."

Jim's eyes misted with tears. "If I could, I'd change what happened. I really would, but . . ."

"I know you would. You did what you had to do," Sara interrupted. She grasped his hand tightly and held it. "God's been good to me, Dad. Don't worry. Please. I'll see you soon—maybe at a ball game. Love you." And she was gone, skipping across the street and ducking into her car. She waved as she drove away.

Jim sat in the emptiness of the Suburban, enjoying the lingering scent of her Peony perfume. He waited for the roller-skating waitress to come and gather the tray. Then he slowly drove back to the office, thinking about the years gone by—they seemed like a mist. He knew one of these days he'd become a grandpa. His mind couldn't quite come to terms with that yet, but like everything else, he supposed he'd adjust.

When he stepped off the elevator on the third floor of the law enforcement center, Emily was having an intense conversation with someone on the phone. It was clear from the pleasure in her voice that it was a person she knew rather well. A sudden giggle threw Jim off base. When Emily twirled in her chair and came face-to-face with Jim, she reddened with embarrassment, although Jim had no idea who she was talking to.

"Lt. Higgins, I didn't expect you back so soon," she said breathlessly, her eyes wide with chagrin. Her bashfulness was uncharacteristic for someone so poised in office etiquette. "It's your brother, Dave. You can take it in your office."

Jim blinked, surprised that Emily would be having an animated conversation with his brother in California. "My brother, Dave?"

Emily nodded. "Yeah, it's Dave."

"Thanks," Jim stammered. He turned and walked down the hall, feeling confused by this whole scenario. He sat down at his desk and picked up his landline.

"Dave? What's up? Carol said you called," Jim said.

"Hi. That administrative assistant you've got there in your office is quite the conversationalist. When did she start working there?" Dave asked.

"Emily?" Jim asked stupidly.

"Yeah, Emily. How long has she been there?"

"Oh, I s'pose it's been at least ten years. She's kind of a fixture around here. Keeps the place going," Jim responded casually.

"Every company I've ever dealt with that's successful has at least one person who's worth their weight in gold. Sounds like she's that kind of professional," Dave remarked.

"We would be hard pressed to replace her, that's for sure." Jim found Dave's focus on Emily to be rather unusual, especially when his brother frequently reminded Jim of his status as a confirmed bachelor.

"Well, you know we got acquainted at Sara's wedding, and now we talk quite regularly for long periods of time," Dave informed Jim.

"You do?" Jim said, surprised. Why was he always the last to figure out these relationships? He'd have to ask Carol about this new development, but he was sure she already knew all about it.

"Yeah. In fact, I may take an extended vacation to Wisconsin in August, and Emily and I are planning on spending some time together."

"It's news to me, but don't get me wrong. She's a wonderful person," Jim commented. "What else is new in your world?"

Jim and Dave caught up on the latest trends in the Silicon Valley world, where Dave was a corporate vice president of a growing technology firm. Half an hour later, Jim hung up. *Am I really that clueless?* he thought.

That evening, after the kids were in bed, while Jim and Carol enjoyed a glass of wine on the back patio, Carol confirmed the fact that even though Jim was a great detective, his ability to see and predict romantic relationships lagged behind his other skills.

"Really, Jim? You didn't realize Emily and Dave were friends?" Carol asked as she sipped her wine, insinuating that the entire city of La Crosse was already aware of this budding romance.

Jim huffed with frustration. "Why would I know that, honey? Dave's in California, and Emily is here in Wisconsin. And just to remind you, long-distance relationships are notoriously hard to maintain. Everybody knows that."

"Well, if there's a common attraction and a few shared interests, unexpected things can happen."

"You didn't have anything to do with this whole thing, did you?" he asked, warming his hands over the crackling logs in the fire ring. Carol smiled mysteriously.

"The only thing we can take credit for is putting on a great wedding party for Sara and Jerome. If Dave and Emily enjoyed themselves at the party and a little spark happened, then so be it."

"Well, they aren't going together or anything," Jim said offhandedly. Then he noticed the sharp look Carol gave him. "Are they?"

"I don't know about the ins and outs of your brother's relationships. Those questions are for you to ask. I always assumed he would stay single. I'm sure in his capacity at the company, he's had plenty of opportunities to date interesting women, and he's still single, so . . ." Carol looked at Jim and flipped her hand upward, "Go figure."

"Right. That's just what I'm not going to do. Until something concrete happens, I'm not making any predictions," Jim said, "or announcements, and you shouldn't either."

Carol held up both hands. "My lips are sealed, honey."

30

Lewis Borden squirmed and flexed his muscles in the tight quarters of the closet in the little cabin near Coon Valley, but nothing helped. For the past several hours he had been trying to extricate himself from the tight little cabin closet where he'd been thrown like a sack of potatoes, duct tape binding his wrists and ankles. His shirt was soaked in sweat from the warmth inside the tiny space and his futile attempts to escape his bindings. His entire body ached from the punches and bruises he'd received when he'd fought and lost the battle to Charlie Tewalt. Besides his other injuries, his neck was cramped at a funny angle, and a wave of claustrophobia washed over him as he sat in the tight space of the closet like a trussed-up turkey. Gulping several deep breaths, he exhaled a desperate sigh and collapsed in defeat.

Charlie's ranger reputation was obviously well-earned. Although Lewis thought he knew his compatriot, obviously, he'd been duped by his charm and charisma and his cunning ruthlessness. Lewis moaned. The sting of betrayal hurt, and being stuffed in this tiny, dark space hadn't improved his disposition in the least.

The little cabin was situated in a coulee east of the tiny village of Coon Valley, and it was remarkably peaceful—that was the problem.

He was hoping the owner of the cabin would pop in when he didn't see Lewis fishing on the creek bank or moving around outside. Mr. Bjornstad promised him a fly fishing lesson, but foolishly, Lewis had not set a specific date or time, snubbing the man's attempts at friendliness. In fact, Lewis had been rather standoffish when the proprietor tried to schedule a lesson, claiming he needed the seclusion and quiet of the countryside to recover from the stress of his life in Chicago. Now Lewis realized he'd made a tactical error. The stress of being immobilized in this tiny closet was far greater than any stress the daily grind of Chicago life could dish out. In addition, there was very little traffic in the secluded valley. The cabin was off the gravel road several hundred feet, up a narrow, rutted two-wheel trail along the creek bed. Since he'd been attacked and restrained last night, it had been very quiet. The kind of quiet that makes you feel like you're the only living soul for miles around—a definite disadvantage now that he was in this situation.

Lewis had a lot of time in the past few hours to think about his life. Having your hands and feet bound, unable to move so much as your little pinkie, made you focus on things that really mattered. He realized he fell woefully short in accurately analyzing other people's character. Despite their disagreements over the years, he'd never felt any ill will toward Charlie Tewalt—until he'd impulsively fired Lewis a week ago. His loyal service to Charlie had been dismissed with a snap of a finger. That his boss could give him the boot without blinking an eye infuriated Lewis. However, in the quiet hours that followed his betrayal, Lewis began questioning his own ethics. Had he tolerated Charlie's shenanigans over the years because he was well-paid to cover for his numerous clandestine affairs and shady deals? Had the money blinded him to the unprincipled appetites of his boss?

Undoubtedly, Charlie's activities were a direct manifestation of the inner man—the qualities of the heart that guided everyday decisions and actions. Small thoughts led to larger certainties. If that was the case, then Charlie Tewalt's heart was the size of a shriveled pea. But suddenly, Lewis stopped. Who was he to judge other people's motives when his own were so shallow and self-serving?

The text from his former boss late yesterday afternoon had been worrisome, and it should have tipped Lewis off to the trouble he found himself in now. Apparently, Tewalt had received a call from some investigator at the La Crosse Sheriff's Department asking about his relationship with Lewis and "some valuable missing antiques."

"Get back 2 me and we'll talk," Charlie texted. "We've always been a good team."

If and when the Tiffany windows were discovered, Charlie wanted a share. Because of the text, Lewis knew the police were aware of his presence in the area. Obviously, they were still trying to discover his whereabouts.

A good team? Not on your life, thought Lewis. *You fired me, and that's the end of it.*

One thing Lewis did know: Charlie had enough information about the windows from their short discussion a few hours ago to find them. Lewis was sure his former boss would take the young archaeologist hostage and take full advantage of Alberg's expertise for solving difficult puzzles. Jamie was well known for his persistence and unremitting determination. Several articles from the *La Crosse Sentinel* touted Jamie's role in a couple of investigations at the La Crosse Sheriff's Department. Apparently, the kid had a nose for finding valuable, missing things. No one could figure out how he did it, but Charlie would hunt Jamie down and undoubtedly tap into his unique abilities to find windows that had disappeared over a hundred years ago. And if the archaeologist refused, Charlie would use his refined skills to convince Jamie to cooperate with him.

Lewis gritted his teeth in frustration, and the muscles of his jawline rippled in anger. *Everything I've worked so hard to achieve will be lost if I don't escape from this cabin and intercept Charlie before he gets to Jamie.* A couple more hours, and it would be too late. Lewis began wiggling again, kicking at the closet door, hoping someone would hear him.

31

Bubba and Kay Starch stood in the sunshine that streamed through the small-paned windows of the dilapidated chapel several hundred yards beyond the boundary of their property on Moon Ridge Road near Ontario. The pine boughs swished softly in the gentle breeze, their fragrance crisp and sharp. Overhead in the clear blue sky, a red-tailed hawk peered down on the tranquil scene searching for his next meal, his wings extended as he soared gracefully on the warm updrafts.

Inside the dusty, little sanctuary, Kay gazed at the stained-glass windows with quiet awe; they were beautiful beyond anything she could have imagined. The colors were vibrant, and when the sunshine hit the images embedded in the glass, they shimmered with beauty. The amazing artistry of the Tiffany craftsmen was evident in every incredible detail—even the individual hairs on the knight's head stood out in stark clarity. It was like looking at a 3D image that miraculously came to life, shook itself out of its reverie, and stepped into real time.

Kay had never seen anything made by Tiffany before. She'd been skeptical when Bubba had told her about the windows after Willie's funeral. "You'll know a Tiffany when you see it," he'd said. At the time, she thought that was quite a statement coming from someone who readily admitted his ignorance of art. When he'd made such a resounding declaration about the windows, Kay hadn't really believed him—until now. Now she understood in a way that was rooted in reality. Seeing *was* believing. The windows were amazing.

"What are we going to do with them?" she asked, gesturing at the iconic treasures lumped together under the tattered tarp.

"We've already talked about this, remember?" Bubba said, his voice gruff with impatience. Seeing the hurt in Kay's eyes, he tempered his brusqueness and spoke in a gentler tone. "Remember our plan? We're going to load them on a wagon and pull them to our place, pack them in the frames I built, and reload them into my pickup. As soon as I finalize the agreement with the church committee, we'll deliver them to St. George's Presbyterian Church in Milwaukee, and they'll cut us a check."

Knowing how enthusiastic Kay was about her faith, Bubba thought this was the perfect solution. The beautiful windows would grace a large church in Milwaukee, where a congregation of over five thousand parishioners could enjoy the windows during worship every week. He imagined this would please her, but he could see she was still disturbed about the whole affair.

Kay nodded, silent and somber as Bubba reviewed the plan again. She didn't know how many times they'd hashed over this plan, but she still doubted that they could sell something that wasn't really theirs. The arguments between them about the ownership of the windows had been heated and intense—something that had not characterized their relationship before. This controversy had unhinged her from the safe, small-town life she'd always enjoyed. She noticed Bubba's eyes shone with a gleam that bordered on obsession. How could some antique windows made by a famous craftsman have such a strong effect on someone as reasonable and cool-headed as Bubba?

Kay's indecision about the sale of the windows boiled down to ownership. *Who really owned them?* she thought for the umpteenth time. Originally, they had belonged to the Howard Ellison estate. Yet now, since her husband had discovered them in a deserted backwoods chapel in Ontario, Wisconsin, they seemed to belong to her, Kay Starch, William Bradford's great-great-granddaughter. Was this an instance of finders keepers, losers weepers? If so, did that make her the owner by proxy because her great grandfather possessed the windows? She remembered that old English saying dating back to the 1700s: "Possession is nine-tenths of the law."

Kay had spent considerable time over the last few days researching various laws pertaining to ownership of items and property. From her vantage point and the results of her investigation, she believed legal documents would probably be required to claim the rights to the Tiffany windows, especially if they were going to sell them. The only thing they had was the letter written by her father to Bubba. Was that enough for them to claim to be owners of something so incredibly valuable in the art world?

In addition, Kay had spent many hours researching other "lost" Tiffany windows. The conundrum of ownership was clarified somewhat by two specific cases she'd read about. A long-lost set of seven Tiffany church windows discovered in New Jersey came to auction in November 2020. The eight-foot-tall windows survived a church fire, the subsequent demolition of the church to make room for an interstate highway, and the precarious transit of the windows from cluttered garages and dusty barns to an auction house in New York City, where they'd sold for an incredible 5.3 million dollars. In another case in Chicago, some Tiffany windows also survived a church fire and a wrecking ball. They were discovered hidden in a Chicago Riverside suburban home after forty years in obscurity. The windows came to light when the owner sold them to a glass restorer for $5,000. In both instances, it seemed to Kay that the ownership of the windows was not questioned but rather was accepted without any legal documentation. She wasn't so sure about these windows Bubba had stumbled across in the old logging chapel in the middle of Wildcat Mountain.

Bubba watched a wave of emotions flutter across Kay's face. He saw doubt mingled with reverence, excitement tempered by common sense. That was his wife—as honest as the day was long and practical to a fault.

"Listen, honey," Bubba began again, trying a different tack. "I know you have misgivings about this whole situation, especially selling something you feel we really don't own. But the sooner we can unload this stuff, the better off we'll be. Hanging on to them is depriving other people of the enjoyment they could give. The windows aren't doing anybody any good lying in this old, deserted chapel." His words hung in the air, begging for further comment.

She tilted her head and stared at her husband. "You forgot to mention the financial freedom we'd enjoy from the money we'd make if we sold them," she said. Bubba was about to protest, but Kay held up both hands in front of her, stopping any comments by her husband. "I know, I know. Two and a half million dollars is a lot of money. It's just that—" She sighed dramatically and lowered her hands to her sides. It was clear to Bubba she was still plagued with uneasiness about their decision. Kay sighed with resignation. "We've already discussed this a hundred times, but sometimes, you know what? I wish you'd never found them." Her frustration was palpable, and she folded her arms across her chest. After a few minutes she continued. "At least they're going where they'll be appreciated . . . I hope," Kay tentatively concluded. Bubba nodded his head in understanding.

Determined to move on from the ownership dilemma, Bubba turned to the windows leaning against the wall, clasped the tarp in his hand, and carefully removed it from the five large windows. "I'll bet these are pretty heavy. I don't know if we'll be able to lift them or not, but we can try," he said.

Kay grabbed the frame of the first window in the pile leaning against the wall, and Bubba got on the other end. They each took a big breath and leaned in as they lifted. The windows were much heavier than they'd estimated. Glass and lead are dense, heavy materials, and they could only lift them a couple of inches off the floor. Moving them out of the chapel would be difficult, to say nothing of lifting them into a wagon and transporting them to their garage.

"They're really heavy," Kay said, letting down her end. "I can't do it." Her eyes clouded with anxiety.

"Yeah, I don't think this plan is going to work. I may have to find a couple of guys to help me get them in the wagon and move them to our place," Bubba said, frowning.

"Remember what you said. We talked about this," Kay warned him. "You said the fewer people who knew about this, the better."

"I know what I said," Bubba snapped, irritated by the reminder. "We'll have to move to plan B."

"Do you have a plan B?" Kay asked, her eyes widening.

"Just trust me. I know what I'm doing," Bubba reiterated, trying to stay calm.

Kay was not comforted by his words. She stared at him until he squirmed. He pushed his Carhartt hat back on his head and swiped his arm across his brow. Noticing his frustration, Kay finally said, "I'm trying to trust you, Bubba. I really am."

"Good, because everything is going to be just fine," he muttered. "Just fine." He adjusted his cap impatiently, pulling it down on his forehead again. Despite his positive words, he didn't seem confident about his plan. In fact, he sounded worried and scared.

Suddenly, Kay was struck with an urgency to pray. *Protect us, Lord, from evil,* she thought. Then she wondered where that thought had come from. A dark despondency settled over her as they climbed back on their UTV and headed for home. She looked back at the tiny chapel, and a shiver of dread ran up her spine. *What kind of mess have we gotten ourselves into?*

32

Leslie Birkstein sat in her red Toyota Prius on the southern end of Winona, Minnesota. The stoplight at the junction of U.S. Highways 14 and 43 changed from red to green, and in the car next to her, a young whippersnapper spewed his blaring hip-hop into the atmosphere. The sounds of the pounding drum and garbled lyrics throbbed in Leslie's ears until she grimaced in pain. When Leslie gave him a dirty look, he gave her a thumbs up, smiled placidly, and bounced his head in time to the music.

Leslie had arranged an afternoon meeting at Gorgeous Glassworks with Benton Zalinsky, the owner of the company. She drove north a few miles beyond the stoplight, turned on Palisades Street, and parked her car in the small lot next to the glass restoration company—a nondescript, tan brick building. She walked into a small reception area that had a counter, and behind it, a young gal sat at a computer. She glanced over at Leslie and asked, "Can I help you?"

Leslie explained her reason for coming, and the girl directed her through a large workroom filled with light boxes. A couple of craftsmen were hunched over them. One had a paintbrush and was touching up pieces of blue glass, and one was adjusting cut pieces of glass on a template, which would later be soldered together. The front office assistant stopped in the doorway of a large office. A man with a trim beard and dark brown hair sat behind a desk studying a template of a window. When the office girl tapped on the door, he looked up and smiled warmly at Leslie. He stood and came around the desk, extending his hand.

"Detective Birkstein. So nice to meet you. I hope I can answer your questions," he said.

"We'll see. My inquiries involve some Tiffany windows that disappeared over one hundred years ago." Mr. Zalinsky's eyebrows lifted in an expression that seemed skeptical at best.

"We've dealt with a few restoration cases over the years that had some questionable history, so you never know." He shrugged his shoulders up and down. "Have a seat and give me the details of your case. Hopefully we can come up with something that will help," he said, pointing Leslie to a chair.

Leslie grabbed her yellow notepad from her bag and clicked her ballpoint pen. She looked up and asked, "Could you explain what you mean by restoration?"

Benton smiled. "Yes, of course. Most people think the restoration of a stained-glass window means replacing glass, but that is the last thing we want to do unless it is absolutely necessary, unless the glass is shattered, chipped, or missing altogether. The true meaning of restoration in the stained-glass industry means restoring the integrity of the lead structure that supports the window, and sometimes that includes the frame that holds it in place. Any restorer worth their salt will preserve the original glass in the window at all costs. If we only restore the lead and frame, then the window can still be categorized as original or 'in original condition.' For collectors and historians, this is a vital aspect to preserving the history and integrity of the piece."

Leslie nodded. She was fascinated by the definition since she, like many others, assumed restoration would involve replacing the glass pieces. "I understand, but I'm sure most people would think of restoration more in terms of the glass rather than the lead."

"Yes, that's a common misconception. We've had restorations that involved replacing glass, of course. But to steal a medical phrase, we subscribe to the 'first, do no harm' approach." Benton explained. "This approach guides our work and ensures that the integrity of the piece can be maintained, and its value will not be diminished by the restoration."

"Makes sense," Leslie said, nodding her head. She explained her work with Dr. Rochelle Drummond, the recovery and restoration of antique works of art in the Middle East during the Iraq conflict.

"How interesting," commented Benton. "So you have a good understanding of the process needed for preservation and restoration to be complete."

"Yes, yes, I do," Leslie agreed. "But let me fill you in on a case we're working on right now that's giving us some headaches. Maybe you can give us some advice on how to proceed." Leslie began explaining the Tiffany lost window conundrum. Benton listened with rapt attention, nodding in agreement until the moment when Leslie suggested a restoration company such as theirs might actually be involved in the heist.

"Excuse my interruption," Benton said suddenly.

Leslie stopped abruptly, visibly cringing. She was afraid that her questions and suppositions might have hit a nerve. From the look on Benton's face, his crinkled frown, wide eyes, and flaring nostrils, the restorer was clearly perturbed by Leslie's probing analysis.

"There is no way that our company would have ever been involved in such a crime. My grandfather started this company, my dad built the business to include the international scene, and I am trying to follow in their footsteps. Over the years, in every restoration we've done, our integrity and pride are evident in our work—from the removal of the windows from a building to the craftsmen who work on the lead and glass to the billing department to the final delivery of a restored project. Integrity and honesty are woven into every project. They are part and parcel of all we do here." By the time Benton had finished, his face was flushed, and he was sitting forward in a rigid position, ticking off his points on his fingers.

Leslie smiled. "Please accept my apology. I did not mean to insinuate that you were involved in the heist of these particular windows. But the facts remain: Someone took those windows out of the Ellison house, loaded them on a train headed for your studio, and they disappeared. We're just trying to come up with some kind of explanation for how that might have happened."

Benton took a deep breath, and his expression softened. "I understand, but I couldn't let your assumptions go unchallenged."

"Understood," Leslie said. "Do your records go as far back as 1904? Maybe we could start there."

"Well, it would take some investigation," Benton started. "Our company began in 1902, but at that time, it was located in my grandfather's garage on the east side of town, over by Winona State University. We didn't move to this facility until 1964. Since then, we expanded and built on in 1993. I could go back into the archives and see what's there, but it might take me a few days to find the time to do it."

"Anything you can do would be helpful," Leslie said.

Benton stood up and nodded his head. "Okay, let's go with that plan then. How about I get back to you in a few days with the results of my search? Say Monday at the latest?"

"Sounds good. Thanks so much for your time. I know Lt. Higgins will appreciate it."

As Leslie drove back to La Crosse, she thought about the elusive search for the windows. In her experience, every investigation had dead ends. Sometimes what you thought would transpire never actually developed into anything remotely related to a crime. Then sometimes, something that was said—an interview, a newspaper article, a photo—could take you in a totally new direction. *Well, I've planted the seed. Whether it will amount to anything is hard to tell at this point,* she thought. *Higgins won't like the timetable, but that's not my problem.*

FRIDAY, MAY 25

33

Geoff LaSarde stood in his kitchen on Friday morning listening to the prerecorded message on Jamie Alberg's phone again. "You have reached the residence of Jamie Alberg. I am not available right now. Please leave a message." Geoff scowled. After trying to reach his friend several times since their disagreement, Geoff concluded Jamie was either out of range, busy at the excavation site, or not answering his cell for some reason. There were other possibilities that he didn't want to think about.

Geoff sighed loudly and leaned against the counter while Sir Lancelot wound himself between his legs, meowing with an irritating yowl. Geoff was familiar with Jamie's history. Several years ago, Lt. Higgins had put him under protective custody to keep him out of danger after Jamie, on a drunken spree, had been thrown into the Mississippi River by an unknown perp and presumed drowned. A few years later, another incident involving a female assassin resulted in Jamie being tied up and hidden away in a cave to rot to death.

Geoff was worried. He hadn't heard from Jamie for several days. They'd had arguments before, and usually the disagreements blew over in a day or so. It had been four days of silence, and his friend's previous record of dangerous escapades made Geoff's stomach clench with anxiety. Was Jamie in another precarious, life-and-death situation?

Sir Lancelot rubbed persistently against Geoff's leg and continued his yowling complaints. Geoff leaned down and stroked the cat's wide back.

"I know, boy. Diets suck, but that's the way it is," Geoff said softly.

Sir Lancelot gazed at his owner, his yellow eyes shifting to his empty food dish. Geoff walked to the cupboard, opened a can of cat food, and emptied it into the dish. Sir Lancelot hungrily lapped up the juicy meat scraps. *Do cats really appreciate their owners?* Geoff wondered. *Highly doubtful.*

Geoff swallowed hard and stared into space while he contemplated the kind of trouble his friend could be in. As he stood in his kitchen, he recalled his conversation with Trisha Fanella on Tuesday morning and his chat with Lt. Higgins later that night. He'd come to the conclusion that the same person who had attacked him had returned and ambushed Jamie. Geoff shuddered when he thought about the tactics that might be used to extract the possible location of the windows from his friend. If that was the case, then things were heating up, and as a result, Jamie was probably in some kind of serious trouble.

Geoff glanced at the clock. It was a little after seven, early but not too early. He plucked his cell from his jeans and punched in Lt. Higgins' number.

"Lieutenant Higgins."

"Lieutenant, it's Geoff LaSarde. Have you talked to Jamie recently?"

"No. In fact, DeDe Deverioux tried to contact him several times yesterday but couldn't reach him," Jim explained.

"Well, I've been trying to call him, too, but he doesn't answer," Geoff said.

"Is he out of town on some archaeology work?"

"He's been working over in Lansing at Fish Farm Mounds."

"Maybe he's over there. Listen, I understand your concerns. He has a habit of getting himself into the thick of things. There's not much I can do about it, other than warn him off, which usually doesn't work too well," Jim said.

"Do you know about his theory?" Geoff asked.

"Yes, something about the Bradford family from Ontario," Jim remarked.

"He has this theory that William Bradford I, the manager of the Ellison household in Oshkosh in 1904, was the one who whisked the Tiffany windows into hiding," Geoff began to explain. "I tend to agree with him since my research seems to point in that direction, too, although I can't verify that it's accurate. He told me Monday night that Bradford's grandson currently lives in Ontario, and he was going over there to talk to him. That's the last conversation I had with him."

"He called me and told me about that, too. I can have one of my team check into that and see what comes of it. In the meantime, I would caution you to be careful. This person who took you out of commission is still in the area. He's dangerous. We're aware of his presence, but until he does something to draw attention to himself and reveal his whereabouts, we don't have time to go looking for him, so stay in contact with friends and with our department if you have further concerns. Understood?"

"Yes, sir. I understand. Thanks," Geoff said.

When the conversation ended, Geoff debated his next move. He went to the bedroom, took his pepper spray out of the dresser drawer, and stuffed it in his pocket. He gave Sir Lancelot a final affectionate pat and walked to the garage. Backing his car out, he turned onto the street, preoccupied with dark thoughts about Jamie's safety.

Driving down West Avenue, Geoff turned left on Jackson Street and drove up out of the valley on Highway 33 toward St. Joseph's Ridge. The countryside opened up before him. The burgeoning greenery of the trees and pastures relaxed him, and he settled back in his seat, enjoying the bucolic scenery. Barns and fields whizzed by the window, but his thoughts were fixated on his destination. He'd never been to Ontario, Wisconsin. From the tiny pinpoint on the map, he knew it was small. Despite its size, he had the feeling the little village was about to be thrust into the limelight.

34

Things had been chaotic on Friday morning at Jim's home on Chipmunk Coulee Road. After Jim's conversation with Geoff, he dressed and headed to the kitchen for his morning coffee. Perusing the newspaper, Jim heard an argument in the hallway leading to the bedrooms. Within minutes, the argument between Henri and Carol had moved into the dining room, where Jim became the judge and jury, much to his chagrin. The kerfuffle all began when Henri refused to wear the button-down shirt Carol laid out for him, opting instead for a new fishing T-shirt Jim had bought him a few days ago at a bait shop in Stoddard. Henri's resistance set off a flurry of rationalizations from Carol about the school dress code at St. Ignatius, which did not impress the little tyke in the least. He refused to budge on his choice of shirt, so in the end, Jim weighed in on the side of Henri, giving his approval of the fishing shirt.

Carol stood in front of Jim's newspaper, her hands on her hips, her brown eyes flashing. "Well, if I get a call from Sister Mary about a violation of the dress code, you won't be here to defend me, will you?" Carol said, irritated by Henri's obstinacy and Jim's casual approval.

Henri looked at Carol with a brown-eyed gaze and a quivering lower lip. His arms were crossed defiantly over his little chest, and tears glistened in his eyes as he listened to the exchange between Carol and Jim.

"I fail to see what is offensive about a fishing T-shirt," Jim said caustically from behind the *Wisconsin State Journal*. "After all, God made fish and put them on this earth for food and enjoyment. Tell that to Sister Mary if she calls."

"Are we parenting from behind the newspaper now?" Carol complained loudly. She reached over and used her index finger to lower the newspaper a few inches. "Jim, I need your support . . . and your participation."

Jim sighed loudly and laid his paper on the table. "Let's compromise. Henri gets to wear the

T-shirt, and you can forward Sister Mary's call to my cell, if and when she actually calls," Jim said, losing patience with this talk of dress codes. "Just remember, I'm experienced with situations like this. After all, I never know what Sam is going to wear to the office. The dress code usually goes up in smoke when he walks in with his undercover drug-dealing getups. I've had to go to bat for him more than once when Turnmile got feisty."

"Okay, I'll consider it a done deal then," Carol said. Turning to Henri, she handed him the T-shirt. He let out a whoop of joy and ran down the hallway to his bedroom to finish dressing.

While the T-shirt discussion raged in the dining room, Lillie pounded away on the baby grand in the living room. Jim heard strains of Shostakovich, Bach, and Mozart waft through the house along with scales and exercises Sister Gertrude had assigned to her. Lillie's piano expertise and performance had improved by leaps and bounds since they had changed teachers. Carol kept Jim up-to-date on her progress. Although his musical expertise was somewhat limited, he could plainly hear her growing finesse on the keyboard improve from month to month. He credited her progress to her daily hour-long practices, which frequently extended beyond the recommended time.

"She's getting pretty good, don't you think?" Jim asked, sipping his second cup of coffee.

"Sister Gertrude says with practice and work, she could become a very accomplished pianist. In fact, she recently told me we may have to enroll her with a different teacher—someone who comes highly recommended from the Twin Cities—a Madame Stroud at the University of Minnesota," Carol answered from the kitchen. "According to Sister Gertrude, her teaching credentials are very impressive."

"The Twin Cities? Madame who? Good heavens, who's going to drive Lillie up there?" Jim asked.

"That would most likely be me, but it would only be once a month," Carol informed him.

"Well, I'm no music expert, but she sounds great to me," Jim said. "By the way, have you talked to John lately? He's left a couple of messages, but I've been so busy I haven't had a chance to connect with him yet. All we end up doing is playing phone tag."

Carol filled Jim in on his older son's activities as she packed the children's lunches and tidied up the kitchen before she headed to work. "They've been looking at a house in the Holmen area, I guess. He really wants to find a day to go fishing in Timber Coulee. You have to call him soon, Jim." Carol gave Jim a wistful glance. "He loves being with you so much, you know."

Jim rolled his eyes toward the ceiling and made a *tsking* sound. "Don't make me feel more guilty than I already am, hon. I promise I'll connect with him tonight." Jim entered a reminder into his phone. Taking a few final gulps of coffee, he carried his cup to the kitchen sink and gave Carol a kiss.

Traveling along Chipmunk Coulee Road to Highway 35, Jim turned on the Great River Road and headed north to La Crosse. The river sparkled with light in the early morning sunshine. A couple of huge tows were working their way north, and a lone jogger huffed along the shoulder of the busy highway. When Jim got to the outskirts of the city, the chaos from summer road construction began and lasted through the heart of the downtown district. The beeping of large machinery, the roar of engines, the piles of gravel and debris, and men scurrying around in blaze orange vests would be a familiar sight for the next several months as three roundabouts were being built. City traffic was congested but manageable, even with the detours around the construction. Jim pulled into the law enforcement center parking lot at eight-thirty.

When he stepped off the elevator on the third floor, Emily was concentrating on her duties. Jim watched as her fingers flew over the keyboard, amazed at her dexterity. How anyone could type and talk at the same time was a phenomenon Jim had not solved yet. Her typing skills alone sent shivers down his spine, to say nothing of her filing and organizational prowess, which left him speechless.

Jim focused his attention on his secretary. After all, she was the reason this place operated with some semblance of professionalism. Sometimes he felt like saluting when he stood in front of her desk, but he knew Emily would be offended by such a gesture. He had to admit, though, that without her at the helm, his bureaucratic duties would be impossible to manage. Obviously, she loved her job, and making his day run as smoothly as possible was always her top priority. He'd heard horror stories from others in the building about their secretarial help, so he silently ticked off his blessings in his head. *She's just one of those exceptionally efficient secretaries,* he thought. *Don't hold it against her.*

"Mornin' Jim," she said simply.

"Good morning, Emily," he said, returning her greeting.

"How's everything?" Emily chirped. Her auburn hair was impeccably styled, and her clothing fit her like a glove, the obvious result of her dedication to regular workouts and a yoga regimen.

"It's going better now," Jim replied laconically, thinking about the muddled argument this morning with Henri.

"Sheriff Turnmile sent some paperwork related to the August court case," Emily began, handing Jim a thick manila folder. "Also, Leslie called. She wants to talk to you as soon as possible. Sam is going to be a little late. He's dropping his Jeep off for service and will walk to the office from the dealer over on Third Street. I haven't heard from Paul, but I assume he'll be here at his regular time."

Professionalism oozed from Emily's pores as Jim watched her tick off items from her mental checklist. *Wow!* he thought. *She could run a major corporation, but here she is dedicating herself to a bunch of detectives who fly by the seat of their pants, hoping things turn out the way they're supposed to.*

"Lt. Higgins?" Emily asked. "Did you get that?"

"Huh? Get what?" Jim replied.

"You're scheduled for a haircut at Great Clips tonight after work—four-thirty."

"Oh, right. Thanks for the reminder," Jim said hurriedly.

"Carol just called and told me you might forget. Something about Henri's shirt?" Emily asked, a frown creasing her forehead.

"Oh, yeah. Just another kink in the morning routine," he said, grinning. "Leave it to a five-year-old to throw a wrench in the works."

Emily returned his smile. "I wouldn't know about that, but there's fresh coffee in the pot, sir. Help yourself."

After getting a cup of coffee, Jim walked down the hall to his office. When he opened the door, the smell of stagnant air hit him. He walked over and cracked open the window. The fresh air revived him as he sat at his desk, returning phone calls and working through a stack of papers on his desk he'd been avoiding. He began organizing the June training session for the team after finding the flyer in his stack of papers. He stared at the title of the seminar: Six Myths of Police Training that Inhibit Effective Learning.

"Oh, brother," he exclaimed. "Just what everyone is going to want to hear about." He chucked the paper aside in disgust and picked up the phone, dialing Leslie.

"Leslie, have you been to Winona yet?" he asked brusquely.

"Yep. I went yesterday. The owner of Gorgeous Glassworks, Benton Zalinsky, will look through his archives to see if he has anything about the 1904 Ellison windows. He got offended when I asked if his company might have been involved in the disappearance of the stolen windows."

Jim grimaced. "Oh, I'm sure that didn't go well."

"Not to worry, Chief. I smoothed it over. He'll get back to us by Monday with any information he might have."

"Well, don't put their possible involvement out of your mind. We've been surprised before by the characters who are involved in criminal activity. By the way, how's working from home? Do you like it?" he asked.

"Like it? Well, let's just say this: I knew there would be some adjustments, but right now, I'd say the positives are outweighing the negatives."

"Good. So you're happy then?" Jim asked.

"I wouldn't go that far, but as a parent, I feel I'm doing what I need to do for Karina."

"I understand," Jim commented, but he stopped there, knowing the conversation could devolve into a lot of personal issues he didn't have time for right now. "I'll talk to you again in a few days. Take care."

His phone rang again.

"Lt. Higgins."

"Jim, it's Tanya. Hey, I hear Paul and Sam found Kevin Chroniger dead in his van the other day. Is that right?"

"Yeah. They'd been looking for him for a while around town. Some homeless guy suggested Goose Island Park, and they found him there. They got a huge load of drugs out of his van, too. I guess it was one of the biggest busts in La Crosse County," Jim explained as he shuffled papers.

"So I heard. That's forward progress. What's the deal on the missing suitcase from the break-in on the north side?"

"Things are percolating, I guess. Nobody can get a hold of Jamie Alberg. He seems to have disappeared. That's got me worried, but it's a typical move for Jamie. Who knows where that will lead."

"One of these days, he's gonna get killed. You know that, don't you?" Tanya said.

"He's a slow learner. I'm hoping that won't happen, but if his history with this department is any indication, then the probability gets higher every time he gets involved in one of our cases."

"I hear you. Hey, I gotta go. Keep me informed on the suitcase deal. Let me know if I can help."

Jim hung up. He appreciated Police Chief Tanya Pedretti's concerns. She refused to participate in the territorial turf wars between the city and county law enforcement agencies, and Jim valued her support.

He worked steadily on his pile of papers until lunch. He walked down the hall and gathered up his team, suggesting they go to Lindy's for subs. They piled into Jim's Suburban and headed downtown to the sub shop. The smell of baking bread wafted into the street, and Jim's stomach growled. They ordered subs and found a table along a wall. As they ate, the conversation turned to Geoff LaSarde.

"You think LaSarde is on the up-and-up, Chief?" Sam asked, tipping his head.

"Whaddya mean?" Jim asked, puzzled by his statement.

"Well, maybe he's pullin' our chain. Maybe he does know where the windows are, and he's leading us away from the area so he can find them and sell them himself," Sam said. "It'd be a feather in his cap as a Tiffany expert to offer 'lost' windows for sale. His reputation in the art world would soar through the roof."

Jim thought a moment, then made a disgruntled face. "Nah, I doubt it. Doesn't explain his encounter with Lewis Borden. He certainly didn't fake the drug-induced sleep on his kitchen floor. That would be pretty hard to do," Jim explained. "When I checked with the ER doctor, he shared the results of his blood test—he was injected with benzos. My sense of the whole thing is that LaSarde was rattled by the attack, but being a Tiffany expert, he can't leave the whole affair alone and let us figure it out. So what he's planning next is . . . well . . . who knows? It's up for grabs."

"And Jamie's next moves are certainly another unknown factor," DeDe said sourly. "That kid is so unpredictable."

Paul spoke up. "That's the only thing we can bank on—Jamie's penchant for sticking his nose where it doesn't belong. If anyone can stir the pot, it's Jamie."

Jim nodded. This whole conversation was depressing. *Leave it to Jamie to lead us to places unknown where we'll probably get in a bind with a bunch of thugs,* he thought. *But sometimes he's better at finding criminals than we are.*

The team finished their subs and drove back to the office. Jim reserved the lecture hall downstairs for the dates of the training session. He called the presenter from the International Law Enforcement Educators Association and chatted with the man for fifteen minutes. Then he turned his attention to more paperwork, but his brain was working in the background, mulling over the possibilities of Jamie's absence. *Wait 'til I get a hold of him,* he thought.

He was surprised when he looked up from his desk work and discovered it was already four o'clock. He shut down his laptop, made an attempt to straighten his desk, and left the building. Walking to his Suburban across the law enforcement center parking lot, he noticed the rain had stopped, but it was still cloudy and cool. Standing by his vehicle, he scrolled through his phone and found the weather forecast from a local TV station for the weekend—cool but sunny. Jim glanced up at the sandstone bluffs in the distance and thought that if the weather held, it would be a good opportunity to take the boat out on the river for a cruise. Then he frowned. He wondered if Doc had checked over the boat engine yet. He never took his boat out on the river for the first run of the season without some necessary, yearly maintenance. He was about to get in the truck and head for home when his cell buzzed.

"Lt. Higgins," he said brusquely.

"Lt. Higgins," a voice hissed. "Are you busy?"

Jim could hear some rustling noises. He frowned. Was this some crank call about some incident the police had handled within the city limits? Or a complaint about one of his detectives? Nowadays, it seemed like the police were either the heroes or the heels, depending on the political persuasion of the caller. Jim groaned inwardly. He was in no mood for a heated, political digression that ended in an exchange of hostile, angry barbs. If that's what this was, he would refer the caller to Turnmile. After all, that's what she was paid to do, even though her skills with the public were dismally inadequate.

"This is Lt. Higgins. Who is this?"

"It's Jamie. I'm being held against my—"

Jim heard some more scuffling noises and then silence. "Jamie? Where are you? Jamie?" Jim realized the phone connection had gone dead. He rubbed his hand over his eyes, then stared at the phone. Mumbling to himself, he tipped his face toward the sky and said, "I knew this was gonna happen. I just knew it."

"Chief? Who are you talkin' to?" Paul asked as he walked up to Jim. When Higgins tipped his head to the heavens as if he were praying, Paul knew things were in a downward spiral. *More trouble is brewing,* he thought. *Probably with Jamie.*

"Well, who do you suppose that was?" Jim asked, his blue eyes flashing with frustration, the anger in his voice unmistakable. "I'll give you one guess, and the first one doesn't count."

"Oh, boy. It's not Jamie, is it?" Paul asked, his eyes widening with concern.

"You got it," Jim rasped. He took a huge cleansing breath. "I can't believe the gall of that kid. From what I was able to make out, it appears he's been abducted, and someone is holding him against his will . . . somewhere." Jim shook his head at the mess Jamie had managed to get into, even after he'd warned the young upstart several times to steer clear of the Tiffany window controversy. "Well, we're gonna need a plan. It looks like we're going on another wild goose chase to who knows where."

"Maybe Ontario?" Paul asked.

"Could be. That makes the most sense since it was the last place he mentioned when he talked to Geoff LaSarde. Fortunately for us, the town is small. Shouldn't be that hard to find him," Jim said sourly as he headed back into the law enforcement building. He stopped suddenly, and Paul practically ran into him. "That kid is gonna drive me nuts!" he finished vehemently through clenched teeth.

Paul backed up a few steps and held up his hands. "Sorry, Chief, but I had nothing to do with this."

Jim's shoulders sagged. "I know that, but you can bet if Jamie's involved, it's gonna be a rough ride."

35

The sun was setting against the backdrop of hardwood trees behind the Higginses' home on Chipmunk Coulee Road. Carol had had an extended conversation with Jim earlier, and now she broke the news to Henri that his daddy would not be home until late.

"You'll already be in bed before Daddy gets home tonight," Carol said.

"But he promised he'd help me build my boat tonight!" Henri whined, tears spilling onto his cheeks. "We were gonna float it down the creek tomorrow!" He stomped his foot vigorously on the hardwood floor and stared up at Carol. "Where is he? Why can't he come home?" Henri asked.

Carol knelt down and took Henri in her arms, delivering a much-needed hug. "I'm sorry, Henri, but you know that when Daddy is called out, he has to go. That's part of being a policeman," she said, stroking his curly brown hair.

Henry's brown eyes flashed with anger. "Well then, I'm never gonna be a policeman," he sputtered emphatically as he folded his little arms across his chest.

Lillie stood to the side and watched the dramatic exchange between Carol and Henri. "Hey, Henri. Maybe I could help you with your boat," Lillie suggested diplomatically. "What kind of boat do you want to build?"

Henri stared at his sister and considered his options. He seemed to be weighing whether he should wait for his dad to appear or allow his boat plan to be hijacked by his domineering sister.

"We were going to make a stick raft to float in the creek," Henri mumbled skeptically, "with a flag like Huck Finn." He looked up at Lillie beneath hooded eyes.

"Well, I could help you gather up some sticks from the backyard," Lillie said. "That way, when Daddy gets home, you'll have everything ready, and he can help you put it together."

Henri's eyes brightened, and for the first time since the crisis began, a smile crept across his cherubic face.

"Yeah! That's a great idea. Let's go!" he yelled, running across the living room and out onto the limestone patio with Lillie following closely behind.

Carol plopped down in the swoopy black chair, letting out a sigh of relief. Sometimes, despite Lillie's increasing independence and dominating personality, she could be considerate and kind to her little brother. *We must be doing something right,* she thought. She glanced out of the window at the two kids tramping through the high grass beyond the tall trees toward the creek in search of twigs to build a toy raft. Latte, the golden retriever, hovered near his two charges, his protective instincts on high alert.

Carol leaned back in the chair, nestled her body into the cushions, and closed her eyes. Although Jim wouldn't be home until later, she refused to worry. He hadn't told her any details about the situation that had changed his arrival time at home, so she tried to ban anxious, unproductive images from her mind. It was useless to try to predict the sticky situations her husband could get into or the nefarious characters he might have to deal with. *I just hope he doesn't get shot,* she thought bitterly. Then she reconsidered. *I have to remember he has a good team who are loyal and capable of returning fire power with fire power if need be. I'll have to let the chips fall where they may.* She did worry, though, but she held out hope for a good outcome—one in which Jim would return home in one piece. Her lips moved silently as she presented her petitions to the Lord. *Prayer is the best thing I can do for Jim.*

36

Sheriff Elaine Turnmile swiveled in her office chair and picked up her desk phone. She quickly dialed and waited for an answer.

"Jim Higgins."

"Higgins, where are you?" the cantankerous sheriff blurted.

"On my way to Ontario," Jim said.

"Canada?"

"No, no. Ontario, Wisconsin. Traveling down Highway 131 as we speak, about two miles out of town. What can I help you with, Sheriff?" Jim asked politely, although he was gritting his teeth at the sound of his boss' guttural voice. He rolled his eyes and drove on.

"911 received a call from someone named Jamie. You know him?" Turnmile asked.

"Yes, I do. What was the gist of the call?" Jim asked.

"Claimed he was being held against his will, but the call was interrupted, and the line went dead. What do you know about that?"

"I don't know anything about that, but I received a call, too, very similar to that one. In my last conversation with Jamie, he was determined to track down those lost Tiffany windows, which he believed were hidden somewhere in the Ontario vicinity. Considering the terrain in the Wildcat Mountain area, that may be more of a challenge than he realizes," Jim said. There was a significant pause.

"Wildcat Mountain? Are you pulling my leg?" Turnmile said in a challenging tone. "I didn't know there were any mountains around here, Higgins."

"Well, that may be something of a misnomer, but the people of Ontario take great pride in the hills located here. I suppose someone who's never seen a mountain range might think the hills in the Driftless Area classify as mountains, but for people from the western United States who really know mountains, the Wildcat area would be considered ant hills."

"The mountain thing is beside the point," she said rudely, shifting back to her original concern. "So why are you headed to Ontario, and who's with you?" Jim could almost imagine her scowling expression. *Is there anyone as grumpy and disagreeable as my boss?* He didn't think so.

At that moment, his thoughts turned to his deceased friend, the former sheriff, Davy Jones, as they often did when he had to deal with the uncivil temerity of Elaine Turnmile. He recalled Jones' friendly demeanor; he could almost see his pleasant, smiling face. Jim missed that smile. He had admired the former sheriff's absolute commitment to the safety of La Crosse area residents. Furthermore, Jones understood the importance of humor and kindness in the day-to-day interactions with his officers—all things Turnmile couldn't seem to wrap her little head around. *God help us all,* Jim thought. *When is she ever going to get it?*

"Actually, ma'am, Paul is with me. We're just coming into Ontario now." Jim glanced at the population sign for the little town as they drove down the main street: Ontario, Population: 554. "We're going to look up a guy named Willie Bradford who lives here," Jim explained.

"Who's he?" Turnmile snarled.

"Well, supposedly—"

"Suppositions don't really come into it, do they, Higgins? I thought we had a conversation about that recently, remember?" Turnmile rudely interrupted. "The attack cat?"

Jim could almost picture a sarcastic grin curling the corners of Elaine's pink, glossy lips.

Jim was a patient man, a man of grace and respectability, but his patience with the cranky sheriff was running very thin. He swallowed hard and gritted his teeth until his jaw hurt. He wondered about the wisdom of continuing to be a gentleman. He dove back into the conversation with an attitude just short of insubordination. "If you'd let me finish, I could explain the situation. But that would require you to listen. Can you do that? Could you just listen for once?" he snapped.

Paul gave Jim a wide-eyed stare when he heard the caustic retort. *Boy, Higgins is goin' out on a limb,* he thought. *Playin' it dangerous with that attitude.*

The line went dreadfully quiet. "Ma'am, are you there?" Jim asked brusquely, hoping they'd been disconnected. Silence ensued for several seconds.

"Yes, I'm here, Higgins," Turnmile said with frosty arrogance. "Explain away. I'm all ears."

Jim proceeded to explain the lost windows situation again, the suspicion that the Bradford family was involved in their disappearance, and how Jamie had gotten tangled up in the whole affair.

"So when Geoff LaSarde discovered this Bradford name in his papers from the suitcase," Jim said, "Jamie did his own research and discovered a grandson, Willie Bradford III, who lives down here in Ontario. The problem is that when Jamie gets something in his head, he's hard to dissuade. And he has an incredible knack for getting himself in tight jams that frequently escalate into life-threatening situations. Believe me, I've dealt with this kid before," Jim said. Paul nodded his head in agreement.

By the time Jim explained the whole affair to Turnmile, Paul had eased the truck into a parking place on Main Street in front of a hardware store. He shut off the engine and waited for Jim to finish his conversation.

"What's your plan now?" Turnmile asked Jim.

Suddenly, Paul lightly touched Jim's sleeve and pointed to a man crossing the street. Jim watched as Geoff LaSarde strolled down the sidewalk toward their vehicle.

"Sorry, ma'am, but something's come up. Gotta go. I'll call you back later," Jim said hurriedly. He disconnected, slipped his phone into his trousers, and climbed out of Paul's Ford pickup.

"Geoff, my man," Jim said as he stepped onto the sidewalk blocking Geoff's path. Paul joined him and stood next to him. Together, they formed a human fence. "Fancy meeting you here in Ontario." Geoff stopped about five feet in front of Jim and Paul, stuffed his hands in the pockets of his jeans, and stared at the two detectives as if they were aliens who'd just stepped off a spaceship.

"I didn't expect someone as eloquent as you to be at a loss for words," Jim said.

Geoff stared at him, his mouth slack-jawed with wonder at seeing the detectives in Ontario.

Jim continued. "It's a small world, son. So what is there to do in Ontario besides fishing and canoeing? Something must have brought you here." Jim waited, but getting nothing from Geoff but a distant stare, he went on. "How about a sandwich and a cup of coffee at the River's End Cafe down the street?" he suggested, pointing to the restaurant with his thumb. "We haven't had dinner yet, and I have a feeling it's going to be a long night. You can help pass the time by getting us up to speed on this window situation." Jim lifted his eyebrows and then scowled at Geoff, who remained silent. "Cooperating with the police would be your best choice right now, Geoff. Let's go," he said gruffly, pointing across the street to the cafe.

Geoff's shoulders dropped, and he turned and accompanied Jim and Paul across the street.

The little eating establishment was a storefront affair, a building with faded siding and a covered porch with a screen door that slammed loudly whenever anyone entered. Above the porch, an illuminated sign swung gently in the soft breeze. Inside, the decor was decidedly outdoorsy—wainscoting on the lower half of the walls and fishing gear, hunting paraphernalia, and a collection of old gas signs were all displayed on the upper half, everything arranged between three six-pane windows, which ran the length of the building facing Main Street. Several patrons were ordering food, while others were patiently waiting for their orders to arrive. The smell of frying fish and spicy, barbecued ribs permeated the air, making Jim's stomach rumble with hunger.

The three men meandered to a booth with windows facing the street and waited for a server to come to their table. While they waited, they perused the menu. Geoff was very quiet, but his knee jiggled up and down with nervousness. Jim didn't push him. Instead, the senior detective took a few moments to observe the pace of life in Ontario through the window.

A shaggy dog lazily trotted across the street. An impatient driver in a yellow Humvee with a kayak strapped on top honked at the dog, swerving to miss it. Hunched with arthritis, an older lady wheeled a shopping cart out of the IGA grocery store, stopping briefly to frown at the rude driving antics of the Humvee driver, then loaded her groceries into a small, rattle-trap pickup, and putted down the road. Along the restaurant side of the street, a teenage boy was headed somewhere on his bike, his baseball glove dangling from the handlebars.

Jim, being a country dweller, sometimes forgot all the daily interactions that happened in a small town like Ontario. Surely someone in this community must know something about the Bradfords, and possibly, about some lost Tiffany windows that might be hidden somewhere in the area. There were plenty of hiding places: caves, abandoned buildings, barns, or somebody's garage or basement. The list went on.

A tiny server came to their table. Her hair was pulled back in a ponytail, and she wore a white, ruffled apron over a black T-shirt and jeans. Jim wondered if she even weighed a hundred pounds.

"Hiya, guys," she said with a friendly smile. "What can I get ya?"

As the men dictated their selections, the young girl wrote down the orders and collected the menus. She came with fresh coffee, and Jim and Paul slowly sipped their hot drinks while Jim studied Geoff across the table. What did the art expert know at this point? Had he been in contact with Jamie? Was this visit to Ontario some kind of plan to throw the detectives off their game so Geoff and Jamie could recover the windows and sell them before anyone became the wiser? Jim knew Jamie presented himself as an innocent bystander only to swoop in at the right moment and subvert the police to gain the upper hand, claiming the credit for himself. While Jim pondered these questions in his mind, Geoff avoided making eye contact with the senior detective.

"So, Geoff," Jim finally said, breaking the uncomfortable silence that had been building like storm clouds in the sky. "Tell us what you've found out about the Bradfords."

Geoff's worried expression relaxed somewhat as he began to talk, but a frown still crinkled his forehead. "I think Jamie discovered the link to the missing windows, namely the Bradford family. I'm pretty sure they're involved somehow in the windows' disappearance, although that's still uncertain. That's Jamie's theory, but it makes sense to me on the surface. Sometime in the last twenty-four hours, someone must have come to his house with the intention of getting information out of him, and now he's disappeared. Could've been the guy who attacked me, but the upshot is Jamie has vanished, and no one knows where he is—although Ontario makes the most sense to me. He told me he was going to come here to investigate. That's why I'm here. I tried to reach him, but I didn't have any luck." Geoff sighed loudly and leaned his elbows on the table, crossing his arms. "He can be so frustrating. How well do you know Jamie, lieutenant?"

Geoff asked with a sour expression.

"Oh, I know him very well," Jim said, keeping his response low-key. "When he gets involved in police matters, things tend to go off the cliff."

Geoff nodded. "Well, I'll give him credit. After doing my own investigation, I agree with him that the windows must have been taken off the train by old man Bradford, and he squirreled them away somewhere in these hills—maybe a cave or something. But where he hid them is anyone's guess."

Paul nodded in agreement. "It's a big, wild area. If the windows are hidden here, they may never be found. So where is this Bradford guy? Have you talked to him?" Paul asked.

Geoff was about to expound on the topic when the server came with a large tray of food and set entrees in front of each man. She then brought salt, pepper, and ketchup to the table. After a few bites of food, the conversation resumed.

"When I got here today about noon," Geoff began, "I went to Willie Bradford's home, but there was no answer there, so I went down to the Wildcat Bar & Grill for a cup of coffee, thinking I'd go back later to see if he was home. That's when I picked up the local Ontario newspaper and saw Willie Bradford's obituary."

Jim's head snapped up, and he met Geoff's gaze. "What? He's dead?" Jim said, holding a french fry midair.

"Usually that's the basic premise of an obituary, sir," Geoff said. The sarcastic tone underlying the comment was not lost on Jim.

Paul made a wry face and let out a sigh. "Why am I not surprised?" he said in a defeated tone. "We finally figure out who might have been involved, and the main dude with all the information tips over."

Jim stared at Geoff. "Well, that kinda wipes out the opportunity to question him, doesn't it?"

Geoff moved his index finger back and forth like a metronome. "Mmm, not necessarily. The obituary listed a daughter, Kay Starch, who lives out of town on Moon Ridge Road. She may know something about the family legacy, or she could be totally innocent in the whole scheme," Geoff said dejectedly. "I thought it'd be worthwhile to find her and talk to her. That was going to be my next move."

"Makes sense," Jim said, nodding his head.

Paul leaned over to Jim. "I think you'd better call Sam and get him down here with the drone—and maybe bring Paco. That dog might come in handy if we have to chase somebody through the woods," he suggested, "or locate a hiding place back in these hills somewhere."

"First, let's see if we can connect with this Kay," Jim said. "If that's a dead end, then we'll canvas the town and try another plan."

"You got one?" Paul asked, looking sideways at Jim.

"A plan?" Jim shook his head. "No, not really. Playing it by ear at this point," he said casually, although he wondered what kind of situation they'd find themselves in over the next few hours. He wasn't up for an all-night vigil deep in the woods with unknown assailants who were most likely armed to the teeth and ready to fight it out for the stolen windows. He thought again of Lewis Borden. He was pretty sure that Borden had taken Jamie hostage and that right now, they were somewhere in the Ontario area biding their time, watching and waiting for an opportunity to locate the windows.

As he finished his meal, Jim recalled Lillie's dream about the ramshackle shed with the beautiful windows. At this point in the investigation, Lillie's dream was a complete wild card, which Jim refused to share with Paul and Geoff. He and Carol had doubted Lillie on occasion and paid a high price for their skepticism, but Jim was pretty sure that a nine-year-old's prognostication about the location of windows that had been missing for over one hundred years would not be met with an ounce of belief by anyone involved in the case. After all, Lillie had no evidence to prove her point; all she had was a feeling and a memorable dream. That wouldn't be enough to convince experienced detectives or erudite art dealers to take advice from a little kid about the hiding place of some famous windows. Furthermore, there were some things Jim would not do, partly because he believed it would muddy the investigative waters and be judged unethical, but also because he wanted to protect his daughter and her incredible gift. And then there was Sheriff Turnmile. He could imagine what her response would be to Lillie's premonition—outright total disbelief accompanied by a strong helping of sarcasm and ridicule.

They were finishing their meal when Jim glanced out the window and noticed a black Chevy pickup truck cruising slowly down Main Street. Jim glanced at the driver, and although he had only seen photos of Lewis Borden from the art gallery at the meeting with Police Chief Pedretti, he recognized his profile immediately. Jim was fortunate that way; he had a memory for faces, even someone he'd only seen once. He leaned forward and watched the truck proceed to the stop sign, then turn left.

Jim grabbed the check from the table, fumbled in his wallet, and flagged down the server. He pressed a hundred-dollar bill in her hand and said, "Keep the change." Then he turned to Geoff and Paul and spoke rapidly, "Come on, guys. Lewis Borden just drove down the street. We don't want to lose him."

Jim ran to the door while the other two men scrambled out of the booth. They trotted rapidly across the street and hopped into Paul's truck. Jim pointed to the stop sign and said, "Hang a left at the intersection. He's driving a black Chevy pickup."

"Are you sure it was him?" Geoff asked, leaning over the seat, his eyes wide with amazement.

"Not one hundred percent, but his profile looked very familiar. Besides, we're not getting anywhere in this investigation, so following this guy can't hurt," Jim said. "Go ahead, Paul."

Paul pulled out of the parking spot on Main Street. When he got to the stop sign, he turned left. Farther down the street, the black pickup braked for a pedestrian who ambled slowly across the street in the direction of the Hoot Owl Bar. The delay gave Paul just enough time to get in position to follow Borden.

Eventually, the black pickup drove south of town until it came to Highway ZZ. The truck turned onto the road. The men drove through the hilly, bluff country where the Kickapoo River wound its way through the valley. Craggy bluffs jutted out next to the road in several places, and despite the tense situation they found themselves in, the setting was beautiful and peaceful. Paul followed the truck and crossed several bridges over the lazy, crooked river. They skirted the north edge of Wildcat Mountain State Park for several miles. About ten minutes later, they came to the junction of ZZ and F. The pickup turned right on F, heading straight east toward Mount Tabor. Paul held back, driving slower than necessary to prevent the truck from noticing him, although most likely, the driver was already suspicious.

When the black pickup came to Moon Ridge Road, the driver turned and picked up speed. Paul accelerated, trying to keep up with him. Jim worried about the speed increase—the roads were curvy and narrow.

"Slow down," Jim cautioned. "He's heading for Starches most likely. I don't think we'll lose him."

They met a couple of cars, but they were few and far between. Rounding a sharp corner, they came to an open valley. A long driveway with a fire number next to it led to an attractive, sprawling log home on several acres. The home was surrounded by lush green lawn and overflowing perennial flower beds, which were just beginning to bloom. Adjacent to the home was a double-car garage and shop, also of log construction. In the distance, the thick hardwood forest rose up from the valley floor and surrounded the open field.

The black pickup turned into the driveway. "Drive past," Jim ordered Paul, motioning down the road. "Park in that lane next to the pasture below the garage." Paul drove his pickup onto a short, gravel driveway a slight distance from the house.

"Yeah, this should work," Jim said, looking around. Their truck was tucked behind the workshop out of view from the house. Anyone who might look out of the house toward the driveway wouldn't see it. While Paul parked, Jim mentally made a plan in his mind. From here on out, it was all a crap shoot, but retreat was not an option.

Jim jumped out of the passenger door, walked behind the truck, and opened the tailgate. He pulled a black tote toward him and opened it. By this time, Paul had joined him, and the two men rifled through the contents of the tote, retrieved their department-issued weapons and Kevlar vests, and strapped them on.

Geoff watched the procedure uncomfortably, his eyes widening at the sight of their guns and equipment. Suddenly, he realized his small bottle of pepper spray was woefully inadequate for the situation they found themselves in. He almost laughed at the ludicrous nature of the moment, but things were too serious to be joking around.

"You aren't going to shoot somebody, are you?" Geoff asked, still staring at Jim's and Paul's weapons. In the quiet that followed his question, he suddenly became aware of the surroundings in crisp detail: the humming of the electrical line overhead, the smell of freshly mown grass, and the chirp of crickets in the nearby undergrowth next to the road.

Jim stopped what he was doing and looked at Geoff. "In these situations, you have to prepare for every contingency," he lectured, meeting the art expert's nervous stare. "I'm recommending that you stay here at the vehicle and wait for us to return. If that's not something you're willing to do, then I must tell you you're taking a serious risk. The people who are involved in this situation are determined. They've already made several questionable choices, including disabling you in your own home and probably abducting Jamie for the information he has. A civilian is not going to stop them from accomplishing their goals. Do you understand what I'm saying?" Jim asked brusquely, snapping his gun in his holster.

Higgins' blue eyes glittered with determination, and Geoff shrank back at this new revelation of Higgins' personality and considered his options. He noticed Paul standing directly behind Higgins, looking over the senior detective's shoulder, his face hard and immovable like granite.

"I understand the risks," Geoff said. "But I also have a vested interest in this whole affair. My friend, Jamie, is in danger. Hell, he might even be dead by now. I can't very well walk away from a friend, can I?" Geoff asked, his impatience flaring.

"Are you telling us or asking us?" Jim asked bluntly.

Geoff squared his shoulders. "I'm telling you. I'm in, and I understand the risks."

Jim slammed the tailgate of the truck. "All right. Here's the plan, loose as it is." In the next few minutes, as the men walked up the shoulder of the road, Jim outlined his plan: approach the house, assess the situation, and make a move on the man in the black pickup.

"Whaddya mean—make a move?" Geoff asked. "Do you even know who this guy is?"

"Like I said earlier, I'm fairly confident the man is Lewis Borden. I recognized him when he drove by the diner from the photos that your friend Trisha took at the art gallery. He followed you here, and he's probably been watching you most of the day. He got tired of waiting for you to lead him to the windows, or he might have recognized Paul and me and decided to strike out on his own and make something happen. Apparently, he knows where Kay lives, and he's come to find out what she knows about the windows. We're going to have to stop him before he hurts someone," Jim said rapidly. "Any other questions? Because time is ticking by, gentlemen." Jim glanced at Geoff and Paul.

"I'm with you, Chief," Paul said. "Let's go."

37

Leslie Birkstein was having a conversation on the phone with her former boss and friend, Sheila Walsh, a prominent officer in the Department of Homeland Security, specifically the Immigration and Customs Enforcement division in Chicago, known to law enforcement as ICE. Leslie had been employed at the department briefly for several months before her return to the La Crosse Sheriff's Department a couple of years ago.

"You wanted more information on a Charlie Tewalt of Tewalt Technologies, and believe me, Lez, this guy has been busy," Sheila said with a sarcastic tone. "It took me several phone calls to my contacts to catch up on all of his suspected illegal activities in the area."

"Okay, let's hear it," Leslie said. She bounced Karina on her shoulder as she held the phone to her ear.

"He's been fairly successful in his small computer component business—seems to have a good business head on his shoulders, but after that, things go south. He's been involved in some sketchy loan shark activities and illegal gambling, and his clandestine affairs with the ladies about town are well known to those who monitor and enforce human trafficking. He's in the process of building an extravagant, multi-million-dollar mansion over by Lake Michigan. When I talked to the general contractor in charge of the project, he revealed that Tewalt has been on the lookout for genuine Tiffany windows for the library of his new home, and he won't take no for an answer. He's determined to locate them. Apparently, he found out about the lost windows from the Ellison mansion in Oshkosh, probably through his personal assistant, Lewis Borden, who went in search of them. That's how this whole deal got dumped on your turf." Sheila stopped for a moment.

"So where is Charlie now?" Leslie asked.

"Well, from the information I've been able to gather, he's off on a business trip to Wisconsin," Sheila explained, "but mark my words, he's in your neck of the woods because he's involved in the hunt for the windows. He's probably in your area as we speak. He's a rough player, Lez. You need to warn Higgins to be careful. How much did you say these windows were worth?"

"Two to three million on today's market," Leslie said. "Maybe more depending on who's interested and how much they're willing to pay."

Sheila whistled softly under her breath. "Given Charlie's history of shady deals and questionable activities in the underworld of Chicago crime, I'd say he's taken matters into his own hands. You'd better contact Higgins and let him know the playing field got a little more crowded—and a lot more dangerous."

"Right. Thanks a million, Sheila. I owe you," Leslie said.

"Just catch Charlie Tewalt red-handed and throw his sorry ass in jail. That's enough of a reward for me," Sheila commented caustically. "Considering all his other criminal activities, he'll be there for a substantial amount of time." Then, in a softer tone, she said, "Hey, call sometime so we can catch up on life—and that new baby girl."

"You got it," Leslie commented. She hung up and speed dialed Higgins. She heard panting and extraneous sounds in the background when Higgins answered.

"Chief. I've got some information you need to know about the Tiffany window thing," Leslie said, cutting to the chase.

"Go ahead, Lez," Jim said, huffing.

"Where are you?" Leslie asked. "What are you doing?"

"Joggin' up a county road near Wildcat Mountain to Kay Starch's home, where we followed Lewis Borden."

"Be careful. I just found out from Sheila Walsh that Charlie Tewalt is probably in the vicinity looking for the Tiffany windows, too. He's a dangerous character, Chief. His reputation follows him, and believe me, it's not good."

"That complicates things here, but we can handle it. Gotta go. Thanks for the heads up." And the line went dead.

As it turned out, Jim, Paul, and Geoff were standing about a hundred feet from the Starch residence when the call came through from Leslie. The men stopped briefly under the shade of a massive pine next to the open cattle pasture and discussed the new information while they assessed their plan.

"That was Leslie," Jim said. "Apparently, Charlie Tewalt is in the area somewhere."

"Who's that?" Paul asked.

"That's the guy who owns Tewalt Technologies in Chicago," Jim said, "He's the guy that Lewis Borden used to work for."

"That's going to complicate things even more," Paul said.

Jim made eye contact with Paul. "When we get to the home, you hang back while I approach the front door. Be ready to assist if things go bad." Jim pointed at Geoff. "You can still go back to the truck. It's not too late to bow out." Geoff hesitated. Jim could see the man was conflicted. "Look, Geoff, I'm going to make a decision here. This new information complicates things. You head back to the truck. Once we've assessed the situation, I'll call you and give you instructions. I can't risk having a civilian involved in a possible violent confrontation."

Geoff jerked his shoulders back, challenging Higgins approach. "You mean you're going to go in guns blazing? What about Jamie?"

"Generally speaking, blazing guns is not our style," Jim said firmly. "That sounds like something from some TV show you've watched. And don't worry about Jamie—we'll deal with him. You go back to the truck and wait for my call."

Geoff resigned himself to the dynamics of the changing situation, pivoted slowly, and began trudging back to the pickup.

"Good call, Chief," Paul said. "The guy is a total greenhorn. He'd probably get us all shot, but I think we're going to need reinforcements. What about DeDe and Sam?"

Jim whipped out his phone and dialed Sam. When he answered, Jim began barking instructions.

"I need you and DeDe down here in Ontario ASAP," he said. "We'll meet you at the canoe rental place on the edge of town. Bring Paco. We may need his tracking abilities." Jim filled Sam in on the news of the surviving Bradford daughter. "We're standing under a pine tree about a quarter mile from the Starch home on Moon Ridge Road. We followed Lewis Borden here, but we're not sure of his intentions. To complicate matters, your wife called, and she seems to think Charlie Tewalt is also in the area. This is a powder keg waiting to explode. Paul and I are going in. Geoff LaSarde is in my pickup about a hundred feet beyond the Starches' driveway on Moon Ridge Road. He'll wait there for instructions. You need to get here as fast as possible. Once we've contacted the Starches, I'll call you. Keep your phone on. Gotta go." Jim clicked off.

Sam hung up the phone and leaned over to start his Jeep Grand Cherokee. As he drove toward his home on Warner's Bluff above Genoa, he dialed DeDe.

"Hey. I know you think you just got off duty, but forget that," Sam started. He explained the situation to her and arranged to meet at the vacant Kmart parking lot on the corner of Jackson and State Road 33 at seven o'clock. "I'll be there as soon as I run home and pick up Paco," he said.

"Paco?" DeDe asked. "He's coming along, too? Why do we need him?"

"Higgins thinks we might need him to do some tracking. Wear practical clothes. Bring a sweatshirt, your vest, and your gun. We'll probably be out all night. See you at seven."

Sam accelerated, driving rapidly along Highway 35, weaving in and out of slower traffic. He could have used his mobile siren and lights but decided to risk the drive without them, praying some newbie traffic cop along the river road wouldn't stop him for speeding. He tore up his steep driveway below Warner's Bluff, left the Jeep running, and jogged into the house.

"Lez! You here?" he hollered.

"In the studio," she hollered back.

Sam walked quickly into the studio and stood in front of Leslie. She noticed his tense demeanor.

"What's up?" she asked.

"Where's Paco?" he asked tersely.

"I let him out back. He's around here somewhere." Leslie rolled her chair away from the large painting she was working on and reached down to pick up Karina. Sam leaned over, gave his baby daughter a brief kiss, then turned and jogged through the house to the back door of the kitchen.

"Paco! Here boy! Paco!" Sam yelled into the backyard then whistled loudly.

In a moment, the energetic black lab appeared, careening through the brush underneath the overhanging bluff in the backyard. He ran up to Sam, his exuberance evident in his wagging tail and loud barks.

"Grab his leash, Lez," Sam instructed. He clipped the leash on the spirited canine, turned to Leslie, and explained.

"I'm headed to Ontario with DeDe. It sounds like a chaotic situation. Jamie's missing, Borden and Tewalt are in the area somewhere—that's just a guess. But it's all coming to a head. Higgins thinks we might need Paco's nose. Gotta go!"

Leslie reached down and patted Paco's head. "Be a good boy," she said. Then she grabbed Sam's arm and kissed him. "Good luck."

"Luck has nothing to do with it, honey, as you well know. Don't know when I'll be back. Keep your cell on. I'll call you," he said as he jogged to his Jeep, dragging Paco with him.

38

While Sam careened at reckless speeds over curving, winding roads and gunned the Jeep up and down the hills of the Driftless Area to Ontario early Friday evening, Jim and Paul were standing on the Starches' doorstep. They discussed a couple of strategies, but in the end, Jim decided that ringing the doorbell would be the most effective way of moving the situation along.

Jim pushed the button and knocked loudly on the front wooden door. They waited beneath the covered front entrance to the log home. The black pickup they'd followed earlier sat next to the workshop. Eventually, a solid, well-built man with a trim mustache and dark brown eyes opened the door. He was wearing a flannel shirt and worn blue jeans. He stared at the two detectives standing on the doorstep.

Jim displayed his ID and introduced himself. "I'm Lt. Jim Higgins from the La Crosse Sheriff's Department, and this is Detective Paul Saner. We'd like to talk to you about the Tiffany windows."

Jim knew he was taking a risk, albeit an informed one, that this man knew about the controversial windows. He thought of something his father had taught him many years ago: "You have to go out on a limb because that's where the fruit is." At the time his father had said it, Jim thought it was just another quaint Norwegian proverb that was unapplicable to any situation in life. He harrumphed and shook his head. He was sure his dad had no idea how priceless that saying had become to him, how he often recited it when he was called to action in a tense situation. *We're about to go out on a limb, Dad,* he thought ruefully.

At this point in the investigation, Kay Starch's knowledge about the windows was a pretty good assumption. Over time, the situation had come to a head, and now a decision would have to be made. Jim wasn't sure what would happen next, but this wild goose chase with its suppositions and innuendos had gone on long enough.

The man stared at Jim, and then sighed as if a terrible load was resting on his shoulders. "Well, you're a little too late, but come in anyway. We have company," the man said. He turned and walked through the foyer into the comfortable home. Jim and Paul followed him.

The foyer opened into an impressive great room with a ceiling of exposed, hand-hewn log rafters. The room was furnished with a couple of leather couches situated in an L shape, and two recliners sat opposite the couch. Seated on one end of the couch was a petite lady, and across from her sat a man Jim recognized as Lewis Borden. Jim thought the brown-eyed man was probably Kay's husband, who introduced himself as he sat down beside her.

"I'm Bubba Starch, and this is my wife, Kay. And this guy," he pointed to the man in the recliner across from them, "is Lewis Borden."

Jim studied the cast of characters sitting before him. How many times in his career had he been in the presence of people who had succumbed to temptation, which led to questionable moral decisions that were not easily resolved or reversed—situations that put others in danger and threatened to explode into violence? Jim sensed that everyone here had compromised a portion of their integrity in a frantic search for the elusive antique windows, and now things had reached a crisis point. There was a mood of somber tension in the room. The two detectives stood side by side, facing the three people on the couch.

"We've been aware of Mr. Borden's presence in the area since the break-in at Geoff LaSarde's home on the north side of La Crosse. What are your intentions now, Mr. Borden?" Jim asked, fixing him with a firm gaze. His blue eyes had a striking intensity as he stared at Borden. "Have you been holding these two people against their will?"

"No, I haven't," Lewis snarled. "On the contrary, I think these two," he waved his hand at Kay and Bubba, "have been hiding their involvement with the Tiffany windows for a long time. I just happened to learn about them from a friend of mine—"

"Charlie Tewalt?" Jim interrupted. Lewis kept a straight face, but Jim noticed a slight tick near his eye that was beating as if it had a pulse of its own. Jim continued. "Charlie's in the area right now and has probably taken Jamie Alberg hostage. We intend to find them, and you're going to tell us what you know."

"I told you this was gonna happen, Bubba," Kay interrupted. She gave her husband a cross glance, then focused her attention on Jim. "We admit that we know about the windows—"

"Kay, we talked about this—" Bubba whispered hoarsely.

Kay held her hand up in a stop gesture. "I'm done talking, Bubba. This is going to be resolved right now. People are in danger, and someone is going to get hurt."

"Finally, a voice of reason in this whole uproar. Thank you for your honesty, Mrs. Starch," Jim commented laconically. "Go on. Tell us what's been happening around here."

While the two detectives stood in front of the expansive windows that faced south, Kay began to reveal the problems that had confronted them over the last few days.

"It all started when my father died suddenly a week ago," she began, "and we discovered a family legacy we knew nothing about." Her voice wobbled with emotion, but she cleared her throat and went on with her story. "Bubba received a letter from our family lawyer on the day of my dad's funeral. In the letter, my dad explained what he knew about the window mystery. Apparently, my great-grandfather was suspected of stealing five very valuable Tiffany windows from his employer in Oshkosh—a Mr. Howard Ellison—after a terrible house fire gutted his home. In the letter, my dad expressed skepticism that this legacy could actually be true. But prior to my dad's death, Bubba, through no fault of his own, discovered an old chapel beyond our property, which probably dates from the days when the logging camp used to operate in the area." Kay waved her hand in the direction of the large window. "He went into it out of curiosity. Inside, he uncovered the Tiffany windows. They must have been sitting there for over a hundred years." She stopped briefly, glancing at her husband. "I still can't believe our family is involved in this kinda . . . *stuff.*"

Jim closed his eyes briefly, thinking about Lillie's dream—an old, run-down building with beautiful windows. *How does she do that?* he thought. A chill ran up his arms as he marveled at her amazing gift.

Bubba rubbed his eyes with his hands, then let them slide down his face until they dropped in his lap. He continued to tell the story. "Finding the windows was a total fluke. I was clearing a logging trail that went beyond our property when I discovered the old chapel. I went into it out of curiosity, and I found the windows stacked in the corner under an old, rotten tarp. As far as I know, the windows are still there. They seem to be intact, although they're covered in dust and grime. We tried to move them, but they were too heavy, and we couldn't do it."

"When did you discover the windows?" Paul asked.

Bubba and Kay looked at each other. "It was the morning my dad died," Kay said, "so it must have been last Wednesday . . . and since then, it's been nothing but a colossal headache."

"I believe it," Jim said tersely. "Let's just hope no one gets hurt before we get this whole thing resolved. It's going to take some coordination."

"Don't you mean cooperation?" Bubba asked, tilting his head.

Jim nodded. "That, too."

During the conversation between the Starches and the detectives, Lewis Borden had been strangely quiet. He sat ramrod straight in the recliner, his silence complete. Jim found his reticence revealing. Was the guy totally taken aback that the police discovered the characters and the plot surrounding the infamous windows? Probably. Most criminals Jim dealt with in his job had a very low opinion of police officers, believing they were clumsy and stupid at their jobs. *Too bad for them,* Jim thought. *That's a serious miscalculation on their part.*

Jim had watched Lewis as the story of the windows unfolded. The question at the forefront of Jim's mind now was whether Lewis was prepared to cooperate, because Jim had DNA evidence of the assault on Geoff in his home on May 15. Obviously, Lewis' reconnaissance and search for the owners of the windows had been somewhat successful, but now the jig was up, and he would be arrested for his attack on LaSarde and the break-in and subsequent robbery he'd carried out in Geoff's home.

"What's next, Lt. Higgins?" asked Kay.

Jim looked at Borden and indicated with his hand that he should stand up. Lewis shot him a look of resignation. He stood slowly. Jim walked over to him, frisked him, and confiscated a Ruger pistol strapped to the inside of his leg. Then he gently turned Borden around and placed handcuffs on him.

"Mr. Borden, I'm arresting you for the assault on Geoff LaSarde and the robbery you carried out at his home in La Crosse on May 15. You will be taken to the La Crosse County jail as soon as we can transport you there," Jim informed him.

"You can't prove it was me," he sneered, jerking his arm away from Jim. Jim smiled, an expression that seemed totally out of place in a discussion that involved assault, robbery, and theft. Higgins' smile unnerved Borden, and he felt a chill as if the air conditioning was set too low.

"Fortunately for us, Geoff's cat, Sir Lancelot, gave us a sample of your DNA that was under his claws. We traced it to you. I'm afraid whatever racket you were planning with the windows is over." Lewis stood mute, his head hung in what appeared to be a penitent pose, but Jim wasn't fooled. The guy was dangerous, although apparently, somewhat incompetent. He motioned for Paul to take Lewis Borden outside.

Jim called the local police department in Ontario and arranged for Lewis to be transported to the La Crosse County jail. Once Jim finished the call, he turned back to Bubba and Kay.

"We need to make a plan," Jim said. Bubba Starch leaned forward, listening intently as Jim began to talk.

39

Charlie Tewalt and Jamie Alberg stared out the windshield of the black Chevy Silverado pickup they'd rented at Enterprise in La Crosse before they headed to Ontario. They were lost. A fact Charlie found to be extremely disconcerting. He'd traveled through every back alley in Chicago and never been lost. How could he be so disoriented in a place where the people were simple-minded country folk, and the scenery was as primary as a two-lane road? Dusk was just an hour away and would soon envelop the hills and castellated bluffs of Wildcat Mountain in darkness, making their mission more treacherous and difficult.

Since arriving in Ontario during the late afternoon, they'd spent time observing the residents of the little town, talking to some business owners, drinking a cup of coffee at the local cafe, and questioning some of the residents along Main Street. After learning that Bradford's daughter lived on the other side of the state park, they drove along State Highway 33, which cut through Wildcat Mountain and crossed Billings Creek. The winding roads and serpentine Kickapoo River disoriented them. Being lost was embarrassing for someone as sophisticated as Charlie Tewalt. He was parked at a pullout literally named Dead End Road, and for the last several minutes he'd studied the map with growing frustration.

"This isn't right," Charlie blurted. "How hard can it be to find Moon Ridge Road?" His face was creased with hard lines. With growing frustration, he grabbed Jamie's arm in a steely grip as a deep frown crinkled his forehead, adding to his menacing persona. "You're about as useless as they come. You know that, kid," he snarled in frustration. Jamie wisely stayed silent. The GPS in the rental truck seemed to be malfunctioning, so Charlie resorted to using Google Maps on his phone. He swore under his breath while Jamie held an icepack against his bruised face. Late in the afternoon, Charlie and Jamie had had a furious argument, and Charlie had slapped the young archaeologist across the face when he discovered his hushed conversation with the operator when he called 911 to report his abduction.

Jamie watched Charlie out of the corner of his eye as he leaned against the passenger door of the pickup. He was starting to feel the smoldering anger building in his gut. He wondered where Lt. Higgins was. He could use his help right now, especially after the harried ride to Ontario and an afternoon filled with frustrating tidbits of information that had gotten them nowhere. The reticent, sleepy town folks of Ontario were no help whatsoever in revealing what they might know about the Bradfords and the lost windows. They seemed to be awfully closed-mouthed, reticent to talk about one of their own to strangers. Jamie remembered one little lady they'd talked to on the main street of Ontario.

"I've known the Bradfords for a long time, and the suggestion that they could be involved in anything criminal or illegal is just plain preposterous," she spouted firmly, jutting out her chin in defiance. "They're some of the best people I know, so don't come around here with these wild stories from who knows where unless you have some hard proof."

She turned abruptly and walked down the street, her shoes slapping the pavement. Jamie watched her leave, disheartened that his theories were going up in smoke before his eyes. They were no further ahead in finding the Bradfords than they were this morning when Charlie had forced Jamie into his truck and driven to the little village situated on the banks of the Kickapoo River.

"Well, that's another person you've pissed off with your wild theories," Charlie had snarled under his breath, grasping Jamie's arm in an iron grip.

"Me? You're gonna blame me for that woman's attitude?" Jamie hissed in return as he pointed at the woman hiking down the street. "Who's the one who did the research—"

"Shut up!" Charlie said, directing him back to the pickup. "You and your big, flappin' mouth are gonna have this whole town in an uproar before we're done!"

Now they were sidelined in the truck, in obvious confusion, directionally challenged, retracing their steps to figure out where they had made a wrong turn. Charlie hunched over his phone and enlarged the screen, tracing the winding country roads with his thick finger, stopping frequently to read the road names. He looked over at Jamie in exasperation. "Someone in this little hick town knows something about the windows and this Bradford character. They've got to," Charlie complained, hitting the steering wheel with a closed fist. His dark eyes jumped with annoyance. "How is it that you know so much and they know so little?" he asked, glancing over at Jamie. "They live here for Pete's sake! You'd think somebody would have heard the story about the windows. Are they just stupid or what?"

Jamie leveled a cool, aloof stare at Charlie. "On the contrary. They are just as smart as you or me," he lectured. "Smarter, maybe. The problem is your low opinion of them, which they can sense immediately. You can't come in here with your slick pickup and your Black Mastercard and think these people are going to be impressed by your upper-class status. You've insulted their intelligence, and they're not buying it. Besides, if they know anything at all, they've probably figured out by now it's best to just let sleeping dogs lie," Jamie said softly.

"Don't give me a bunch of philosophical bullshit," Charlie snarled. He went back to studying his phone. Suddenly, after several moments of concentration, he said, "Oh, wait a minute. Here's where we are. We're almost there. Moon Ridge Road is just beyond the intersection of Raccoon Drive and Cheyenne Road. We drove right by it." He pointed vaguely in the distance.

"And how is that going to help us?" Jamie asked, dreading the answer before it was spoken.

"That's where the Starches live. Don't tell me the granddaughter doesn't know something about the windows. Once we take them hostage, we'll recover the windows and get this show on the road," Charlie said.

"I'm not taking anyone hostage," Jamie said loudly. "If you think—"

Charlie leaned over and grabbed Jamie by the collar of his shirt. He pulled him roughly across the seat toward him and, in a threatening voice, growled, "Shut up. You will do as I say, or we'll have another session in which I kick your everlovin' little ass to the curb again. You got that?"

"I got it," Jamie peeped meekly.

40

By seven-thirty Friday evening, Sam and DeDe were standing in the parking lot at Duck's Canoe Rentals on the edge of the village of Ontario with Jim, Paul, Bubba Starch, and Geoff LaSarde. The sun was sinking toward the horizon, and darkness was just an hour away. Jim decided to come back into town to meet with Colleen Feske, the ranger at Wildcat Mountain State Park. She agreed to meet with the group to add anything that might be helpful as they planned the move of the Tiffany windows to a secure location. However, Charlie Tewalt and Jamie Alberg were still on the loose, and Jim had no idea where they were, which complicated the situation. *It's not over 'til it's over*, he thought.

Sam and DeDe had arrived from La Crosse with Paco in tow, and now the black lab was sniffing and woofing, his nose quivering with new smells and unfamiliar people. He skirted the edge of the group until he came to Jim. The dog shoved his massive black head into Jim's hand, begging for attention. Jim leaned down and petted his head and thumped his side.

On a personal level, Jim felt guilty when he thought about his rather callous attitude toward Jamie and his grandiose ideas. The kid *was* smart, but he was also a smart aleck. Still, when all was said and done, Jamie was an adult, and the choices he made he also had to own. Jim shook his head at the thought of the young archaeologist's careless, headlong plunge into the window mystery. He'd been missing for over twenty-four hours. No one had seen him, but Jim was pretty sure Charlie Tewalt had abducted him. The only proof they had of the possible kidnapping was the two desperate phone calls he'd made earlier in the day, one to Jim and one to 911.

"So the windows are in this old, broken-down chapel just beyond my boundary line here," Bubba said as he pointed to a detailed map of the area provided by Colleen. Jim had tuned out for a moment, but now he pulled himself back and concentrated on the conversation.

The park ranger nodded her head, studying the map intently. "That's part of the logging camp that used to exist here in the late 1890s. It's been defunct for decades. We've uncovered some other buildings in that area that have since disintegrated, so that makes sense," Colleen said. "I never knew there was a chapel, though."

"There are a couple of rock outcroppings close to the chapel that could be used for lookout points in case Tewalt shows up. We can take my UTV and trailer to haul the windows safely to my garage," Bubba explained.

"We've got a first-aid kit in the truck, we'll pick up some bottled water and snack bars," Jim said, "and let's hope we don't get into a standoff before we can get the windows out of there." The conversation was interrupted by a sharp bark from Paco.

A couple of teenagers were passing by the canoe rental lot on their bikes, and when they saw the group talking and pointing to a map spread over the hood of Sam's Jeep, they slowed and studied the adults from a distance, hesitant to approach. One boy was tall and lanky and wore a yellow T-shirt and black jogging shorts. The other boy was of medium height and had an intensity about him that Jim found interesting. He had on a pair of camo pants and an Under Armour T-shirt. Both boys had a fishing pole strapped to the handlebars of their bikes and a tackle box hung from one of the boys' handlebars.

Everyone looked up when the boys parked their bikes and strolled over to the group. Paco bounded up to them, woofing and sniffing.

"Hi, guys. What's up?" Jim asked.

The boys introduced themselves. "I'm Rusty," the boy in the yellow shirt said, "and this is my friend Lance. Just wondering if you're in town about the lost windows?" Rusty asked.

"We're conducting an investigation into that," Paul replied. "You know something about that?"

Paco barked loudly as if to say, "We're on it. The professionals have arrived." Sam shushed the dog and clipped on his leash.

"There was this dark-haired man and another younger guy in town today asking a bunch of questions," Rusty explained. "They went up and down Main Street."

"Wait a minute," Jim said as he pulled out his phone. He scrolled briefly, then showed the boys a picture. "Does this look like the man you saw?"

"Yeah, that's him," Rusty said.

"Did you talk to them?" Jim asked.

"Yeah. They waved us down when we were riding our bikes down to the river. They wanted to know where Bubba Starch lived," Lance said.

"What did you tell them?" Bubba asked the boys.

"We said he lived out of town on Moon Ridge Road," Rusty said. "We thought they were just some dumb tourists or something, you know, lost, trying to find someone they knew. We found out later from some other kids that they'd been asking around town about some old windows. It all sounded kinda weird. We thought they were some kind of antique dealers or something."

"When was this?" Jim asked.

"Mmm . . . this afternoon until about four or five o'clock," Lance said.

"Thanks, guys. You've been a big help," Jim said. "If you see these guys again, don't talk to them and report it to the local cops, okay?" The boys nodded, looked everyone over again, then turned and pedaled their bikes back into town.

Bubba whipped out his cell phone. The original plan they'd made before coming into town was for Kay to pack a few clothes and head to her dad's residence in the village for the night. Everyone felt she would be safer there. The new information from the two bikers threw Bubba into turmoil. He worried that Kay would get caught in the middle of the conflict, especially when the boys said that Charlie and Jamie might be heading to his home on Moon Ridge Road. Bubba stepped away from the group and dialed his wife.

"Kay, call me when you get this message," Bubba said tersely.

"No answer?" Jim asked, breaking away from the group's conversation.

"No, but that's not unusual. Kay usually shuts her phone off when she's busy outside. She's probably feeding the animals."

"We're going to go back to your place, load up everything we might need on your four-wheeler and trailer, and head to the chapel. We'll check on Kay when we get there," Jim explained. Noticing Bubba's worried look, he clapped him on the shoulder. "You look pretty worried. She's probably already at her dad's. We'll swing over there before we leave town and check it out."

"Yeah. That sounds good. She might have forgotten to turn her cell phone on," Bubba said.

Jim turned back to the group. Paul was folding up the map, and Colleen walked to her pickup, waved to the group, and started back into town.

"Okay, let's get everybody on the same page," Jim said tersely. "We're heading back to Bubba's place, where we'll meet and gather up our supplies. Sam, DeDe, and Paul—you head to Starches now. Bubba and I will go to the Bradford house here in Ontario and check on Kay, and we'll meet you at the Starches as soon as we can get there," Jim ordered. He turned to Geoff. "I would strongly recommend that you head home and stay there. We'll let you know how everything turns out later." Geoff nodded his head slowly, turned, and walked to his truck.

Paco barked loudly as if to say, "What about me?"

Jim bent down and patted the dog's head. "And Paco, you be ready for action," he said seriously. Paco barked as if to say, "The professionals have arrived. I'm on it!"

41

Kay Starch fumbled in her closet, rifling through her clothes, and grabbed a sweatshirt, a pair of jeans, a pair of panties, and a nightgown, which she threw in a small travel bag. She rushed to the bathroom and hurriedly deposited a toothbrush and toothpaste, hairbrush and some hairspray, and her weekly medication dispenser that sat on the top of the bathroom vanity for her overnight stay at her dad's house in Ontario.

Kay was shaking, dreading what the next few hours might bring. Those Tiffany windows had brought Bubba and her nothing but trouble, and she sincerely wished Bubba had never discovered them in the old chapel. "It's too late to worry about that now," she mumbled under her breath. She should have departed at least an hour ago, but the cats, goats, and two horses needed to be fed and watered, which had slowed down her departure.

At that very minute, she heard footsteps in the hallway outside the bathroom, and her heart leaped into her throat. A young man appeared in the doorway of the bathroom. He was beaten up. Kay noticed a purple shiner developing around his left eye, and his upper lip was swollen. He looked petrified. She supposed she did, too.

"Who are you?" Kay whispered softly.

"That's not important, but let me assure you that we need to work together and have each other's back, or we're not going to get out of this alive," he whispered to her.

A deep voice yelled from the kitchen. "Get out here, Jamie, and bring the woman with you."

The young man was intense, yet beneath the intensity was a calm determination. He winced at the sound of the gruff voice, then tilted his head toward the kitchen in a gesture that meant Kay should follow him.

Kay and Jamie walked into the kitchen. Charlie Tewalt, the man who had yelled, stood next to the kitchen island. His eyes smoldered with frustration, and in his hand, he tightly gripped the handle of a Ruger pistol. Kay was used to rifles and shotguns. Bubba had several in his collection that he used to eliminate pesky varmints around the farm, but she wasn't used to having a pistol pointed at her. The threatening man who was standing in her kitchen was unsettling, but this whole window affair had pushed Kay to the brink of her legendary patience, and now she felt a hot anger rising in her throat. What she said next surprised her, and she wondered where she'd gotten her bravado.

"How did you get in here?" Kay asked the man, returning his belligerent stare. "Who gave you the right to invade my home and threaten me with a pistol?"

"We came in while you were out feeding your horses," Charlie said. Kay remained calm and unflappable despite the fact that her knees were trembling and she thought she might throw up. Jamie looked over at her and caught a hint of defiance in her stance and expression.

"Listen up, little lady. You're going to lead us to the windows," Charlie snapped, suddenly all business. The next statement was a calculated risk, but he said it anyway. "I know you know where they are, so don't even try to deny it. It may result in you being harmed, and we wouldn't want that to happen, would we? Just take a look at Jamie if you doubt my ability to inflict injury."

Several moments of silence ensued as Kay glanced at Jamie again, noticing his bruised face. She turned her gaze back to Charlie as she calculated the odds of surviving whatever ordeal he had in mind. "What's your plan?" she asked quietly.

Kay's calmness in the face of the wild threats seemed to confuse Charlie, and her question seemed to confuse him. Instead of presenting an organized plan for the recovery of the infamous windows, as Kay thought he would, he stammered and seemed flummoxed. His face flushed a deep pink from embarrassment. "Well, first of all, I need to know the location of the windows. Then I'll develop a plan for getting them back to my truck and out of this god-forsaken county."

Kay realized at that moment the power of leadership had changed hands. This man, whoever he was, didn't know where the windows were. Did the other kid know? She looked at Jamie. He appeared to be a greenhorn, but appearances could be deceiving. The kid, whoever he was, didn't look like he was more than twenty, barely out of his teens. His injuries told Kay that he was probably an uncooperative hostage, maybe someone this guy had abducted and slapped around. What was a kid like him doing with a desperado like this guy, someone who was waving a pistol at a harmless woman?

Kay knew where the windows were, but whether she could keep these men from the hiding place until help arrived was a terrible gamble. She thought of something Bubba had told her once about his warfare experiences in Vietnam: Every advantage is temporary, so when it presents itself, seize the opportunity. If help didn't arrive soon, then eventually she would have to lead these two men to the small chapel. But at the moment, she seemed to have a slender thread of control over the situation, plus she had another advantage—knowing the surrounding area like the back of her hand. Driving through the woods and up onto the bluffs would eat up a lot of time, and crossing the Kickapoo River several times would add to the diversion as they traveled to the location of the hidden windows. She might be able to hold off their arrival at the chapel for a couple of hours at the most. Maybe that would be enough time for the detectives and Bubba to remove the windows and load them onto a wagon. Kay said a silent prayer as a plan gelled in her mind.

"Our UTV is in the garage. We can take that," Kay said in a business-like tone. "I'll grab some water and energy bars. We'll be going through the backwoods, maneuvering through thick brush and forest, so I hope you're ready for a long, rough ride." Despite the threats from Charlie, Jamie could see Kay had a calm, purposeful plan. If she was scared, she wasn't showing it. She lifted her chin and stared Charlie down. Jamie watched her and thought, *I like this gal. She's got spunk. My chances of escaping from this mess just got a whole lot better.*

Charlie flicked his wrist and waved the gun toward the back door. "Let's get this show on the road," he snarled.

After the meeting in the parking lot in Ontario, everyone went their separate ways according to their plan/ Sam, DeDe, and Paul headed to Moon Ridge Road, Geoff drove back to La Crosse, and Jim and Bubba drove across town to Willie Bradford's home since Kay could not be reached by phone. The group would reconvene for another powwow at the Starches as soon as they all arrived.

Jim drove through the small village to Bradford's home, which was located on a quiet back street of the town. When Jim arrived at the house, he parked in the driveway and left the motor running. After a five-minute search inside, Bubba returned to Paul's pickup, his face tight with anxiety.

"She's not here. She's either on her way to town, in which case we'll probably meet her on the road, or she's still at our house, and she hasn't left yet," Bubba told Jim. There were other possibilities Jim thought of, but he stayed quiet.

Backing out of the driveway, Jim gunned the Ford pickup in the direction of Moon Ridge Road. As he drove, he thought about his police experiences throughout the years. The consequences of several criminal confrontations still rattled around in his memory like a skeleton in a closet. The day Paul was critically wounded in a search for a fugitive, and his own brush with death in a gravel quarry in Vernon County with a violent drug dealer came back into his mind with surprising clarity. Jim was constantly amazed at the lengths people would go to steal money, drugs, or stolen treasures. Throw in some evil ulterior motives and volatile emotions, and you had a disaster on your hands. Suddenly, his mind turned a corner and an image of a map formed in his brain—a map in which all roads led to Wildcat Mountain. In his mind, the road was etched in red with a big black star at the center where the Tiffany windows lay under a rotten tarp in an abandoned chapel. He shivered with foreboding at what might happen.

After several minutes of silence, Jim said, "Let's hope Kay didn't meet up with Charlie Tewalt. That could get nasty."

"Kay is tougher than you think," Bubba said. He pushed his hat back on his head, scratched his scalp, and pulled the hat down tight around his ears again. "She rescued my sorry butt when I came back from Vietnam and helped me get my life back on track. As surprising as it might seem, she's resilient and smart. To think that her quiet nature is a sign of weakness would be a big mistake." He looked out the window at the scenery rolling by. "She might do better than you think," he added thoughtfully.

But Jim was not convinced, and he shook his head in silent disagreement. The normal guy or gal standing on the street corner was not prepared to deal with the likes of Charlie Tewalt. His shooting skills and physical prowess alone would be challenging even for the trained detectives on his team.

"I hate to disavow you of the confidence you have in your wife's ability to defend herself, but most people would be overwhelmed rather quickly by the likes of Tewalt," Jim said.

"Well, there's one other thing you don't know about Kay," Bubba said, staring through the windshield into the growing darkness.

"Oh yeah? What's that?" Jim asked, glancing over at Bubba.

"She prays," he said simply.

Jim's eyebrows shot up, and he focused on the road ahead. "You'd better join her then because if Charlie Tewalt got a hold of her, she's going to need all the prayers she can get."

42

Yea, though I walk through the valley of the shadow of death, I will fear no evil for thou art with me, Kay thought, recalling the familiar Bible verse. *Even the evil of this awful man in my garage.*

The UTV parked in the garage was loaded with supplies that had been placed in a cardboard box: a heavy-duty flashlight, a small stash of energy bars, a couple of bananas and apples, a water jug, and a few sweatshirts. Kay looked everything over while Charlie nervously paced the perimeter of the vehicle, kicking the tires and inspecting the chassis. Jamie helped her fill the gas tank from a can that sat along the inside wall of the garage. For some unknown reason, Kay felt she could trust Jamie. She repeated her prayers for protection and guidance over and over until they felt like a broken record running through her head. *The Lord is near to those who call on him . . .* Kay silently prayed, her lips moving without any sound.

"Let's get going," Charlie said loudly. "It'll be dark in fifteen minutes."

Kay carefully backed the UTV out of the garage, and Jamie and Charlie hopped in. Kay drove down the gravel driveway, opened the gate to the expansive southern pasture, and drove across the field until they came to another gate and the dense woods that bordered their property. Clumps of Indian switch grass rustled against the sides of the UTV as they headed into the woods. Spring peepers chirped cheerfully, and somewhere in the dense forest, Kay heard an owl hoot a long, low trill. As they moved down the trail through the dense undergrowth, two white-tailed deer leaped across the path. Musk and lilac scents wafted on the air currents. The moon was rising, peeking through the openings in the trees. Kay noticed a few stars flickering in the darkening sky.

Bubba and Kay had spent many hours each spring, summer, and fall grooming trails, advancing into mature tracts of woods to make new paths for their horses and recreation vehicles. She had several routes to choose from, but she decided to head east on a particularly steep trail that would lead them away from the small chapel. It was rocky, but as far as she knew, it was clear of major obstacles like fallen trees and large boulders. She knew these trails like the back of her hand. In several places, the Kickapoo River meandered in crooked, serpentine patterns, swift in some places, slow, lazy, and shallow in other spots. Sandstone bluffs jutted to heights of ten or fifteen feet at random spots along the route. On any other day, these features would have thrilled Kay. She especially loved the rocky escarpments; they were like sentinels of the forest watching over everything that happened there. They had stood the test of time, and Kay loved the idea of their permanent presence on the landscape. But now the very things she loved about the land seemed laden with menace. In the growing darkness, she faltered. How was she going to pull off her plan? Would it work? She didn't know. Shaking her head silently at the uncertainty of the situation, she felt a spasm of fear twist inside her chest. She whispered more desperate prayers, avoiding eye contact with Charlie, who sat next to her exuding a threatening, murderous energy.

They forged ahead into the deep woods. It was still early in the spring, and the bushes and shrubs that normally hung across the two-wheeled track had not grown much yet, making the trail easier to negotiate. Once they were under the shade of the trees, it became much darker, so Kay turned on the UTV's headlights. She drove carefully, although Charlie squirmed with agitation and several times urged her to drive faster. When they came to a place where a washout had carved a deep gully in the trail from the recent spring rains, Charlie sat back in his seat, realizing Kay knew the terrain better than he did. She carefully maneuvered the UTV around the ditch and continued along the trail. Charlie quit giving orders, and despite the tense situation they were in, Kay relaxed a little bit.

After half an hour of slow but steady progress in which they crossed a couple of shallow sections of the Kickapoo River, Kay came to a dead end on the trail. She knew another trail was only about two hundred feet away, but she would have to push through dense undergrowth and rough ground to get to it. That trail would lead them up on the bluff where they could travel somewhat faster.

"Hang on!" she said loudly over the grumble of the UTV engine. "This might be kinda rough."

She turned into the dense thicket and proceeded to bulldoze her way through the brambles. Branches from thin trees whipped by their faces, and rocks that had washed down the steep hillsides jumbled their insides when Kay drove over them. Eventually, after fifteen minutes, they reached the lower trail, which gradually wound steeply upward again to higher ground on top of the bluff.

Kay turned the UTV onto the trail. Suddenly, Charlie grabbed Kay's arm and squeezed tightly. She winced from the pain, but she refused to acknowledge his control. "Listen, I was a ranger in the U.S. Army. I'm not stupid. You're leading us in circles," Charlie barked. "You get our ass on the right trail to wherever we're going, or I'm dumping you and the kid off in these woods. I'll hide you so good, no one will ever find your dead bodies. You understand?"

Kay jerked her arm away from Charlie's iron grip. Suddenly, he slapped her hard across the face. The shock of the blow brought tears to Kay's eyes, but in the darkness she gritted her teeth, fighting against the urge to cry.

"If you're unhappy with my navigation skills, I'll give you the reins," she said quietly while the motor hummed beneath them.

Yeah, right, thought Jamie in the back seat. *He couldn't even find Moon Ridge Road, let alone some building out here in the forest.* She took her hands off the steering wheel and laid them in her lap, waiting for Charlie's decision.

Charlie grabbed Kay's sweatshirt and pulled her across the seat. When her face was inches from his, he spewed more threats. "No more evasive moves! I'm onto your plan! Get us to the location of the windows. I'm through with this crap!" He shoved her roughly toward the steering wheel. "Let's go!" Charlie snarled, pointing down the path. "Drive!"

Kay carefully put the UTV in low gear and started down the path. It went smoothly for several minutes, and they seemed to be making good progress. Kay thought through her strategy again. She decided she couldn't be responsible for the injury or death of another person, namely Jamie. It was time to lead Charlie to the chapel, despite her misgivings that the whole situation was a powder keg waiting to explode. What would happen if Bubba and the detectives were already there? She blinked rapidly and gritted her teeth at the thought of a gunfight at the chapel.

They traveled along the smooth, flat two-wheeled path for several more minutes until they came to another trail that descended into the valley below. Suddenly up ahead, Kay could see a pile of large rocks strewn across the path, the result of a washout in a recent storm. She stopped just short of it and looked over at Charlie.

"Well, what do you want to do?" Kay asked as the engine grumbled beneath them. "Turn around?"

"Hell, no. Everybody get out and start chucking rocks off the path," Charlie ordered.

They all got out of the UTV and began lugging several large rocks off the trail. It was hard work, and despite the cool night temperatures, they all began sweating. Half an hour later, the trail was cleared, and the way forward seemed free of rocky debris. Charlie shoved Kay out of the way and plopped himself into the driver's seat. He roared the engine to life and began driving rapidly down the trail. Kay put her seat belt on, hoping Charlie's reckless handling of the UTV wouldn't result in a rollover.

The trail continued to ease downward. Jamie had been quietly obedient and compliant during the trip up and down the bluff, but his thoughts were dark and frantic. *How do I always manage to get into these life-threatening situations?* he thought. *One of these days I'm going to get killed.* He just hoped that Kay would not become an innocent victim of Charlie's rage and pent-up aggression.

As they roared down the trail in the dark, Kay leaned over toward Charlie and said, "You might want to slow down a little. The windows are up ahead about a half mile."

Charlie shifted the UTV to a lower gear, slowing down slightly. He stared through the darkness, gripping the steering wheel tightly while rounding a wide bend in the track. Up ahead, a huge sandstone outcropping protruded ominously close to the edge of the trail. Beyond the outcropping, a dilapidated, weathered building came into view. It was leaning precariously toward a swale filled with cattails.

"Stop here," Kay said. Charlie braked hard and shut off the engine. The darkness of the forest surrounded and engulfed them. In the intense silence that followed, a horrible sense of dread came over Kay. She had no idea what Charlie might do now that the windows had been located. Would he eliminate them and try to complete his mission alone? If he did, he'd have a hard time loading the windows by himself. They were very heavy and large. She doubted one man could move them and load them alone. Moths fluttered in the headlights of the UTV. For several minutes, they all sat still and listened to the night sounds. Finally, Charlie spoke.

"So? Where are they?" he asked brusquely.

Kay pointed at the chapel. "In there," she said.

"Are you serious?" Charlie snarled, disbelieving that something as valuable as Tiffany church windows could possibly be hidden in a place like this.

"Yes, I'm serious. I've seen them myself," Kay said calmly. "I don't know how they got here, but that's where they are." Her face still stung from the slap Charlie had delivered earlier, and she absentmindedly rubbed her cheek, deeply resenting the violence he had inflicted on her.

"Show me," Charlie ordered.

Kay unbuckled the seat belt and jumped out of the UTV. She grabbed a flashlight from the storage box behind the seat, turned it on, and walked confidently toward the chapel. The two men followed closely behind. When Kay got to the door of the chapel, she pointed to the pile of rotten steps thrown in a heap off to the side.

"Be careful. Bubba knocked down the rotten steps. You'll have to hoist yourself over the threshold to get inside. The windows are against one of the walls under a tarp," Kay said, pointing to the interior of the chapel. Charlie grabbed the flashlight, and the two men hoisted themselves up onto the sash of the door and went into the chapel. At that moment, Kay turned, ran quickly to the UTV, started it, and spun the wheels on the trail, making a beeline for her home.

When Charlie heard the engine start, he jumped out of the front door of the chapel, drew his pistol from beneath his sweatshirt, and aimed into the dark. He fired several shots at the taillights, but the UTV did not stop as it continued roaring down the trail.

Charlie swore a string of obscenities. "Dammit, I don't believe this!" He shook his head in disbelief. How could a seemingly timid, middle-aged woman have the bravado and guts to outsmart him at his own game? "Now what am I gonna do?" he moaned.

Jamie smiled as he watched the UTV recede down the trail in the dark. *You rock, Kay,* he thought. *Be safe.*

43

The detective crew and Bubba Starch arrived back at the Starch home Friday evening at about nine-thirty. Full darkness had descended, and as they gathered in the kitchen to discuss their plan, Bubba voiced his concerns.

"Kay's not here, but her vehicle is still in the garage. That black pickup in the driveway is Lewis Borden's, and the other one—I have no idea where that came from. One of our UTVs is gone, and the gate to the south pasture is open. So where is Kay?" he asked. His face was lined with furrows of worry and anxiety. He blew out a puff of air as he watched Jim's face.

"Most likely she's with Charlie Tewalt and Jamie Alberg," Jim said. "She has nothing to fear from Jamie, other than his wild, crazy ideas about how he's going to escape his current situation." Jim sighed loudly. He was reluctant to discuss the implications of being a prisoner of Tewalt, but the situation could not be ignored, so he continued. "Charlie, however, is a different story. From what Leslie told me, his involvement in the Chicago underworld is well known to law enforcement there. He's an experienced criminal who will stop at nothing to accomplish his goal of getting the Tiffany windows,"

Jim explained. "According to Lez, what Charlie wants, he generally gets by any means necessary."

At that moment, there was a thump against the door that led to the garage. Bubba jerked and everyone looked startled. Sam asked, "What was that?"

The sound of the bump sent Paco into full alert. Barking loudly, he scrambled to the garage door and stood cocking his head, listening. He woofed several times, looking back at the crew as if to say, "Hurry up! Someone needs help!"

Bubba turned and walked rapidly toward the garage entry. Flinging the door open, he cried out when he saw Kay slumped on the garage floor next to the door. He knelt beside her as the rest of the team hurried to the garage and hovered over the wounded woman.

"Paul, call an ambulance!" Jim ordered loudly, kneeling next to Bubba. He talked over his shoulder as he assessed Kay's condition. "She's been shot. Can't tell exactly where. DeDe, get hold of the Vernon, Crawford, and Monroe County Sheriff Departments with a description of Charlie and Jamie and issue a BOLO with the warning that Tewalt is armed and dangerous. Call Leslie and Ruby and let them know what's going on."

Bubba hovered over his wife. "Kay, honey. What happened? Can you tell us?" he whispered.

Kay's eyes fluttered open briefly. Her voice was quiet, but steady. "I took Charlie and Jamie to the chapel . . . I had no choice. When they went inside to look at the windows, I jumped . . ." She paused a minute, grimaced from pain, catching her breath. ". . . on the four-wheeler and . . . and I drove away . . . but Charlie shot at me and hit me."

"Where are you hurt?" Jim asked. He could see a trail of blood splattered and smeared across the garage floor.

"I think . . . my thigh and my shoulder," she said weakly, laying her hand across her chest. She closed her eyes again.

"Let's move her—" Bubba said, but Jim interrupted.

"No, no. Leave her here. Sam, run into the house and get a blanket. She is shivering, and we need to keep her warm." Then he looked at Bubba. "We don't want to move her and cause more damage. She got this far. She needs to stay quiet to prevent further bleeding. We'll wait for the ambulance to get here. They can assess her wounds and get her to a hospital."

Sam returned with a warm quilt, and Bubba made her as comfortable as he could on the cement floor of the garage.

"When the ambulance gets here," Jim said, "you go with your wife, Bubba. The rest of us will get organized and go after Tewalt."

Sam pulled Jim away from the wounded woman. Standing by the garage wall, he expressed his concerns in an intense voice. "Chief, we're going to have a hard time tracking down Charlie and Jamie in the dark. We can try, but it's gonna be tough," Sam said.

"Yep, it is, but we're going after him, dark or not. He won't be expecting some country cops to organize a manhunt for him, but that's just what we're gonna do," Jim said tersely. His face had taken on a hard edge, and the determination in his voice calmed Sam's foreboding. "In fact, his opinion about us might be the very thing that gives us an advantage." Jim looked over at Sam and noticed the sheen of perspiration around his hairline.

"I'm with you, Chief. All the way," Sam said quietly.

"Atta boy," Jim said. "Let's get organized."

Charlie Tewalt trudged silently through the woods in the black darkness of night. The only light he had was the flashlight on his phone, but he'd been saving his battery by hiking with the light from the moon. Overhead he could hear the rustle of leaves in the gentle breeze, and the stars above were bright pinpoints of light in the velvety sky. It reminded him that not all the world was in upheaval and pandemonium. Out here it was quiet, dark, and still. In any other situation he might have called the situation peaceful, but unfortunately, even with starlight over his head, peace for Charlie was in short supply tonight.

After Kay took off on the UTV in her daring escape, he'd bound up Jamie with duct tape and some rope he'd found in a box in the corner of the chapel. The kid wasn't going anywhere soon, although eventually he would probably escape. Charlie continued walking, considering his options as he went, using the compass on his phone to keep moving in a northerly direction toward the little town of Wilton. The obsession with the Tiffany windows, like most of his appetites, had gotten him into a boatload of trouble he was not prepared to handle by himself. Where was Lewis, his front man, when he really needed him? *I should never have fired him,* he thought. *That was stupid and arrogant.* His shoulders slumped dejectedly as he picked his way along the rough, rocky ground, trying not to stumble in the dark. He stopped briefly, sat on a large rock, took an energy bar from his pocket, and guzzled water from a bottle inside his jacket.

As he snacked, he flicked on his cell flashlight and studied the map on his iPhone. He decided the northern route toward Wilton provided the best chance of escape, although the direction he chose was irrelevant—North to Wilton or south to La Farge. He was unfamiliar with this rugged territory. He was just passin' through. He thought of the ranger motto: Rangers Lead the Way. *Yeah, right,* he harrumphed bitterly. *Just lead the way, you idiot.* This whole plan from the beginning had been on shaky ground.

The situation he found himself in this evening, however, did have one note of familiarity. During his stints in Afghanistan and Iraq, he'd had plenty of practice carrying out nighttime excursions through hostile territory—hiking across stretches of desert sand for over fifty miles, crouching behind huge rocks when random vehicles appeared on the scene loaded with a bunch of wild, barbaric banshees screaming at the top of their lungs, brandishing their weapons. On those missions, he'd commanded a small group of elite soldiers who were in top physical condition—soldiers who used only their wits, physical strength, and instincts to survive. Those scenarios came back to him in full living color. The only difference now was that he was alone.

His captive, Jamie Alberg, had been an entertaining piece of work, but in the end, the young kid would only complicate things. Too bad. Charlie had come to enjoy Jamie's intellect and insights, but he knew the kid would be a dead weight around his neck, preventing a quick, efficient escape from this rugged country. In addition, Charlie sensed a strong moral fiber in Jamie that sooner or later would have bumped up against his own criminal instincts. Violent, immoral acts were not carried out by people who had a responsive, tender conscience. Charlie knew Jamie would eventually argue about the moral ramifications of his actions, and as a hardcore, seasoned soldier, he was not about to listen to a rambling discussion about ethical, responsible choices from a teenager. No, Jamie had to be left behind. Charlie had a niggling fear he'd made a mistake leaving the kid alive, but knowing Jamie's weaknesses in self-defense and survival skills, he rationalized that he was harmless, still wet behind the ears. Charlie stood up and began hiking through the woods again. The sooner he got out of here and got back to Chicago, the better.

Up ahead, Billings Creek bubbled over a layer of limestone rocks. Charlie plunged across the shallow stream and climbed up the opposite bank. He headed into a thicket of brambles, cussing and swearing as he went, hoping to reach a major highway by daybreak. From what Jamie had told him as he'd tied him up, Lieutenant Higgins would come after him with guns blazing, especially if he'd injured Kay when he shot at her in the dark. The farther he could advance in the darkness tonight, the sooner he could be out of the reach of this supposed law enforcement wonder. Jamie's babbling about some Podunk, small-town detective team whose reputation exceeded all expectations seemed preposterous. Charlie smiled in the dark and thought, *I'll believe it when I see it.*

44

By eleven o'clock Friday night, Jim and his team were in the Starches' kitchen, meeting with Vernon County Sheriff Cecil Bjornstad and several of his deputies. More law enforcement personnel were heading their way from Monroe and La Crosse Counties. Jamie Alberg was still missing along with Charlie Tewalt, and Jim was beginning to believe the animated, overconfident archaeologist might be dead. The overhead light hanging above the kitchen island cast a harsh white halo over the worried expressions of the team. Everyone looked bleary-eyed and exhausted. A few half-empty coffee cups littered the kitchen island along with a brown banana peel and an open package of Oreo cookies. Paco, ever vigilant, sat next to Sam as if he understood the discussion underway. *All of this hullabaloo over some famous stained-glass windows hardly seems worth it now, considering Kay's injuries and Jamie's disappearance,* Jim thought bitterly.

"From my vantage point, I'd say that Tewalt has to either go north toward Wilton or south toward La Farge," Sheriff Bjornstad said. Everyone leaned over the map that was spread on the kitchen island, watching Bjornstad trace the possible routes on the map with his stubby finger. "Ontario is almost equidistant from Wilton and La

Farge, and since he started from Moon Ridge Road on the west side of the Wildcat, he's going to go one way or the other. That makes the most sense to me."

"That sounds reasonable, but Tewalt is not your average Joe Blow when it comes to reconnaissance," Sam said. "He's very experienced at surviving challenging situations, and for what it's worth, he's probably ditched Jamie by now. He'd only slow him down." Jim cringed at the thought of Jamie, wounded or dead, somewhere in the thick, impenetrable woods. If that were the case, he might not be found for several days.

"Other ideas?" Jim asked.

"He could be headed to Hillsboro straight east," DeDe suggested. "That leaves us with three possible escape routes."

"True," Jim agreed. "But there's a lot of other rough country between here and his destination that he might be willing to navigate to avoid detection." Jim glanced at the sheriff. "His survival skills as a ranger are considerable. How many men do we have at our disposal?" he asked.

"You've got four—" Sheriff Bjornstad started, but Sam interrupted.

"Don't forget we've got Paco," he added. The sheriff frowned conspicuously.

"Yeah, we've all heard about Paco's escapades," the sheriff said with disinterest.

"You may doubt his abilities and reputation, but he's a decorated veteran," Sam said, bristling. "You have to see him in action to believe it."

"Whatever," the sheriff commented under his breath, dismissing Paco's presence with a wave of his hand. "So, you've got four officers and a dog, and I've got four men," the sheriff continued. "Monroe and La Crosse Counties will send a few people, too. If we plant patrol teams on Highway 131 north of the Wildcat and another team south on 131, and another team east on Highway 33, we have a decent chance of intercepting him and tightening the noose around him. He might eventually come out on a highway somewhere, but still . . ." His voice tapered off.

"The odds are not in our favor," Sam said, finishing the sheriff's thoughts. "He'll avoid open country and stick to the woods. When he gets near a highway, he'll probably steal a car. Walking in the open along a highway would be too risky. Someone would see him and remember it."

"We don't have many choices at this point," Jim said sternly, throwing Sam a frustrated glance. "I'm not willing to let this guy shoot and injure an innocent civilian and kidnap someone and then simply walk out of this county without a concerted effort to stop him." There were several nods from the group around the kitchen island. "Are you with me on that?" Jim asked, his voice fraught with challenge.

Sheriff Bjornstad looked at Jim and nodded his head. "I'm with you, Jim," he said resolutely. Jim's deep, baritone voice and steady resolve seemed to infuse the team with confidence. "We've got to at least make an attempt to capture the guy," Bjornstad continued. "You never know, we might get lucky."

"We might," Jim said, straightening to his full height. He spent a moment gathering his thoughts into a cohesive plan. "All right. Let's get out there and patrol these highways. Sam brought our drone, and if we haven't found Tewalt by morning, we'll launch that and survey the area. There's a chance we could spot him from the air."

"What about the park area? Shouldn't we have a team there as well?" asked Paul. "You said this guy is creative and determined. If he finds a hole in our loop, he's going to take advantage of it."

Sheriff Bjornstad nodded. "Agreed. We'll put a couple of guys in the park, too," he said.

Jim took over again. "Keep your cells on and communicate with everyone if you spot Tewalt. It'll take more than two people to actually capture and subdue him. If he heads into the woods, follow him and stay in communication. We'll all be within a few miles of each other, and we'll drop everything and come to your aid if you find him. Remember your training—a suspect is around every corner until you discover he's not. Tewalt's not going to expect us to hunt him down, and that's to our advantage. He's armed, and he's already tried to kill one person, so be aware of your surroundings at all times. Look up and out, and wear your vests."

Jim locked eyes with each team member around the island. He saw fear in the eyes of some of them, but he was encouraged when many of them nodded, their expressions serious and determined. *All right then—into the fray we go,* he thought. Then another thought came to him. *He who dwells in the shelter of the Most High will rest in the shadow of the Almighty. You will not fear the terror of the night, nor the arrow that flies by day.* Jim closed his eyes, took a deep breath, and sent a prayer heavenward.

"Let's check in with each other on the hour. Stay with your team," Sheriff Bjornstad reminded everyone. "Everybody be sharp."

The group walked out of the kitchen, where the planning continued out on the driveway in front of the garage as people divided into search teams and gathered their equipment. Jim's cell phone beeped.

"Lt. Higgins," he answered brusquely.

"Hey. It's Bubba."

"Yeah. What's up?" Jim asked.

"We're in La Crosse at Mayo. Kay just went in for surgery. I'll keep you informed. Have you discovered where Tewalt and Jamie are yet?"

"No. We're not sure of the situation yet, but Jamie hasn't been found. One of our teams will go back to the chapel and check the area there. The rest of us are going after the guy who shot Kay," Jim said firmly.

"Well, I hope you catch him," Bubba said angrily, his voice cracking with emotion. "He tried to kill my wife!"

"Did Kay give you any information about where Tewalt might be heading?" Jim asked.

"No, by the time we got to the hospital in the ambulance, she was very weak. She's lost a lot of blood," Bubba said.

"Listen, gotta go. If Kay tells you anything that might help, call me," Jim said.

"Will do."

"One more thing," Jim said.

"Yeah? What's that?"

"Keep praying," he said brusquely, and hung up.

45

The night air was cool as Jim and Sam rode the UTV back into the woods toward the chapel. Somehow, crazy as it seemed, the darkness was comforting like a warm cloak wrapped around their shoulders. Paco sat between the two men on the front seat on high alert, his ears erect. His nose twitched, and his dark brown eyes scanned the path in front of them. Occasionally he let out a low, threatening growl, and the hair stood up on the back of his thick neck. He was on patrol, and he seemed to know instinctively that people's lives were at stake. Sam fluffed his ears and patted his side. Paco reciprocated with a massive lick on Sam's cheek.

As they rode across the pasture and entered the thick, dark woods, Jim contemplated all that had happened. It seemed crazy that someone would abduct a person and shoot somebody else over some famous windows, but there you have it—that's exactly what had happened. Jamie was still missing, and Kay was in surgery for the wounds she had received at the hand of a desperate, cynical man who would stop at nothing to get what he wanted. Jim harrumphed to himself when he thought about Tewalt's shallow motives. The former ranger's greed and self-serving hypocrisy left Jim feeling angry and frustrated.

"You say something, Chief?" Sam asked.

"Nope. Just thinkin' about the selfishness of some people, that's all," Jim said with a bitter resignation in his voice. "What's the matter with people anyway? Has everybody gone off the deep end?"

"Well, you know the answer to that as well as I do," Sam said, his eyes fixed on the trail ahead.

"Yeah, I guess I do," Jim sighed. "Sin keeps rearing its ugly head, doesn't it?"

"Sure does, Chief," Sam said.

The night sky was clear, and away from the big city lights, the stars seemed closer and brighter. Jim had read something recently about a new effort among conservationists to protect the dark skies. Apparently, with all the electricity generated in cities to keep them lit and bright, the sky was no longer dark enough to even see the stars. Jim leaned back in his seat and lifted his eyes upward, and for just a moment, the wash of sparkling stars flung across the black expanse of the night sky made him pause. God was still in control despite man's conniving plans to wreak havoc upon His creation. As Jim thought, Sam drove through the quiet forest toward the chapel, both men hoping against hope they would find Jamie alive.

Thanks to Bubba's hard work, the path to the chapel was well-worn and cleared of brush, rocks, and debris. Sam approached the old chapel slowly, parked in front of the structure, and shut off the engine. It was ominously quiet, but as Jim and Sam knew from previous stakeouts, there were plenty of night sounds—crickets chirping, frogs croaking, the brush of the wind in the evergreens that sent needles swishing in a gentle rhythm, the creaking of tree branches swaying in the breeze, and the occasional howls from a pack of coyotes.

"What's our plan?" Sam finally asked after a few moments of silence.

As if in answer, Paco emitted a low growl and a single woof as if to say, "We're on the scene, and we mean business."

"Let's check out the chapel," Jim said. "Let Paco run loose in the area. He might sniff out Jamie and save us a lotta time."

"He's done stuff like that before," Sam said nonchalantly. He thought back to the snowy day several years ago when Paco had tracked down Leslie, his owner and wartime companion. Injured and in shock after her psychotic boyfriend had beaten her and hidden her in a wooden box in an abandoned barn, Paco had single-handedly used his incredible sense of smell to locate her and save her life. Sam smiled in the dark. That was the beginning of their love story, rough as it was. *I wouldn't have it any other way,* Sam thought. *Nobody else has a story like ours.*

Jim and Sam stepped out of the UTV and approached the chapel. Paco jumped down and began sniffing the ground, working his way around the site, his tail high in the air. He struck a pose and listened, then put his nose to the ground again, searching. Sam was pleased the dog hadn't lost his edge. He couldn't count the times the canine had assisted them in locating missing victims or the occasions when he'd interrupted nefarious plots by lowlifes who were determined to cause damage and injury.

Hoisting themselves across the threshold of the chapel, Jim and Sam uncovered the windows lying in the corner under the tarp. Sam aimed his flashlight at the multi-colored glass masterpieces and breathed in sharply.

"Will you look at that," he whispered. "Here's what the whole commotion is about."

Jim looked over Sam's shoulder and made a *tsking* sound. "Somebody's big idea of hoarding the windows and hiding them all those years ago has sure caused a ruckus. Let's just hope we can stop all this before someone gets killed."

Suddenly, in the distance, Sam and Jim heard Paco barking aggressively. Sam could tell that the dog had discovered something. He wasn't letting up; the barks were getting more intense.

Sam turned and launched himself out of the chapel with Jim following close behind.

"Come on, Chief! He's found something!" Sam shouted as he trotted toward the sound. "It's probably Jamie!" The light from his cell bobbed erratically in the dark woods as he ran, the path illuminated by the unsteady, bouncing beam.

"Be careful!" Jim warned. "It could be Tewalt!"

The two men worked their way along the path, past a huge outcropping of sandstone along the trail, the barking getting louder.

"We're close, Chief!" Sam said. He cupped his hand around his mouth and shouted, "Paco! Here boy! Come on, boy!" He whistled loudly.

Suddenly out of the darkness of the woods, Paco bounded into the light of the cell phone, his eyes bright, his tongue flopping in and out of his mouth.

"Whaddya find, boy? Show us!" Sam said.

Paco barked several loud, agitated barks, turned, and ran into the darkness again with Sam and Jim following close behind.

Sam and Jim ran after Paco, although the dog was much faster. Sam stopped when he saw Paco standing over someone huddled against a huge tree trunk. He pulled his pistol out of his holster and approached the scene. His anxiety escalated when he thought about Jamie, possibly dead or severely injured. Was Charlie nearby waiting to ambush them? As he got closer to the tree where Paco had focused his energy, he could see Jamie bound tightly to the tree with a rope around his chest, his arms behind his back, his mouth plastered with duct tape. It looked like Charlie had done a bang-up job of securing Jamie, so there was little possibility of escape.

Jim ran up to Jamie and knelt beside him. Jamie's one eye was wild with anxiety and fear. His other eye was black and swollen shut, but other than that, he seemed to have weathered the storm pretty well. Jim fished his jackknife out of his pants pocket and began cutting the thick rope that bound him to the tree. When his hands were free, Jamie reached up and ripped the tape off his mouth.

"Oh, Lt. Higgins! I knew you'd come!" Jamie whispered intensely.

"I told Charlie all about you. He didn't believe me when I told him you'd hunt him down, but here you are! Where's Kay? Did she get hurt? Where is she?"

Paco hovered over the young archaeologist, licking his face enthusiastically. Jamie reached up and hugged the dog to his chest.

"Sam, go get the UTV. Let's get this kid loaded and back to the farmhouse," Jim said. "How long have you been tied up?" Jim glanced at his watch—12:48.

"We left the house about nine-thirty, and Kay took us on a rough ride trying to kill time, but Charlie figured out her scheme, and he got rough with her," Jamie said breathlessly. Jim handed him a water bottle from his jacket. The young man gulped the water so fast it ran down his chin, then he swallowed hard and continued his story. "Kay brought us to the chapel, and while we were inside looking at the windows, she hopped on the four-wheeler and took off. From the minute I met her, I knew she had some spunk."

"Well, Charlie did a number on her—he shot her in the shoulder and thigh—but she made it back to the house. She's in La Crosse having surgery as we speak," Jim explained.

"Charlie's a tough character, Chief, but Kay outwitted him—"

"Well, she almost got herself killed!" Jim interrupted angrily. "That's a long way from outwitting somebody like Tewalt." He heard the UTV coming down the trail. Jim stood, leaned down, and pulled Jamie to his feet. He wobbled unsteadily as Jim helped him into the vehicle. Paco jumped onto the back seat next to Jamie.

As they rode back to the log home on Moon Ridge Road, Jamie explained everything that had happened: the man who followed him from Fish Farm Mounds archaeological site, his capture and abduction by Charlie at his home in La Crosse, their hurried, desperate trip to Ontario to find Willie Bradford, and the break-in at Starches' house where they had come face-to-face with Kay. To Jamie, it seemed like a long time ago, although only twelve hours had passed.

Jim's shirt was wrinkled and sweat-stained, and his face reflected the exhaustion he felt from the day's activities. Suddenly he felt old and tired. His back ached, and his eyes felt gritty. He blinked rapidly, then analyzed Jamie's physical condition as they stood outside the Starches' garage. "What am I gonna do with you now?" Jim snapped after listening to his litany.

"Well, I'm going with you," Jamie said, rubbing his wrists. "I'm not stayin' here by myself." A serious expression settled across his delicate features. Jim was familiar with the fierce resolve reflected on the young man's face. After all, his own daughter, Lillie, possessed an unswerving stubbornness and determination very similar to this kid standing in front of him.

Jim hesitated. He debated the wisdom of allowing this upstart to accompany them on their search for Charlie, but when he thought about it, he supposed the kid deserved to see his captor arrested and put in handcuffs. Sam interrupted, bringing everyone up to speed.

"Chief, we've gotta get to our post. The rest of the crew is scouring the area lookin' for Tewalt, and here we are standing in the driveway arguing. Are we takin' Jamie or not?" he asked gruffly.

Jamie gave Jim a dejected look.

"Well, I thought we should probably load up the windows and get them to a safe place, but catching Tewalt is more important at the moment. The windows will have to wait. They've been in the chapel for a hundred years already. They're not goin' anywhere. As for Jamie . . ." Jim gave him a sideways glance and then blew out a breath of frustration. "At least if you're with us, I'll know where you are. Let's roll," he said as he walked briskly to Sam's Jeep.

SATURDAY, MAY 26

46

Organizing a manhunt in the Wildcat Mountain area was a daunting task, but as the night wore on, and no one spotted Charlie Tewalt, Jim knew the morning would bring a flurry of activity that he hoped would tighten the noose around the fugitive and result in his capture. Although the odds were against them ever seeing Tewalt again, Jim thought back to other seemingly impossible situations his team had faced in the past. He refused to acquiesce to fear and overwhelming odds. After all, when their backs had been against the wall, his people had come through. Evil and wrongdoing had been confronted; justice had been served.

Jim, Sam, and Jamie hunkered down in Sam's Jeep along the side of the road on County Z between Crouch Valley and Sterling Ridge. Sam cracked open an energy drink and guzzled a few swigs. Jamie munched noisily on an energy bar, and then, thankfully for once, he became quiet.

The intrepid archaeologist had given them a blow-by-blow account of his escapades in the clutches of Charlie Tewalt—how he'd tried to reason with Charlie and develop a personal relationship with his captor, how he'd called 911 and Jim and then gotten beat up for it, how he'd opposed Charlie's plan to take Kay hostage, and how Kay had escaped by distracting Charlie when she'd led them to the Tiffany windows hidden in the ramshackle chapel. Finally, with a loud sigh, he was talked out. He lay down in the back seat of the Jeep and fell asleep, exhausted by his review of the day's stressful activities and his injuries.

Sam had remained alert for some time, but now he was fighting the sleep he desperately needed. It was close to three o'clock in the morning. He rubbed his neck, trying to ease the tension. Jim looked over at him.

"Tired?" he asked.

"Yeah. Can you handle it for a few minutes so I can take a quick power nap?" Sam asked.

"Sure. Get a few winks. This thing might last longer than we thought," Jim commented. Sam reclined in the passenger seat and closed his eyes, instantly falling asleep.

While Sam and Jamie slept, Jim called Carol. He was about to hang up on the fifth ring when Carol answered.

"Jim?" she asked sleepily.

"Hey, baby. Just checkin' in. Are the kids okay?" he asked.

"Yeah, they're fine. Henri was very upset that you didn't come home, but believe it or not, Lillie helped me out and took him outside to hunt for sticks for his boat." There was a slight pause. "Do you know what time it is?" Carol asked with a hint of irritation in her voice.

"You said you wanted me to stay in touch, so that's what I'm doin'," he muttered. "Besides, I'm trying to stay awake while Sam and Jamie get a few winks."

"You found Jamie?"

"Yep. Beat up and tied to a tree up in Wildcat Mountain," Jim said matter-of-factly. "I should really give Paco the credit. He's the one who sniffed him out."

"Wonders never cease. How does that kid get himself into these predicaments?"

"Don't ask. It's a long story, which I'll tell you later. Right now, I wish I was in bed with you."

"Oooh . . . my mind is going to some very nice places, but that would be futile since you're not here in the flesh to fulfill all my fantasies. But we can catch up later, right?"

"Absolutely, but not 'til I've had a stiff brandy and about sixteen hours of sleep," Jim said, smiling.

"Thanks for calling, honey, and stay safe. I'll say some more prayers," Carol said.

"Love you," Jim said softly.

"Love you, too," Carol said, and she hung up.

Farther south on Highway 33, Paul and DeDe were driving slowly along the highway toward the city of Hillsboro, a trip they'd made about three times already this evening. During their excursions, several deer had crossed the highway in front of their vehicle, and they'd spotted one skunk, two raccoons, and a mother opossum, her babies clinging to the fur on her back.

"Who knew this stretch of highway was such a thoroughfare of activity?" DeDe said in a sarcastic tone, clutching her coffee mug.

"Well, it's busy, but animals don't count when you're conducting a manhunt," Paul said grumpily.

"How long do you think we'll be at this?" DeDe asked.

"Hard tellin'," Paul answered. "But if nothing develops tonight, we'll need a new plan in the morning."

Meanwhile, Vernon County Sheriff Cecil Bjornstad sat behind the steering wheel of a black and tan Tahoe, his two deputies from his department in the back seat. They'd been driving the county roads that encircled Wildcat Mountain State Park, and driving slowly through the park, occasionally shining their spotlights into the thick woods along the roadside. So far, their attempts to locate Tewalt had come up empty.

Discouraged and weary, the sheriff recalled the determined resolve etched on Jim Higgins' face while they'd stood in the Starches' kitchen. He shuddered. There was something about the senior detective's demeanor that made him pause. He was aware of all the hoopla that surrounded Higgins' reputation, and up until today, he'd considered it nothing but a bunch of idle talk. Some hotshot detective outta the big city comes out here to the sticks and thinks he's gonna show everybody else the what for. That changed as he watched Higgins organize the search team, inspiring them with his quiet, focused leadership. He suddenly realized Higgins *expected* to catch Tewalt despite the overwhelming odds. And it was that expectation—that "we can do this" attitude—that inspired others to give their best and buy into the plan. Even if they never got a glimpse of the fugitive in question, Sheriff Bjornstad learned a valuable lesson: Your mindset gave you the ability to set a ripple effect into motion—a little pebble tossed into the pond creates an undulating wave that quickly spreads to others. He thought of a saying that was popular many years ago: It only takes a spark to get a fire going. Yeah, Higgins was the spark. He was the pebble that set the wave in motion. Somehow, the lieutenant, in a few brief statements in the Starches' kitchen, had been able to communicate a higher purpose that had inspired the entire team.

"Hey, boss. How long are we gonna keep circling the park?" Officer Larson asked from the back seat.

"As long as we have to," the sheriff answered brusquely. "Or until Higgins comes up with a better plan."

47

Early Saturday morning, Jim's phone buzzed. He fumbled to retrieve it from his pants pocket, shaking the grogginess and exhaustion away. He wondered when he'd fallen asleep, but then realized there was nothing he could do about it now. The cab of the Jeep smelled stuffy and vaguely like Paco. The indomitable canine had spent the night in the back seat, his head resting in Jamie's lap. Now, at the sound of the cell phone's ring, he raised his massive black head and woofed.

"Higgins," Jim mumbled into the phone, his voice deep and weary. Paco leaned over the seat and licked the side of Sam's face. Sam mumbled, frowned, and sat up abruptly, confused by the early morning light and Higgins' gruff conversation.

"He did what?" Jim asked loudly, still trying to shake off the fogginess of the night's long stakeout. He adjusted the driver's seat forward, forcing himself into a sitting position. His hair stuck up in a wild mess, and he absentmindedly rubbed the stiff stubble that shadowed his chin. Sam scanned the landscape, but everything outside the Jeep seemed quiet.

"Wait, wait. Say that again," Jim said impatiently. He switched his phone to speaker and laid it on the front seat.

Sam recognized the voice of Colleen Feske, the ranger at Wildcat Mountain State Park. "A couple of bikers came into my office early this morning about six o'clock," she said. "They'd been camping in the park and were planning on doing some biking today, but one of their bikes was stolen early this morning. Apparently, one of the neighbors in the next campsite got up to relieve himself, and he noticed someone—he said it was a large man—take one of their bikes. I'm wondering if the guy was Charlie Tewalt. The description the camper gave fits him to a T."

"Did this person get a good look at the guy?" Jim asked, wondering if this was another wild rumor that would lead to a futile chase through the dense woods.

"Well, it wasn't fully light yet, but he described the guy as large, physically fit, and dark-haired with a swarthy complexion. Does that sound like Tewalt?"

"Unfortunately, yes, but if he's riding a bike through the countryside, we should be able to spot him somewhere," Jim grumbled.

"I thought you should know about the bike, but you have to realize, Higgins, that we have a lot of trails within the park," the ranger explained. "If he's any kind of biker at all, he could get on a trail and disappear within the confines of the park pretty easily, and from there into the broader landscape. By the way, I've been telling all my campers and visitors to be aware that a fugitive is on the loose, possibly within the park. I managed to get a photo of Tewalt from the internet, and I've posted it outside on the office bulletin board."

"That's good. Which way was he heading?" Jim asked brusquely.

"The person who reported the stolen bike was in the group camping area in the middle of the park. It's only accessible by a gravel road," Feske said. "Where the guy headed after he stole the bike is unknown. All we can assume is he's heading out of the park so he can connect with a highway, but if you can post teams on Highways double Z, F, and 33, you might have a good chance of intercepting him."

"That's good. Thanks for the call, Colleen. I'll relay it to the team," Jim said. He turned to Sam.

"Someone spotted Tewalt?" Sam asked, swiping a hand through his hair, yawning widely. Jamie stirred in the back seat, then leaned his arms on the front seat and listened intently.

"Colleen said a couple of campers came into the park office to report a stolen bike early this morning. From the description of the guy, it sounds like it could be Tewalt. Pull up a map of the park on your phone while I call the teams," Jim ordered Sam. Suddenly, the atmosphere inside the truck was bristling with purpose.

Jim notified the teams, and during his conversations, Sam located a map of the park and studied it. Jamie leaned over the seat and pointed to the group campsite on the phone screen. When Jim finished, he leaned across the seat and looked at the map.

"Here's the group campsite," Sam said, enlarging the area. "If we can concentrate our efforts in that area, we might be able to spot him."

"Maybe, but remember he's pretty slippery, and he's got a head start on us." Jim sighed, trying to shake off the exhaustion he felt. "But it's the only thing we've got, so we'd better press our advantage and get a move on."

"My bike's on the Jeep in the rack. If worse comes to worse, I could pursue him," Sam said. His hazel eyes glowed with the anticipation of chasing a perp over the steep hills on a bike.

"You're going to pursue a killer on a bike?" Jim asked, tipping his head, his eyes wide with concern. "Are you serious? You do remember he's armed, don't you? He shot Kay Starch, for Pete's sake. If he did that, he won't hesitate to shoot someone chasing him on a bike."

"Well, if he's gone off-road, I could keep him in our sights. You could coordinate the teams and

. . ." Sam's voice faded away as Jim continued staring at him. Sam squirmed with discomfort, his expression ripe with frustration. He noticed Jim's skeptical expression. "Well, you got a better idea?" he snapped.

"Actually, no, I don't," Jim said calmly. He started the Jeep and drove onto the road heading into the park. He glanced over at Sam. "If you're going on some fantastic bike odyssey, then you'd better get your vest on and load your weapon. The chances of you ending up in a shoot-out are pretty good."

"I'm aware of the risks. Let's get this show on the road," Sam said, pointing toward the distant expanse of thick woods.

From the back seat, Jamie piped up. "Do you guys always make plans on the fly, or is there a rhyme or reason to your strategies?"

"Shut up, Jamie." Jim and Sam replied in unison.

⊠

Charlie Tewalt was tired, hungry, and cold, but pedaling the mountain bike he'd stolen from the campers in the park got his blood pumping, and soon he was sweating with exertion navigating the hilly trails of Wildcat Mountain State Park. He stopped after about fifteen minutes and studied the map of the park he'd brought up on his phone. Things were quiet in the park this morning, and he hoped he could get out on a country road soon and get to a nearby town before all hell broke loose. Last night, he'd made a call to his personal administrative assistant, Sarah Fletcher, at her home in Chicago while he was propped against a tree trunk in the dark woods trying to catch a few winks of sleep.

"Sarah?" Charlie asked when someone came on the line.

A deep male voice asked brusquely, "Who wants to know?"

"Her boss, Charlie. Is she there?"

"Yeah. Can't it wait? We were busy," the voice said, insinuating some kind of sexual tryst.

"Put her on," Charlie demanded.

"Are you serious?"

"For what I pay her, I'm dead serious," Charlie said, his voice raspy with frustration. "Put her on the phone! NOW!"

There were some fumbling, rustling sounds, and Sarah finally came on the line.

"Mr. Tewalt? Where have you been? I've had a hundred calls—"

"Never mind that now! I need you to contact Larry Fischer. You've got his number in your system somewhere—"

"You mean right now?" Sarah interrupted in a whining tone. "It's two o'clock in the morning, sir."

"I'm well aware of the time. And yes, I mean right now! Have him call me on my cell. You know my number," Charlie ordered impatiently.

"Are you all right, sir? You sound awfully stressed," Sarah said with polite concern.

Charlie drew in a deep breath and dredged up as much patience as he could. "I'm fine, Sarah. I just have a very important job for Larry. In fact, it's an emergency, and I know you'll do a great job convincing him to call me, won't you?"

"I'll do my best, sir," Sarah answered professionally.

"As I knew you would. This is why I hired you, honey, and it's why I pay you such a good salary. Now you call Larry as soon as I hang up, okay?"

"Yes, sir," Sarah said. "I'll give him—"

Sarah heard the phone line go dead.

"—your number," she said softly into the phone.

48

At six-fifteen in the morning, Jim's team, Sheriff Bjornstad and his two officers, and several other personnel from Vernon and La Crosse Counties law enforcement were standing in an open field bordered by a forest of huge pines, mature oaks, and maples. Nearby, the Shinnick Valley Observation Point overlooked the panorama of the Driftless topography. It was a beautiful morning. A haze of fog drifted lazily through the valley along the Kickapoo River, which wound its way through the landscape like an ancient, sinuous serpent. On the horizon, the pink hue of sunrise gave way to a layer of blue that held the promise of a clear, sunny day. Layers of old pine forest were interlaced with stands of hardwoods. Suddenly brilliant sunshine broke through the drifting clouds and illuminated the landscape below.

Sam pulled his mountain bike from the rack on the back of the Jeep. He struggled into his Kevlar vest and holstered his pistol under his armpit. It was clumsy, but he was a competent biker with a lot of experience, so being weighed down with protective equipment was something he was prepared to do—cumbersome, but necessary considering the task at hand.

Jim Higgins stood next to Sam's Jeep, a map of the park spread over the hood as he talked to the group of cops. Earlier in the morning, Sheriff Bjornstad had spent time on the phone contacting law enforcement personnel in Vernon County to help in the search, and Sheriff Elaine Turnmile sent several officers to the park as well. Most of them were sipping cups of hot coffee while Jim reviewed the plan. *From the looks of it,* he thought, *we all should be sacked out in bed.* Nevertheless, he tried to look alert and in charge.

"All right, here's the plan, loose as it is," Jim began. Using his finger, he pointed on the map to the group campsite in the northeast corner of the park. "Tewalt was spotted here about a half hour ago," he began. "That's where he stole the bike. If he's looked at a map, he'll most likely head along Red Trail making his way toward Highway F. Of course, that's just a guess, but we've got to start somewhere." Jim looked around at the group; so far, they seemed alert and focused.

Sam leaned over the map and tapped his finger on the paper. "I'll head down Green Trail until I come to Red and see if I can intercept him," he said.

From the edge of the group, Paul commented, "I'll launch our drone and start scoping the area. I may be able to spot him on one of the trails."

Sheriff Bjornstad pointed his thumb over his shoulder at one of his officers. "Jeff will patrol Highway F while we're conducting the search in the park."

"All right. That sounds good," Jim responded. "Think fluid, people. Things will change rapidly if he's spotted. Let's spread out at points along the trails. Everyone, be alert. This guy has already injured a civilian. He's desperate and exhausted, which is not a good combination." Jim paused, thinking about the ramifications of their plan. He'd never had an officer chase a suspect on a bike before, and he fidgeted nervously when he thought about all the things that could go wrong. In addition, the densely wooded areas in the park provided endless possibilities for concealment. An ambush accompanied by gunfire was not out of the realm of possibility. The search could go on for quite a while, possibly days, and then, there was the likelihood that Tewalt had already gotten away and was headed back to Chicago.

"Some of us will go down Blue Trail," Jim said after a slight pause, "and a couple of groups can hike the Purple Trail, here and here." He pointed to the trails on the park map. "Let's rendezvous at Johnnycake Overlook at ten o'clock. Keep your phones on and communicate with the team so we know when and how to assist if Tewalt is spotted." The team remained mute, but Jim was encouraged when several heads nodded in agreement.

"I'm off," Sam said as he jumped on his bike and pedaled steadily toward the opening of Green Trail. Soon he disappeared into the forest.

Standing next to Jim, Paul looked over at his boss, his face furrowed with worry. "Think he'll be all right, Chief?"

"Yep. He'll be fine. Of all of us, he's probably the only one who has a decent chance of spotting

Tewalt . . . except you with that . . . thing," Jim said, pointing to the drone. To everyone, he said, "Let's get to our posts and start searching. DeDe, you're with me."

Jim's phone vibrated. Ranger Colleen Feske asked, "What's the plan, Higgins?"

Jim filled her in. "That's a good plan," she said when he finished. "Jed and I will back you up. We'll start here at the horse camp, and we'll proceed down Red Trail on horseback and head to Johnnycake Overlook. With everyone out, we have a good chance of spotting him."

"You armed?" Jim asked.

"Yes, sir. Always am. We're prepared to assist in any way we can," Colleen said.

"Great. Talk to you later," Jim said.

The group dispersed. Some went down Green Trail, some veered off to the northeast on Purple Trail, and some stayed on Blue Trail.

Jim, Jamie, and DeDe began hiking vigorously down Blue Trail.

Paco trotted ahead of them, at times with his head up and alert and other times with his nose to the ground, sniffing and snorting. The morning sun left dappled patterns of sunlight on the shaded path. Somewhere in a nearby tree, Jim saw a flash of yellow and heard the warble of a common yellowthroat. There was something comforting in the little bird's song, a cheerful optimism that Jim sorely needed at the moment—he took it as a good sign. Despite the grim circumstances, he was struck by the beauty of the natural world. In the face of the last-ditch efforts by law enforcement to capture a violent criminal, the park's solitude was a peaceful backdrop. Jamie and DeDe trudged along behind Jim while Paco led the charge. The dog's indomitable attitude lifted the group's spirits as they tramped through the mute forest in the early morning hours.

Farther ahead on the trail, Sam pedaled steadily until the path merged with Red Trail. He stopped briefly and took a swig of water, wishing he'd brought Paco with him. He thought of his beautiful wife and daughter at home sleeping in their beds, and he whispered a prayer for his protection. He knew his chances of intercepting Tewalt were pretty slim. Still, he had to try. The guy had tried to kill Kay Starch. Sam gritted his teeth in anger at the thought of the damage Tewalt had already done, and he pushed off again, pedaling furiously, scanning the forest and undergrowth for any sight of the elusive desperado.

He was moving along at a good pace when suddenly, off to his right, he noticed a flash, some kind of shadow. At first, he thought it might be a deer, but then, as he glanced back to where the Red and Purple Trails intersected, he saw a flicker of metal and heard the swish of tires on the dirt path, the flash of something black. Tewalt!

Sam backtracked and saw the sign for the Purple Trail. He turned on it and began pedaling faster, exerting himself, pumping hard up and down the hills and around the frequent curves on the path. Up ahead, quite a distance away, he saw Tewalt madly pedaling in his bid to escape. Sam fumbled in his jacket pocket for his cell. Speed dialing Jim as he pedaled, he waited for an answer.

"Higgins."

"Chief, I've spotted Tewalt," Sam huffed. "He's on Purple Trail heading northeast. Check your map. Any place we could meet?" he asked, waiting for Higgins to respond.

"Hang on. I'm looking . . . the only thing I see is Billings Creek Lookout."

"Okay. I'm following him—get some people over here." And he hung up.

Up ahead, Sam caught another dash of black clothing moving fast through the woods. He pumped intensely. Suddenly, Sam heard the pop of gunfire, and an overhanging tree branch just above him splintered, sending pieces of bark and wood into the air. Instinctively, Sam ducked, pulled his pistol from the holster, but then he realized gripping the gun while steering the bike would be too clumsy and would slow him down, so he tucked the pistol back under his armpit and pumped harder. The gunshot ticked him off. In his anger, he pumped madly, and he began to feel the familiar burn of exertion in his legs. He was sweating profusely, and his lungs felt like they'd explode.

Up ahead, a sharp curve on the trail almost upended him, but he hung on as he rounded the corner. *Tewalt must be a pretty good athlete. He's movin' fast,* he thought. *Maybe the guy stopped and is waiting to ambush me.*

A few moments later, the trail dipped steeply downward in a series of log steps that descended to a flatter area below. Sam hesitated, then stood on his pedals and pointed his bike down the stairs, hoping the logs weren't slippery. He bumped precipitously over the rough steps and ended up at the bottom upright and in one piece. He looked ahead. Tewalt was only about a hundred feet in front of him.

"Stop!" Sam yelled hoarsely. "You're under arrest! You won't get away with this, Tewalt! You're surrounded." After he yelled the last words, Sam felt foolish. Surrounded hardly described the situation Tewalt was in. After all, he was being chased by one cop on a bike.

In response to Sam's warning, the former ranger continued to pedal, then turned and fired his pistol again. Dirt exploded on the trail in front of Sam, splattering him with grit and pebbles.

Sam poured it on, and soon only a few feet separated him from Tewalt. He gritted his teeth as he caught up and pulled even. The two men rode tandem down the narrow trail. Tewalt looked over at Sam, an expression of sheer panic on his face. He swore, then lifted his pistol and pointed it at Sam.

In an audacious leap of self-defense, Sam launched himself off his bike, his legs arching up and over the handlebars as he threw himself on Tewalt. The tackle knocked the two men into the air as they somersaulted to the ground and lay in a heap, panting with exhaustion. The bikes flew off the trail and landed in a pile of tangled metal, the wheels whirling aimlessly. The pistol Tewalt had brandished a moment ago flew through the air and landed twenty feet away.

Tewalt was not through resisting, however. He reached over and punched Sam in the stomach. Rolling on top of him, he continued to pummel Sam's face and upper body with well-aimed blows. In a move reminiscent of his high school wrestling days, Sam continued to roll and work his way free under Tewalt, finally breaking loose and jumping up into a fighting stance. Tewalt scrambled to his feet, and the two men squared off, eyeing each other with murderous intent. Tewalt circled Sam, analyzing his chances of escape.

"Give it up, Tewalt," Sam whispered intensely. "Law enforcement is on the way. Even if you escape from here, there's more of us comin'. You won't get away with this."

Tewalt considered his options as he danced around Sam. He'd been in hand-to-hand combat before. He was surprised by the strength and tenacity of this young man who'd chased him relentlessly through the hilly wooded terrain and tackled him from a moving bike. *Of course,* Tewalt thought, *I am aging, and my fighting skills are a bit rusty.* Sitting behind a desk all day tended to dull the sharp edges of a person's reaction times. *Now what?* Tewalt thought. *Negotiation?* Maybe. *Go for the gun?* Another possibility. *Give up?* Inconceivable.

Suddenly, two horses appeared on the trail, galloping quickly toward the scene. With guns drawn, the officers pulled the horses to a dramatic stop, dismounted, and quickly approached Sam and the fugitive.

"Charles Tewalt, I presume?" Ranger Feske asked, aiming her Glock pistol at the fugitive's midsection.

"That would be correct," Sam piped up. He was beginning to feel the areas on his body where Tewalt's blows had landed. *Boy, I'm gonna be sore tomorrow,* he thought. He grimaced when he ran his hand across his midsection.

Sam heard a light buzzing sound and looked up. The drone from the law enforcement department hung effortlessly in the sky above them like an aerodynamic whirligig. It hovered there, watching and recording the capture.

Tewalt scrutinized the proceedings as if he were a spectator—like an out-of-body experience. His mouth hung open, and he thought, *What else are these bozos gonna pull out of their hats?*

At that moment, Deputy Tom Still from the Vernon County Sheriff's Department came jogging down the trail with Paul Saner close behind. Tewalt shook his head at the inevitability of the situation. He was surrounded. His capture was a foregone conclusion. The retired army ranger groaned, thinking of the consequences of his crime spree, his ignoble arrest recorded in detail by the hovering all-seeing drone. He was sure the events of the past few days would garner the attention of the national press—all because a bunch of Keystone Cops took their jobs seriously. *I guess my luck has run out,* he thought bitterly. As the handcuffs were snapped around his wrists, Tewalt heard words he thought he'd never hear.

"Charles Tewalt, I am arresting you for the abduction of Jamie Alberg and the kidnapping and attempted murder of Kay Starch. You have the right to remain silent . . ."

49

By the time Charlie Tewalt had been loaded in a cruiser for his ride to the Vernon County jail, Jim, DeDe, Sam, and Paul were sitting in Sam's Jeep, tying up loose ends. Jamie Alberg hunched down in the back seat, a look of smug triumph etched on his boyish features as he stroked Paco's thick fur and fed him kibble treats.

"So, Tewalt is being taken to La Crosse eventually, right, Chief?" Sam asked. He rubbed his stomach muscles gingerly. The bruises from his take-down of Tewalt were already causing him considerable discomfort. In addition, his mountain bike had been loaded on the back of the Jeep. It was a mangled mess. Sam didn't even want to think about the price tag for the repairs it would need to be functional again.

"Tewalt will be charged with the crimes he committed in La Crosse County, namely the abduction of Jamie. Vernon County will file its own charges of the attempted murder of Kay Starch. He'll appear before Judge Walcott on Monday to be formally arraigned," Jim said wearily. "By the way, I talked to Bubba, and Kay came through her surgery well. She's on the mend and should be home within two or three days. Her full recovery will take quite a bit longer."

"The windows? What's happening with them?" DeDe asked from the back seat.

"The ownership issue is still front and center," Jim explained. "From what I understand, the old rule about possession being nine-tenths of the law will come into play, but that's something for the lawyers to fight over. In the meantime, the windows have been moved to the Starches' garage, where they will remain for the time being under the watchful eye of a couple of Vernon County deputies."

Paul yawned widely and stretched out in the back seat. "All I know is, I need some sleep and some food, in no particular order. Breakfast in Ontario, anyone?" he asked.

"Sounds good by me," Sam replied, leaning over and starting the Jeep.

"Pancakes, eggs, and sausage will go a long way toward my recovery," Jamie chirped cheerfully from the back seat.

Jim shook his head. "Drive, Sam," Jim said wearily, wiggling his finger at the road ahead of them.

"What?" Jamie sputtered. "What did I say?" His eyes widened in false innocence.

DeDe patted his hand in a motherly gesture. "If you don't know, buddy, we're not telling you."

Jim slept away most of late Saturday afternoon in the confines of his quiet bedroom. Lillie could no longer wait for her father to appear. Bursting into his room at five o'clock in the evening, she stood by the bed and rubbed Jim's shoulder. He was still groggy from two days without sleep, but he rolled over and sat up in bed.

"Hey, peanut," he said to Lillie.

"Dad, your hair is sticking up all over," she said with a frown, giving him a long, penetrating stare.

"Been a tough couple of days, toots. What's on your mind?" he asked. "Where is everybody?"

He was still feeling the effects of the exhausting manhunt in the park. Waking up, the facts of the Tiffany case crowded into his mind again and weighed him down. He shook his head trying to dismiss the nagging facts while he gazed tenderly at his daughter. She always grounded him, and he was happy to see her. Lillie's physical features reminded him of the Nordic genetics that ran deeply through his family—fair skin, blonde hair, and blue eyes. But it was her searing questions that kept him on his toes. Lillie stared at her father, undoubtedly composing a series of penetrating questions about the Tiffany window case. She didn't disappoint.

"Did you find the beautiful windows?" she asked. She crossed her arms over her chest and waited for Jim's response. Her gaze was accompanied by a preternatural calm that made Jim sit up a little straighter.

He patted the bedspread. "Come up here. I need a hug from my girl," he said.

Lillie crawled up on the bed, wriggled under the blankets, and snuggled next to Jim. "You're growing up way too fast, Lillie," he said, pulling her closer. "You need to stop growing. Can't you just stay this size forever?" He buried his nose in her blonde curls.

"You can't hold back nature, Dad," Lillie said with a patronizing tone. "It has a mind of its own. I'm already forty-four inches tall—that's almost four feet."

"Wow! Like I said, you're getting way too big for your britches," Jim said softly with a trace of sadness. *Where have the years gone?* he thought. It seemed like only yesterday when four-year-old Lillie had stood in the bathroom and watched him shave, asking a thousand questions.

"You didn't answer my question," Lillie persisted. "Did you find the beautiful windows?"

"Yep. And they were in an old shed like the one you saw in your dream."

"Really?" Lillie's eyes grew big with the accuracy of her prognostication.

"Yes, really. They were hidden in an old lumber camp chapel over in Wildcat Mountain."

"Where's that?" Lillie asked brusquely.

"Over by Ontario," Jim explained. "I'll take you there sometime."

"Today?"

"No, no," Jim said brusquely, shaking his head. "I've had enough of that place for a while, but it does have some beautiful trails. Maybe one day we'll go hiking and have a picnic. How does that sound?"

"When, Dad?"

"Well, we'll talk to Mom and—"

At that moment, Henri exploded into the bedroom dressed like a cowboy. His felt hat was tipped at a jaunty angle on his head, and his cowboy boots were scuffed, but he had a determined look on his face as he swung his lariat in a circle over his head. "I'm gonna lasso you, Dad!" he shouted, "and tie you up!" He twirled the lariat over his head and threw it toward Jim and Lillie, but the rope missed the mark and landed on the bedside lamp, tipping it precariously. Jim quickly leaned over and saved it from falling onto the floor.

"Hey, pardner!" Jim said. "What's with the cowboy stuff?"

"I'm an old cowhand," he said seriously, "from the Rio Grande."

"Do you even know where the Rio Grande is?" Lillie asked sarcastically.

"Lillie, give him some freedom to imagine," Jim cautioned. Carol walked into the room, came over to the bed, and gave Jim a tender kiss. "Have you gotten roped yet?" she asked with a grin.

"Just about, but Cowboy Henri needs a little more practice," Jim said, chuckling under his breath.

"Supper in about a half hour," Carol said. "Your favorite—roast chicken, smashed potatoes, salad, and blueberry pie."

"Wow! Sounds great. I'll jump in the shower," Jim said, placing his feet on the floor. Lillie jumped down from the bed, grabbed Henri's lariat, and began advising him on his roping tactics. "See Henri, you've got to get a rhythm going," she advised as she began twirling the rope over her head, her hips gyrating wildly.

"Hey! Out on the deck with that before you do some major damage," Carol warned loudly, pointing toward the backyard.

The children ran out of the bedroom through the house to the patio. Suddenly it was quiet. Carol sat down beside Jim and gently rubbed his back. "How're you feeling, honey?" she asked.

"Old and tired." He ran his hand through his hair.

"Anybody get hurt?" Carol asked.

"Jamie got a black eye when he smarted off to Tewalt after he abducted him from his place in La Crosse. The guy is well known in the Chicago criminal underworld. He shot Kay Starch in the thigh and shoulder when she tried to escape from the chapel, where the windows were hidden, but she drove home on her UTV and collapsed in the garage. Sam took a Tour de France ride on his bike through Wildcat State Park and chased down Tewalt, tackled him, and captured him. I think Tewalt was surprised, but not as much as Sam was when he managed to pull that one off. Kay came through surgery with flying colors. She's tough, despite the fact that most people think she's a pushover. I think Jamie's got a new heroine—Kay Starch—if a sixty-something woman can be a heroine."

"Hey, I could be offended by that statement," Carol said, frowning at Jim. "Older women can definitely be heroines."

Jim made a wry face and shook his head. "Yeah, I guess I would have to agree with you on that." He thought about the miraculous escape Kay made on the UTV in the dark and wondered how Bubba was handling the crisis with his wife. "Other than that, the rest of us are still in one piece," Jim explained.

"Wow! That sounds like an amazing sequence of events," Carol commented. "Once again your team came through, but don't overthink all of this. Just take it at face value. I'm sure you'll have some time to put it all in perspective later."

Jim nodded in agreement and looked over at his wife. Despite the fact that they had landed solidly in middle age, Carol was still a very beautiful woman. He always felt privileged to be in her presence after he'd been away from her for a few days. It was in those moments when she sat close to him or showed him affection that he realized how much he loved her. Her physical beauty, her concern for him, the kindness reflected in her brown eyes, her gentle touch. They were all the things he treasured about her but rarely appreciated in the hectic day-to-day activity of everyday life. He knew everyone could become blasé at times about the normalcy of life, but as a cop, he'd seen how life could be shattered in an instant by a violent confrontation—a traffic accident, a stray bullet, a chance encounter with a desperate criminal, a heart attack, a freak accident. Normal might not be exciting, but it was the fabric of everyday life, and he was so thankful for the simple moments when things were ordinary.

"Do you know what a blessing you are to me?" he asked. His eyes misted with tears.

"Are you going all sentimental on me now?" Carol asked brusquely, cocking her head at him. Then her expression softened. She laid her hand on his thigh, and she smiled shyly. "I know what you mean." She held up her hand in a scout salute. "True confession: I don't know what I'd do if something happened to you."

Jim nodded his head. "Lots of stuff has already happened to me, and you handled it just fine."

"Well, let's not put that theory to the test." Carol laughed softly and stood up. "You'd better get in the shower and just remember, we'll do something about all this tonight after the kids are in bed."

Jim stood up and began walking to the bathroom. "Is that a promise?" he asked over his shoulder.

"I'll hold you to it," she said smiling.

MONDAY, MAY 28

50

In the days that followed the capture of Lewis Borden and Charlie Tewalt, the Tiffany window saga took on a life of its own. An amazing discovery of lost treasures by an unassuming Vietnam vet and the subsequent capture of the perps responsible for the mayhem in the area by Jim's team had propelled the story into state and national attention.

Charlie Tewalt—the highly trained army veteran and successful Chicago businessman—probably never imagined that his foray into the Wisconsin countryside would be a disaster of epic proportions. Jim harrumphed, then smiled when he thought about Sam hightailing it through the woods after Tewalt on his bike. Charlie's refusal to take his opponent seriously had had devastating repercussions. Jim was sure the cocky criminal was still reeling in disbelief at the unconventional methods of "a bunch of country cops from the sticks," a phrase he had muttered under his breath when he was taken into custody by the Vernon County Sheriff's Department.

On another positive note, Jim's team had captured Lewis Borden and arrested him for his attack on Geoff LaSarde in his La Crosse home, and they'd located the elusive, missing Tiffany windows, which provided a certain degree of satisfaction. Organizing the evidence around the case would take months of evaluation, and the preparation for the trials that would follow later would include a considerable amount of time, organization, and expertise.

The discovery of the windows also resulted in attention from state and national press. Since the discovery of the national treasures, reporters had arrived in droves, inundating the small college town of La Crosse, crowding its restaurants and hotels to capacity. The city streets were jammed with news vehicles from the Tri-State area, and reporters were everywhere, wanting exclusive interviews with members of Higgins' detective team, and of course, Jamie Alberg, treasure hunter extraordinaire. Hordes of reporters swarmed the new art gallery, the law enforcement center, and the Mayo hospital in town, where Kay Starch was still recovering from her surgery. The insatiable thirst for anything bordering on the fantastic or extraordinary was nothing unusual. The team had endured its share of uncomfortable moments in the spotlight before. Jim watched the news reports on a few local TV stations in his living room over the weekend with an attitude of insouciant tolerance.

In addition to the irritating presence of hundreds of reporters and videographers in and around La Crosse, art critics had descended on the small college town like a horde of angry bees. To Jim, it seemed like everyone and their dog were trying to determine the location of the infamous windows—the proverbial needle in the haystack. Curious onlookers and other sensationalists were spreading out over the city and countryside in a desperate attempt to get a glimpse of "lost" history rediscovered. As a result, Vernon County Sheriff Cecil Bjornstad and his crew of loyal deputies had to move the windows from the Starches' garage in Ontario to an undisclosed location in the cover of dark while trying to avoid any undue attention from pesky reporters. Jim and the team holed up in their respective homes over the weekend, avoiding the limelight and hysteria over the priceless treasures. Jim couldn't count the times he'd answered his phone only to say, "No comment" before he rudely hung up. Jamie Alberg, true to form, conducted several interviews from his home on Madison

Street, complete with details of his abduction and subsequent rescue by Jim and Sam. YouTube was voraciously feeding the public's curiosity about the case with tantalizing tidbits that Jamie had so openly shared, much to Jim's chagrin.

By Monday morning, life at the Higgins' household had leveled out to some degree. Jim had caught up on his sleep, the kids were bickering at the breakfast table like they usually did, and Carol was scurrying around getting school lunches made and organizing the kids' backpacks before the school bus drove up.

Jim's cell buzzed in his pants pocket as he was about to get another cup of coffee.

"Higgins."

"Chief, wondering if you saw Turnmile's news conference this morning on Channel 8?" Sam asked.

"Nope, but I've seen her in action before, so I'm not going to waste my time listening to her rambling analysis of what we did, or what we could have done better, or what we should have done instead," Jim said caustically. "Besides, she never has anything good to say about us anyway, so why should I give her attention she doesn't deserve?"

"Well, she actually gave us a few backhanded compliments," Sam informed him.

"Will wonders never cease?" Jim said grumpily. "So what were these earth-shattering accolades?"

"As I recall," Sam continued, "she said something about her 'crack' team of investigators and their 'inventive' tactics in capturing Tewalt."

"Was she referring to your hair-raising ride through the Wildcat Mountain trails on a bike while you were dodging bullets?" Jim asked.

"I would imagine that was what she was referring to when she used the phrase 'inventive tactics,'" Sam said, chuckling. "By the way, are we meeting today?"

"I'll be in the office by nine, and we'll meet at ten or so and start wading through the evidence."

"That's gonna be a big job," Sam commented dismally.

"Yeah, I know, but you have to admit that when we started this whole Tiffany thing, there was hardly enough evidence to even consider it a case, remember? We've come a long way since then. See you about ten," Jim said tersely and hung up.

Jim continued his morning routine, indulging in an extra cup of coffee with Carol before he left for work. Driving along Chipmunk Coulee Road to the law enforcement center in the city gave him time to reflect on the hustle and bustle of another case with its surprising twists and turns and dramatic finale. At the office parking lot, Jim stepped down from his vehicle and began walking to the back entrance of the law enforcement center.

Suddenly, from around the front of the building, a reporter hurried toward him, his cameraman following, trying to keep up. The reporter raised his hand in the air in a kind of salutation. Then in the next few seconds, another swarm of people appeared around the corner of the building, rushing toward Higgins, some with microphones and others shouldering heavy cameras.

"Lt. Higgins! Wait! Could we have a comment?" Matt Calhoun shouted.

At the sound of Matt's voice, Jim cringed inwardly. He'd been hoping to avoid a major scene with the media. There was already plenty of scuttlebutt circulating on social media about the discovery of the Tiffany windows, but most of it was grossly inflated to inaccurate levels of untruth. Jim turned and weakly raised his hand in a greeting and waited near the entrance at the back of the building while the swarm of reporters caught up to him. He recognized Matt Calhoun from the *La Crosse Sentinel* leading the pack.

"Matt, what's up?" Jim asked. The reporter stopped in front of him, pushing a mike in his face.

"What can you tell us about the Tiffany windows?" one voice shouted.

"Where are they being stored?" another yelled.

"Who found them?" Matt asked. "Are the men—"

"Whoa, whoa, whoa!" Jim said, holding up his hand. The crowd quieted down. "I will make a brief statement. That's it. I've got a meeting to get to."

"Just a statement? Nothing else?" Matt said, the frown on his forehead deepening. A rumble of voices behind him threatened to upend the interview.

Jim held up his hand in a stern warning. "You want information or not?"

Matt nodded his head sheepishly.

"Okay. Here we go," Jim continued. "The Tiffany windows were found in an old building near a private residence in rural Ontario. They are now in safekeeping until their ownership can be determined." Jim hated the intrusion of the cameras and microphones in the background recording his every move. "A woman was injured during the hunt for the windows, but she has since had surgery and is recovering. Two individuals were apprehended during the incident. We are still trying to piece together the chain of events that has led to this unfortunate event." Jim stopped, and the reporters stared at him.

"Is it true the windows have been missing for over one hundred years?" Matt asked.

"Yes. That is true," Jim responded calmly.

"And they're genuine Tiffany windows?" another asked.

"Yes, they're the real deal."

"Who owns them?" someone else asked.

"We're not sure yet. The lawyers involved in the case are still trying to determine that."

"Can you reveal the name of the injured party?" a petite woman asked.

"No, she wishes to maintain her privacy," Jim said.

"Come on, Lieutenant," Matt said crossly. "It's all going to come out anyway."

"Well then, let's give her a few more moments of privacy, which she richly deserves." Jim shuffled his feet and moved toward the door. "That's all, people." Jim swiped his ID through the card reader and pulled the door open.

"Wait! One more thing," Matt yelled.

Jim turned, wedging his foot inside the door. "What now?" he snarled.

"Is it true that Sam Birkstein captured one of the individuals by chasing him through Wildcat Mountain State Park on a bike?"

"Yes," Jim said. He stepped inside the building and walked down the hall. He could hear the buzz of conversation beyond the closed door as he walked away, and he felt the heat of his flushed cheeks as he stepped into the elevator. Dealing with the media was a crapshoot at best, but he realized it was a necessary part of his job. His thoughts shifted to the task before him. He leaned against the wall of the elevator as it ascended to the third floor. "I hope I fed them enough so they leave me alone," he said to himself.

51

Bubba Starch leaned over the railing of the hospital bed where his wife, Kay, lay sleeping. He looked at her plain face and graying hair. She wasn't a raving beauty. In fact, she'd always been something of a wallflower in other people's estimation. But to Bubba, since her daring escape from the chapel in the woods behind their property on their UTV while wounded, she seemed like a modern-day Joan of Arc and Marilyn Monroe all rolled into one.

"Don't make me out to be a hero, Bubba," she said softly, her brown eyes filling with tears. "You would have done the same thing if Tewalt had threatened you."

"Well, the point is, you were the one who had the balls . . . whoops, wrong metaphor." He corrected himself. "You were the one who had the nerve and grit to pull it off. Everybody is talkin' about it, honey." Leaning over to pick up the *La Crosse Sentinel*, he pointed to the title of the lead article on the front page, "Unassuming Woman Escapes Desperate Criminal on UTV." "See? It says right here you're a bona fide hero."

Kay read the headline and waved her hand weakly in his direction. "It doesn't say anything about being a hero. That's all just a bunch of hype. Some reporter needed something to plaster on the front page to sell a few extra newspapers. I just did what I had to do, and you would have too." She rolled over and drifted back into a drug-induced sleep.

Bubba lowered the newspaper and watched her placid face. He couldn't reconcile his wife's nonchalance with the bold headlines about her that jumped off the page of the *Sentinel*. Sooner or later, he realized they would go back to their quiet, country home and pick up living where they'd left off, before all this crazy stuff had invaded and run rampant over their ordinary lives. Somehow, for Kay, her life did not include heroic tales that had been elevated to levels of exaggeration and hyperbole. She just wanted to go back to life as it used to be.

Kay's surgery had been successful for the most part. Dr. Gerhig explained the procedures he'd used and the repairs he'd done to piece together Kay's hip and shoulder. Despite the significant amount of blood she'd lost before her arrival at the hospital, Kay had been tough and had made a remarkable recovery. The surgeon explained the need for intense physical therapy to regain the full range and use of her leg and shoulder, but with several months of focused exercise, he was confident she would make a full recovery and continue the active life she'd enjoyed before all of this had happened. Every day, she seemed to gain strength and confidence, although the fear and trauma of the escape in the dark on the UTV continued to haunt her dreams and torment her.

Bubba turned and left Kay's room. He walked down the hallway in search of a freshly brewed cup of coffee. Suddenly, from behind him, he heard a familiar voice.

"Bubba! Wait up."

Bubba turned to see Jim Higgins walking briskly toward him. He was casually dressed in a pair of blue jeans, Hey Dude loafers, and a plum-colored pullover sweater. Jim reached out his hand, and the two men shook.

"How's Kay?" Jim asked.

"She's getting stronger every day. Hopefully, we'll go home in a few days and try to get back to normal." Jim met Bubba's intense gaze and held it.

"Fair warning. It might take more than a few days to process everything that's happened," Jim said brusquely.

Bubba noticed the steely-eyed gaze and the determined set of Jim's jaw. "You sound like you're speaking from experience," Bubba said.

Jim nodded his head, and he looked off into the distance, remembering his painful recovery from his shoulder injury a couple of years ago. "I am speaking from experience, unfortunately. My daughter is still recovering from her abduction by a merciless criminal a couple of years ago. The physical wounds will heal, but the psychological damage can run deep." Jim looked directly at Bubba again. "I'm just saying from experience, it takes time and patience. Don't try to rush it along. The brain and emotions have their own timetable for healing."

"When we get back home, Kay wants to have you and your family over for a meal," Bubba explained. "She wants to thank you for all you did."

"I didn't do that much. She's the one who used her wits and escaped, but that sounds great. You've got a beautiful place. My kids would love it." Jim smiled widely. "Hey, listen, I was just in the neighborhood and thought I'd check on you. Glad to hear things are moving along," Jim continued, "but I've got a meeting back at the center."

"I imagine you're still trying to connect all the dots in this mixed-up affair," Bubba said.

"Dots that are missing, mostly. But we've come up with a few details that might help, although we're a long way from knowing what really happened. The years between the theft of the windows and your discovery of them in the chapel is an awfully big space to fill with facts that are . . . well . . . nonexistent."

"I never did show you the letter from Willie, did I?" Bubba asked.

"No, you didn't. Would it help?"

"Everything that's in it you already know. I honestly don't believe Kay's dad knew that much either. I guess old man Bradford covered his tracks so well, he was the only one who really knew what happened."

"Looks like it," Jim said. He placed his hand on Bubba's shoulder. "I've gotta get going. Take care of Kay. The good Lord was watching over her, that's for sure."

Bubba nodded thoughtfully. "He still is," he whispered softly.

52

Larry Fischer arrived at the Wildcat Mountain State Park office about nine o'clock on Saturday morning—a bit too late to rescue his boss, Charlie Tewalt, from the mess he'd gotten himself into. Larry thought about the frantic phone call he'd gotten from Tewalt's secretary in the middle of the night. As usual, it had been a bit over the top, but that was Charlie. He tended to over-dramatize his problems. But when Larry received another phone call from Charlie late Saturday afternoon detailing his apprehension by police, Larry realized his boss was in some very serious trouble.

After Charlie was taken into custody and transported to the Vernon County law enforcement facility Saturday morning, Larry holed up at the Comfort Inn on the edge of Viroqua over the weekend and made some phone calls. Now on Monday morning, he stepped into the shower and lathered up. When Lewis Borden was fired three weeks ago, Larry never imagined that Charlie would consider him a potential personal "fixer." He thought about the one chance he had to impress his boss, and a tight knot formed in the pit of his stomach.

Larry Fischer was a legitimate licensed lawyer in the state of Illinois, but, in reality, he'd never practiced any kind of law other than corporate law. He'd been indispensable at Tewalt Industries preparing paperwork for patents, handling personnel complaints to avoid lawsuits, negotiating contracts with subsidiary companies, and a variety of other corporate legal work that required a quick mind and dogged attention to detail. But personal defense attorney? That was way out of his league. However, as he considered his options, he was confident that with practice and significant personal effort, he could deliver for his boss. His heart fluttered in his chest when he thought about the substantial pay increase that would accompany such a position in the company. It was well known among the administrative office staff that Lewis Borden had been rewarded very well for his work on Charlie Tewalt's behalf, although no one really knew exactly what he did or how much he'd been paid to do it. Of course, right now Lewis Borden was sitting in jail in La Crosse on charges of burglary, theft, and battery—all felonies in the state of Wisconsin.

Larry thought about the current incarceration of Tewalt and Borden. He was confused and troubled by the thoughts and questions that swirled in his mind. Borden's legendary reputation as an exceptional soldier was well known throughout the small Chicago company. So, what was he doing operating undercover? If he was so good at his job, how had he been so easily followed and apprehended by the local police force? And what was he doing stalking someone and attacking them in their own home? That seemed odd and unsettling, but more importantly, it was criminal. And the capture of Charlie, his boss, was even stranger, but the charges were much more serious. Perhaps the rumors floating around the office of Charlie's association with Chicago's modern underworld gangsters were true. How could a decorated army officer like Charlie, familiar with reconnaissance and survival tactics, be so easily duped and captured—for kidnapping and attempted murder? Larry shook his head in bewilderment. Either the local police had some kind of exceptional detection skills, or they were extremely lucky, or Tewalt and Borden were starting to lose their edge. Larry shrugged his shoulders as he knotted his purple silk tie. *Maybe all of them at once,* he thought. *The ranger expertise must be overrated. Just a lot of bull and bravado.*

He plucked his lightweight wool navy suit coat from the back of the chair and pulled it on. He stroked the lapel of the Zegna suit he'd ordered from Saks Fifth Avenue earlier last month. It was worth every penny he'd spent on it. It made him look like a million bucks. Taking a final look in the mirror, he leaned in and flicked his fingers through his thick, auburn hair. Satisfied he looked like the astute lawyer he was, he suddenly had a chilling thought. *What am I getting into by taking on this new role in the company?* The notion unsettled him, but he shrugged it off. The financial rewards far outweighed any moral quandaries he might face on the job. His wife, Suzie, would relish his new status, and the money could make some of their wildest dreams come true—it might even shore up their somewhat rocky relationship. He relegated his nitpicking, worrisome tendencies to the trash heap, turned and grabbed his leather briefcase, and walked out the door.

At the Vernon County law enforcement facility, Larry Fischer presented his ID and credentials asking for a few minutes with his client, Charlie Tewalt. He was buzzed into the facility and led down a narrow corridor to a cell where he walked in and sat down next to Charlie. When the jail attendant was out of earshot, Charlie began his tirade.

"Where've you been?" Charlie snarled under his breath. "Don't you answer your messages?" His dark eyes flashed with irritation as he glanced at the top shelf suit Larry was wearing and his freshly scrubbed, innocent face. "You should have been here days ago! When are you going to get me outta here?"

Larry nervously fingered his tie and shook his head at his boss in a sad sort of way. "No can do, I'm afraid," he said, "unless you're willing to pay bail, which has been set at three-quarters of a million dollars."

"What?" Charlie sputtered, slapping both knees with his large hands. He jumped up from the bench he was sitting on and spun around to face Larry, poking his finger in the lawyer's face. "That's . . . that's outrageous! You need to get me out of here! Preferably today!"

"Can't do it, sir," Larry said apologetically, looking at his boss with a hangdog expression. "The charges against you are very serious. Judge Walcott set the bail very high because of your past criminal associations in Chicago. When they found the marijuana in your rented truck, they upped the drug charge to possession with intent to sell so they could hold you longer. You're lucky they didn't deny bail altogether. You've been charged with kidnapping in La Crosse County, which, if convicted, is punishable in Wisconsin with up to forty years in prison and a $100,000 fine. Then there's the other, more serious crime. Vernon County has charged you with first-degree attempted murder of Kay Starch, which is nothing to sneeze at. It's a very serious crime, I'm afraid." Larry stopped speaking and glanced at his boss.

"I don't believe this!" Charlie spat, deploring his current state of affairs. He plopped down on the bench again next to Larry and angrily crossed his muscular arms across his chest, his face glowering in a fit of outrage at his current circumstances. "It's that damn Jim Higgins. Jamie warned me about him, but I didn't believe him. And then that other cop came along. Who knew he was an expert biker and a former high school wrestling champ?"

Larry suddenly realized what his job might entail, and the prospects did not excite him. He spoke in a low, yet confident, voice. "As of right now, you are considered a threat to public safety and a flight risk," he informed his client. "Speaking frankly as your lawyer, sir, I don't think your focus should be on the police who captured you."

Charlie glanced at Larry. "What should I focus on then?" he snarled.

Larry sighed loudly. "I think you'd better start thinking about a plea deal to lower your sentence," he said quietly, "or you are looking at a very long stint in a maximum-security prison and some hefty fines that might bankrupt you."

Charlie slumped against the wall, his face a mask of disappointment and defeat. "Where's Lewis when I need him?" he whispered.

"In jail, sir," Larry said softly.

TWO WEEKS LATER . . .

53

In the weeks that followed the capture and arrest of Lewis Borden and Charlie Tewalt, Jim and his team spent time trying to piece together the story of the missing, now rediscovered, Tiffany treasures. From multiple conversations with Bubba Starch, the amateur historians at the Oshkosh Museum, and the owner of Gorgeous Glassworks, things were still fuzzy, more theoretical than honest-to-goodness solid evidence.

The Tifanny window saga was another story in the files of the detectives' track record. Charlie Tewalt—the highly trained and determined Chicago businessman—probably never imagined that his foray into the Wisconsin countryside would be a disaster of epic proportions. Jim harrumphed, then smiled when he thought about Sam hightailing it through the woods after Tewalt. Refusing to take your opponent seriously had had devastating repercussions for Charlie. Jim was sure the cocky criminal was still reeling in disbelief at the unconventional methods of "a bunch of country cops from the sticks," a phrase he had uttered under his breath when he was taken into custody by the Vernon County Sheriff's Department.

"So, you're telling us that the William Bradford I was responsible for removing the windows from the train?" Jim asked. The team had gathered in the classroom down the hall from Jim's office to try to come up with a timeline that would explain the chain of events that led to the discovery of the windows and the capture of Charlie on a bike chase through Wildcat Mountain State Park, resulting in his subsequent arrest.

"Nothing else we've come up with explains how the windows got to the chapel," Leslie said as she bounced Karina up and down on her knee.

"Well, nothing that we know for certain," Jim countered. "And you have to remember, we may never know."

"True, but Chief, the windows were obviously hidden, covered with a tarp, and through the next hundred years or so, sat in the chapel unknown to anyone else except the person who hid them there," Leslie explained. "They didn't get there by themselves. No one at the time of the disappearance, not even the Oshkosh police, was able to locate the windows. Of course, without Jamie's wild theory, we might have dismissed the whole affair as an absurd possibility."

"Jamie," Jim said under his breath. "That kid . . ."

"Did you say something, Chief?" Paul asked. "Because at some point in time, you're going to have to give Jamie some credit for his help with the case." Anger flashed across Jim's face, and his index finger began jabbing the air between him and the team as he talked.

"It'll be a cold day in—" Jim stopped abruptly when the rest of the team gave him blank stares. He thought back to his conversation with Lillie about cursing. He tucked his finger into his fist and bit his lip. "Let me restate that," he began again after an embarrassing moment. "Despite numerous warnings from me, Jamie plunged headlong into another police case that could have gotten him killed. I admit I don't understand why he isn't buried somewhere in Wildcat. From everything I've learned about Tewalt, I'd say Jamie is extremely fortunate. After all, Tewalt did try to kill Kay Starch and Sam, so what stopped him from killing Jamie?"

Sam shrugged his shoulders. "The protection of the Almighty?"

"I'll accept that as the only possible explanation for Jamie's survival," Jim retorted, taking a deep cleansing breath.

"Getting back to it, Chief," Paul injected.

"Go ahead," Jim said, hoping someone would come up with a logical explanation of the whole conundrum.

"Leslie learned some stuff from Benton Salinsky at Gorgeous Glassworks that might clarify things a little bit," Paul said, turning to Leslie.

"Benton explained the route of the Burlington Northern Railway in 1904," Leslie began, "and I found a map in my research that helped me understand a few things." Leslie reached into her bag and unfolded a map on the table. The team gathered around as she began explaining.

"I should begin by telling you that ten rail systems were operating in Wisconsin at the turn of the twentieth century. Benton found records—an old work order from the Ellison family—that showed the windows were to be shipped on the Great Northern from Oshkosh with a few transfers along the way to their destination in Winona. The Great Northern served points in central and northern Wisconsin. To the east, it came as far as Trempealeau and New Lisbon. The Tomahawk Railway was a spur line that began at Camp Douglas, and had stations at Tomah, Fort McCoy, and Sparta, ending near La Crosse." Leslie pointed to the map, making a circular motion with her finger, and continued. "This area—north to Tomah and south to Muscoda—was basically a railroad desert. So the windows must have been taken off somewhere near the Camp Douglas area and then transported south by wagon to the lumber camp and eventually to the chapel. It's the only thing that makes any sense."

"Well, the point is," Jim interrupted, "we'll never really know. We weren't there, and we don't know everything. What we do know is that Gorgeous Glassworks found a work order and repair estimate given to the Ellison family, but other than that, there is no other known documentation that supports the theory currently on the table." Jim looked around at the team.

Sam spoke up. " Are you saying we're on shaky ground trying to explain the appearance of the windows near Wildcat?"

Jim shrugged. "All I'm saying is let's not waste our time trying to explain something that has no explanation," he said gruffly. "It'd be satisfying to know how the windows got where they were, and it would probably make us all feel better, but facts, or the lack of them, are something we should all be familiar with in our line of work. When you're dealing with history, and you mix it with people's motivations, and add one hundred years of the past, things can get murky real fast."

"That's true," Paul said. "There's a lot of supposition as to how the windows were transported to such an obscure place. I tend to agree with you, Chief. Forget how the windows got to the chapel. We've seen them. They're the real deal. We've recovered them. Now it's time to move on."

"That sounds like a good dose of common sense to me," Jim said flatly.

"But what about the issue of ownership?" DeDe asked. "Do the Starches own the windows? They really weren't even on their property, so how can they claim them?"

"Possession is nine-tenths of the law . . . maybe?" Sam stated. "As far as I know, in other cases similar to this, that law is still upheld in courts across the country."

"It is still relevant in today's legal landscape," Jim added, "but it doesn't always guarantee absolute ownership. Sometimes further legal action—in this case, a claim by a member of the Ellison family—might be taken to protect their rights of ownership since the windows were stolen from their family."

Leslie shook her head. "I'm glad I'm not the lawyer trying to figure out the next course of action."

"I'm glad I'm not the Starches who *think* they own them," DeDe said.

"Well, I've talked to Bubba," Jim started to explain, "and he says that Kay's dad, Willie, had no idea about the whole scheme—to him it was just some off-the-wall story that seemed more like a fairy tale than anything that could have been true. Little did he know. And I believe that Kay is totally innocent in all of this, too."

Jim's cell vibrated in his shirt pocket. He walked away from the team and stood near the window, looking out onto the street below.

"Higgins."

"Sir, a lady named Josie DeChamp is on line one in your office," Emily explained. "Something about the Tiffany windows."

"Right. I'll get it," Jim said. He walked quickly to his office and picked up the phone.

"Hello. This is Lt. Jim Higgins. Can I help you?"

"I hope so," a woman on the other end said. "I'm standing at the front door of Bubba and Kay Starch out on Moon Ridge Road, but nobody is home. Do you know where they are?"

"Yeah, Kay is still hospitalized, but before I say more, why do you want to talk to them? You're not a reporter, are you? Someone looking for an exclusive on their story?" Jim asked.

"Oh, no! But I'm probably not the person they're going to want to see right now," Jodie said.

"And why would that be?" Jim asked gruffly.

"I'm a great-granddaughter of William Bradford, and I'm here to claim my rights to the Tiffany windows."

"Oh, I see," Jim said.

"Do you?" Jodie asked brusquely.

Jim bristled at her curt reply. "Look, the ownership issue is one that I'm not qualified to comment on. But if you want to meet with them, you'll have to get permission from the personnel at the Mayo hospital in La Crosse. I couldn't say when they're going to release Kay, but even if they do let her go home, she's going to need a lot more recovery time and therapy. I'm not sure they're going to want to discuss the ins and outs of the window ownership at this time," Jim explained. "But that's not for me to decide. That would be an issue you'll probably have to discuss with the Starches' lawyer."

"Yes, I understood that some negotiations would have to take place. I guess I'll have to drive to La Crosse and see if I can get in to see them," Jodie concluded.

"Yep. I think that's your best bet," Jim said.

As soon as he hung up, he dialed Bubba and explained his conversation with Jodie.

"Who is this person?" Bubba asked after Jim finished.

"Her name is Jodie DeChamp, and she claims she' s a great-granddaughter of William Bradford I. Beyond that, I have no proof that she is who she says she is, or that her claim to the windows is valid." Jim heard Bubba sigh deeply. "My advice, Bubba, is to funnel all calls about claims to your lawyer. Let them figure out if these people are who they claim to be. To me, that seems like a good logical first step. But I have a feeling this is going to be what your life will be like for a while 'til everything can get sorted out."

"Yeah, I think you're right, but thanks for the call anyway," Bubba finished.

Jim hung up and walked back to the group. "Any more wonderful insights, or are we just spinning our wheels in the muck and mire?" he asked Sam.

"We're in a rut so deep we may never get out," Sam said, but his grin debunked the negativity of his words. "Just kidding, Chief, but we're all in agreement. We nailed the dudes who were out to cause harm, they're in the slammer, and I say we should celebrate our victory, even though it seems relatively small in comparison with what still needs to be sorted out."

"I'm in agreement. I'll talk to Carol about a cookout at my place, over the weekend."

"All in favor?" Paul asked.

"I," they all said in unison.

"Case closed," Jim said. "My place Saturday night around five-thirty."

SATURDAY EVENING

54

The evening air was balmy, the trees were still, and the sun was heading toward the western horizon, casting shadows on Higgins' expansive lawn. The irises and roses were in full bloom, wafting a delicate fragrance into the air, and laughter and discussion buzzed in the air. Twinkling lights strung across the patio created a backyard atmosphere of relaxation and camaraderie. Jim built a fire in the fire pit out on the stone terrace, and Carol organized the food in the kitchen. Jim would grill brats and hamburgers later while their guests snacked on the relish trays and some refreshing drinks.

Despite the tension the Tiffany window case had brought to the Higgins' household, much of it had resolved when Charlie Tewalt and Lewis Borden were captured and incarcerated. Lillie had quieted down. No more predictions had erupted from her lips lately, which put Jim and Carol at ease for the moment. Carol thought about the long road to recovery for Kay Starch in the next several months. She was hoping they would stop tonight before they headed home to Ontario.

By six-thirty, the patio was hopping with energy. Children ran in and out between groups of adults. A volleyball net had been set up under the big maple trees, and several kids were tossing the ball back and forth in a loud, spirited game. Jim and his investigative team were present with their spouses and children. Doc Wycowski had arrived with a friend, Jamie Alberg and Geoff LaSarde came with a few of their acquaintances from MVAC, and Bubba and Kay Starch arrived for the meal. Food was served, and the conversation continued.

"So, Doc, what've you been up to these days?" Sam asked.

"Well, I bought the boat business in Stoddard. So far, I've only been at it about three months, but it's going well," Doc explained. "We've got a number of restorations in the works, and I hired a new young guy with lots of talent and, believe it or not, a willingness to work long hours."

Sam nodded and took stock of the man who'd helped them solve a mysterious case of an elusive thief and arsonist just six months ago. Doc looked healthy and happy. Of course, the attractive woman on his arm might have been a factor. "Who's your friend?" Sam asked, shifting his gaze to the woman.

"Oh, I'm sorry." Doc turned, and his eyes softened as he gazed at his companion's serene face. He grabbed her hand and pulled her close. "This is Darlene Offenbach. She's an artist who has a studio on Main Street in Stoddard."

Darlene flashed a beautiful smile. Her blonde hair was piled on top of her head in a casual style, and her hazel eyes sparkled with good humor. "Oh, you're the detective who recovered from a lightning strike, right?"

Sam grinned. "Yeah, I survived, but . . . well, let's just say I'm not the person I used to be."

"I'd say you're lucky to be here at all," she replied, lifting her eyebrows.

At that moment, Leslie strolled up to Sam's side carrying baby Karina. Sam wrapped his arm around her waist, then said, "Have you met my wife, Leslie?"

"No, I haven't," Darlene said, "but I've heard about you. You're the artist who lives in Genoa up on the bluff, right?" Leslie nodded pleasantly.

"This is Darlene Offenbach from Stoddard," Sam said by way of introduction.

"Yes, I thought I recognized you. I've seen your work in a couple of galleries in La Crosse and Winona. It's nice to finally put a face with a name," Leslie said, shaking her hand. She handed Karina off to Sam. "Let's get a drink, and you can tell me what you're working on right now." The two women walked off toward the patio while Sam and Doc stood by and watched.

"It's sure nice to have a woman back in my life," Doc replied dreamily.

"Sometimes they can complicate things, but most of the time, they're undoubtedly an asset," Sam said. "I don't know where I'd be without Lez."

Before Doc could reply, Lillie ran up to Sam, put her arms out, and took baby Karina. "I'm going to give her a ride in the wagon. Is that okay, Sam?" she asked.

"Sure, that's fine."

The two men wandered to the patio and found a couple of chairs. As they sipped their drinks, Jim strolled over and pulled up a chair, too, then sat down cradling a beer in his hand.

"So, Doc, I've been wanting to catch up on the news about the boat business. Tell me the story," Jim said. He noticed the lines and creases that wrinkled Doc's face somehow seemed softer and less noticeable.

"Well, there's not much to tell. I hired a young kid who looks promising, we've got several boats to restore, everyone's paying their bills, and I might even make a little money this year instead of just breaking even," Doc said with a smile.

"And he's got a lovely lady in his life," Sam said, pointing to Darlene.

"Really?" Jim said. "That's great." *Look what love can do,* he thought.

"Who's the lady in the wheelchair?" Doc asked.

"Have you got a couple of hours to listen to a story?" Jim asked.

"I've got nothin' but time," Doc said with a wry expression.

Jim leaned back in this chair and studied the trees arching over the lawn. The sky was turning a dusky purple, and a few twinkling stars were poking through the night sky. "Well, it all started when a guy on the north side of La Crosse had an intruder break into his house . . ."

55

(FOUR MONTHS LATER)

It was hot for a September day in Wisconsin. The traffic rushed by on West State Street in Milwaukee, kicking up fallen leaves and blowing them helter-skelter across the sidewalk. Jamie Alberg and Geoff LaSarde stood in front of St. George's Presbyterian Church waiting for the arrival of Rev. Townsend, who had promised to meet them there and give them a tour of their new parish hall.

"Think he'll show up?" Jamie asked, squinting in the bright sunshine. He pulled his hat lower to shade his eyes.

"Sure, he'll show up," Geoff said. "He was very anxious to show us the new Tiffany windows in the hall. According to Townsend, the congregation is very proud of them, although they paid a hefty price to the Starches."

The Starches' lawyers had fought a bitter genealogical battle and finally prevailed in court when they proved that Kay was the closest living relative to William Bradford I. Josie DeChamp was disappointed that her arguments had not prevailed in court, especially when

Bubba and Kay were granted ownership of the infamous treasures.

"Yeah, 2.7 million is a lotta sheckels. They must have some very faithful, well-endowed benefactors," Jamie responded, "but, really, when you think about it, without our help discovering the windows' location in the first place, they'd never have been able to buy them from the Starches. Those treasures would still be under that rotten tarp in that run-down chapel on Wildcat Mountain, hidden away in obscurity forever."

"Don't get on your high horse, Jamie," Geoff warned. "We had a lot of help from Higgins. Without his team . . . and Paco's nose . . . you'd still be tied to a tree somewhere in Ontario."

"I know. I know," Jamie said, reluctantly agreeing with his friend. "That is true, but you helped, too, and I intend to get a lotta mileage out of this whole affair," he spouted self-righteously. "I've been asked to write an article about the lost Driftless treasures for *National Geographic*, and in January I'll be shooting a couple of episodes for *Wisconsin's Treasured Past* on PBS. I'm hoping Lt. Higgins will join me, and I want you to come, too. You'll give the program some much-needed expertise and authenticity with all your Tiffany knowledge."

"Well, I do have to admit this whole incident has boosted my reputation as a Tiffany expert," Geoff began to explain. "I've gotten phone calls and job offers from quite a few agencies, but I'm going to take my time and carefully consider all my options."

"Yeah, take your time. There's no hurry. Your skills are in demand now, so don't sell yourself short." Pointing to a man approaching them from the side of the church, Jamie said, "Oh, that must be Rev. Townsend." The man waved them over, smiling widely.

"Hello, fellows," Townsend said. "Glad you could make it. I think you're going to like what you see today. Come this way, please. I'm anxious to show you the final installed product on display for all to see." The man turned and chattered amiably as he led Jamie and Geoff around the side of the church to a large brick fellowship hall. They entered the hall through an old, heavy antique door, its dark patina burnished from years of exposure and wear.

Inside the hall, the temperature was cool and inviting after the intense heat of the bright sunshine outside. They walked through a spacious vestibule into the hall. Beams of light shone through the Tiffany windows, sending radiant cascades of color that reflected on the floor, walls, and ceilings. Jamie and Geoff stopped in their tracks and gaped. The two young men felt the shifting beams of color envelop them, bathing them in a miraculous display of elegant splendor.

Rev. Townsend watched their rapt expressions as they took in the beauty of the windows. Since they'd been installed late this summer, the reverend had been privy to the ecstatic expressions of his parishioners and several other members of the community when they saw the incredible story of the Tiffany windows and heard the tale of intrigue that surrounded their amazing discovery. Visitors had come to see if the windows' beauty was truly as spectacular as the experts had reported. Apparently, if facial expressions were any indication, the windows were indeed a rare and beautiful example of the craftsmanship and magnificence of Louis Comfort Tiffany.

Geoff moved closer to one of the windows, which depicted a knight kneeling at the foot of a cross, his sword unsheathed and lying on the ground in front of him. The colors were brilliant, and each detail was exceptionally crisp. Geoff tentatively reached out and touched the glowing figure.

"They are spectacular," Geoff whispered in awe as his fingers caressed the intricate pieces of glass.

"Yes, every day I seem to see something new in them," Rev. Townsend said. "They've certainly lived up to their reputation."

"You can't say that about too many things in this world," Geoff said.

Jamie stayed silent, completely taken in by the beauty in front of him. Geoff marveled that his friend, who was always ready with a quip or quote, was speechless. That didn't happen very often, and he took note of it.

After several minutes in which Jamie and Geoff inspected the windows, they thanked Townsend for his patience in showing them the treasures. Walking slowly to the car, Jamie was thoughtful and reflective.

"What are you thinking about?" Geoff asked him.

"Those windows are incredible, but without light, they're just dull, boring, ordinary pieces of glass."

"That's true," Geoff replied, "but the best thing about stained-glass windows is that when darkness sets in, their true beauty is revealed only if there is light within."

After several moments, Jamie turned and said, "How'd you get so smart?"

"I hang around with people like you," Geoff said with a grin.

THE END

ABOUT THE AUTHOR

Sue Berg is the author of the Driftless Mystery Series. She is a former teacher, and enjoys many hobbies including writing, watercolor painting, quilting, cooking and gardening. She lives with her husband, Alan, near Viroqua, Wisconsin.

The Driftless Mystery Series

The Driftless Mystery Series set in the beautiful Driftless region of the Upper Midwest does not disappoint. With complex characters, intriguing plots, and surprising twists and turns, this series will delight you with its ability to entertain while upholding the values we all treasure; love, faith, loyalty, and family. It is destined to become a beloved and enduring legacy to the people and culture in this unique part of the country.

The Dirty Business Mystery Series

From the author of the award-winning Driftless Mystery Series comes a sharp new sleuth with a mop in one hand and a mystery to solve in the other.

Meet Sonja Hovland—smart, observant, and not one to ignore what others overlook. Alongside her husband, Trygve, and police chief Tanya Pedretti, Sonja finds herself drawn into cases where everyday messes lead to something far more dangerous.

Set in the Midwest and grounded in small-town grit, the Dirty Business series delivers blue-collar thrillers with big-time stakes, unexpected twists, and a heroine who knows that cleaning up is sometimes just the beginning.

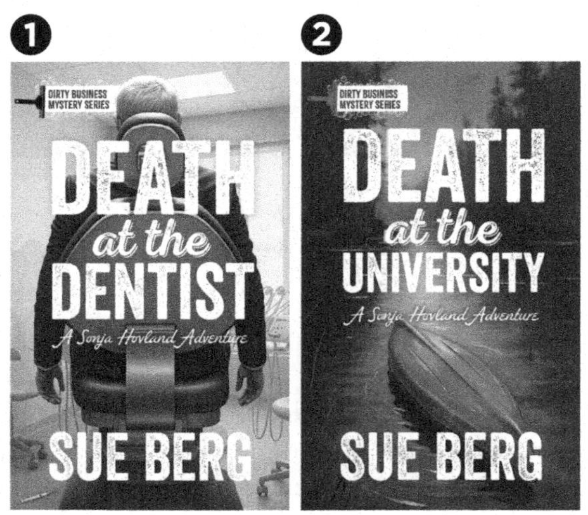

COMING IN MAY 2027

JIM HIGGINS'
ADVENTURES
CONTINUE...

Look to the next page for an excerpt from *Driftless Gamble.*

1

Paul Saner, investigator for the La Crosse Sheriff's Department, sat at his desk Tuesday morning in a cramped cubicle on the third floor of the Law Enforcement Center on Vine Street shuffling papers and organizing the results of the crime scene reports from the Devon Williams' case. The evidence the team had collected would convict Williams on multiple charges including robbery, assault, kidnapping, first degree murder, drug trafficking, and arson. Williams, a particularly nasty criminal, had been captured south of La Crosse near Victory, Wisconsin, in a decrepit camper late last summer. Despite wild shots from a 9mm pistol within the camper during the stake-out, no one had been injured except the perpetrator himself whose girlfriend wrestled the gun from him and shot him in the ribs. Since recovering from his injuries, Williams was being held in the La Crosse County jail awaiting the trial scheduled for July.

Paul had been a member of Lt. Jim Higgins' investigative team for several years. His financial savvy in uncovering kinky deals including money-laundering and fraud had sent several perps to the Boscobel prison for lengthy terms. He was calm and unflappable in tense situations. Although he was initially skeptical when he met his colleague, Sam Birkstein, he had come to appreciate his cohort.

When the chips were down and they were backed into a corner, they were brothers in blue and had each other's back.

Paul turned his office chair toward the window on Vine Street and pondered the investigative team's latest sting. He wondered how everyone had managed to escape unharmed. *That was a miracle,* he thought. A knock at the door got his attention. He turned and watched fellow investigator Sam Birkstein enter his tiny cubicle. Sam plopped down in a chair close to Paul's desk, studied his fingernails intently, rubbed his chin with his thumb, and looked at Paul with curious, hazel eyes.

Sam had been through momentous changes the past year. Surviving a horrendous lightning strike during a raging thunderstorm in August near the tiny river town of Stoddard, he still struggled with terrible migraines, and at times his mood swings were unpredictable and downright nasty. But, as Paul had learned over the last few months, victims of lightning strikes rarely survived without some kind of physical or psychological fallout. Sam's emotions had finally leveled out to some degree thanks to the arrival of baby daughter Karina in November.

"How's it goin'?" Sam asked nonchalantly.

"It's goin'. You look like you've got somethin' on your mind." Paul continued sorting and straightening the paperwork on his desk. "Higgins give you some kind of orders?"

"Sort of. The Chief wants us to go over to the Social Security Office and interview an employee who called about a situation of possible fraud . . . or something like that. You up for that?"

"Do I have a choice?"

Sam shook his head. "Nope.

"Okay, just give me a minute," Paul said. After several moments of sorting and answering a few phone calls, Paul stood, grabbed his suit coat, and walked to the door. He reached over and shut off the lights. "You comin?"

The two investigators walked down the narrow hallway and waved to the department secretary, Emily Warehauser, as they stepped into the elevator.

"How's Ruby feeling?" Sam asked, making small talk while the elevator descended to the first floor. Paul and Ruby were expecting their third child in less than a month.

"Fat. Bloated. Ornery," Paul said, frowning. He sighed. "Life's just a barrel of laughs these days." Pausing, he thought of Ruby's auburn hair and silky skin, and he smiled recalling her beauty. "Actually, she's on right on target—she's due next week. Gettin' the nursery ready. Hopefully, she'll deliver in the next few weeks."

"Better you than me," Sam said as they walked across the Vine Street parking lot to Sam's Jeep Patriot. Sam drove several blocks until he came to the U.S. Social Security Administration Office on South 7th Street. He parked the Jeep, and the two detectives entered the building and stood in line behind an elderly man with a walker. The receptionist looked up expectantly when she finished with the aged gentleman.

"Can I help you?" she asked.

Sam and Paul displayed their ID's. "We need to speak to Phoebe Iverson," Sam informed her.

The receptionist pointed to a cubicle across the room. "That's her space right over there," she said.

The large open room consisted of a series of small cubicles built along one wall which were designed for private consultations. In the middle of the room were groups of casual stuffed chairs and a scratched-up coffee table with out-of-date magazines lying on it. The two detectives walked to Iverson's cubicle, and Sam poked his head around the door opening. Phoebe looked up from her paperwork.

"Yes? Can I help you?" she asked. "Do you have an appointment?"

"No, we don't. We're investigators from the Sheriff's Department. You called about a concern you had?" Sam said.

"Oh, yes. Please come in," she said. "I didn't think you'd respond so quickly. I just called yesterday."

"We aim to please," Sam said. Paul rolled his eyes. The two detectives sat down, and Phoebe began telling them her problem.

"A man named Lester Smithfield lives with his mother over on Old Vineyard Road," she said pointing in a southerly direction, "past the bluffs beyond the city limits. He's been in our office several times this year, and I helped his mother with some paperwork when she applied for Supplemental Social Security."

"I know where Old Vineyard Road is. Nice area," Sam commented. "It's near Mt. La Crosse, right?"

"Yes, it's near there. Anyway, a neighbor of Lester's came in the other day on some Social Security business, and we were talking," Phoebe explained. "She told me she's been a friend of Lester's mom—her next-door neighbor, actually—and has visited her at least once a month for the past several years. But recently, in the last year, whenever she goes to the house, Lester meets her at the door and says his mother isn't feeling well and can't have visitors. Sophie found that to be rather odd since previously she'd always been welcomed into the home by her friend. Now, in the last several months, Lester won't let her in the house, and the mother seems to have disappeared . . . according to Sophie." Phoebe stopped speaking and looked curiously at the two detectives. She blinked rapidly and waited for a response.

"So, this neighbor lady hasn't seen Lester's mother in over a year?" Paul asked, a quizzical expression passing over his features.

"That's right. She hasn't seen her neighbor for several months. Lester always tells Sophie his mom isn't feeling well. I mean, you can't just barge into someone's home and demand to see them, can you?" Phoebe asked, her eyebrows lifting slightly.

"Well, you can, but it might not get you the results you'd hoped for," Paul said thoughtfully. "One question—is Mrs. Smithfield still cashing her Social Security checks?"

Phoebe nodded. "Well, most people just have their checks deposited directly into their account, so technically she doesn't cash her checks. But to answer your question, her checks are being deposited every third Wednesday of the month."

"Okay. That makes things appear to be normal." Paul hesitated and looked at Sam. "We'll talk to this neighbor lady and see if we can figure out what's going on. Do you have a name and address?" Paul asked.

"Yes. The neighbor lady's name is Sophie Davidson. She lives at 5409 Old Vineyard Road. From her description it's on a cul-de-sac." Paul scribbled the name and address in his memo pad. "She says she keeps an eye on Lester's house, so she must live close to him. Does that help?" Phoebe asked.

"Sure does. We'll check into it. Thanks for the call," Sam said. Outside on the street, Sam and Paul talked as they sauntered to the Jeep.

"Things are slow if this is all we've got to investigate," Sam said under this breath.

"We could hand it off to DeDe," Paul suggested, "and then go rattle some cages. Maybe make a drug bust down in Hoska Park."

Sam pointed his key fob at the Jeep and unlocked the vehicle. "No, we can't go make a drug bust, because Higgins would find out we didn't do our due diligence and our butts would be in a sling. We all get our share of boring stuff, and I guess this is ours."

"So we just have to buck it up and do it, huh? Is that what you're saying?" Paul said resigned to the boredom.

"Yep, but you've got to admit it beats getting shot at," Sam said as he got in the vehicle and started the engine.

"Or sitting at your desk sorting papers and random evidence for trial. You can't argue with that," Paul sighed, buckling his seat belt, "but there's nothin' like a good old-fashioned sting to get your blood pumpin'."

The beautiful spring sky that had graced the morning hours now turned gray with a raw east wind. Thick clouds gathered and soon a gentle misting rain began falling as the temperature plummeted. Sam peered upward through the Jeep windshield, his face knotted with frustration.

"So much for my bike ride tonight. Looks like it might be an all-day soaker," Sam said. He headed south out of town, turned left onto Old Vineyard Road, and drove through a quiet neighborhood with alternate expanses of open lawn and patches of thick woods, everything bordered on the south by towering sandstone bluffs and rolling hills. Grandad Bluff, the iconic geographical feature of the La Crosse area, was just a couple of miles to the north. The neighborhood had a secluded feel to it, and Sam found the area appealing. There were eight residences along Old Vineyard Road according to GPS. Sophie Davidson occupied the seventh residence which bordered the Smithfield property, the last home on the dead-end road.

By the time Sam pulled into Sophie Davidson's driveway, the rain had intensified falling steadily on the Jeep making little pinging noises. The detectives looked through the windshield at the dark ranch-style home. Whenever they made cold calls, they adopted a vigilant attitude. Acting on someone's tip didn't always produce the desired results. Most of the time, a visit to a home included a customary question-and-answer session, but both men knew domestic calls could be fraught with high emotion and intensity. Frequently, verbal arguments between family members could intensify leading to physical altercations. That meant someone could get hurt. At this point in the investigation, Sam and Paul weren't sure Sophie Davidson had any evidence that something criminal was happening at the house next door; she just suspected something. It seemed trivial to the two investigators, but responding to someone's concern of possible wrongdoing was part of police procedure. Paul doubted an elderly woman would give them any trouble, but they'd been surprised before on a couple of occasions.

Sam opened door of the Jeep and stepped onto the driveway. The trees and vegetation dripped with falling rain. It was ominously quiet, except for the quiet drumming of precipitation on the roof of the house. With senses on high alert, the two men cautiously approached the front door. Sam walked up to the door and rang the bell. Paul stood behind him shuffling his feet, impatiently scanning the woods that surrounded the dated home. Nothing happened. Sam rang the bell again as they waited under the eave where it was dry. They were just about to leave when a light snapped on in the interior of the house. A few moments later, a diminutive lady hunched with age opened the door and blinked rapidly. At that very moment, Sam noticed the .22 shotgun tucked under the woman's arm.

"Are you selling somethin'?" she asked crossly. "'Cause I'm not interested, and I don't want any religious tracts either." The scowl on her face deepened, and she raised the gun until it was pointed at Sam's midsection. Sam quickly flipped his ID open, extended his arm to the woman so she could read it, and politely said, "Ma'am, I'm a police officer. Would you please lower that gun? I don't feel like getting shot this morning."

The woman studied Sam's ID with careful concentration, the gun clasped firmly under her arm. Then she said, "Now listen here, sonny, I've been huntin' in these hills for fifty years. Do you think I'd be stupid enough to shoot a policeman? Besides, the safety's on." She turned and began walking into the house, waving the two detectives inside. "Come on in. Sorry about the gun, but the way things are these days, you just never know what might happen. People are shootin' each other for the stupidest reasons. Livin' all alone on this road, I've got good reason to come to the door with my shotgun. It's always been my best friend. Come on in. I'll make some coffee."

Sam took a few deep breaths, willing his heart to slow down. They stepped into the house. It was like morphing into a seventies time warp. Gold carpet, olive green couches and chairs, brown throw pillows, and an iconic painting of the woods in autumn—more gold, orange, green and brown. The heads of two massive whitetail bucks with huge spreading racks hung on the wall on either side of a large picture window, their glassy eyes staring down at the two detectives. Sam was sure nothing had changed in the living room for over forty years. The kitchen was a repeat of the color scheme: gold appliances, green linoleum, and a black wrought iron potholder hanging over an island in the middle of an out-dated kitchen. The potholder was loaded with cast iron frying pans of various sizes hanging from large hooks. Despite the retro décor, the kitchen was welcoming and cozy. Sophie propped the shotgun in the corner by the refrigerator, then scurried around opening cupboard doors. Soon she had a pot of coffee brewing. The aroma filled the room, and Sam began to relax a little.

"Have a seat, boys. Now what can I do for you?" Sophie asked. She set mugs in front of them and then began rummaging in a cupboard until she found a tin of cookies which she opened and arranged on a plate.

"We understand you're concerned about your neighbor, Mrs. Smithfield," Paul said.

Sophie stayed silent until she sat down opposite the two detectives. She had petite features; a tiny mouth, a button nose, and very alert, blue eyes. Curly white hair framed her face. Although her hands were gnarled by arthritis and her knuckles were swollen, she gracefully poured three cups of coffee. The old woman wore a pair of worn, patched blue jeans and a button-down gray sweatshirt with red cardinals embossed on the front. She took stock of the two detectives before speaking, studying them carefully. *Nothing much gets past Sophie Davidson,* Sam thought when her blue eyes stayed on him for a long moment.

"You look familiar to me," she said as she gazed at Sam. Suddenly she snapped her fingers. "I know who you are. You're the cop who was suspected of that robbery and murder in Stoddard awhile ago, right?"

Sam's face darkened with anger. "For your information, I was framed and wrongly accused," he said as his mouth twitched with frustration. "The real killer is in jail awaiting trial."

Paul glanced nervously at Sam whose disposition had soured instantly when the old woman mentioned the fallacious scuttlebutt from their latest case.

"Sophie, could we get back to your concern?" Paul lightly tapped the table, and the old woman focused her attention on him. "You reported there was something odd going on with your neighbor," he said. "Could you tell us about that?"

"Oh, you mean Rachel . . . Rachel Smithfield." She leaned back in her chair and took a bite of a cookie and sipped her coffee. "Well, here's the story, boys. I've been Rachel's friend for over twenty-five years," she explained patiently. "The Smithfield's moved into this neighborhood back in 1996. Rachel's husband left her high and dry, and since they moved here, her bachelor son, Lester, has always lived with her. My husband, Dr. Davidson, was a vet here in town. We became good friends with Rachel over the years. We tried to help her with things around the house—you know, little fix-it projects. I've been having coffee and playing a Scrabble game with Rachel every second Wednesday of the month for over twenty years," she explained. Her bright eyes sparkled as she talked about her friend. "We've kept those Scrabble dates religiously even though she usually beats me—she does The New York Times crossword puzzle every day. She's smart, very, very smart," Sophie said in a clipped tone. A hint of a smile softened her worried expression. "She held a position at the university, something to do with genetics. We never missed our Scrabble game," she finished wistfully, taking another sip of coffee.

"So, what changed?" Sam asked.

Sophie pointed a gnarled finger at Sam. "Now that's a good question," she said emphatically, shaking her finger up and down. "Before Covid hit, I'd go over to the house every Wednesday for coffee and our game, and I was welcomed into the house. Now when I go over, Lester always says the same thing—'Mom's not feeling very good today. We'll have to cancel'. Now correct me if I'm wrong, but don't you think it's a little strange when someone is always sick on the second Wednesday of every month?" She shook her head vigorously, and her blue eyes flashed with frustration. "It's not likely, is it? That's why I'm suspicious." She pointed her index finger toward the Smithfield residence. "There's something goofy going on over there."

"It does sound a little strange," Paul remarked. The two detectives exchanged a glance.

Sophie stared at them, then said, "Something's happened to her." Suddenly tears misted in her eyes. "I think she's dead," she said quietly.

"So, you haven't actually seen her for over a year?" Sam asked.

"No, but I haven't seen anyone carry her outta there, either," Sophie said with a tinge of anger in her voice. "If she's dead, how come there wasn't a funeral or something?"

"What kind of person is her son, Lester?" Paul interjected, quietly writing down his observations.

"He's quiet. To himself. Personally, I think he's a little tetched in the head. He's not very friendly, but in his defense, I think he's a little slow. He just retired from the brewery about a year ago. That's when all these shenanigans started with Rachel. I just don't understand it," the old woman said. "Something's happened to my friend, and there's nothing I can do about it." By now, Sophie was crying softly, and she gently wiped the tears from her cheeks.

Sam leaned over and grasped the old lady's hand. "I'm sorry you're upset about your friend. We'll look into this. If anything changes here in the neighborhood, you can call one of us. We'll leave our cards. If you notice something suspicious, just give a holler, okay?"

Sophie smiled, and her lips quivered as she regained control. "I can do that. Thank you for listening. Nobody believes me, but something has happened to Rachel. I just don't know what it is," she said, "but I can feel it in here." She patted her chest tenderly. Sam laid their business cards on the dining room table.

"We understand, Sophie," Paul said as he stood. "We'll look into it. Thanks for the coffee."

"Be careful now with that rifle," Sam said as he walked to the front door. "Don't go shootin' anyone. . . especially a cop." He grinned tentatively.

"Oh, you're a rascal," Sophie said, grinning back, "but I only shoot varmints—woodchucks, skunks, and squirrels—and a rabbit now and then for supper. Cops don't count unless you consider them varmints." She chuckled heartily at her own joke. "You take care now, boys. Thanks for stopping. I appreciate the visit." She closed the door softly behind the two detectives.

Down the street at the Smithfield home, Lester watched with binoculars from the back bedroom through a copse of maple trees as the two detectives climbed back into the Jeep. Who was visiting Sophie? They looked important. Cops? Insurance agents? What was she blabbering about now? Was she telling them a pack of lies about his mom? Lester thought about the argument he'd had with Sophie last week, and he let the curtain fall back into place. *Somebody might have to do something to shut her up. Maybe I should call Floyd.*

A few minutes later, there was a series of loud knocks on the front door. Lester froze in the darkened hallway between the bedrooms and living room, pressing against the wall, waiting. More knocking and some muffled talking. Then it was silent. Hurrying back to the bedroom, Lester peeked carefully through the sheer curtains. The two men were driving away. *No doubt about it. Sophie needs to mind her own business.*